Bucket Full of Stars

Penny Cavanaugh

Glasswell Cavanaugh, Romeoville, IL, USA.
ISBN: 0692338950
ISBN 13: 9780692338957
Library of Congress Control Number 2014921270
Glasswell Cavanaugh, Romeoville, IL

Acknowledgments

Eternal love and thanks to my dearest wife Kathleen for believing in me every second of the day. Thank you for letting me read each chapter to you as I wrote it, and more importantly for listening as I read (most of the time). Thank you for being my sounding board, the president of my fan club, and for doing the dishes and folding the washing on those days when I didn't move from my chair unless it was to pour myself more coffee. You are my light.

Mum and Dad, thank you for helping me become the person I am, and teaching me not only how to dream, but how to achieve. Sorry about the naughty words in the book!

Jemima, thank you for being my best friend and the world's best sister. Not only have you given me my awesome nephews, but a lifetime of childhood memories that have shaped me into the person I am. I could not be me without you.

My deepest thanks and appreciation to Rosa, the champion of this novel. Anyone reading this would do well to thank her too, for without Rosa this story would not be what it is (she will deny it, but she is being humble). Thank you, Rosa, for all of your hard work, as much as you would like to downplay it. I ardently believe that you are a gift from God and you have changed my life. There is not one single person in the world who could have done the job that you did...not the way you did it, for they do not have the same heart as you. You are so much more than an editor Rosa. Muchas gracias, mi amiga.

Thank you to MaryD, Nancy, Ash, Jackie, Sinèad, Jessa, and Sherri for reading this story in one incarnation or another. I am so grateful for your thoughts. Eva, your artistic ability blows my mind. Thank you for creating a cover that is literally my dream come true.

Finally, I'd like to thank you (yes, dearest reader, you) for deciding to read this book. I do so hope you love reading it as much as I loved writing it. Get yourself a cup of your favorite beverage and snuggle into the comfiest chair you can find, shut yourself out of whatever world you are reading this in, and enjoy your time in Richmond, Australia in 1856.

This novel is dedicated to everyone who has ever loved someone.

Chapter 1

1856, Tasmania, Australia.

The Suds Bucket rested alone at the bottom of Richmond, in an eternal shadow cast by nothing but disdain from the disapproving townspeople, who avoided it at all costs. In daylight, that is. When night fell, the Bucket crawled with an array of creatures spanning from the scum of the town to the most well-to-do gentlemen, who, of course, paid well, and very well, to ensure lips were locked, not only while they were there, but also when they left.

What had once been a happy home filled with flowers, laughter, and the smell of freshly baked bread, now reeked of alcohol, sex, and hopelessness. The brittle wood creaked constantly, as if even standing was an effort for the old structure. A shaded veranda wrapped around the brothel, access to which was by a staircase so worn that it looked like it could collapse at any second. Luckily for the Bucket, its patrons were educated in which steps to avoid thanks to an incident that had occurred one early Thursday morning. A rowdy young man just old enough to drink, but not old enough to hold his liquor, left the bar in a rage after spending all of his money on alcohol and not saving enough to have the privilege of taking one of the girls upstairs for the evening. He stormed out of the Bucket; too busy yelling to remember to skip the third step down. His leg slipped through the wooden plank, and there he was stuck until daylight, when the local authorities found him on their morning rounds. The step was repaired, but no patron ever stepped on it since then.

In contrast, Richmond was bursting with color as the early days of autumn began to make themselves known. The main strip of town bustled with people in the morning, and friendly smiles were not difficult to come by. That is, unless you were Sherie Kelly.

The blonde prostitute, just one year past twenty, stood at the front of the line in the post office. Blatantly out of place in a cheap, second-hand dress and worn out brown leather boots, she clutched a deteriorating canvas bag full of vegetables, a bottle of milk, and a letter. The customer in front of her had just finished his business, but as Sherie stepped forward to approach the counter, she was shoved out of the way by a well-dressed woman who clearly had far more important business than Sherie could possibly have.

Knowing by now that it wasn't worth her time to even consider making an issue of what had just happened, Sherie continued to wait quietly. She played nervously with the envelope she held, and made an effort to keep her eyes lowered. Willing the time to pass faster, Sherie tried to calm herself by tracing the lettering on the envelope. It was smudged ever so slightly, but she had faith the letter would reach its destination.

> *Mr. Daniel Kelly;*
> *In care of Sandhurst Post Office*
> *VICTORIA*

She wished her father were with her now. He had always been a respected villager of Richmond, and people were proud to call him a friend. Not much time had passed since the days where she would skip into this very same post office with him, sending letters back to her grandparents in Ireland. The greetings she had received when she was with her father were very different to the ones she received these days. It had taken a while for her to realize that she was no longer considered an equal in the community she had called home since she was born, but those days were gone, and she well understood her place in the town now.

Over at the far right counter, another customer finished his business, and the post office attendant signaled for the next person in line to come forward. Before anyone else could push in front of her, Sherie walked up to the counter and placed her letter down gently, trying to hide behind her soft actions. The harsh lines on the attendant's face became even more rigid when she looked up and recognized Sherie. In a fluid motion, she reached over and picked up a sign, which she placed in front of her with a cold smile. 'CLOSED.'

"I just need you to stamp it." Sherie pushed the envelope around the sign. The attendant picked up the 'CLOSED' sign and, for a second, Sherie's heart fluttered with the hope that she had changed her mind, but the moment was fleeting as the attendant only slammed the sign down harder on the counter and then walked into a back room that was hidden by a curtain. Not surprised, but all the same dejected, Sherie stood still for a moment and took a long, pronounced breath. She picked her letter up and left the post office without protest, defeated. She knew it had been a bad idea to think that she would be able to get service from anyone in Richmond other than the few people who already helped her, and even then some of those told her to come back late at night and would shun her publicly. Her sister Molly had been right—it was silly for her to expect anything more from these people, and putting herself out there in the hopes that someone would act differently to the rest of them would only hurt her. She cringed when she thought of how Molly would react when she heard what had happened. She would gloat about being right, as she always did, and then she would send a few of their clients around to 'send a message' by means of vandalizing the post office—a message which would only serve to reinforce the negative opinions held by practically each and every individual in Richmond. No, perhaps she would keep this incident to herself this time. She paused on the front step outside the post office while she waited for her eyes to adjust to the sunlight. When the world grew brighter, she instantly noticed a new addition to the wall beside her: *"Earn your fortune on the gold fields today,"* it suggested, the words emblazoned across a background of dangerous promises. The poster showed a smiling bearded man with greedy eyes. He stood in a tidy camp area holding a metal pan littered with golden nuggets of temptation. Behind him, a rainbow plunged deep into the blades of grass that covered the campground. Lost in the image, Sherie stood motionless for a long time, and stared at the man's face, which had long since transformed into the kind face of her father. She imagined him right now, barefoot and ankle deep in a muddy river, thinking of her and her sister every time he plucked a piece of gold from the bottom of his pan. She tried to think of how it would feel to see the glitter through the sludge, and she felt a sense of accomplishment. She tucked her letter to him into her bag. She didn't need to post it anyway—he would be home soon.

Sherie wandered down the street in the direction of the Suds Bucket with her head down, and it wasn't until she had collided into the group of men that she even realized she was walking toward anyone. She mumbled an apology (all too knowing that her words meant nothing) as she looked up, instantly flooded with more than just remorse for who she had walked into. John, Josh, and Thomas were the type of men who went further than just shooting dirty looks at the women who worked and lived at the Bucket. They actually practiced what they preached in terms of disapproving of the whorehouse, as opposed to others who would very publicly voice their disgust for the establishment in daylight, but slipped away from their wives in the night for a visit. Not these men. These men had foul sneers on their faces while they took in the offensive sight of Sherie, as if she were a ten-day-old dead kangaroo rotting on the side of the road.

"Watch it, whore." Josh spat as he addressed her by a name she was used to by now. She shook her head, and pushed through the middle of them, all pretense dropped. She no longer wished to apologize, nor did they wish to hear it. The only thing she was sorry for right now was existing. Eyes lowered, she didn't need to see the young couple a few meters up cross the street prematurely in an attempt to avoid her to know that they had done so. This was exactly why she was trying to grow vegetables out the back of the Suds Bucket. The less time she had to spend in town, the better...for everyone. Life hadn't always been this hard, and if not for the discovery of gold on the Mainland five years earlier, Sherie's eyes might still have had that sparkle they once did.

Chapter 2

Sherie

Five years earlier...

The night was so still that Sherie could hear the river running kilometers away as it traveled down through the cemetery toward the Richmond Bridge. Sherie knew exactly when the water was flowing around the occasional rock in the riverbed, when it forked off and trickled into smaller streams, and when it would crash against the mossy sandstone of the bridge. She had been listening to that river flow for so long now, that she could even isolate the sounds of the water that ebbed at the embankment, pooling in the mud and forming drinking holes for the rabbits, or the occasional Kangaroo. When she closed her eyes and really concentrated, she could hear the sounds behind the sounds—the pebbles below the surface that moved back and forth, dancing with the grains of sand that formed the riverbed.

"We should go down to the river tomorrow," Sherie said, voicing her train of thought.

Daniel nodded. Despite her father being a man of few words, Sherie was surprised that they had been sitting on the hill for hours now without any conversation whatsoever. She was used to her father's quiet demeanor. He said what needed to be said and very rarely much more, but when he switched his gaze from the skies and looked into Sherie's eyes, she could tell he was holding something back.

"It should start any minute now," he said.

"This is my favorite night of the whole year."

"This is everyone's favorite night of the year."

"Yes, but ours is more special," Sherie said. She had no interest in the annual festival Richmond celebrated, which happened to be on the same night that a shower of stars rained over their heads through her favorite constellation.

"Sherie, dear, you shouldn't judge which is more special. Our night is just as special as theirs," Daniel said.

"So wise, Daddy," Sherie replied sarcastically. "I just mean, what is the point of getting so drunk that you can't even walk home? It's just silly."

"Well, some might ask what is the point of watching hundreds of stars shooting through the…" Daniel fell silent as the first meteor sliced through the night sky, lighting the hill so brightly that for a second they could see the green grass that they were sitting on.

Sherie gasped when a second and a third star flew overhead, not as bright as the first, but enough to create a glow that cast a shadow of herself and Daniel, illuminating the very special moment.

The last star shot across the sky, but Sherie continued to look up, hopeful for just one more. After a minute or two of staring at the regular stationary albeit sparkling stars, she turned her attention back to Daniel. "What aren't you telling me? You're acting strangely."

Daniel sighed and met her eyes again. Sherie knew him well enough to know that he was searching for the perfect words. "I'm going to join the others in Victoria," he whispered.

Sherie studied his face, taking in the creases that had started to form faster than ever before, since her mother died. So this was why he had been acting so peculiar all week. She thought his behavior had been something to do with the gold rush. News that Tom Burnes had struck gold and was coming back to Van Diemen's Land after being away for less than six months was traveling through town faster than ever, and all of Richmond was abuzz about it.

"The fields are planted and will be ready to harvest soon, and I've spoken to Ed, who said he will help you and Molly when it's time to harvest. You will have enough to manage, and he can help you re-plant if I'm still gone by then."

Sherie processed what Daniel was saying. She didn't like his decision one bit. "I can get a job. Please, don't go, Daddy. I don't want any gold. We don't need any gold. Stay, please," she begged him.

"I'll be back before you know it, my dear. I love you, and I love Molly, and I wish I could give you more than what we have. The house will need repairs soon, and I can't afford the wood to reinforce the stilts, or replace the rotting beams on the roof. If something doesn't change, we will be in trouble."

Sherie tried to imagine her home falling apart. She definitely didn't want to see the place where she had grown up rot away, but she couldn't help feeling that if her father wasn't there, it wouldn't be much of a home to her anymore. "What if we run out of money?" she asked.

"Ed will make sure you have what you need. I've told him he can take anything he wants from the crops in return for looking out for you girls."

"Ed…Edward Smith? Your cousin?"

Daniel nodded, and Sherie shuddered at his confirmation. She instinctively disliked Ed. She was unsure why, since he had never really given her any reason to justify her feelings, but whenever he was around, she felt unsettled. "He said he would look after us?"

"He did, and of course, don't forget there is always Maggie too."

Sherie smiled, relief washing over her as she thought of her aunt. Maggie had been in her life for as long as she could remember, and was one of her very favorite people. She was a gentle soul, and Sherie could see in her eyes that she had been beautiful when she was younger. Not that she wasn't still beautiful in her own way now, but she lacked the flawlessness that came with youth. The lines around the corners of her eyes and mouth gave away the fact that despite the smile that often graced her face, she had experienced things that no woman ever should.

"Daddy, I'm going to miss you."

"I'm going to miss you too, dear. I'm doing this for you and Molly. I'll be back soon enough."

"Promise?"

"Cross me heart," Daniel said, his Irish accent still as strong as the day he stepped off the boat. "But you have to promise me something too."

"Anything."

"Look after the house. Ask our friends to help you if you need to. The Richmond folk are kind, and they will be good to you."

"I will," Sherie promised.

"Always make sure there are flowers in the vase, like your mother used to," he said.

"I'll make sure I buy only the best from Flanagan's," Sherie assured him.

"Good girl." He ruffled his hand through her hair.

Sherie scowled as she attempted to flatten her hair back down into place.

"Come on, let's get home." Daniel pulled her into the kind of all encapsulating hug that only a father could deliver. Sherie's heart felt as warm as his hug, despite the knowledge that he would be leaving soon. She had faith that he would keep his promise and be back before she knew it, and with any hope, he'd bring a mountain of gold back with him.

Molly

The comfort that came with the promise of Daniel's return faded as the days passed and his departure drew nearer. Molly was not happy one bit and had barely spoken to Daniel after he told her of his plans. She refused to meet Edward Smith the day before Daniel left, and chose to skip dinner that night rather than share the meal with what remained of her family.

Maggie brought her a plate of steaming lamb and rosemary stew, and tried to reason with her. "Why don't you come downstairs, Mol? It's your father's last night."

Molly gratefully accepted the plate from Maggie and stuck a fork into a fluffy potato with vigor, as if the potato were to blame for this whole mess. "That's his choice. This is mine."

"Choosing not to say goodbye to him?"

"I thought he was coming back? It's not goodbye if he's coming back, Maggie," Molly said through a mouthful of lamb.

"It's farewell though, isn't it? See you soon? Be safe?"

Molly grunted as she shoveled another forkful of stew into her mouth. "I'm angry at him," she stated plainly.

"I understand," Maggie replied.

"Yeah, I don't think you do. Until someone you love makes the decision to leave you, I don't think you get an opinion. Sorry."

Maggie took two slow breaths and said softly, "What about someone you love who decides to beat you? Hurt you on purpose? I get an opinion, Molly. You know that."

"He is choosing to leave us!" Molly shouted. "How is that not hurting us on purpose?" She stabbed her last mouthful of lamb and tore the meat roughly from the fork prongs with her teeth before throwing the plate and fork at the door. "Get out!" she yelled.

Sherie watched from the crack of the almost closed door as her older sister gave in to the rage that Sherie herself was fighting with everything she had. In that moment, she decided that she was going to have to be strong enough for the both of them. At least for a little while, anyway.

Chapter 3

The next morning, after packing a small bag, Daniel left. Molly had given in and joined Sherie and Maggie at the top of the steps to the house, where they stood and watched him walk away towards the coach station. Before he left, Daniel kissed the girls and hugged them tightly. None of them could speak for fear of losing control of their emotions. The silent farewell created an energy on the staircase that lasted for months after Daniel had gone. Each time the girls walked through the opening in the balcony railing, they could feel the buzz left over from the day that Daniel left.

Edward came the next day, and took some of the wood that was chopped and stored under the house. He was not completely unpleasant, but certainly did not display the same friendly demeanor he had when Daniel was around. Sherie invited him in for a cup of tea, which he declined by way of a short grunt and a dismissing wave of his hand.

"He's drunk," Molly said, her arms folded as she watched him load their firewood into a crude wheelbarrow, leaving without a goodbye. She looked at Sherie, whose face was branded with concern. Molly shared her sister's unease. They had faith that their father believed he had left them in good hands, but not so much faith that his trust in Edward was well placed. It was very obvious that he was drunk, if not for the wobble in his step, then for the stench of rum on his breath.

The next time Edward returned, he brought a friend. By the look of him, he hadn't bathed in months, possibly years, unless you counted the liquor that had missed his mouth and spilled down the front of what looked like his one and only shirt.

It was late, and Sherie and Maggie were already in bed. For a fleeting moment, Molly was hopeful that Edward was stopping by on his way to (or from? She couldn't quite decide) the tavern to give them some money. It had been a little while since their father had left, and Molly had spent the last of their money that morning. She had planned to visit Edward the following day to ask for help. After he had uttered only one word, Molly knew that he was not there to give her any money.

"Molly," he rasped, his voice low and unsettling.

"Ed. I'm glad you're here. I—"

"She's glad you're here, Eddy," Edward's dirty friend said with a perverted snort.

"Look, Ed, we need some more money," Molly said.

"Interesting. You need some money and my friend here needs some relief." Edward held out his hand in front of the man, who reached into his pants. Appalled, Molly looked away as he pulled out a pouch of coins. Edward opened the pouch and tipped the contents onto the table beside him. He scooped up half of the coins and slipped them into his pocket, then put the other half back into the pouch and pulled the string closed.

Molly held her hand out for the pouch.

"Now hold on just one minute; this isn't free money here," he said.

Molly stepped back when Edward stumbled over a chair in an attempt to move around the table and get a little closer to her. "You promised my father that you would take care of us," she said.

"I did, and I will. That's what family does, Molly, they take care of each other. I'm going to give you some money…" Edward shook the small pouch, rattling the coins inside. He held out his hand flat, the pouch of money ready for the taking. "So what will you give me in return?"

Molly was completely unsure of what to do. She knew she needed the money. She had really let down Sherie when their father left, and not a day went by where she didn't regret not spending their final night together as a family. She needed to show Sherie that she was the big sister and that she was strong. She needed to prove not only to Sherie, but also to herself, that she could take care of them and the house until their father returned. She nodded nervously as she reached out and took the pouch of coins.

Edward's yellow teeth showed when he curled his lip back and pushed his drunken friend towards Molly. The feral man rubbed his dirty hands together and reached out to touch her. She pulled back instinctively, but almost as if he were expecting her to do so, the man reached a little further and squeezed her hard.

Molly yelped in pain, but was unable to move as she was struck with fear. She didn't want Sherie to wake up and come downstairs, so she just closed her eyes and waited for it to be over. She wasn't even sure what 'it' was, since there had been no discussion on what a few measly coins would buy the man whose name she never wished to learn. Molly kept her eyes shut. She could hear his labored breathing and knew he was getting closer when she could smell his stagnant swamp-like breath hot against her lips. His tongue pushed into her mouth and his hands traveled up her skirt at the same time, sliding her under-garments down roughly.

Molly's eyes opened wide when it happened. She felt a venom spread through her body as she was jolted about. Unable to ascertain whether the incident had lasted five minutes or five hours, she woke up to find herself alone, lying on the cold, wooden floor. Her pants were still around her knees, and her whole body was stinging. She lay there smelling like sweat and disgust, and allowed her tears to trickle down her cheek.

Molly didn't move until the moon did, replaced by the sun that crept into view from the window above her. The world she woke up in was very different from the world she had woken up to the day before, and she felt the change run through her as did the events of the previous night—both uninvited and unwanted. She stood slowly and noticed the coin pouch that she must have dropped at some point. She picked the pouch up and poured the money into her hands so she could count how much she had earned. She couldn't say that her experience had been worth the coins, but a very tiny part of her was happy that they had money at least.

Molly spent the morning alone in her bedroom and didn't make an appearance downstairs until much later in the day. She wandered into the lounge room, where Maggie and Sherie were sitting, laughing. The difference within her was undeniable, and she expected her sister and her aunt to notice immediately, but they did not.

"Afternoon, sleepy head," Maggie said, pouring her a cup of tea.

Molly said nothing as she sat down beside her and took a sip. She allowed the woody taste to calm her in a way that she remembered her mother telling her it would. *"There's no problem a cup of tea and a cuddle can't fix,"* her mother used to say. Molly thought she would be happy to go without the cuddle for now. She took a bigger gulp of tea and decided that she would be perfectly happy with not having any physical contact ever again for the rest of her life. She jumped when Sherie leaned over and hugged her, as if she could hear her thoughts and was blatantly ignoring them.

"He'll be back soon," Sherie said.

Molly reeled back from Sherie's unwanted touch, and though her stomach was empty, she felt the distinct threat of vomiting knocking at the back of her throat. It took her a moment to realize that Sherie was referring not to Edward, but to their father.

"He better be," Molly finally said, her stoic expression preventing suspicion from the other two.

"I wish I was like you," Sherie said.

"What do you mean?"

"So strong. I cried myself to sleep last night, the same as the night before. I don't know how I'm going to cope without him."

Molly was grateful that Maggie had wrapped an arm around Sherie, saving her from having to. She took another mouthful of tea, and as she tipped the cup up, she caught her reflection staring back at her in the bottom of the teacup. She looked into her own eyes and noticed that they were still shining. She squinted at herself, curious as to how that could even be possible after last night. *It's probably just the surface of the china,* she thought.

She kept the cup to her lips for a moment more while she stared at the girl at the bottom of her teacup. She swallowed the rest of the tea and put the cup down on the saucer.

"I'll look after you, kiddo," she told Sherie. She gave her a detached pat on the leg despite her effort for the gesture to come across as affectionate, and then stood up.

"Where are you going?" Sherie asked.

Jesus, not even two days without him and she is acting as if she was eleven years old again, Molly thought. "For a walk," she said aloud.

"Can I come?"

"I'd rather walk alone."

"I don't have to talk."

"I doubt that."

"Please?"

"Molly, take your sister with you," Maggie said.

"Come on then," Molly said with a sigh as she started toward the front door.

Sherie leaped up as if she were attached to Molly by a very short rope. "Can we go down to the bridge? Or, ooh, maybe we can go and visit Sam? His father's sheep had TWO lambs last week."

Molly could not contain her sarcasm. "Really?!"

Sherie didn't appear to notice her tone, or more than likely, Molly mused, she chose to ignore it. She bounced down the stairs, both feet jumping onto each step before she launched herself down to the next one. "Yes! They weren't expecting two because she wasn't very fat, but then, after the first one popped out, they saw more legs and then a little while later, there it was, a twin lamb!"

"Do you think they'd give us one?" Molly asked.

"Since when have you wanted a pet lamb?"

"I mean for dinner!" Molly said.

Sherie was quiet for the rest of the walk.

That night, Edward returned with a different, equally foul man. Molly accepted the coin purse, but this time requested that they meet below the house, in an effort to shield Sherie and Maggie from what she knew was about to happen. This man was aggressive, and he held on to Molly's wrists tightly while he kissed her.

"Relax, Dan, you're paying her. She isn't going to fight back."

Edward's words made Molly feel more disturbed than she already was, for two reasons, the first being that this man shared the name of her father. The second was the way Edward was re-assuring Dan that she wasn't going to fight back, as if it was something he was used to. Molly jumped when she felt a hand between her legs. She was certain that Dan's hands were both holding hers tightly, which would mean that the hands between her legs belonged to Edward.

"Get out, you bastard," she spat.

"Calm down, Molly," Edward said, laughing off her warning.

"Just get it over with," she said.

"Relax, you little whore. Look, here, I'll throw an extra shilling in for the feel up." Edward laughed and tossed another coin on top of the purse.

When Dan had finished, Molly pushed him off her and ran outside. She grabbed a nearby bucket and hugged it to her chest as she vomited violently. The men left shortly after, not bothering to acknowledge her. When she had emptied the contents of her stomach, she dropped the bucket and walked over to the coin purse. Dan had paid more than the previous nights' visitor had. She held the money tightly and her knuckles turned white as the coins pressed into her skin. She walked upstairs slowly, each step more effort than the one before it, and finally made it to bed, collapsing onto the top of her blankets, not bothering to pull them back and get in underneath them. Despite her attempts to forget what had happened, her mind replayed the evening while she tried to fall asleep. She kept hearing his name over and over, and she suppressed the urge to throw up for as long as she could, but when it was clear the contents of her stomach were not going to settle down, she climbed out of bed and allowed herself to vomit out her bedroom window.

This was her father's fault. It was his fault she was being raped, and she hated him for it.

Weeks passed, and Edward's visits became more frequent. Molly learned to control her disgust for the acts she was subjected to, and eventually she grew numb to it. She found solace in the coin purse that was left behind after then men disappeared. The men varied, and so did the price they paid for her. One night she tried to put some rules in place with Edward, but he slapped her in the face, knocked a back tooth out, and took away one of the shillings from her pouch. It was clear Edward had no desire to consider this a business arrangement between the two.

Molly's anger grew in conjunction with Sherie's utter obliviousness of the situation. What made her even angrier was her sickly sweet positive attitude, coupled by the fact that not only did Sherie maintain the hope that their father would return, but also that she verbalized it on a daily basis. Molly's feelings festered and mutated into a bizarre ambivalence to the entire state of affairs. She was furious that she had allowed herself—no, that her father had allowed her to be violated by the town he claimed was full of 'good people,' but the money she received from these people was a tangible reinforcement that she had the power to do whatever it took to look after her family. The money made her feel safe and in control of things. It even made her smile again.

Molly had planned to confront Edward when he visited her alone next. This time though, she didn't want to lose another tooth, so she took her time to devise her plan, and made sure she executed it with perfect timing. Occasionally he would come without a man, and demand to be looked after for a quarter of what the other men paid. If she tried to deny him, he punished her by not returning with another man for a week, which meant she didn't receive any money that week. When Edward arrived that evening, Molly greeted him with a bottle of liquor.

"What is this for?" he asked.

"A thank you. For everything."

He frowned at her, but sat down on a nearby chair and drank the bottle in almost one go, burping as he slammed it down onto the table. "Don't think we are going to be making any deals. I've already told you. You get what you get."

"I know. I get what I get, and you get what you get," Molly said. She stared at his eyes intently, waiting for his pupils to dilate to the point where she was sure he would not have complete control of his motor skills.

"That's right." He reached out and pinched her roughly.

Molly snapped. Fine motor skills or not, she refused to put up with Edward for a second longer. She picked up the bottle and brought it hard down onto the edge of the table, smashing it in half. It shattered, and, much to Molly's pleasure, sharp glass spiked from the neck of the bottle, which she used as a handle. She pushed his filthy hand away from her and thrust the bottle forward, pressing it to his throat. Stunned, Edward blinked and teetered on his chair, and Molly took the opportunity to move behind him and drive the sharp glass into his throat, drawing blood. She made sure not to press too deeply.

Edward began to scream. Of course, Molly had no intentions of killing him, though she was tempted.

"Like I said, you get what you get, but I'm starting to realize, Eddy," Molly growled into his ear, "that I'm contributing an awful lot more to this than you are. In fact, I can do this without you here at all. So, here is how it's going to work—"

Molly was cut off when she heard Sherie's gasp from the bottom of the stairs. Sherie stood in shock as she took in the scene before her. Blood trickled down Edward's throat, mixing with his sweat and staining his shirt.

"Molly! What are you doing?"

"Go back upstairs. Now," Molly instructed calmly.

"Stop! What's going on? Molly, stop!" Sherie was becoming frantic, and Molly knew she wasn't just about to go upstairs and pretend nothing had ever happened.

"He's evil, Sherie. He's evil and he needs to go away."

"What will happen to us if you kill him? He's helping us. We can't live without that money."

"I am the one helping us!" Molly screamed, her rage unleashed by Sherie's utter ignorance of the entire situation. "He gives us money because he lets men rape me."

"What are you talking about?"

"Tell her!" Molly instructed, pushing the bottle harder into Edward's throat.

Edward looked close to passing out, but he nodded weakly. Molly watched Sherie's eyes scan the scene, finally settling on Edward's unbuttoned pants, and realization washed over her face.

"I want to slit his throat, Sherie," Molly said.

Edward howled under the glass, reduced to a pathetic mess.

"Don't, Molly. Just let him go. He won't come back, will you, Edward?"

Edward shook his head, whimpering when the movement pushed the glass sideways into his wound.

"I can't let go. I want to, I think…but I can't. I need to drag this glass through his throat. I need him to feel pain Sherie," Molly said.

Sherie walked slowly over to her and placed a gentle hand on top of Molly's shaking one. "Come on," she said softly. She pried Molly's rigid fingers from the bottle.

Edward stumbled and moved as fast as his blood loss would allow him to stumble to the front door, and when he was out of sight, Molly let herself relax a little.

"You're bleeding," Sherie said. Molly's tight grasp on the broken bottle had caused the glass to pierce her skin.

Sherie led Molly upstairs and sat her down on her bed. She used a towel to wrap Molly's hand up. "Stay here. I'm going to heat some water for the tub," she said.

Molly slept while Sherie heated enough water to fill the bath. When it was ready, she woke Molly and guided her into the tub. She gently sponged the blood off her hands, and cleaned the wound, which was luckily not too deep at all. "I had no idea," she finally whispered, breaking the silence.

"I know. I wanted it to stay that way," Molly said.

"I feel so guilty. Why would you put yourself through that?"

"Why do you think? We didn't have any other choice."

"What are we going to do now?" Sherie asked. "For money?" she clarified.

"The men will come back," Molly said plainly.

"We need to call the police then!" Sherie was alarmed.

"Or we just establish ground rules, and allow them to come in on our terms," Molly said.

Sherie stopped short, unable to comprehend what her sister had just suggested.

"I've been making a small amount of money, but Edward always took half of it. Sometimes more."

"Okay…" Sherie waited for her to go on.

"I don't think he'll be coming back anytime soon. Without him taking a cut, I can double what I was earning," Molly said.

Sherie wasn't convinced. "It doesn't seem safe. We have crops to sell still. There has to be a better way to earn money."

"The field is drying up. Ed took most of what hasn't already died. What's left isn't good enough to reseed, and we don't have any money to buy more," Molly said.

Sherie sat silent.

"You don't think I haven't spent hours thinking of different ways? You seriously think I want to do this? It's the only way."

Sherie shook her head. "Not possible. It can't be. We'll talk to Maggie in the morning. She'll have some thoughts."

"You keep your mouth shut, understand? There will be no telling Maggie." Molly raised her index finger as Sherie opened her mouth to protest. "And there will be no trying to convince me otherwise. This is how it's going to be. End of discussion."

Sherie looked into Molly's eyes, searching for the familiar twinkle she was used to seeing, but something had changed. She wondered how she hadn't noticed earlier. Molly lay back in the bath and slid down under the water until she was fully submerged. Sherie looked at her sister's naked body, peppered with bruises along her wrists, ribs, and hips. Her eyes traveled up to her face, serene and expressionless under the water. Small bubbles escaped from her nose and mouth and floated to the surface. Molly was a woman now, not just her big sister, and Sherie knew well enough that once her mind was made up, that was the end of it.

Business started slower than what they had hoped it would, thanks to word spreading of what Molly had done to Edward. Choosing not to let one little incident set her back, Molly made personal visits to some of the men who Edward had 'introduced' her to, and encouraged them to come back, promising an increase of services to go along with the increase in price. A fair few of the men agreed to her terms before they had even heard her proposition—some were really just that desperate to get their hands on a woman, and others in an effort to get rid of her before the unsuspecting wife could overhear the conversation. She found herself flirting with the men who seemed unconvinced about the adjustment of rates, and it didn't take much more to have them agree to return. Before long, Molly was 'entertaining' steadily almost every night, and it had reached the point where she could no longer hide the situation from Maggie.

One evening, three men had arrived at the same time, and despite Molly's attempts to reason with them, none of them wanted to wait his turn. Reluctantly, Molly told Maggie what she had been doing.

Maggie looked appalled when Molly told her, naturally, but she didn't have time to explain in detail.

"Please, Maggie. Three showed up, and one of them has a freaking sovereign," she begged her.

"Well, this explains why you were able to get the roof fixed so quickly."

"Is that a yes?" Molly asked.

"Absolutely not!" Maggie said. "And tomorrow we are going to talk about how to get you out of this mess."

"Why stop? Maggie, we're making a killing!"

"WE?!" You don't mean to tell me you've dragged your younger sister into this?"

"No, of course not. She knows what's going on, but she doesn't...you know. We can afford for just me to do it."

"At what cost, Molly?"

"At no cost! That's the beauty!"

"The beauty?! Selling your body for nothing but a few shillings is nothing beautiful, Molly Kelly," Maggie admonished her.

"It's more than a few shillings. I told you, one of them has a sovereign!"

"Molly!" Maggie was entirely unimpressed.

"You're missing the point. This body is nothing beautiful. This life is nothing beautiful. My father left us, and I'm doing what I need to in order to get by." Molly was getting annoyed now. She was looking for help, not judgment.

"Look, if you don't want to help, fine. Just know that means I'm going to have to ask Sherie to help, because I really won't be able to take all three by myself. I mean, I can try, I've done two before, but..." Molly trailed off and waited for the guilt to seep in. She didn't have to wait long.

"Fine," Maggie said. "Once, and only once."

Molly smiled. "Deal!"

Maggie cringed. "This isn't what I had in mind when I promised your mother on her death bed that I would look after her daughters."

"Well, I'm sure this isn't what my father had in mind when he promised us that Edward Smith was going to look after us...but we adjust."

Maggie shook her head. "This is one hell of an adjustment."

It took less than a month for Maggie to give in and participate a second time. She suspected Molly had been encouraging certain men to frequent the house more often in an effort to overrun herself, leaving Maggie with no choice but to step in and help. It worked, and before long, she was working every night as well. They continued to live as normally as they possibly could, despite the significant changes that had taken place. Sherie played her part by making sure her mother's vase was always filled with the most beautiful flowers, as per her father's parting request. Eventually, they had enough money to buy the most stunning bunches, fresh from Flanagan's. It gave Maggie some comfort to know that, despite the ugliness that was going on under the roof of the home that had sheltered the Kelly girls for so long, Sherie could still capture the loveliness of life in something as simple as an arrangement of flowers.

In the beginning, the men would arrive at the house loaded with liquor and a bottle to drink while they were there, but Molly had floated the idea of turning their living room into a bar and selling alcohol to make even more money. Maggie agreed that it certainly couldn't hurt.

"Maybe it would generate enough of an income so that you could stop what you are doing, and we could just sell liquor?" Sherie suggested.

"Why stop?" Molly asked.

"I just never thought things would turn out this way," Sherie said.

"Of course you didn't. Aren't you proud though, that we found a way to look after ourselves?"

"I suppose. I don't know. I don't think I'm proud of what we are doing."

"You're not doing it," Molly snapped. "I'm proud. This house is falling apart and we are the ones saving it. You know those stilts won't hold it up forever. Dad said it himself—they need replacing. Isn't that why he left us in the first place? What do you think he would say if he got a letter from us telling him to come home because we had fixed the house? He could drop his gold pan and catch the next coach to Richmond."

"I don't want him to know what we are doing," Sherie said, her head lowered.

"You don't really still think he's coming back, do you?" Molly asked.

"Part of me hopes he doesn't," Sherie whispered, not looking up.

Maggie decided their bickering had gone on long enough. "Girls! Come on...let's have a bit of faith. I think opening a bar is a great idea, and I definitely like the idea of not touching any more men in the near future," she said. She didn't like the current tone of the conversation, nor the direction it was headed. She had come to expect such remarks from Molly, but hearing those kinds of words come out of Sherie's mouth was something new and it unsettled her. As far back as she could remember, Sherie had always possessed the ability to see the good in even the most horrific of situations, and her current lack of hope concerned her greatly.

"What if the coppers find out?" Sherie asked.

"They won't. We are opening a bar, not a brothel. You really think Dan and the others want word to get out around town that they are paying for sex?" Sherie shook her head.

"Of course not," Molly continued. "No one will know."

"Based on the way Constable Smith looks at me whenever I pass by the station, I'd say we might even get a bit of business out of a few of them," Maggie said.

"So what are we going to call it?" Sherie asked.

"Call what?" asked Molly.

"The bar. If we're going to open a bar, it's going to need a name." Sherie nudged her toe against a bucket of water sitting beside her, causing the reflection of the stars to ripple and appear as if they were moving.

Maggie noticed Sherie's unbroken stare. "Pretty."

"What? Oh. Yes…Pavo." Sherie looked up at the constellation and Maggie followed her gaze, the stars twinkling amongst the hues of the navy midnight sky. "When I look at the stars, I can almost feel Dad's presence," she said.

Maggie reached out and placed a comforting hand on Sherie's arms, which were folded across her body. "You can't feel the presence of someone who is still alive. You're just remembering how you felt when he was here," she said.

Maggie hoped her reassurance had consoled her. It wasn't the first time they had discussed the possibility that Daniel might never return, and Maggie couldn't shake the feeling that he was no longer walking the same earth as they were.

Sherie nodded. "You're right. He'll come back. He promised." She looked back down to the bucket on the ground and gave it another nudge with her toe. She didn't look convinced, and Maggie didn't blame her. She wasn't either.

"What about 'The Bucket Full of Stars'?" Sherie suggested.

"Too long," Molly said. "And too romantic. But you're on the right track..." She looked at the bucket. "What about 'The Suds Bucket'?"

Sherie's eyes lit up. "Perfect."

Maggie agreed too, and so the Suds Bucket was born.

Chapter 4

The Suds Bucket overflowed with success due to a number of reasons. There was a buzz about Richmond as the villagers flocked in to see what had happened to the old Kelly home. Of course, there were a number of people who were beyond shocked at what Molly and Sherie had decided to do, none of whom kept their opinions to themselves, but the girls brushed off the criticism, most of which they were too busy to listen to anyway. The fact that Richmond itself sat conveniently in the middle of the route from Port Arthur to Hobart meant that more than enough convicts and soldiers stopped overnight, and sailors and soldiers alike were hardly known for their reputation to search for a good cup of tea. There was only one other bar in the town, and it certainly could not compete with the unspoken services of the Suds Bucket. It wasn't long before the other bar transformed into an inn, as a last ditch effort to remain open for business. While sales at the Suds Bucket skyrocketed, the villagers' opinion of Sherie, Molly, and Maggie plummeted in the opposite direction as rumors spread like wildfire about their underground shenanigans.

"Surprise" raids by the police were unsuccessful, due in part to the fact that Constable Smith had developed a slight conflict of interest, also known as a crush on Sherie.

Throughout the rapid success of the business, Sherie remained untouched, despite the bemoaning from many a customer who offered more than a few sovereigns to be the first man to take her to bed. She was torn, feeling both thankful and helpless about the fact that she was not contributing her body to the operation. She watched Molly's eyes lose their sparkle completely, duller than the scythe below the house that had once harvested the crops, now forgotten. She felt guilty for being the reason why Maggie cried herself to sleep every night over the broken promise made to her mother long ago—to keep her and Molly safe. She felt helpless and overlooked when she did speak up, ignored when she asked if she could help. More than once, Molly had told her unequivocally that under no circumstances was she allowed to do anything but serve the liquor.

"But I hate feeling like I'm the only one not doing it."

"Can you just listen to yourself for one second, please? You're actually asking me if you can be a prostitute. A whore, Sherie," Molly said. Her blunt choice of words would not deter Sherie.

"It's not about that. It's about seeing you and Maggie doing what you do, and feeling like I'm not pulling my weight. Just because you're older than me doesn't mean I'm not allowed to want to look out for you. I want to help."

"Look, you don't understand. I know we laugh down here, but that's part of it! We're meant to look like we're having a good time, because that's what these pigs want. Do you really think for one second that I enjoy what they do to me upstairs? Of course I don't! If you saw what went on, we wouldn't even be having this conversation. You don't see what some of those disgusting men makes us do up there. You don't understand," Molly said.

"The other day one of the sailors offered three sovereigns to take me upstairs when he found out I was a virgin," Sherie told her.

"Good! Let them keep trying. Tempt them with the unattainable! Flirt with them, turn them on, but then send them upstairs."

"You hear them all begging for me, don't you? You know they want me the most," Sherie bragged.

"You're sixteen years old! Of course they want you, but I'm telling you now: they will never have you. I will never let that happen to you." Molly put down two empty glasses of beer on the bar. "Wash these, and then go to bed," she instructed.

Sherie scowled as she picked up the glasses and plunged them into the bucket of soapy water beside her. Molly was being noble and protective, and it pissed Sherie off. Only two years her senior, Sherie felt it was pretty rich of Molly to be treating her like such a child. She surveyed the area that had once been a quiet family room, and felt a wave of nausea rush over her when she saw the overweight and far from sober cobbler standing in the corner where her mother used to sit and read books to her and Molly. The very same cobbler who made her squeal with delight on her ninth birthday when her mother had ordered her a pair of custom made leather boots, which he had gone out of his way to dye red for her. The cobbler's greasy hand had disappeared up Maggie's skirt, roaming wherever it pleased. Sherie's lip curled as she watched, wishing she could turn away but unable to convince her eyes.

"We're closing," Sherie called, finally able to focus on something other than the cobbler.

"Get up or get out!" yelled Molly, winking at a group of men who were visiting the Suds Bucket for the first time. They had been fairly rowdy all evening and Sherie had seen the same situation more than enough times to know that at least one, if not two of them, would be reaching into their pockets any moment. Maggie disappeared silently upstairs with the cobbler, and Sherie made a mental note to purge all happy memories that had anything to do with her red leather boots.

The front of the house was set up in such a way that the entrance of the bar opened straight into the old family room—one long room with stairs at the end of it, opposite the front door. Facing the stairs, standing at the entrance to the left was where the kitchen once stood, now a fully functioning and terribly popular bar. Beside that and leading outside was a makeshift kitchen that was hidden by walls that were recently added. Opposite the bar, the family room flowed seamlessly through a wooden archway to what used to be the lounge room. Patrons could hide around the corner behind the wall that separated the family room from the lounge room, where they would drink copious amounts of alcohol, nominating the least drunk to go to the bar and buy more drinks when Sherie had decided any one of them was too drunk to continue drinking. It had worked initially, but after the girls caught on to what they were doing, they made sure at least one of them was at the back of the lounge at all times, to keep an eye on things.

Molly made her way over to the group of men who were just peeking out from behind the corner. Sherie watched carefully, as she always did with unfamiliar patrons, reminding herself to talk to Maggie and Molly about the possibility of hiring someone to help with security. After all, three women alone in a bar full of drunk men who not only wanted to have sex but expected it…it was only a matter of time before something went wrong.

"Hey! If you're going to touch, you're going to pay," Molly said, her voice dropping all sexual undertone.

"How much?" the drunk man closest to her slurred.

"What do you have?" Molly asked.

The man held out the coins that he was holding ready and waiting.

"Yeah, okay." Molly took the coins from him and tucked them into her skirt pocket.

"Is that for just me? Or all of us?" the man asked.

"All of you? All four of you?"

The man nodded.

"I want the same amount from each of you, and two of you will have to wait. The bar's closed though, sorry. You'll just have to hope your friend here is quick," she said. The two men who were being told to wait did not look happy at all. Sherie saw Molly take a step back, and she felt an energy rush through her body as she realized the seriousness of the situation when the man closed the distance between them again.

"Can't we all come up? We can pay you more," the man said, pulling out more coins and pressing them into her hand. "Come on. We don't have long until we have to be on the road again."

Molly shook her head.

"We can watch, sweetie. I'll give you a shilling if you just let me watch," another said.

"You have two hands, don't you?" the third man said, stumbling as he pointed to Molly's hands, which were propped up on her hips. "Two hands, two of us." He gestured to himself and one of the others. "Alf on top, and Ruán here watching," he suggested.

Molly looked down at the money Alf was holding out. Sherie couldn't believe she was considering it. *Not even Molly could be tempted by the money to take four men at once*, she thought.

Sherie was wrong.

Molly held her hand out and Sherie watched it shake as she took the money. "Let's go, boys!" Molly called, her mood changing the second the coins dropped into her pocket. One thing was for sure—Molly certainly did her job well.

She made her way toward the stairs, waving at Sherie when she passed by the bar. Sherie wanted to vomit as she watched her sister lead the way for the four burly men. Molly was half way up when Ruán stumbled on the stairs, falling down hard and causing Alf to trip over him.

"Hurry up, boys, we don't have all night!" Molly called down as she continued across the landing, the other two men close behind her.

Sherie had to act quickly; she had to make a move in the few seconds it would take the men to pull themselves off the stairs and follow Molly. She didn't want to miss her opportunity to save Molly from what would happen to her if all four men followed her up to her bedroom. She raced around the bar, and squeezed herself past the two men who were still struggling to stand up.

"Are you okay?" Sherie asked, feigning concern as she leaned her body back and slid seductively down the railing. Ruán didn't reply, and only attempted to push past Sherie in an effort to rejoin Molly. Sherie moved in front of him to block his path and force him to pause and consider her. "Did you know I'm a virgin?" she asked him.

Ruán's eyes lit up and instantly traveled down her body. Sherie felt dirty when she watched his eyes stop at her breasts.

"And I'm sixteen," she said to Alf.

They stared at her, dumb. Sherie wasn't really sure what to do next. She reached a hand out and placed it tentatively on Ruán's shoulder.

"Would you like to come upstairs with me?" she asked, her best efforts put toward growling the same way she had heard Maggie do a thousand times before.

Alf looked at her with a cocked head, and Sherie could tell he wasn't convinced by her timid actions. Before she could let them reconsider, she pushed past Ruán, keeping her hand on his shoulder, and pressed her body against Alf's, sliding her hand down his chest, continuing down until she found what she was looking for. She did her best to ensure her face did not convey the fear within her.

Neither man was able to speak as she guided them slowly upstairs to her room. She pushed the doll from her mother off her bed in one fluid motion, hoping they hadn't seen it. She was fairly certain their eyes were elsewhere.

Molly was outraged at first when Sherie told her why the other two men had never joined her, but she admitted to Sherie later on that she found consolation in the knowledge that her sister loved her enough to intervene in such a way. Sherie knew that Maggie was upset, because it took at least a week before she would even look at her, let alone discuss what had happened. Maggie refused to admit that she understood why Sherie felt the need to interject and stop the men from following Molly upstairs. Sherie, however, knew deep down that Maggie knew exactly why, because she had done the very same thing in the beginning. In the end, the whole ordeal brought the girls closer together and established the foundation for the Suds Bucket, which was far stronger than the physical foundations would ever be. It took a long time for that first night to stop appearing in Sherie's nightmares, the repeating scenes unfortunately being replaced by new ones, as opposed to fading away as she had hoped they would. With each night that passed, new and very different experiences would supersede those from the night before. After a while, even the most outlandish evenings became typical.

As time passed, lost women looking for somewhere to call home would come upon the Suds Bucket and fall in love with the false promise of 'staying a few months' to build a better life. Five years on, six beautiful women, who had long said farewell to their pasts, existed with nothing but the shadow of who they used to be. They were women who believed in hopelessness more than they did in hope, and who loved none but each other and the Bucket in which they lived: Sherie, Molly, Maggie, Claire, Olivia, and Georgina.

Chapter 5

The six women who lived and worked at the Suds Bucket spent their days lazing about on the veranda. Topics of discussion varied from the strange fetishes of the clientele or the rashes that were finally clearing up, to the dreams they conjured that allowed them to forget the work that they did. When it was too hot, there was no conversation at all. Today was one of those days.

Molly sat on the two-man swinging chair that backed the front of the Suds Bucket and looked as if it could snap and fall at any moment. The seat beside her was currently vacant, reserved for Sherie. Molly's hair was as dark as her general demeanor. Growing up in the Suds Bucket before it was named so and experiencing its downturn firsthand had left her with a resentment for life that could not be easily hidden.

Maggie rested on the railing of the veranda, her back to the dirt road behind them as she faced Molly. She leaned against a pole and her leg swung back and forth from under her baggy dress. She was the eldest of the women, and though her blonde hair did well at concealing her age, the wrinkles at the corners of her eyes and mouth gave it away. Her lines were not laugh lines. Maggie would sing with Rachel, Molly and Sherie's mother, while they hung the washing out to dry over the balcony, on the very railing where she now sat. Maggie never spoke of Rachel, as it not only upset herself to remember, but the girls too, and that was something she attempted to avoid at all costs. She had given up on the idea that there was a better life out there, and instead devoted herself to looking after Molly and Sherie as best she could. To the left of Maggie sat Claire, stretched across a weathered couch, her face hidden by a book. Gentle loose curls of brown hair that would be soft if given the right attention hid whatever of Claire's face was not already hidden by her book. Her green eyes darted back and forth constantly, as the more time spent reading was less time spent thinking about the life she found herself in, and perhaps more critically, the life she had left behind.

Opposite Claire and to the left of Molly sat Olivia, behind a small spinning table. The pottery wheel spent most hours of daylight spinning, spinning, spinning. Olivia's hands molded the clay into the perfect vase, which would be lucky to see it through till midnight, depending on the rowdiness of the clientele that evening. Her brown hair was covered by a red scarf that protected her locks from the frequent clay splatter.

At the far end of the veranda, a little behind Olivia, was where Georgina sat beside a large copper cage of bright yellow canaries, three in total. With raven black hair and not a single curl, she appeared as a shadow within a shadow, with an unseen but certainly felt dark aura surrounding her. Unspoken pains peeked out from behind her dead golden eyes, but when she spoke to her canaries, it was as if she was free from the burdens of her memories.

The darkness that surrounded the Bucket did not save its occupants from the unforgiving sun that beat down upon them. Too hot to gossip, they sat and listened to the creaking of the swinging chair, the whirring of the pottery wheel, the pages of the book when Claire turned a page (rather infrequently, as her learning to read meant a lot of time spent on one page), the fan that Maggie flicked back and forth in front of her face, and the scratches of canary feet as they fought for the pieces of peach that were offered to them from Georgina's mouth.

Sherie approached the Bucket with her shopping. She smiled when she saw her makeshift family sitting as they always did on the balcony. As she had done a thousand times before, she dropped her bag to the ground and sat in the empty space on the swinging chair beside Molly. She picked up Molly's hands and placed them on her shoulders, hinting for a massage. Molly complied without any further coaxing needed, which surprised Sherie. Perhaps Molly had picked up on the fact that something had happened in town…It was less about intuition and more about the frequency of such occurrences. Molly squeezed Sherie's shoulders slowly, and Sherie relaxed under her grasp.

Sherie settled into her chair and the chorus of background sounds resumed. After a few moments, Claire tipped her head backwards and looked at Maggie from upside down. Maggie returned the look endearingly and Claire shoved the book into the air to roughly Maggie's eye level. "What's a cap-tane?" she asked.

Maggie read the word Claire was pointing at and chuckled. "Captain, hon."

Claire brought the book back into her lap and studied it for a moment. Sherie watched her consider the word, clearly happy with the new information as she grinned triumphantly at Maggie before turning her attention back to the page.

Sherie let her head roll back while Molly massaged her neck. "Mmm. Best sister ever," she said.

Molly smiled and squeezed her shoulders extra tight with affection. "And don't you forget it!"

The day continued much the same, as had the past week, the past month, and the past five years. The sun began to leave, but the heat made no such promise, and the girls eventually moved indoors to prepare for the evening of work ahead.

As the day ended, the Bucket stood in darkness, except for a dim light that flickered through the windows. Inside, Sherie was stationed behind the bar, serving another drink to one of their regulars, Tom Burnes. At thirty years old, Tom had definitely already had his fair share of adventure. He had arrived in Hobart fifteen years earlier on a boat from England. Tried and convicted of a crime that varied depending on who you spoke to about town, Tom had served a seven-year sentence before being released as a man free to settle if he wished. Sherie had heard that he stopped in Richmond on his way from Hobart to Port Arthur with the intent to return to Great Britain. He had stayed for a few weeks before joining a group of men who were headed to the gold fields in Victoria, and after being there for less than six months, he struck gold. Sherie had also heard that he stole the gold from a sleeping Chinese miner, but the stories were all spectacle from bored townsfolk who had nothing better to do. Whether or not the story was true, Sherie wasn't sure. She didn't have the slightest inclination to ask him because she wasn't sure she was prepared to hear the truth. The rumors around which crime he committed that resulted in having him shipped to Australia ranged from theft to indecent assault to murder, and Sherie was happy to remain in the dark. He appeared normal enough to her, always polite, and one of the few men who visited the Bucket for the purpose to drink as opposed to any of the 'extracurricular' activities secretly on offer.

Molly walked past Tom and bumped him slightly, knocking his beer into his lap. He leaped up instantly.

"Oops! Sorry! Sherie, you should get that." Molly winked at Sherie, who rolled her eyes in conjunction with a grin, as she grabbed a towel and made her way around the other side of the bar to dab at Tom's crotch. She wasn't entirely comfortable with her instructions from Molly to 'encourage' Tom as much as she could, but she trusted Molly and knew that her intentions were for the good of the Bucket. The fact that Tom had not only a lot of gold, but no interest in paying any of the women for sex made him an excellent candidate for a husband. It was no secret that Molly wanted Sherie to marry Tom, and while they hadn't discussed the arrangement specifically, Sherie was sure that the idea had more to do with Tom's money than her own happiness. She also knew that having a man in the family would ensure the ownership rights of the Suds Bucket would remain with them, should anything officially happen to her father.

A drunk Chinese man who was apparently still in control of his fine motor skills sat at the piano, belting out a raunchy tune that the patrons encouraged the girls to dance to. Georgina danced slowly between the rows of tables— her ability to make every man think she was dancing for him and only him was unlike any others'. For this reason, she was one of the most popular girls despite her unstable demeanor. The drunken men cheered wildly for her as she slid her body against the invisible music notes. Appearing from the shadows, Olivia snaked her arms out in time to the music, a hand brushing along the leg of the nearest patron. It happened to be Constable Smith, who paid large sums of money to ensure his name did not leave the establishment when he did. Better known as 'Smitty' in the Bucket, he let out a whoop and nodded in approval of the way Olivia's body was moving to the music.

Claire joined the two in a line as they each picked up a seat and twirled it around to sit on it backwards. They had performed this dance a hundred times over. It was clear that the patrons, whether they had witnessed the show a hundred times over or not, were enjoying themselves immensely. While the girls were dancing, the men took the opportunity to gather their money, not only to ensure they had enough to spend on the woman who greatest took his fancy, but also to ensure there was enough money left at the end of the night so that his wife did not notice the funds significantly depleted. It was a game well played by most of the men in the town, whose only other option was spending money at the horse races. Either way they came home with a lighter wallet, but at the Suds Bucket, they were guaranteed a little more than the joy of betting on a fast horse.

James, a young man who would be handsome if he knew how to hold himself, was a regular patron of the Bucket. He leaned against the wall, his eyes on no one but Claire. Another regular, Billy, walked up beside James and let out a hoot, pumping his beer in the air and spilling plenty of it. Billy threw an arm around James and nodded his approval of Claire. "How much longer are you gonna stare at her before you take her upstairs, mate? Ya don't have to convince her!" he guffawed.

James frowned but said nothing as he pushed Billy away from him. Obviously too drunk to care, Billy fell backwards onto a conveniently placed chair behind him and turned his attention back to the girls.

The dance continued as Maggie and Sherie walked behind the three girls sitting on the chairs and twirled slowly and seductively around them. The suggestive moves had clearly been designed to encourage the men to be less than frugal with their cash. When the song reached its crescendo, Molly appeared. Sherie and Maggie dropped to their knees and Molly placed her hands on their heads, forcing them lower to the ground and putting a foot on Maggie's back as she fell forward onto her stomach. Clearly, Molly was the queen bee. The patrons cheered drunkenly as the girls moved from their current positions and began to dance as a group. Their soft hands caressed one another, and this was all it took to convince the few patrons at the back of the room who were uncertain of whether it was worth their money—they moved their hands from their pants to their wallets.

The evening progressed as usual and the girls traded choreography for particular attention to the men who showed the most promise of taking them upstairs. Georgina was giving a lap dance to a very happy man, and she reached out and swiped a full mug of beer from a tray that Maggie was carrying as she walked past. Maggie paused when Georgina swigged from the mug, not bothering to attempt to stop her from drinking what had obviously been bought and paid for by another customer. Georgina placed the mug, now only three quarters full, back down on the tray and returned her attention to the man between her legs on the chair.

Across the room, drunken and excited men chanted in unison, "KISS! KISS! KISS!"

Billy and Smitty joined in with the chant that was directed at Claire and Olivia, who were clearly enjoying teasing them. Claire reached out and removed the hat from a man, before moving towards Olivia. They kissed, open mouth, to a loud cheer from the men. Claire put the hat on Olivia's head mid-kiss. The sound of wallets opening was practically deafening as Olivia bit Claire's lower lip with a wicked flair. When they broke apart, Olivia held the hat out to the boys, who all happily dropped coins into it.

James watched the group from afar and jumped when Maggie grabbed his cheeks as she floated past him with an armful of empty glasses. "Smile, James! You'll make us feel bad!"

He managed a weak attempt at a smile, before turning his attention back to Claire and Olivia, who were now flicking tongues with one another in exchange for more coins.

A weathered old man who was missing more teeth than hair approached Molly with a stagger that was enhanced more than likely by a lot of alcohol. He held up his fist, which clenched a handful of money. He gestured in Sherie's direction, too drunk to even form a sentence. Molly roughly counted the money in his hand. "For the hour or the night, mate?"

The man managed somehow to articulate that he wanted Sherie for the night. "Double it and she's yours," Molly said.

He rubbed his hands together in anticipation, before a snap of Molly's fingers reminded him to dig into his pocket and pull out another few coins. He handed them over with a toothy grin as Sherie made her way around the bar. He wrapped his arms around her as they made their way toward the stairs. Sherie turned to the room and waved. "Goodnight, everyone!"

The bar responded, patrons cheering for the old man, who had clearly done well for himself in his state. Olivia and Claire were sitting on Billy's lap, one knee each, as they called out to Sherie a few seconds later than the rest of the crowd. "Goodnight Sherie!"

Tom turned to Molly, who was polishing glasses. "I hate him," he said.

Molly flicked him with her towel. "You hate all the men here," she said.

Tom screwed his face and muttered his disgust, "That ain't no man…paying for a woman."

"Oh, Tom, you're so noble for such a crim!" she said.

"Don't call me that," Tom said with a scowl. Molly flicked him with her towel again.

"Well, you know we have to make a living somehow. Not all of us are striking it rich on the gold fields!"

Tom nodded.

"I think it's cute, you being all protective of Sherie," said Molly.

"It's not just Sherie, it's all you lot. It's a damn shame," he said, pulling the towel out of her hand before she could whip him again.

"We do what we have to," Molly shrugged. "We're lucky to have you here to look out for us if we need it."

"You do, you know?" Tom looked her dead in the eyes. "I'm here for you. Anything you need," he said.

"I'll keep that in mind," Molly said with a wink.

"I'm gonna head home. You need anything?" he asked.

Molly shook her head. "Not right now," she smiled.

Tom leaned over the bar and gave her a kiss on the cheek. "Night Molly," he said.

"Such a tough crim, handing out kisses to ladies of the night. Next time I'll charge you, you know!" She laughed.

"No, you won't! You love it. And don't call me that!" he said as he waved goodbye and left the bar.

Maggie walked behind the bar to drop off some dirty glasses. James approached the bar and tipped his head close to Molly in an attempt not to be overheard. An amusing concept, considering the bar was so loud. "Can I book Claire for tonight?" he mumbled.

"What's that, honey?" Molly asked, leaning in and plugging her ear in an attempt to hear better.

"Claire. For tonight?" James asked. Maggie interrupted. "She's taken tonight, James. You're too late, sweetie. I'm free though." She flashed a smile at James, who nodded.

"What? She's not ta—" Molly was cut off when Maggie put her hand up to halt the words about to come out of her mouth.

"She's taken. I'll look after this one," Maggie said. She grabbed James' hands and pulled him onto the dance floor. He stumbled as they began to dance, knocking Maggie into Georgina, who was dancing with Smitty. Smitty bumped into the piano, and the clay vase that was resting on it tumbled and smashed when it hit the ground.

Instantaneously, the music stopped and the patrons all groaned in disappointment.

"Good one, Smitty!" snarled Billy, highly unimpressed. Throughout the room, men shot dirty looks in Smitty's direction, and Billy thumped him on the arm.

Molly made her way from behind the bar and climbed onto the piano, her hands on her hips. "That's the evening, people! You know the rules. Drinks down, get out!"

Billy looked at his empty glass. "Aw, come on, Mol, you didn't even call last drinks!"

Molly was unswayed. "Too bad! You've been coming long enough to know that when the vase is done for, so are you!"

The drunken patrons moved disappointedly toward the door, downing the last of their drinks. Maggie and James headed upstairs together. Smitty gave Georgina a smack on the ass, causing her to squeal.

"Smitty, next time we'll charge you for that! Paul, if you look up my skirt, it will be the last thing you ever see!" Molly issued her warnings to the boys as they walked out the door. Paul was ruffled by his mates as they left. Olivia traipsed up the stairs with her 'gentleman' for the evening, and Claire made her way over to the pianist. "You want your gobbie now, or save it for a rainy day, Mr. Yinyue?" she asked him.

"Georgina free?" Mr. Yinyue asked.

Paul called goodbye to Georgina, who blew him a suggestive kiss. He paused for a moment, digging through his pockets. "Hey, Ned, loan me a shilling?"

"Loan him two shillings, Ned," Molly told him.

Ned pulled two coins out of his pocket and handed them to Paul, who gave them to Molly.

"She's yours," Molly said. She winked at Georgina, who wrapped her arms around Paul, and dragged him in the direction of the stairs. He cheered with excitement as he half stumbled and was half dragged up the stairs.

"Sorry, Yinyue, not tonight," Claire said. "D'you want me? Come on."

Mr. Yinyue nodded and followed Claire upstairs for his free blow job in return for his services behind the piano.

With the Bucket in silence (on the first level anyway), Molly turned her attention to the money behind the bar, and mused over what Tom had said to her. She wondered if he was sincere, whether he really would do anything for them. She pulled the cash bag out from under the bar and filled it up with the night's takings. She could count the money tomorrow, but the conversation she wanted to have with Tom could not wait.

Molly knocked on Tom's door and it took a while for him to answer. She cringed as she waited. He was probably asleep. As soon as he opened the door, she spoke. "I'm sorry if I woke you."

"Don't be. It's fine. Are you okay? Did something happen?"

"Can I come in?" she asked.

"Of course." Tom stepped aside and let Molly in. His house was small and rather empty. She looked for somewhere to sit before deciding to just lean against an old wooden table in the middle of the room.

"You know how you said you'd do anything for us? Earlier?"

Tom moved closer to Molly, looking confused. "Er, yes?"

"Well, what do you think about marrying Sherie?"

Tom spluttered, clearly blindsided. "What?"

"Have I ever told you that if anything happens to my father, we lose the Suds Bucket?"

"No."

Molly nodded. "It's true. If, or actually I should probably say when people realize that he isn't coming back, ownership will pass to whatever relative is around. Male relative, I should clarify, and if there's no one, the government can just take it back. Us women aren't qualified to own property."

"Well, to most people women are property," said Tom.

"You don't think so?"

"I'm not most people."

"So will you help us?"

"Geez Molly, I don't know. Does Sherie even want to marry me?"

"She wants what is best for the Bucket."

"Yes, but does she love me?"

Molly laughed. "Wait, you're serious? Well, sure, of course she does!" She knew Tom didn't believe her, and rightly so. "Look, I see the way you look at us. It's been a long time since you've...you know..."

"What?" Tom looked at her.

"Held a woman. Been with a woman,"

"I'm not going to answer that question." Tom blushed.

"You just did. Look, mate, if Sherie can prove to you that she loves you, would you consider marrying her? Please? For me?"

Tom looked at her. "For you, huh?"

Molly flashed him a grin. "Why don't you start with a date? Court her properly!"

Tom nodded. "Alright. That sounds reasonable."

Molly kicked anything without roots as she walked home. This was not the life she would have chosen for herself. She hated that she was selling not just her sister's body, but her future now too. It was for the best though, and a marriage was a necessity. Despite his background, Tom was a good man and she knew that was an important part of setting Sherie up for the long run. She wondered what she would change if she were given the chance to go back and make different decisions. A few things came to mind, but every scenario had the same core problem: money, or rather the lack thereof. No, if given the opportunity, Molly would have done everything exactly the same way.

Chapter 6

A month had passed and Tom and Sherie had been on several dates. Despite Molly's persistent nagging, there was still nothing solid between the two, though Sherie insisted that the relationship was still a work in progress.

With the heat in full force, the girls sat out on the balcony as they had done the past month, in silence. Olivia's hands moved up the wet clay, and she sighed dramatically out of nowhere. "I don't care that my vases get smashed, honestly. But it would be so nice if for once they could fulfill their life purpose, and actually hold a bunch of flowers."

The girls looked sympathetic and Sherie nodded. "I noticed the other day that Flanders Flowers has the most amazingly beautiful daffodils." She lamented over the fact that it had been at least three years since there had been fresh flowers inside the Bucket. Molly looked at her, as if she was daring her to ask the question. Sherie knew better and held her tongue.

"You know you could just pick the yellow flowers that are on the side of the road," Molly suggested.

Sherie scoffed, insulted. "Those are weeds!"

"Well, you're not spending our money, if that's what you think," Molly shot back.

Sherie stood and walked over to Olivia, and pinched her cheeks. "Look at this face. This hard working face," she pleaded. Olivia was covered in clay, and the lines in her face suggested stress far greater than she should be enduring at her age.

"Hard working, yes. To put food on the table and to pay our bills. We can't afford luxuries like flowers. You know that." Molly gave Sherie a stern look, completely unnecessary, however, since Sherie knew well enough the unfortunate financial situation that the Bucket was in.

Claire looked up from her book. "I thought we had a big night last night?"

Molly looked at Claire, eyes ever so narrowed, and it was difficult to tell if she was squinting from the sun or giving her a dirty look. "Big bills too."

Claire shut up, returning her attention to her book. Maggie stood up and disappeared into the Bucket before the conversation continued.

Sherie and Olivia looked at Molly with downtrodden faces. Sherie knew it was lost on her though, as she picked up her beer and drank it without looking at them. Molly was not one who could be easily convinced to do anything she didn't want to do.

"Don't look at me like that. If you want to blame someone, blame Dad for leaving."

Sherie's face changed from a playful attempt to guilt her sister into buying flowers to one of anger. "He didn't leave. He went to earn money. To find gold. To give us a better life," she reminded her.

Molly threw her now empty beer bottle into a crate beside the chair, and it crashed against other empty bottles. "Yeah? And how's that workin' out for you? 'Cause I'm sure as hell not loving it."

Sherie got up and started towards the stairs, finished with the conversation. "I have to meet Tom," she said bluntly.

Molly opened another beer and took a swig. She kicked her feet up onto the chair. Raising her voice to reach Sherie, who was halfway down the stairs, she called in frustration, "You know if you put a little more effort into that relationship, the Bucket could have all the flowers you could dream up!"

Sherie stormed down the steps, ignoring the statement. The words hurt because she knew there was an element of truth to them.

She was walking away from the Bucket when she stopped for a second to consider the yellow flowers that littered the side of the road. *Bloody weeds*. She kicked dirt in frustration as she started down the road to town.

"Sherie!" Sherie stopped and turned back towards the Bucket balcony, but she couldn't determine who had called her name. Claire was buried in her book, Olivia was potting, Georgina was playing with a canary, and Molly was drinking and sulking into her beer.

"Sherie!" The voice was coming from above her. She looked up and saw Maggie hanging out of the window on the second story. Sherie took a few steps closer to the Bucket.

Maggie held up her hand, something small inside it. She made a motion that she was going to throw it down, and after a quick nod from Sherie, she pitched it in an arc, and Sherie caught it perfectly in her palm. She opened her hand and saw a coin resting there. Before she could protest, Maggie blew her a kiss and disappeared back into the Bucket. Sherie shot a quick glance to Molly, who seemed unaware of this exchange as she continued to drink.

Sherie turned around, an added bounce to her step as she made her way to town.

Maggie

Ten Years Earlier...

Rachel opened the door and caught Maggie just in time as she collapsed forward, the handle no longer holding her up.

"Maggie! Goodness, what on earth happened to you?" Despite her slight frame, Rachel somehow managed to carry Maggie across the room and into the sitting room, where she laid her on the nearest couch. A lot of Maggie's blood had already started to congeal, matting her hair and sticking it to her face, but some of it still trickled, and dripped without hesitation onto the cream cushions Rachel laid her on. Rachel was beyond shocked, but she knew better than to show it. She pulled a handkerchief from out of her blouse and began to dab at the cuts on Maggie's face.

"Daniel?" Rachel called calmly to her husband. "Could you please mix some warm water with salt, and bring it to me?"

"What for?" came the voice from the other room.

"Please, just bring it as quickly as you can." Rachel stroked Maggie's hair as gently as she could. "And wake the girls. Send them to fetch Doctor Patterson," she told Daniel when he entered the room with the salt water, but he just stood there staring at Maggie's bloodied face. "Daniel, the girls, quickly please," Rachel reminded him as she dipped the handkerchief into the water. This time, Daniel managed a nod before leaving the room to wake Sherie and Molly.

"I'm sorry, Maggie, my sweet, this is going to hurt," she whispered as she touched it to one of the more nasty cuts.

Daniel returned after sending the girls on their way to fetch the doctor, this time holding a glass that was filled with a cloudy liquid. "Warm water and sugar," he said, and set it down on the table beside the couch.

"Thank you, dear." Rachel smiled at him. "Though I don't think she's quite up to drinking it yet…" She paused and surveyed Maggie's face. "She's barely conscious."

Rachel pulled Maggie's eyelid back to look at her pupils, and Maggie groaned in agony when she touched a particularly tender spot on her brow bone.

"Sorry, Maggie," Rachel said, her tone hushed and gentle, dabbing even more softly than before.

It took a good few hours for Maggie to be able to sit up, and only once she had swallowed most of the sugar water was she able to talk. Even then, it sounded like she was speaking with a mouth full of acorns.

"Doctor Patterson must have told him," was all she said, which apparently she felt was a sufficient enough explanation for Rachel and Daniel. Completely clueless, they looked at her in anticipation of additional information.

It didn't come, and Maggie lost control of herself, bursting into tears and throwing herself into Rachel's arms. Rachel let her sob, and just held her tight until the girls arrived back with the doctor. Sherie and Molly led him into the sitting room.

"Maggie?" Dr. Patterson asked gently, touching her on the shoulder.

Maggie looked up, her face hidden behind blood soaked hair. Her face was a rainbow of purple and red, and one eye had swelled so much that it was completely closed. Her lips were twice the size they should be, and cut in multiple places. Sherie gasped.

"Daniel, get them out of here, please," Rachel asked. He ushered Molly and Sherie out of the room and they left without protest.

"Did you tell him?" Maggie asked, her words difficult to understand through the swelling.

"I didn't realize you hadn't mentioned it, Maggie. Yes, I did," the doctor said.

"Tell him what?" Rachel asked. This was not the first time Maggie's husband had beaten her, but it was certainly the most horrific.

Maggie and Frank got married after they discovered that Maggie was pregnant. Halfway through the pregnancy, she suffered a miscarriage. Frank was furious, claiming that Maggie had tricked him into marrying her for nothing. He tried to get her pregnant again very soon afterward, but was unsuccessful. They tried time and time again, but eventually Frank accepted the fact that he was stuck married to a woman who he did not love, and who was unable to give him any children, and that made him a very difficult person to be married to. Frank refused to stop trying, but Maggie had her suspicions that there was something wrong. Rachel had suggested she visit the doctor, to talk about what the problem might be.

"Maggie came to see me a few days ago, and we discovered that she is unable to conceive," Dr. Patterson said.

Rachel shook her head. "Mags, I'm so sorry."

Maggie looked up at Rachel. Her one open eye was welling with tears.

The doctor knelt beside Maggie and opened his bag. Rachel moved back to give him some room, but she didn't let go of Maggie's hand.

"This has gone far enough," she said in a firm voice.

"Your face is very badly damaged, in case that wasn't already apparent to any of you," the doctor said. "If I'm understanding correctly, you're saying Frank did this to you?"

Maggie shook her head. "No. He loves me."

"Maggie!" Rachel reprimanded her. "Stop protecting that asshole."

The doctor appeared shocked at Rachel's choice of words, and looked at Daniel, who shrugged. "You should stay somewhere safe for a few days, until your face heals."

"And then what? Go back for round two? I don't think so!" Rachel said.

"I don't have anywhere else to go. My parents haven't spoken to me since I got pregnant."

"Don't even get me started on your parents. Anyone who decides not to go to their daughter's wedding just because of one tiny slip in judgment doesn't deserve a beautiful daughter like you," Rachel said.

The doctor closed his bag and stood up. "I've cleaned you up the best I can. Come and see me in a week and we'll see how that bruise is doing." He motioned to the large purple mark on the side of Maggie's face. "Do you have any arnica?"

"No, but I can pop in to town later on today and pick some up," Rachel said.

The doctor reached into his bag and pulled out a small jar of ointment. "Here. Have this. It should keep you going for a while."

Rachel took the jar with a nod of thanks.

"Take care of her," said Dr. Patterson.

"Always have, always will." Rachel looked down at Maggie, whose face may very well have had some color return to it. Whether that was the case or not would forever be a mystery, thanks to the shades of purple and red that splattered from her temple, across her nose, and down to the opposite cheek bone.

Rachel watched Daniel show the doctor out of the house. She waited until he was out of earshot before muttering under her breath. "Idiot."

Maggie hit Rachel in a lame attempt to admonish her for abusing the doctor. "He wasn't to know," she said.

"Oh, sure, because every happily married woman visits him with broken ribs and fractured cheek bones." Rachel scoffed.

"I didn't tell him how I got them."

"He's a doctor, Maggie, and it's his job to notice that. Whatever on earth happened to 'do no harm'?"

"I don't blame him," Maggie said.

Rachel smiled again, and wiped away a strand of hair that had fallen across Maggie's face. "I love the way that you see the best in everyone. Even that jerk husband of yours."

"Where do you think I learned it from?" Maggie asked her, taking Rachel's hand in hers and giving it a squeeze.

"Certainly not your mother."

"Mmhm. Did Daniel tell you they're leaving?"

"Yes. I wasn't sure if you knew. Can you believe it? What on earth would possess someone to go back to Ireland?"

Maggie shook her head. "They can go to the moon for all I care. The further away the better."

"You don't really mean that," Rachel said.

"Yes, I do. As far as I'm concerned, the only thing they ever did right was move to Australia. They're idiots to leave." Maggie flinched.

"Don't forget the fact that they made you and your brother…they got that right."

"They got Daniel right. Not me. Look at me. I'm a mess. I married a man who doesn't love me, I can't have babies, and I'm too stupid to leave him because I'd go broke without him and I have nowhere to go."

"That's the second time you've said that. Of course you have somewhere to go, you fool. Do you know how many empty rooms we have upstairs? We never use the reading room, and you know that the nursery isn't going to be used again any time soon," Rachel said, breaking eye contact with Maggie.

"You've stopped trying?" Maggie asked.

"Guess you're not the only one who can't have babies," Rachel admitted, allowing the sadness to flood her voice.

"At least you have two. I've got none," Maggie said.

"You can share them with us."

Maggie chuckled. "I feel like I already do. I love them like they're my own. I'll never be able to thank you and Daniel enough for bringing two such beautiful girls into my world."

"Your nieces love you as much as you love them, you know that, right? They'd love to have you living here."

Maggie nodded. "I do."

"It's settled then. You're moving in with us."

"What am I going to tell Frank?" Maggie asked, fear returning to her eyes.

"You aren't going near that rat ever again. Your brother will deal with him. I'm sure he knows a mate or two that he can take along in case Frank needs a little 'convincing.' I know for a fact your cousin will jump at the chance to lay into him."

Maggie chuckled and coughed. "You're right there. Ed's always looking for an excuse for a good brawl."

"Feisty bloodline you've got, Miss Maggie. Fighters, the lot of you. Survivors," she said with a wink.

Maggie wrapped her arms around Rachel. "My brother could not have married a more incredible woman. I love you, Rachel Kelly."

Rachel loved hearing her full name like that, reminding her that she was married to the kindest Kelly man this side of the equator. She returned the hug, being careful not to squeeze the wrong places. "Love you too, Molly Margaret."

Chapter 7

Once in town, Sherie headed straight to Flanders Flowers. She wasn't due to meet Tom for a while, but the conversation about her father was not one she was interested in being a part of, so if that meant being in town a little sooner than she was supposed to, then so be it. As she approached the flower stand, she felt the condemning looks that were being shot at her from all directions and she began to regret her decision to spend more time in town than she needed to.

Standing in front of the daffodils, Sherie tried to block out the people around her and took her time observing each flower before selecting the one she deemed good enough to grace Olivia's vase. After picking it up carefully, she walked over to pay the shop attendant. Little did she know she was being watched through a window.

Inside a dress shop stood a woman with long, dark brown hair that fell down over her shoulders, and bangs that framed her strong-featured face, with dull blue eyes akin to a shattered mirror that refused to reflect anything. She watched the small blonde woman take her time over something as simple as buying a flower. Kate was bemused by what she could only assume was attention to the most perfect detail, something she couldn't comprehend at all. A young, robust twenty-four-year-old woman, Kate Flanagan acted first and asked questions later, lacked the ability to pay attention to anything for longer than a few minutes, and certainly would not have found herself wasting valuable time picking out a singular flower, or even considering flowers in the first place. Despite this, she was inexplicably drawn to the woman she knew nothing about. She watched as she offered money to the store attendant, who took the flower out of her hands while shaking his head and not accepting her money. He treated the flower with such a lack of care that one of its yellow petals broke off and fell to the ground when he shoved it back into its bucket with the other daffodils. Kate blinked, unsure of what she had just witnessed. She narrowed her eyes to get a better focus on the scene through the window. The man was now shooing the woman away, and despite her protesting and holding up the money, he refused to take it and motioned for her to leave.

Kate's attention wavered as she was manhandled by the seamstress in the shop, who grabbed at her hips and turned her to the left. No longer facing the window, Kate was forced to participate in the excruciating matter at hand—dress shopping with her aunt.

The seamstress held the measuring tape around Kate's waist before writing a figure down. Kate's aunt, Mrs. Flanagan, looked at the scribbled number and cringed, and Kate decided right then to have seconds at dinner later that evening. Possibly thirds.

Far too well dressed for just a trip into town, Mrs. Anne Flanagan stood as tall as she could and prodded Kate to do the same while the seamstress ran the measuring tape down her back. Utterly bored, Kate complied with her aunt's pokes to keep her happy, but also arched her neck to try and locate the woman from outside again.

"What kind of material were you thinking?" asked the seamstress as she wrote down another number on her pad, and moved the measuring tape to Kate's arms.

"Oh, whatever you have extra of is fine enough, Judy. Unless you have any preference for material, Katie?" said Mrs. Flanagan. Kate's concentration was not broken for a moment as the woman outside walked away from the flower cart, dejected. Kate's eyes followed the woman's, who appeared to be looking at the yellow petal on the dusty ground. Could it be that she was more upset about the damage to the flower than she was about the fact that she was, for some reason, denied the pleasure of purchasing that which seemed so perfect to her? Kate considered this for a moment, before noticing that the woman was no longer alone. A man had appeared beside her, and had offered her a handful of flowers, only they were far less beautiful than the daffodils for sale at the flower cart. Kate recognized them as the flowers that grew on the side of the road all around town. The woman appeared to smile as she accepted the flowers as well as a kiss on her cheek from the man, but the way in which she let these flowers drop to her side made Kate wonder if her gratitude was forced. They began to walk away from the dress shop, and were soon out of Kate's view.

Frustrated that she could no longer watch the woman, Kate reluctantly returned her attention back to the shop.

"Kate?"

Kate made eye contact with her aunt, indicating that she was listening.

"What kind of material would you like for your dresses?"

Kate shook her head. The entire situation was completely foreign, and she was not interested in being a part of it for a second longer. She pushed Judy's hand off her shoulder "I don't care."

Mrs. Flanagan looked apologetically at Judy, who shrugged and offered a reassuring smile.

"No worries, how about I pick them, eh?" Judy said.

Kate shrugged and took a few steps toward the door of the shop in an effort not just to distance herself from Judy, but also to relocate the woman she had been watching.

Judy wrapped up the measuring tape and walked back around to behind the counter. She turned to look at the different fabrics stored behind her, and selected a roll of rich burgundy. "How are you settling in, Kate? Do you like Richmond so far?"

Kate chose not to answer Judy. She was standing so close to the window now that her nose was touching the glass, but she still couldn't see the woman.

"She's settling as best she can. It's a lot to take in though, isn't it? Coming to a new town, to a family she barely knows." Mrs. Flanagan sighed. "But family we are, so we will make sure she has a good start at a new life."

"I'm going to get some fresh air," Kate announced, pushing the door open and disappearing before she had to endure the conversation any further.

Having escaped the perils of being measured for dresses (something Kate hadn't worn since she was ten years old), she stood near to where she had seen the woman and her companion just moments before. She looked up and down the main street, but she couldn't see them anywhere. She surveyed the town a little more slowly, taking it all in. Surrounded by emerald hills that varied in incline and height and that Kate promised herself to explore at some point, Richmond bustled with people of all sorts. She was drawn to a Chinese gentleman, the first she had ever seen, who was dressed very differently from everyone else around. He looked at his feet as he hauled a cart covered by a blanket down the street toward the granary. Young women came in and out of a beautiful sandstone teahouse on the corner of the main road. They wore layers of clothing that made Kate wonder how on earth they managed to carry themselves with such grace, considering not just the weight of the material, but the heat of the sun that turned the town into an oven. They were chattering as if it were their one and only opportunity to be heard all day, and Kate winced at their strident giggling as they passed her without so much as a nod of acknowledgment. They did not, however, have any trouble acknowledging the group of red coats just across the road, who were more than likely on their way to the barracks. Kate noticed the soldiers' perfectly polished shoes and wondered how they managed to keep them so clean with the amount of dust they kicked up while they walked importantly through the streets.

Further ahead, Kate could see the steeple of the Catholic church in the distance, and she felt desperately jealous of the birds that landed atop the spire and went anywhere they pleased. She was jealous too of the melodies they sang as they flew overhead and settled on the tin rooftops nearby, taunting her with their up and down sing song. Kate blinked the dust from her eyes, not allowing the inconvenient grit to tarnish her view, and then inhaled deeply and looked up to the sky. The sun forced her to close her eyes and she switched her focus from the visual to the auditory as her favorite sense took over. The sounds of Richmond formed an orchestra made up not only of the birds, but of the trees, the breeze, the people, the horses, and the echoes of the sounds that bounced off the surrounding hills and carried back down the main street. It was busy but not overwhelming, something Kate was surprised to discover, and she savored the response her body gave the wind as it caressed her cheek. Refusing to be dragged into a memory that tapped on her heart, she bit down on her tongue and ignored her spirit's sudden ache to return home, courtesy of the pleasant feelings brought on by the little town.

The time for grief has come and gone. This is your home now. Kate took another breath.

"I'm home," she whispered to herself, as if saying it out loud would help her validate the truth of the words.

The shrill voice of her aunt yet again called her back to reality. "Kate, come on, we're done."

Kate clutched a white cake box in her lap as she sat in the back of the family wagon, which was pulled by two horses. Her uncle, Mr. Angus Flanagan, was driving the wagon, and her cousin Josh sat next to him up front, his little sister Anne on his lap. Mrs. Flanagan sat further back, but despite her background position, still managed to rule the conversation, moving animatedly as she talked. "Judy seems to think she can have the bulk of the clothes ready by Tuesday."

Kate smiled in a genuine attempt to show appreciation. Two days before she had never met these people who had so generously taken her in after events in her life so horrid that she refused to let herself even think about them. "Which means you will have something nice to wear for the festival!" Mrs. Flanagan was obviously far more excited about this fact than Kate.

The wagon passed a pond and Kate instantly recognized the woman from town sitting on the rocks beside the man. He was talking away and skipping rocks across the surface of the pond while she looked down at the boulder she was sitting on. Mrs. Flanagan scoffed as they drove past the couple. Kate noticed her recognition of the two. "Who's that?"

Josh answered first, his voice full of disdain, "The scum of the town."

"Scum means they are dirty," Anne explained to Kate, with an equal amount of disdain in her voice, sounding rather unusual coming from the almost four-year-old child.

Mr. Flanagan tilted his head back from the driver's seat. "You'd do well to stay away from them."

"Why?" asked Kate. She had known them for less than a week and these two people were the first Kate had come across that her aunt and uncle apparently disliked.

"We'll be passing the bar where the woman works in a little while. I'll point it out for you," said Mr. Flanagan.

"That's it? She just works at a bar?" Kate asked.

Mrs. Flanagan shot a quick look at Anne, and Kate realized there must be more information than they were willing to provide in front of her little cousin.

"She *works* at the bar, if you catch my drift," said Josh, tipping his head back in Kate's direction.

"Joshua Flanagan, that's enough!" Mrs. Flanagan warned. Kate pondered the way Josh had emphasized the word 'works.' He had wiggled his eyebrows and given her a wink, and that alone was enough to make Kate want to press for more information, but the look on her aunt's usually cheerful face was reason enough for her to keep her questions to herself. She turned her head to keep the woman in her sights as the wagon drove further away, making her mind up to investigate a little further whenever she next had the chance.

Sherie and Tom sat in silence. It was usually like that, and Sherie thought that Tom seemed to find it easier to talk to her and be a little more outgoing when there were other people around to bounce off. That was probably her fault; she didn't really give him much to work with despite Molly's direction. Tom was skipping stones across the surface of the pond and he was pretty good at it. Sherie didn't know much about him at all, mostly because she was too afraid to ask. It wasn't that she believed the rumors about him—it would be impossible to do so, since the most outlandish ones tended to contradict one another, but it was more so that she didn't believe he could be interested in her, and that made her suspicious.

For the most part, Tom was ignoring her. He looked for more stones to skip, and he was rather selective when it came to which ones he would choose to cast out to the pond, tossing away stones for what Sherie thought was no good reason. So why would a man who was reasonably attractive and could likely have his pick of any woman in town be pursuing her for the consideration of marriage? She knew Molly didn't give a damn about the answer to that question, assuming that Molly saw an opportunity to encourage and exploit his apparent feelings and use them to their advantage, but Sherie wasn't like that. For the most part, it really came down to the fact that she honestly couldn't understand why he seemed to have chosen her, over every other woman in Richmond, especially when there were far more 'desirable' women available to him. Her line of work was rather useful when it came to assessing the intentions of any young man that attempted to engage her in more than just sexual banter and actually looked at her eyes instead of just her breasts. Men who really wanted to be with her would not pay for the privilege, something she had witnessed firsthand through James, a sweet patron of theirs who was at the bar practically every evening to drink and pine over Claire. Claire had only just arrived in town when she walked into the apothecary where he worked, and he was instantly smitten. She told him where she worked and, bless him, he had no idea it was anything more than a bar. She remembered the way his face fell when he walked in and asked to see Claire, and Molly told him to cough up his dough. He had asked if he could just buy her a drink, not appearing to care when Molly told him she drank for free. Of course, seeing his heartache, Maggie came to the rescue, and Sherie recalled that this was around the time she realized that Maggie's urge to protect extended not only to her and Molly, but also to any soul who needed it.

Tom sighed and Sherie realized she had been silent for a little too long. Maybe he really was attracted to her but was too shy to do anything about it, just as James was. *Only one way to find out.*

"Why are you so picky with what stone you choose?"

Tom jumped when she spoke. "You can't get them to bounce off the water with just any old stone." He showed her the stone he was holding, his thumb running across the surface. "You want it to be as flat and thin as possible."

He handed the stone to Sherie and she turned it over in her hands. "It's rough. You said it had to be smooth?"

Tom shook his head. "No, flat. There's a difference. Actually, my older brother used to tell me that the bumpier it was, the better. Something to do with when it's in the air, I think."

He took the stone from her and wound his arm back. "You have to get the right angle, and you have to throw it hard but not too hard." He hurled the stone toward the water, and it skipped a number of times before it slowed and submerged, leaving behind a trail of gentle ripples. Sherie watched as they subsided, breaking against the edge of the pond, and she suddenly understood why Tom enjoyed this little activity.

She noticed a stone that fit Tom's description and she held it up to show him. "Would this one work, do you think?"

"Try it yourself and see," Tom said with a smile. Sherie noticed that his smile reached his eyes, and she felt herself relax a little more.

Sherie pulled her arm back and did her best to copy the angle at which Tom had thrown his stone into the pond. She released it from her fingers with a small squeal, and they watched in anticipation as the stone cut through the air toward the water with promising direction. It hit the water and disappeared beneath the surface with a plop.

"Oh." Sherie's face fell.

Tom laughed, not unkindly, and then handed her another one. "Here, try again."

Sherie's second attempt was just as terrible as her first.

"I guess you'll just have to come out here and practice with me a little more often," Tom said.

Sherie looked at him, unsure of the intent behind his advances. She could stand it no more and decided the best way to find out was to ask him. "Do you want to marry me?"

Tom dropped the stone he was holding and his face flushed. "Uh, gee, um, gee, Sherie, I was sorta waiting for a little while longer before I asked you, and you know usually it's the man who is meant to ask…uh, are you even allowed to ask me? I, Uh…well, yes. I do. But I haven't got you a ring yet."

Sherie pushed him backward, noticing the muscles in his chest.

"You fool, I wasn't asking you to marry me. I was asking you IF you wanted to marry me, you know? Is that where all of this is leading?" She motioned to the pond, the stones, and the two of them.

Tom sat in silence, still flustered. He played with a stone that didn't fit his description for skipping, hiding his face from Sherie.

"I'm just curious, if it's your intention to ask me to marry you."

Tom looked up at her. "I hope so, Sherie."

This time Sherie was the one who had no idea what to say.

"I'm trying to get to know you, which I'm finding to be a little difficult, but you keep saying yes when I ask you to join me places, so as long as you keep saying yes, I'll keep asking you. Is that okay?"

Sherie nodded. "Why me?" she asked.

Tom's hesitation brought back all of Sherie's uncertainty, which had almost been washed away with his previous answer.

"Do you want a family?" he asked her.

"I have a family."

"A family of your own? Children, I mean…and a husband to look after you."

Sherie understood the question, and she wondered why she was being so difficult with him. He did seem genuine, but she couldn't shake the feeling that there was something more behind this. *Perhaps he really does like me*…a concept Sherie was fast realizing was difficult for her to comprehend.

"I suppose, one day. Right now I've got Molly to look after me."

Tom smiled at her. "I noticed."

Sherie laughed. "She can be a little overzealous at times, but she really does mean well. I hope that doesn't bother you."

"Not at all. I love that about her. She definitely wants the best for her sister, that's for sure."

"What did she say to you?"

"Nothing. I mean…no. Nothing really."

Sherie wondered why he was suddenly not as forward with information. "So you're the one who decided that you wanted to pursue me then?"

Tom nodded, appearing to be unwilling to say anything else that may incriminate Molly. Sherie was unconvinced.

"So why me? You didn't really answer that. Most women want families. Even the ones who don't want families know that it's what they're probably going to have to do eventually, so they may as well pick someone who they like well enough, you know?"

"Do you like me well enough?"

"Answer my question, you sly fox. Why me? Unless you're stupid enough to not have realized that I'm a…" She trailed off, embarrassed for the first time since she could remember, to refer to herself as a prostitute.

"You've a pretty face, Sherie Kelly. I hate your job, but I understand why you do it. When you marry me, you won't be doing that anymore. I'll take you away from all of it. Your sister too."

"The Bucket is my home. Richmond is my home. I don't care how many people hate us—it's my home and I'll never leave."

"I mean I'll take you away from this lifestyle. We can stay in Richmond, of course. I love it here too. Why do you think I chose to settle here?" Tom looked at the hills on every side of them and nodded to the gum trees that lined the street in the distance. "This little town is the most beautiful place on earth."

"Well, that's certainly one thing we agree on."

"It reminds me of home. England."

"Why don't you go back?"

Tom took a deep breath and Sherie realized that she had unwittingly asked him what appeared to be a very difficult question.

"I have a family back home. A wife and a son. I was sent here because I was trying to save them from starving. We were far from being sacks of bones, but work was getting harder and harder to find, and it had been weeks since we'd had a proper meal. I'd been thieving bread from a man in town, but a growing boy needs more than bread." He stopped speaking for a moment, and Sherie noticed that his body was shaking.

"He wasn't growing right. My little man wasn't getting what he needed and it was my fault. Prue wasn't well either and she was begging me every day to find work. I would stay out all night sometimes, just waiting around the bins for food to be thrown away for the night, but it was tough, and there were people a lot hungrier than I who would fight me for what were really just scraps. So I did what I had to, for my family. I went to see a man that my father had worked for when I was a boy, hoping he would remember me and help me. The bastard was so rich I really thought he would help us. But it turns out that my father had, how do I put this politely...?" Tom paused.

"Tom, I'm a..." She paused. Why did she feel so guilty all of a sudden? "I'm a prostitute. You don't have to watch your words," Sherie said. She was touched by his gesture of wanting to watch his words, but she was sure she had heard worse on a daily basis, and she was desperate to hear the end of his story.

"My father had been fucking his wife for years, thinking no one knew about it, but it turns out the whole town did."

"Oh. So obviously he wasn't going to help you then?"

"Hah! Help? Not only did he not give us any meat, but he told me my father deserved it when he died of consumption, and that my son's suffering was punishment for being the grandson of an asshole."

"My mother died of consumption," Sherie said quietly.

Tom reached out and put his arm around her, but she did not feel any comfort from the gesture. "Horrible, isn't it?"

They sat in silence for a few minutes before Sherie realized there was still more of Tom's story to hear. "Sorry, I didn't mean to change the subject. So what happened?"

"I went back that night, when he was in bed and—"

Sherie gasped. "You killed him!?"

Tom burst out laughing, the sound ringing across the somber cloud that had surrounded them, destroying it. "God, no! You've been listening to the rumors, haven't you?"

Sherie blushed and ducked her head out from under his arm, pushing him playfully. "No! I just…okay fine, maybe a little."

Tom chuckled a little more before continuing. "I was meant to be just stealing one pig. A little piglet that he wouldn't even notice was missing, you know? Enough meat to tide us over until winter, when I knew I would be able to get myself a job delivering coal. But when I got there I just kept hearing his damn voice in my head, and the way he talked about my son and my father made me so angry that I lost control. I killed his pigs. Every last one of them. Slit the throats of his two giant sows and all of their little piglets."

Sherie shuddered.

"It wasn't some mad crazed slaughter, I promise. I was angry, yes, but this was…I'm not sure how to explain it. This rich bastard sat in his giant house stuffing his face with food while good people watched their families starve to death. So I took all the pigs down into town and gave them away. Every single last one of them…I didn't sell them; I didn't make a profit. I just kept two for my family and gave the rest to the people who needed them the most."

Sherie didn't know what to say. "You're like the Robin Hood of bacon."

Tom laughed. "I suppose so."

"So they knew it was you?"

"I was the first person the Bobbies came to visit, yes. I might have gotten away with it if Prue hadn't been cooking bacon at the time."

"Prue is your wife?"

"Was my wife."

"I'm sorry. What happened to her?"

"I'm not sure. To be honest, I'm too afraid to go home. When I was sentenced she was allowed to visit me once before I was to be shipped out here, and I told her to remarry. I told her to find a man who could look after Thomas properly, but I don't want to find out if she did. I pray to God that she did, but at the same time I really don't want to know. I can't picture her with anyone else, or my son calling another man his father."

"But you've got all that gold now; can't you go and get her back? Or send some of it home?"

"Sherie, if I put gold in an envelope and posted it back to England, it would never make it out of Richmond, let alone Australia."

"Oh. Of course." *Idiot.*

"The whole time I was doing my time I swore to myself I'd go back the second I was a free man. I dreamed of it every night, but when they let me off, I had no money, no way of buying a ticket home. That's why I went to the gold fields, and that's when I got lucky."

"So why didn't you just get straight on a ship home?"

"I had a lot of time to think, out on the fields. Lonely place, there. Full of different people from all over the world, and none of them would hesitate to gut you in your sleep if they knew you were sitting on land full of gold."

Sherie shuddered and tried not to think about her father being gutted in his sleep.

"I knew almost right away that I had a good patch. It wasn't even that big, since I could only afford a few feet, but that was all I needed. I had to be smart about it, you know? Mining and storing the gold, because if I had cashed in on my first day, I wouldn't have lived to see my second. I just spent a lot of time thinking out there, about Prudence, Thomas Junior….about life. I decided that if they managed to settle down and find peace after all the problems I caused for them, then who was I to disrupt that? I told myself I didn't want to go back for them; I wanted to go back for me, and I loved them too much to destroy whatever they might have built while I was away. So I stayed."

"Really?" Sherie wasn't sure she believed him. "If it were me, I'd stop at nothing until the woman I loved was beside me and my son was in my arms."

Tom stood up, climbed off the rock they were sitting on, and took a few steps toward the pond. From nowhere he let out a loud and agonizing scream, and the noise carried with it a pain that Sherie could feel as it reverberated through her body. Tom bent at the knees, his hands gripping tufts of his hair as he screamed long and hard until it faded away, his voice cracking.

Sherie stood up and walked over to him. She placed a hand on his back softly.

"The truth is I'm scared that they're both dead."

"I understand," Sherie said. "Every inch of me understands,"

Tom turned and looked at her, his eyes red but without tears. "I just want to move on."

Sherie pulled Tom into a hug and it did not escape her notice that she didn't feel a single ounce of electricity pass between them. She knew then that she did not have feelings for Tom, but that if spending time with him meant that she would help him to move on, then she would be happy to do so. She thought about the Suds Bucket, and why Molly had asked her to lead Tom on in the first place. If their father never returned, their land title and their beloved home on it would pass into the possession of their closest living male relative. Unless, of course, one of them were to marry.

So she didn't love Tom, but perhaps he didn't love her either. Regardless, this relationship would serve a purpose for both of them. Tom could let go of his past, and Sherie could marry a man who could assume the title of their house and land, were anything to happen to her father.

"Come on, Tom, let's go get a drink."

Chapter 8

It had been a week since Kate had been into town to get measured for her new dresses, and nothing remotely exciting had happened since. Until today. It was Anne's birthday, and they were holding a party at the house. Kneeling at a small table in the center of the room, Anne, who was wearing a floral patterned dress, blew out four candles on a small birthday cake. She was met with a round of applause from the family. She watched excitedly as Mrs. Flanagan picked up a large knife and helped her make one cut into the cake. Kate stood as far into the corner of the room as she could, wearing a full-length dark burgundy skirt and a flowing lilac shirt. Despite feeling incredibly uncomfortable in the garb, she appreciated the intentions of her aunt, as well as the compliments from her family about how well she was looking. Standing beside her was a sturdy and tanned young man named Sam. Unable to think of anything that would be interesting to him, Kate decided to comment on the cake. "I hope it's chocolate."

Sam nodded. "I have a horse called Chocolate."

"Yeah? What breed?" Kate felt herself stand up a little straighter and lean in toward Sam. This was the first conversation she had been interested in since she arrived in Richmond.

"Aussie stock horse. Bit slow, but smooth as ever to gallop. She's my second favorite horse."

"How many do you have?" she asked.

"Oh, gosh, too many to count. I have four absolute favorites though."

Emerging out of the kitchen holding a platter of birthday cake, Mrs. Flanagan eyed the interaction between Sam and Kate and then all but skipped over to them.

"My main man is Derwent. He's a purebred Arabian and the best I own. Then there's Silky; she's an Arabian too but not as big. I'm training her to be a gentle ride. I reckon I'll give her to my little sister when she's ready," Sam said. They paused their conversation as they each accepted a piece of cake from the tray. Mrs. Flanagan stayed put, as if she was chained to the awkwardness that appeared at the same time she did. She smiled a painfully obvious smile, and lingered for a fraction of a second longer than Kate wished she had before it became uncomfortably clear that it had been long enough. She disappeared, to offer cake to other less exciting guests. Kate and Sam watched her leave and shared a knowing smile, before returning to their conversation.

"And I have a palomino that I just bought last week two towns over, but she doesn't have a name yet."

Kate had a mouthful of cake, but that didn't stop her from blurting out with excitement when she heard the word 'palomino.' "Would you sell her to me?"

Sam frowned, his face a mixture of amusement and confusion. "I only just bought her myself."

"Which means you can't be all that attached to her, right?"

Kate watched Sam consider her unexpected proposal. "You haven't even seen her."

"I could come by tomorrow to check her out. I'll pay you five sovereigns more than what you paid for her," she said.

"You don't know what I paid for her," Sam said with a chuckle.

"I don't care," Kate replied. She took a bite of her cake and waited for Sam to make up his mind. She gave him a few moments before she held out her hand, looking at him with a cheeky grin. Sam smiled and extended his arm to shake her hand. Kate knew Mrs. Flanagan was watching her from across the room, her smile as wide as her bottom, and so for good measure she turned her palm up and spat in the middle of it before pressing it into Sam's hand and sealing their agreement. Sam looked incredulously at her as she squeezed his hand, and Kate made sure not to let go until he did.

"Firm handshake," Sam said.

"Nothing worse than a weak handshake," Kate said, and tapped her nose with her index finger. She took Sam's empty plate from him and disappeared into the kitchen. She cringed when she saw Mrs. Flanagan scuttle across the room and follow her in.

"And what were you two talking about?" she asked. She didn't look very happy about what she had seen. "Kate, did you…did you SPIT? In his hand? Did you spit, is that what I saw?"

Kate smiled back. Not a single thing went unnoticed under this woman's watch. "He's going to sell me his horse. We just sealed the deal."

"Sealed the…" Mrs. Flanagan looked flabbergasted. "Kate, goodness, if you wanted a horse, your uncle would have been more than happy to find you a suitable…" She paused for a moment. "…I thought you had found a potential beau."

"Isn't he family?" Kate asked.

Mrs. Flanagan chuckled. "He has been Josh's friend for as long as I can remember, but no, he's not family. Not yet, anyway." She nudged Kate suggestively. Kate took a deep breath, visibly concerned with her aunt's train of thought.

"We were just—"

"Buying horses! Indeed. And spitting in hands…Lord save me!" Mrs. Flanagan looked thoroughly unimpressed. "No matter. This is fixable. He will be at the festival tomorrow along with everyone else, and you can talk about much more appropriate things then." She nodded.

Kate opened her mouth to protest, but lost the opportunity when Anne leaped in front of them with her tongue poked out and rolled up. She pulled her tongue in to speak. "Can you roll your tongue?"

Kate looked down at her, bemused. "Can I do what?" Anne moved closer to Kate and stood on her tiptoes as if the extra inch off the ground would help her explain.

"This. Can you do this?" Anne stuck her tongue out again and rolled it in half to form a tunnel. Kate stuck out her tongue, and it moved to the left, but it didn't fold. "I guess not," she said. Anne stuck her tongue out again. It looked as if she was having trouble trying to decide if she wanted to speak or keep her tongue stuck out. It appeared to be a struggle to do both, but she almost managed it.

"I'm special. I'm the only one in the whole family who can do it," she said.

Kate stuck her tongue out again. It moved, and struggled, but it didn't manage to curl. "You are pretty special!" she said.

Anne beamed at the compliment, tongue sticking out again. "Could your mother and father do it? Before they died?"

Kate went pale at the mention of her parents. "Oh, I don't know, Anne."

Clearly, Anne was not satisfied with this answer and she pressed further. "What about your brother? Could he?"

"Anne!" Mrs. Flanagan stopped her youngest daughter from continuing. "Enough of your questions! Scoot!" Anne leaped off at the command. Kate didn't blame Anne—she knew she was completely oblivious to any of the hurt she had just caused. Mrs. Flanagan looked at Kate sympathetically. Kate half smiled but was lost in her thoughts for the rest of the afternoon.

From where she was sitting in the middle of her bed, Kate couldn't see anything out of her window but the night sky that was scattered with stars. She wondered what it would feel like to lie in it. The sky was not yet completely black but a silken dark blue. Minutes ago, what had been a magnificent contrast of red and purple tones offset by the warm amber that glowed from the sun had seeped into one another, creating a kind of magical blue Kate wished she could capture and pour into her bathtub until it brimmed, threatening to, but never quite overflowing. She imagined even if the tub were to overflow, it would not spill or splatter like water, but drift to the floor in a soft, silent cascade.

Kate closed her eyes and stepped into the tub in her mind. She did not sink or float as the night sky enveloped her naked body, which only showed the physical scars left behind. As her eyelids shut completely, she was greeted by the rest of the damage that far outnumbered the few scars on her body that she could easily hide with clothing. She heard the screams of her family for a moment before she let herself slide under the surface of the cool sky, muffling the cries. Her body tingled when the stars dabbed her skin gently, buzzing with an enchanted current that calmed her completely. She soaked in the sky for a long time, and with each breath that she drew in, she sank deeper into the night, drifting farther and farther away from the Earth until it was a tiny insignificant dot. She felt that nothing on the surface of something so small could hold any power over her. Slowly, she allowed gravity to pull her back to earth and she broke the surface of the sky with a long exhale, blowing indigo bubbles that rippled a pathway for her to follow, up and out of the bath.

Kate opened her eyes and found herself in the middle of her bed again, but this time with a sense of peace. She reveled in the comfortable feeling, knowing it wouldn't last long but that she could call the quiet back again the following night if she needed…and she knew she would.

She allowed a little smile to form and looked over at the piano that sat covered in the corner of the room, seemingly forgotten. She could fool everyone else, but the piano was always on her mind. It was always in her view; even if it were only peripheral and even when her back was turned, Kate could feel the piano pulling her toward it. She had always resisted though, refusing to touch that which had the power to conjure happy memories of her family, but in this moment she wanted nothing more than to hear the sound of her past. She stood up slowly and stepped carefully over to the piano, pulling back the tattered calico that covered most of the instrument.

She hovered above the chair for a moment before sitting down, and lifted the heavy lid that covered the keys. She placed a single finger on a cool, ivory key and pressed down firmly. The note cut across the air and slammed into Kate's chest, slicing through her flesh and punching her in the heart. She stood up immediately and slammed the cover down. She pulled the calico back over the piano and collapsed down onto her bed.

She stared at the ceiling, desperately searching for something to focus on before the melancholy started to creep back in. She pictured Anne grinning as her tongue curled into a tunnel, rocking back and forth on her heels. She pictured Sam, handsome, and strong. She wondered if her aunt would be successful in joining them, deciding it would take her to give in and open up first before she let anyone love her. She supposed it did make sense—he liked animals, seemed to be kind, and most importantly, his smile extended to his eyes. She closed her eyes and pictured them alone together. It took her a moment to place her discomfort, but she put it down to the residual feelings from the piano. Sam reached out and took her hand, pulling her closer. He pressed his lips against hers and she flinched in reality as she imagined what it would feel like when his rough chin grazed hers. She let the kiss continue and she relaxed as it started to soften. She pulled her arm free and wrapped it around the body before her, drawing herself closer as the kiss ignited. No longer rigid, Kate collapsed into the embrace as she reached up and ran her fingers through the long hair of the person she was kissing. She froze instantly when she realized that she was no longer thinking about Sam. She pulled back and found herself looking into the eyes of the woman she had seen in town a week before… Sherie.

She let herself whisper her name, letting the syllables roll off her tongue. She was surprised that this unknown woman had such an impact on her, and she wondered what it was that she was drawn to. The few things she knew about her were hardly positive, and if it was true that she was a prostitute… well, Kate wasn't even sure what to make of that, and why would she be dreaming about kissing her?

Utterly confused and deciding to blame it on her decision to play the piano, even if it were only one note, Kate pulled her bed sheets over her head and covered herself from the world completely.

Chapter 9

The Suds Bucket creaked under the morning sun, greeting its inhabitants good morning as they made their way out onto the balcony.

In their usual places, Olivia was throwing a tall rectangular vase and Sherie sat between Molly's legs, letting her sister play with her hair mindlessly. Georgina sat on the edge of her chair, pressed up against the copper cage that reflected golden bands of light onto her face. Her tongue curled into a tunnel and poked out from between her lips sporadically, giving tiny kisses to her treasured birds. A new canary was perched in the cage, singing gaily and stealing kisses as if he had always been there. Stretched across the sofa was Claire, closer to the end of the book she had been reading for a while now. Maggie sat on the railing of the veranda, leaning against her pole, her leg swinging back and forth and her hand flicking briskly in front of her face, gripping her fan.

"The town's starting to look good for tonight," Sherie said, breaking the comfortable silence.

Maggie snapped her fan shut. "I'm not going," she said.

Olivia rolled her eyes and flung a handful of clay in Maggie's direction. It missed by a mile and hit Claire's book.

"Aw Christ, Liv! How am I supposed to learn to read if my book is covered in clay?"

Olivia rolled her eyes and tossed a rag at Claire, who mopped the clay off the book before turning her attention back to Maggie. "Every year you say you're not going, and every year we end up having to drag you home by your dress at the end of the night."

"If she's still wearing one," Olivia piped in.

Maggie pulled the rag out of Claire's hand and tossed it at Olivia. It hit her in the face. "I'm serious," she said. "I'm taking a page out of Sherie's book this year."

Molly snorted. "Yes, while the whole town is out drinking, you can go and lie on a hill."

Sherie laughed and turned her head toward Molly. "I don't just lie on a hill!"

"You're right. I'm sorry. You get bitten by bugs too." Molly laughed loudly at her own joke as she finished her beer and got up for another. Sherie slapped her behind as she climbed out of the swinging chair and disappeared into the bar.

"Get me another beer too!" Olivia called out to Molly, whose head appeared back outside almost instantly.

"Is that how you speak to your boss?" she asked.

Olivia shook her head and grinned. "Get me another beer, Wench!" she elaborated. Molly shook her head, muttering something about insubordinates as she went back inside to retrieve more drinks.

Claire turned a page in her book and looked up suddenly. "What's this word?" she asked as she passed the book to Maggie, who looked where Claire was pointing.

"Suspicious," Maggie read. Claire blew a kiss in Maggie's direction and took back her book to continue reading. The chatter died down as quickly as it had started and the girls relaxed in silence while they enjoyed the quiet that came with daylight. Their reflection was interrupted when two men on horseback rode by, slowing as they passed the girls on the balcony. All of the women tensed immediately as they recognized the riders, except for Georgina, who was too busy playing with the new canary that she had coaxed out of the cage to feed it a piece of peach.

The vile rider was Dan, a nasty ex-patron who had been banned from the Bucket for one too many indecent acts. The same Dan who had paid Ed Smith to have sex with Molly under the house long ago before the Suds Bucket even existed.

"Georgina, baby…" Dan called, finally getting Georgina's attention. She looked up, but rather than at him, her gaze seemed to stretch through and beyond him, as it did with most things other than her birds. "Wanna play with my cocky, sweetheart?" he taunted.

"It's a canary, cocksucker!" Georgina screamed, standing up with rage, her eyes now definitely focused on him. Maggie was instantly up and at Georgina's side, followed closely by Claire, her book abandoned.

"Beat it, assholes," Olivia demanded.

"Always, honey. And you're on my mind when I do," Dan said with a snigger.

Molly came striding out of the bar, livid, with two bottles in her hand. She hurled one in the general direction of the men. Dan caught the bottle easily. He laughed, and then he opened the beer and took a long drink before spitting it back out. "Tastes like piss! But I guess your customers don't come here for the drink!"

The other man laughed, and Molly threw the other bottle toward his head. This one was thrown with slightly better aim and the bottle only just narrowly missed, knocking his hat clear off his head. "You sure you can afford to be giving that away?" he asked.

"I heard that's the only way they can get rid of the shit," Dan said, and both men laughed.

In her anger, Olivia squished the vase that she was so close to perfecting, her hands turning white as they curled into fists.

"Hey, Dan, I hope you slip through your arsehole and break your bloody neck!" Maggie yelled. Dan threw the bottle back toward the Bucket, where it smashed against the wall, inches from where Sherie was sitting. She jumped and pulled her knees up to her chest. Georgina put her bird back into its cage and disappeared inside as quickly as she could, shrieking insults as she went.

Molly took a running jump toward the balcony, placed both hands on the railing, and vaulted over the edge. She started toward the men, who kicked their horses into motion and rode off quickly.

"Next time the only thing you're gonna get for free is my fist in your damn face!" she yelled at the cowards who galloped toward the town center. She watched them to make sure they were definitely gone before she stormed back up the stairs and walked straight in the bar, returning moments after with more beer.

Olivia looked at the clay mess in front of her and snorted in anger. Claire had since returned to her couch, book back in hand. "Forget 'em," she suggested.

Molly threw bottles to Maggie and Olivia, and opened one herself, draining it with one long swig. "Already have," she said.

Maggie sipped at her beer as she attempted to settle back down against the pole, positioning her body so that she had a better view of the road this time. "So what time are we leaving for the festival tonight?" she asked.

Molly laughed and raised her beer toward Maggie, tilting it in approval. Olivia picked up her pottery materials and went inside, followed by Maggie, and shortly after, Molly, who collected the empty beer bottles on her way.

Claire picked up a bookmark and placed it in her book before closing it and sitting up. Sherie sighed, looking into the distance, her knees still tucked up to her chest. Claire looked at her. "You'll be okay? Tonight, I mean."

Sherie forced a smile. "Gets easier every year."

Claire scratched at a piece of clay that seemed to have dried on her book. She put the book down and leaned across to brush a strand of hair away from Sherie's face. Molly came back outside to collect the last few empty beer bottles.

"He's probably just digging up so much gold that he's forgotten to write," Claire said.

Sherie nodded and kissed her on the forehead. "Have fun tonight. Make sure Maggie behaves herself," she said as she stood up and disappeared inside.

"You gotta stop getting her hopes up. You know he's not coming back," Molly said.

Claire picked up her book and pulled it into her chest defensively. "The girl needs something to keep her going, can't you see that?"

"She's got me…and Tom," Molly said. Claire raised a skeptical eyebrow, but said nothing further.

Molly looked over at Georgina's cage. "A new canary?"

Claire nodded.

"Time flies. Four years now, huh?"

Claire nodded again, moving over to the cage and poking a finger through the bars.

Georgina

Four years earlier

Georgina walked slowly along the road that would wind around a large weeping willow before her house appeared. She took her time, kicking the dust up with every step that she took. Her thoughts drifted, as did the burnt orange dust that formed clouds in her trail. She felt sick to her stomach, and she couldn't tell if it was because she was in love, if it was because she was pregnant, or if it was because, whether or not she plucked up the courage today to tell her parents that she was pregnant, they would find out anyway soon enough.

She had been keeping the secret for a long time, and so far her body had not betrayed her. She wasn't sure how far along she was. She was the kind of fourteen-year-old who didn't bother keeping track of her periods, or anything else to do with her body for that matter. It wasn't until she met Will Trapp that she even took notice of the fact that she was female. It had taken her a little while to realize that her stomachaches were something a little more serious than indigestion. She knew her parents didn't like her spending time with Will, and she supposed, looking back, that it had been for good reason. Her hand absentmindedly cradled her belly, which was still surprisingly flat considering how close she figured she must be to giving birth. She remembered that when her aunt was pregnant, she looked as if she had swallowed a watermelon whole. Lucky for Georgina, such swelling had not occurred, though part of her wished it had, so that she could free herself of the anxiety that came along with keeping such a secret quiet. She wasn't sure what she was more afraid of—the fact that her father would know that she'd had sex, the shame she would bring on her family for being stupid enough to get pregnant out of wedlock, or that she was giving her parents at best about two months' notice that they were going to be grandparents for the first time.

She took a deep breath as she rounded the bend, her house appearing in the distance. A thousand questions ran through her head. *How should I say it? Should I tell them it was Will? What if Will finds out? Is it going to hurt when I give birth?* Her anxiety caused her steps to quicken, and she had to force herself to walk at less of a pace if she wanted to figure out exactly what words she was going to use to break the news. She had absolutely no idea.

She stopped when she got to the front porch, catching her reflection in the window. She smiled at herself and looked down at her stomach. She could see the baby bump, even though there was nothing to see, and she couldn't help but feel proud of herself for creating life. Being fourteen had nothing to do with it. She could feel the child moving within her, and she felt a pride she didn't even realize could exist. She knew being proud was wrong—they told her that all the time at church. She also knew that she wasn't meant to lie beside a man until she was married, but she hadn't realized what she was doing until it was happening, and it felt too good to stop. Will was going to make a great father… if she could actually manage to inform him of the fact. She looked back up to her face, which was blushing as it always did those days, looking much fuller than it had roughly seven months before. Her thoughts were interrupted by her mother's voice.

"Georgina, is that you?"

"Yes, Mama, I'm home," Georgina replied, re-hoisting her bag securely back onto her shoulder. She walked into the house, feeling like she was going to throw her baby up at any second.

"Can you help me, please?" her mother asked from the other room.

Georgina walked through to find her mother folding clothes. She picked up a skirt and began to help. *This is the perfect chance. Just say it,* she thought. "Are you and Daddy going out tonight?"

"I don't think so. We've got nothing planned. I thought we could all have dinner together tonight for a change." Her mother smiled.

Georgina nodded. "That sounds nice."

Her parents never stayed in. Being a lawyer meant that her father was always being invited to one place or another, and contrary to her parents' beliefs, Georgina was old enough to look after herself without getting into any trouble.

"Are you okay dear?" her mother asked.

Georgina noticed she was still holding the same skirt that she had originally picked up.

"Oh. What?"

"Whatever is the matter with you?" Her mother stopped folding the clothes and crossed her arms.

"I'm..." Georgina struggled to find the right words. "I don't feel well," was all she could say.

Her mother resumed folding. "You were up late last night, weren't you?"

"Yes, but I wasn't playing. I swear. I just couldn't sleep."

"You weren't talking to that boy through your window?"

"No!" Georgina was telling the truth. She had been avoiding Will recently, for fear he would try and touch her somewhere that would reveal her secret. She did have the window open, and her head was hanging out of it for most of the night, but it was because the smell of fresh air was the only thing that calmed her down. More and more frequently, she found herself alone in bed, unable to breathe as she allowed herself to get worked up over the entire situation. Her parents were the most important people in her world, apart from her baby, and she knew that they would be ashamed of her. It occurred to her in that moment, as she picked up one of her father's shirts and began to fold it methodically, exactly the way her mother had taught her to do, that she had been fighting an uphill battle with herself, trying to find the right words to tell them. There were no right words, and with this realization came not so much relief, but definitely ease. There were only two words she needed to utter to inform her parents that she had let them down. *I'm pregnant.*

She opened her mouth and took a steady breath. She felt the blood rush from her face and her heart beat erratically as she willed the words to form.

"I'm..." She couldn't do it. "I'm tired."

Her mother looked at her with great concern, and Georgina knew that she must have been paler than a ghost.

"Go to bed. I'll bring you some tea," she said, laying a hand on Georgina's forehead. "You're burning up."

Georgina said nothing as she slinked toward her bedroom, her head lowered in shame. Not only was she pregnant, but she was a coward too. It wasn't just that she was scared to admit she had done something wrong. She had certainly developed a solid level of experience in having to advise her parents of her antics, usually of the utmost trouble making, of which there had been plenty during her younger years. This was different though. This time her parents weren't going to give her a cane on the hand and tell her to behave herself. This time there were serious consequences to consider. Like, would they ever speak to her again? Would they make her give her baby away?

Georgina knew she wasn't being dramatic. She had been raised to be seen and not heard, but it hadn't stopped her from listening while her mother glee-fully gossiped with the other lawyers' wives about all matter of things, and she hadn't even begun to think what God might think of her.

Collapsing on her bed, Georgina took a moment to think about what Jesus would say to her. She knew He was nice no matter who you were, but did that include silly girls who got pregnant? The priest said that Jesus loved everyone, so surely that included her and her baby? She wrapped her hands around her stomach again and caressed her child.

Night took forever to fall as Georgina waited for the familiar sound of the horses to pull up at her house, which meant her father had arrived home. She knew her mother would mention her illness to him, and she made up her mind to tell them the second they walked through the door. No thinking, no nothing. *Just blurt it out Georgina,* she told herself.

Her father passed by the door to ask how she was, but he didn't come into her room. This threw her, as her plan had involved him physically walking through the door and sitting on the foot of her bed as he usually did when she was sick. *He is probably worried he might catch something,* she thought. Her father was always busy, and as he told her often, "I don't have time to be sick!"

A short time later, her mother crept into her room holding a tray. "I thought it would be better if you ate your dinner in bed, so you didn't have to get up," she said.

"Thanks, Mama." Georgina loved her mother so much. "You're the best mama in the world, you know."

Her mother smiled at her and kissed her forehead. Georgina noticed her look down at her breasts, which were bigger than they had ever been before.

"It looks like we need to take you into town for some new undergarments. You're definitely becoming a woman, no matter how much you might wish to hide it," she said with a quick wink.

"I know," was all Georgina could say quietly, as her mother walked out of her bedroom, closing the door behind her.

Adelaide Parker was putting the folded clothes in an airing cupboard, humming softly to herself while she worked, completing a few chores before bed. She paused when she heard what sounded like a dog barking further up the hallway. She closed the cupboard doors quietly and walked up the hall, following the noise until she realized the sounds were coming from her daughter's bedroom. She waited outside the room for a moment, trying to figure out what the noise was. It sounded like Georgina was throwing up. She pushed the door open a fraction and through the small gap she could see Georgina standing up at the window, her head hanging over the ledge. She watched as Georgina violently vomited up the dinner she had served her not even an hour before.

She stepped away from the door, closing it as gently as she had opened it, and walked back down the hallway to find her husband.

Eugene Parker was enjoying his first quiet evening in a long time. It wasn't often that he got to sit in his chair and do nothing but admire the gum trees that were really starting to flourish and mature. He took a sip of hot tea, the steam wetting his nostrils as he brought the cup up to his mouth, and watched the moonlight flicker through the gum tree's branches that flailed in the evening's gale. The shadows were spectacular, and he savored the chance to use his imagination for something more than a new excuse to justify why someone should not be punished for a crime that they more than likely had committed.

Something in the corner of his peripheral made him look further out past the trees in his front yard. He saw a possum chasing a small, injured bird. Of course, the bird had absolutely zero chance of survival, but it was still flapping as hard as it could to protect itself from the possum. Eugene wondered what was going through the bird's mind, if anything at all, as the possum finally caught it, clamping his teeth down hard into the creature, which slowly stopped fluttering. Perhaps it was time he considered a change of specialty to family law. Penning wills for an exorbitant amount of money could surely bring about the same amount of satisfaction found when he successfully argued for the freedom of men who were so clearly guilty that it may as well be written on their faces. This criminal law business was starting to get tedious. Eugene yearned for a challenge. Something to make his life more interesting than it already was.

"Eugene." His thoughts were interrupted by his wife. "I think Georgina is pregnant."

If Eugene had not just swallowed his final mouthful of tea, he would have spat it all over Adelaide.

"What on earth makes you say that? Did she tell you?"

"She hasn't said anything. I can't explain it. I just know."

Eugene shook his head, refusing to believe what his wife was telling him. "Adelaide, she's tiny. There's no way that girl is pregnant. She wouldn't even know what to do with a man," he said, with such an emphasis as if his words could make it so.

"She's pregnant. I know it." Adelaide wobbled as she spoke, and kneeled down to steady herself.

Eugene looked her in the eyes. He knew her well enough to know when she was right. "You're certain?"

Adelaide nodded. "Maternal instincts."

Georgina rounded the corner and saw her house. It looked like there was a horse out the front, but it was attached to an unfamiliar carriage, and Georgina wasn't sure who it was. The same thoughts were going through her head as the day before, plus a few new ones. The orange dust turned into pebbles as she crossed over onto her family's property. She hummed to her daughter while she walked, the melody an uplifting promise of happiness to her child. She had decided it was a girl the previous night. She didn't know how she knew, but she just did—she was growing a little girl inside of her.

She got closer to the carriage and was doused in nausea when she realized it was the doctor. She broke into a run instantly, terrified to discover which of her parents was so sick that the doctor was needed. She pelted up the front steps and burst through the door.

"Mama! Daddy!" she yelled out, desperate for an answer.

The answer that came was calm. "In here, Georgina."

Her father had called her from his study, a room that she was never permitted to enter. She spoke to him from outside the door.

"Is everything okay? Why is the doctor here? Is Mama okay?"

"Why don't you come in here, Georgie?" Eugene suggested.

Unsure of what was going on, she pushed open the study door and stepped over the threshold for the first time. In the room was a man she assumed was the doctor. He was well dressed and fairly scrawny for a man who could probably afford more food than the whole village combined. She didn't like the look in his eyes, or the way he was leering at her as if she had done something to offend him.

"Come in, Georgie, and say hello to Dr. Bailey," Eugene said again, motioning for her to come closer.

Georgina moved slowly forward, her steps loaded with apprehension. Eugene walked over to the door and closed it behind her. Her uneasiness increased by the second as she scanned the room that she had never been allowed in before until now. It was then that she realized the doctor had set up some equipment on her father's desk. She eyed the equipment, which looked like the type of instruments she imagined would be required to climb a mountain of ice. A metal ice pick type rod with a nasty looking hook at the end of it, clamps, ropes...she took it all in, unable to process what it meant.

Georgina jumped when Eugene grabbed her roughly from behind with a grip so forceful that she was scared he was going to crush her daughter inside of her.

"Daddy, don't hurt me, please."

Eugene maintained his grip as he picked her up and lowered her onto his desk, holding her down. Dr. Bailey picked up a syringe full of liquid that had a very sharp needle attached to it.

"You know," Georgina said, terrified.

"There's nothing to know," Eugene said.

Dr. Bailey jabbed the needle into her arm with a total disregard for any bedside manner whatsoever.

"You know I'm pregnant!" Georgina cried.

"You are not pregnant," Eugene told her.

"I am!"

"No, you are NOT!" he shouted. She felt his grip tighten on her, and she quickly realized her struggles were useless.

Georgina arched her head, the only part of her currently not held down, in an attempt to see what was happening. She felt her skirt being pushed up, and her legs being pulled apart despite her every effort to keep them closed.

"Please, don't! It's too late! It's too late!" she begged for her daughter's life while she watched the doctor pick up the large ice pick instrument.

Fear and the instincts of a mother afraid for her child took over, and Georgina found a strength from deep within, unparalleled to the two men who were holding her down. She threw her arms up, releasing herself from the grasp of her father. She reached for the first weapon she could see, a scalpel.

She screamed as she drove the scalpel into the doctor's shoulder, penetrating his skin and pulling it down so that it tore a bloody gash through the joint. She only stopped when the screaming doctor slapped her across the face, instantly drawing blood. She released the scalpel, leaving it embedded in his shoulder, and made her escape for the study door. The doctor dropped the instrument he was holding and collapsed in pain.

Georgina was out the door before her father could get anywhere near her. She sprinted across the entrance and threw the front door open, not bothering to shut it. She heard her mother calling out from behind her. Although the little girl in her heart wanted to do nothing more than to turn back, collapse into her mother's arms and cry until everything was okay, the mother in her knew that she had to get as far away from this place as possible. It was no longer her home.

Tears flooded, and her heart thudded in time with her feet as they slammed into the dust path. She wanted to break down, her mother's wailing striking her wounded heart as she ran from the agonizing cries for her to return. She refused to look back, even once.

Georgina ran until the liquid from the syringe started to affect her to the point where she could no longer walk in a straight line. She detoured off the path she had been following, walking as deep into the brush as she could until she passed out.

Georgina woke as the next day was breaking. Her head was foggy from the after effects of whatever had been injected into her, and her arm was swollen where the needle had pierced her skin. She stood up slowly and looked in both directions to get her bearings. She could see the snapped branches that led a path from where she had run in from the road, and she followed it back out. Standing on the road, she considered for a fraction of a second the possibility of returning home, but the thought was disregarded in almost the same instant it entered her head. Her father's reaction was so extreme, and she doubted he would give her a chance to explain herself, especially given the fact that she had stabbed the doctor. At this point, she wasn't even sure if it were only her parents she was running from, if the police had been told what she did.

She was hungry, and despite sleeping all through the night, she was exhausted. She began to walk away from the only town she had ever known. What lay ahead of her was unsure, but she was certain it had to be better than where she had come from.

Cradling her daughter, she put one foot in front of the other and walked all day until the sun started to tuck itself away behind the trees up ahead. She kept an eye out for any road signs that might indicate how far away she was from the next town, but there was nothing. Deciding it was time to stop, she walked off the main road and into the brush again. She dropped to the floor, and her eyes started to close almost instantly in spite of the fact that there were twigs sticking into her body at all angles. As she drifted into slumber, she heard a low humming sound slowly getting louder. Her eyes flew open, and she saw an amber glowing over the top of the bushes. She stood up and saw the light was coming from a lamp that hung from the front of a large horse drawn carriage. She raced to the side of the road, brandishing her arms and shouting as loud as she could. Given that there was nothing else around, she was easy to spot, and the carriage slowed down, and eventually stopped, just ahead of where she was standing.

A young man jumped down from the driver's seat of the cart. He was burly and walked with a slight limp. "These roads aren't safe. Why are you out here?" he asked as he approached her.

Georgina noticed his eyes were wild, despite his placid and almost clumsy mannerisms. "I know. Could you give me a ride?"

The man nodded and moved aside to reveal a step that she could use to step up into the front of the cart. Taking his hand for assistance, she climbed up and settled herself down. It wasn't as nice as her father's carriage, and she was fairly certain the man was transporting some form of manure by the smell coming from the covered load behind her.

"How far until the next town?" Georgina asked.

"You're not from around here, are you?" he asked.

"No," she lied.

"I'm John. Where are you headed?"

"Georg…" She stopped herself, not sure if she wanted to give this man her real name in case it got back to her family. "Hazel. Hazel George," she said, thinking quickly. "And I want to go somewhere pretty. And safe," she added.

"These areas aren't safe, Hazel," John told her. "It's about four more hours until we get to Oatlands. I'm stopping over there to deliver this load to the miller."

"What's in the back?"

"Half of it's grain, half is cow shit."

"That's disgusting. He's going to mill cow…" She hesitated, since she used the kind of language she would usually be beaten for, "…cow shit?"

John laughed. "The grain is in bags, and the cow shit is separate."

"Oh." She felt like an idiot.

"When I leave Oatlands, I'm headed to Hobart, and that will take me another day. You're welcome to stick with me til then; otherwise I could drop you in Richmond…if you're lookin' for somewhere pretty."

Georgina nodded. "Richmond," she said, letting the name roll off her tongue. It sounded beautiful. The perfect place to raise her daughter.

"You can sleep back there on the grain if you want," John offered.

"Thank you." She climbed over the back of the cart. As she pulled her leg over, she accidentally kicked one of the lamps that was hanging at the front of the cart. It swung wildly, casting a jumping light across the dark road.

"Sorry," she said.

John watched the light flicker, and he seemed captivated by it. Georgina watched him become instantly lost in the dancing light, and she grew increasingly uneasy. Something inside her whispered that she should not have accepted his offer to ride with him, but she was here now, and if worse came to worst, she could always get off at Oatlands and wait for another traveler to pass through to take her to Richmond.

As they started their journey onward, Georgina allowed the gentle rocking to lull her to sleep, where the screams of her mother awaited her.

When Georgina woke in the middle of the night, John was on top of her, his hand up her skirt. The roughness of his actions removing her pants had startled her from sleep, and when he noticed her eyes open, his free hand shot up and over her mouth, silencing her.

The ordeal was absolutely nothing like the experience she had shared with Will, and she wept while John raped her. She lay still and tried to imagine she was in Richmond, in a cottage of her own, holding her daughter beside a crackling fire.

When it was over, John climbed off her and pulled his pants back up, struggling with his belt buckle as he regained control of his motor skills. He climbed back over into the front seat of the cart and slapped the reins, kicking the horses back into motion.

Georgina cleaned herself up as best as she could. She looked down at the road that was passing beneath her. She could jump, but where would she go? More importantly, would the jump harm her daughter? Her only other choice was to wait until they got to Oatlands, and make a run for it then. She climbed back over and sat beside John, refusing to look in his direction.

"You shouldn't be alone out here," he said, his voice strangely calm after what had just occurred.

"Obviously."

"There are bad people out here, very bad people who will do bad things to you."

She looked at him incredulously. She wasn't quite sure what he thought he was doing, warning her against who? Him? "Like you did," she told him.

John's calm demeanor switched abruptly. His eyes widened and he started to shake his head. "No. No, I didn't hurt you." He bashed his hands into his face. "No. No, no, I'm keeping you safe. No, no! I'm sorry I hurt you!"

Georgina moved as far away from him as the small seat allowed her. He was completely mad, and she couldn't believe she hadn't noticed it sooner. All she cared about was the safety of her baby. The thought didn't cross her mind that the first person who offered her help might not actually intend on delivering it.

"Can you stop the cart, please? I'd like to walk," she asked, far more politely than was required, given the circumstances.

"I'm going to make it up to you. I wasn't hurting you. I'll keep you safe."

For the next hour, John repeated those same short sentences over and over while Georgina kept her eyes on the road, hoping that with every corner they turned she would see the next town appear.

"I wasn't hurting you." John hit himself in the head again, pounding his brow bone. Georgina was surprised he hadn't knocked himself unconscious by the looks of the blows he was delivering.

"I'll keep you safe." He looked sideways at her, making her skin crawl. "Such a pretty little girl needs to be kept safe."

Georgina folded her arms across her stomach, feeling her. The last time she had eaten was lunchtime two days before but right now she didn't care that she was hungry. She just wanted to get away from John. She shivered and prayed to whoever was listening that Oatlands was just around the corner. Her prayers were answered as Georgina saw a large windmill turning, next to a quaint cottage in the distance.

"This man is a good man," John muttered as they approached the windmill, nodding his head toward the farmer, who had appeared through the door at the cottage with the most gorgeous brown sheepdog by his side. Georgina was not going to take his word for it, and kept her arms wrapped tightly around her unborn daughter. The cart stopped, and suddenly her plans to run screaming from John were halted. She wondered how far she would get, or if she would just run into another 'John,' or if she would be able to make it to Richmond on her own. Besides, she was starving, and she hoped that this so-called good man would offer them food.

As it happened, the farmer's wife was visiting her sister, so there was no food in the house. He apologized profusely as he paid John for the delivery, and after they had unloaded the cart, he pointed in the direction of an inn where they could spend the night and enjoy some of the best food Oatlands had to offer.

"Their bread is made from flour that comes straight from this mill!" the farmer proclaimed proudly.

Georgina smiled, acknowledging his achievement. He did seem to be a good man, so while she certainly did not trust John's better judgment, she was happy to take the farmer's advice and journey over to the inn for a meal. The problem was she didn't have any money.

She looked over at John, who was counting out the coins into two bags.

"One for my father. One for me," he said, dividing the coins evenly.

"Kettle!" The farmer called after the sheepdog, who had left his post beside his master to chase a kangaroo that was grazing in a field nearby. Georgina watched the dog dart every direction the kangaroo did. He was very quick.

The farmer left the pair to go after the dog, who clearly had no intentions of returning to his side.

Georgina's stomach growled so loudly that she felt her daughter startle inside her belly. She rubbed her tummy and tried to settle her.

"You hungry?" John asked.

She nodded, still unable to bring herself to speak to him. Kettle raced past them, and John spun around to watch as the farmer ran by them shortly afterwards, very much out of breath. He chuckled while the farmer failed miserably at bringing his sheepdog back to his side.

"Kettle!" John called the dog's name, clapping for her as she raced around, snapping at the heels of the poor kangaroo, whose futile attempts to change directions with every jump were thwarted by the nimble border collie.

Georgina actually felt sorry for John while she watched his clumsy actions. He was most definitely mentally disabled, of that there was no question, but he also seemed to have almost a sweet sort of innocence about him. It sounded ridiculous to her, labeling the man who had just raped her as sweet and innocent, but lustful exploits aside, she noticed that he found joy in very small things, like the swinging lamplight, the dancing shadows, and now the kangaroo being chased by the dog. He might not have realized what he was doing, she considered, all the while knowing she was kidding herself by even thinking that was possible. He knew it. He said it himself—bad men who do bad things. He had gotten her where she needed to be so far though, and their travels had taken them through numerous forks in the road. If her parents bothered to look for her (she suspected they might), it would be difficult for them to find her right away. She decided that by the time they were close to Oatlands, she would be long gone, and in order for that to happen, she needed John. She reached out and touched his arm, calling his attention away from the dog.

"Do you want to get something to eat with me?"

"Okay, let's go," John said happily, still laughing at the poor kangaroo.

Georgina had severe pains in her stomach. She lay at the foot of the bed, willing herself not to throw up. She wasn't sure if the pains were pregnancy related or more to do with the fact that she hadn't eaten anything in almost two days. She knew that couldn't be good for her daughter, or herself for that matter. She tried her best to hide it from John, who seemed far too concerned when she had mentioned earlier that she didn't feel very well.

They were to sleep in a very small room above the tavern, whose food did not quite deliver on the promise of being particularly tasty, and Georgina hated to wonder what other food tasted like if this was some of the best that Oatlands had to offer. She was starting to realize just how much of a wonderful upbringing she had been blessed with. The people in this town were not as wealthy as the people back home, and she certainly couldn't imagine how it would feel growing up in a place like this. She hoped Richmond was nicer.

Even though her discomfort around John eased after she started to get to know him better, she still found it difficult to relax and fall asleep while he was in the room. She was exhausted though, and it frustrated her more than it should have.

John left the room after a little while, not saying where he was going. Not a minute after he had left did Georgina's eyes finally begin to droop and the pain faded away as she neared sleep. A few hours later John returned, the sweet scent of port accompanying him in the room, and Georgina woke immediately. Completely tense, she waited for him to lie down before she could relax. John took his pants off, and Georgina prayed his next move would be to climb into his bed, but it wasn't. He walked over to her, and tapped her gently on the shoulder.

She pretended to be asleep, but she knew it really wouldn't make a difference. She moved slowly, and tried to roll over so that she was facing the wall, but he held on to her shoulder and she was stuck on her back. His legs were close to her face, and she felt something sticky and rancid smelling touching her lips. He pushed forward, and Georgina gave in, parting her mouth. She let him do most of the work, and he was thoughtful enough to step away from her just before he finished. Georgina closed her eyes, thankful that it was over.

John woke her a few hours later, and for a moment she was worried he had come back for more, but he simply said, "Time to go, Hazel."

The next leg of their trip took much longer than it should have, since John had to stop every twenty minutes or so for Georgina to throw up. He would pull the cart over and help her down from the seat, walk her to the side of the road where she would vomit while he held her long black hair, and pat her back.

After there was nothing more to throw up, their pace quickened, and Georgina would just stick her head over the edge of the cart and retch stomach acids to the road below.

It got dark before they got anywhere near Richmond, and while they drove as far as they could before John started to fall asleep, they were unable to make it to a town to stop at.

"We can stop here," John said, pulling over on the side of the road. He pointed to a clearing through the trees. The last thing Georgina wanted to do was sleep outside, but she was grateful they were no longer moving, and she took the opportunity to regain control over her digestive system.

Neither of them was carrying any water, and Georgina politely declined the flask John offered to her, but the smell of the liquor was enough to tip her over the edge of sickness again and she fell to her knees in pain as her retching caused her stomach muscles to cramp.

John bashed his head as punishment for setting her off again. "Stupid idiot!" he said, dragging his fingernails through the skin on his forehead.

"John, stop!" Georgina stood up slowly and pulled his hands away from his head.

John looked into her eyes, and she looked back into his. He tilted his head slightly to one side and she wondered what he saw. Now more than ever she hoped her eyes still twinkled as they used to. Despite everything that had happened to her over the past few days, she was still filled with hope for her baby girl. John's eyes were strange. Glassy, vacant, terrifying, as the madness glinted beneath his cloudy pupils, encouraging his carnal desires. She looked at the bag she knew the coins were in.

"Will you give me a shilling if I let you..." she trailed off, knowing that he would understand. It was going to happen anyway, she knew it would, but by making it clear that she wanted something for it in return, Georgina felt the slightest bit better about it all. She felt more in control, and that calmed her. John nodded, slowly at first but then more pronounced, a wild grin spreading across his face. Georgina dropped to her hands and knees, and pulled her skirt up above her waist. He didn't need any further instruction. He pulled a coin out of the bag and dropped it in front of her. It didn't last long, it never did, and he was as sleep moments after it was done.

Tonight Georgina found it much easier to fall asleep. She even managed a little smile as she drifted off, full of anticipation about arriving in Richmond the following day and knowing John would be leaving her behind.

John woke her in the middle of the night.

"What's the matter? Are we going?" she asked, looking up and seeing that the moon was still high in the sky. It must have been about midnight.

"No," John said, moving closer to her.

Ah. Again, she thought, unsurprised that he wanted to go again before they parted ways. She fumbled about in the darkness until she found what she was looking for, and lowered her head. She did her best to please him in the hopes that he would consider giving her a few extra coins. She wasn't sure how long the money she had was going to have to last her, and she had absolutely no idea how she was going to earn more once it had run out. She thought about the different things she might be able to do to earn some money. She had always liked the idea of being a schoolteacher, but she knew she was too young. She wondered if she could get away with telling people she was sixteen, since her breasts were bigger than most girls her age. She might be small, but it was still worth a shot. She was torn from her thoughts by John.

"Hazel?"

Georgina picked up her head and looked at him. "Yes?"

"Why are you doing this?"

She wasn't sure how to answer. "Because you asked me to," she replied, preparing herself for one of his little outbursts.

"So? Why do you do what I ask?"

Georgina was unsure of why he was suddenly asking her these questions. She decided to be honest with him. "I'm doing it because you give me money."

"Oh."

"I'm doing it because I need to look after my baby."

"Where is your baby?"

"In my tummy," she replied.

"You're pregnant?" he finally asked, after a long period of silence.

Georgina nodded.

"How old are you?"

Why stop with the honesty there? It felt good being able to tell the truth finally. "Fourteen."

When John said nothing, Georgina lowered her head again, pulling her hair back behind her shoulders.

John pushed her head well away from his lap. "No, stop." He buttoned up his pants. "Go back to sleep."

Georgina obeyed him. She wiped her mouth and pulled the sack he had given her for a blanket over her face.

Georgina woke late. She looked over to where John had been sleeping, but he was not there. The strong stench of urine cut through her nostrils, and she turned her head in the direction of the wafting scent, ready to abuse John for not moving further away to take a piss.

John was dead. He hung lifelessly from the lowest branch of the tree beside their camp. His body swayed gently on the breeze, his belt cutting into his neck and pushing his head backward. Georgina could tell that his neck had snapped from the unnatural angle that it was stuck. He had also pissed and shit himself, and the feces were dripping down his pants leg, escaping through the bottom and plopping onto the ground below.

Georgina stood up and turned to run away. She stumbled on the sack and fell, hitting her head on a rock. Yelping out in pain, she pulled herself back up and kept running. After a little while, she began to calm down—almost. She stopped briefly to throw up on the side of the road. When she had finished, she looked up, and to her utter disbelief and extreme happiness, she saw the place further up the road that she had been dreaming about since she heard its name: Richmond.

It had taken her almost two hours to reach the sign indicating that the town coming up, and while she didn't think her body would be able to handle much more running, she kept at it, full speed ahead toward her new home. The first thing she was going to do was buy a giant loaf of bread and a chunk of her favorite cheese. She would find a place to stay for the night, and hopefully a steaming hot cup of tea. She started to imagine how good it would feel to sink her dusty body into a warm bath, and wash the day away. She hoped she could find a reasonably priced inn.

Suddenly, she stopped. *I left the coins at the camp.*

Refusing to give in now, she reluctantly turned her back on Richmond and began walking the way she had come. It took her much longer to return to the camp, now that she wasn't running, and her energy was far too low to force anything more than a brisk walk. Twilight was settling in while Georgina approached the campsite. The silhouette of John's body hung in the foreground of the most spectacular scattering of the sun's beams across the early evening sky.

She could hear the flies buzzing around his body, which had already begun to decay under the day's hot temperatures. The stench was almost unbearable, and she had to push through the odor while she tried to locate her coins. Finding them exactly where she had left them, she scooped them up and into her pocket. She turned to leave again, but in the corner of her left eye she saw John's bag, where he kept his money. She picked it up and rustled through it. Something wasn't right. The bag wasn't jingling the way it usually did. The coins weren't there. Slowly and for the last time, she forced herself to look at John. He did not look peaceful, his face screwed up in an uncomfortable expression. She walked gingerly toward him, terrified that he would move at any moment, irrespective of the fact that he had been dead for almost a day. She reached out to him, her head pulled back as far away as possible, as if that would help her nose avoid the pungent aroma. Pulling his coat jacket open, she reached inside and fumbled through his pockets. It was rather difficult because his body swung in every direction when she made even the slightest touch. Finally, she found the coins. She shuddered and pulled them out. Wishing now more than ever that she could just curl up in her mother's arms, Georgina raced the light back to Richmond.

By the time she arrived it was late, and every inn was closed for the evening. There was only one establishment still open, a bar by the name of the Suds Bucket. She didn't really want to go inside on account of the less than courteous people she met at the base of the stairs on their way out, but she had no other place to go.

"The Suds Bucket it is," she said to herself, and walked up the stairs. As the neared the top, the third last step creaked from under her, and for a moment she thought it was going to give way, but it didn't. Riddled with anxiety at the type of people she was preparing herself to meet, Georgina was completely thrown when she pushed open the doors and was greeted by the smiling face of a beautiful young blonde woman.

Chapter 10

It was early evening and the town's Fall Festival was in full force. There was music, laughing, dancing, and a carefree feel on the breeze.

Kate was not carefree as she walked through the festival, wearing a dress with far too much fabric and way too many ruffles for her liking. A young boy ran past her with a flaming torch in his hand, and it made her jump, kick starting her racing heart. Two other boys ran past her in close succession, chasing the first. Their playful laughter sounded sinister to her, and the fire torches that were meant to light the town only made the place feel darker to Kate.

She whipped her head around as she heard a scream coming from behind, but when she turned she saw a young girl being scooped up into a cuddle by her father, both laughing. Something crackled behind her and she jumped again as she spun around, this time looking up at the fire torches that lined the streets above her. The shadows cast from the dancing flames took her mind to a place she had desperately been trying to avoid since she had arrived in Richmond. The noises got louder and Kate became more and more overwhelmed by the second. Her head spun as she turned yet again, faced with more fire, more laughter, and squeals that transformed into screams of pain inside her head. Unable to think or breathe and with tears streaming down her face, Kate turned and ran as far away from the festival as possible.

Some distance away, Sherie was lying on a gently sloped hill, watching the stars. She could hear the din of the festival as it carried across the evening breeze, but it may as well have been silent for all the notice she was paying to it. The focus of her attention was directly above her on a small constellation of stars that were not particularly bright and certainly did not stand out amongst the other stars, but they were special and spectacular in personal meaning, and for Sherie that made them the brightest stars in the universe. As she stared at the sky above her, she allowed herself to lose focus, letting the stars blur and she became completely oblivious to the sound of approaching footsteps behind her, hearing nothing. She was seconds away from a long overdue and very special moment.

Kate's run slowed to a walk as she felt there was enough distance between her and the town. She rubbed her soggy cheeks and took a few deep breaths while she continued walking. She wasn't really sure where she was going as she put one foot in front of the other, but she knew that she was at the base of a small hill which overlooked some of the surrounding meadows, and she was far enough away from the festival that she wouldn't have to worry about any of her family coming to find her. She pushed away some of the branches from the bushes that covered the top of the hill, and as she broke through the final barrier she was surprised to find that she was not the first person there. She hesitated for a moment, unsure if she should interrupt whoever it was, but as the woman turned her head just enough so that her face caught the light of the moon, Kate realized that it was Sherie. Suddenly she did not want to go. She inched closer, wondering what she should say. She paused to take note of her heart, which had only just now started to calm down after the frantic scene at the festival, but as she found herself twenty feet from the woman whom she could not seem to get out of her head, it began to race again. Kate was sure that she had made enough noise for Sherie to notice her, but she seemed to be so engrossed in her stargazing that it was likely she may not have even heard her, or perhaps she was ignoring her. Kate felt an urge to be closer to Sherie and, however irrational and inexplicable her feelings were, she needed to honor them.

When she walked a little closer, she noticed that Sherie's face was almost innocent, dusted with some very faint freckles, and highlighted by her rusty mahogany eyes. Kate could see the detail even from where she was standing as the moonlight cast a glow across Sherie's face and made her eyes shine. It took Kate a moment to determine whether the golden tawny flecks in her eyes were a reflection of the stars or just another beautiful detail to what she had already decided was Sherie's best feature. The fact that Sherie had still not yet acknowledged her presence now made her more intrigued than ever, and she could not go any longer without speaking to her. "It's quiet up here."

Sherie still did not turn around. "It was quiet," she said, emphasizing the word 'was.'

Kate got the hint immediately, but, unfortunately for Sherie, she wasn't interested in being pushed away now that she was this close to her. She walked through the cold reception and sat down beside her. They weren't touching, but Kate could feel an energy between them, raising goose bumps on her arm. She wondered if Sherie felt it too, getting her answer almost instantly when Sherie rubbed her arm briskly and edged herself away from Kate, not once taking her eyes off the sky. Kate looked up too, smiling at the familiar feelings the evening atmosphere stirred within her.

She looked back to Sherie again. "What are you looking at?"

Sherie ignored her, so Kate tried to follow her gaze to the sky. She couldn't see anything specific or interesting enough to capture her attention. She recalled how much time Sherie had spent looking at the daffodils on the flower cart in town, and wondered if she was looking at something Kate just wasn't taking the time to see. Unable to create eye contact with her, Kate gave up and began picking at the grass beside her. A loud cheer in the distance reverberated toward them from the festivalgoers.

"You're missing out on all the fun," Kate said, using sarcasm to hint to Sherie that they might have something in common.

Sherie's gaze remained fixed on the night sky. "I'm not looking for fun," she replied.

Bingo. They were talking. Kate felt a tiny bubble of delight in the realms of her chest. "That's hardly any way to go about life," she said, suddenly feeling playful.

Sherie finally turned and looked at Kate. She appeared incredibly wired and frustrated by her presence. "The last thing I need right now is trouble from your lot, okay?"

"My lot?" Kate asked, genuinely confused.

"You're a Flanagan, aren't you?"

Kate nodded and wondered what kind of trouble her family could possibly cause. They were one of the most highly respected families in Richmond… *And she works in a brothel, you fool,* she thought. They were oil and water…or at least that was what Sherie thought.

"You don't know me," Kate said.

Sherie stood up and walked toward the bushes that led toward town, putting some distance between them. "I don't need to know you, Flanagan." She spat the words.

Kate realized that her reception wasn't getting any warmer, but she refused to let that affect her. It reminded her of the time she had found a possum trapped under a fallen rock when she was a little girl. She was jumping from rock to rock when she noticed it, struggling and terrified. She tried to help the possum, but every time she got close, it would growl and bare its teeth. She called for her father to help, and he explained to her that the possum was afraid, and that's why it was trying to scare her away. Kate remembered what he had told her: *"You have to show him that there's nothing to be afraid of. Ignore his growls, because when he realizes you aren't going to hurt him, he will let you help him."*

Kate stood up and moved slowly toward Sherie, softening her voice. "I think you're wrong. I think you do need to know me."

"Look, I told you I'm not looking for trouble."

"Jeez, not looking for fun, not looking for trouble…what are you looking for?"

Sherie walked to the edge of the hill, a foot back from where it dropped off suddenly and a few more feet away from Kate. She sat back down. "I'm looking to be left alone. You leaving would be a good start."

Kate walked forward toward Sherie, closing the distance again when she sat down beside her. She lay back and let out a little groan as she stretched with an air of relaxation. Despite the fact that her heart was thundering as if it were a galloping horse, her delivered reply was as cool as the night air. "What a shame. I'm not looking to be told what to do."

Sherie shook her head. She turned her head back to the skies. Kate stared at her for a long moment, and then looked to the sky again. After a few minutes of nothingness, she finally saw what Sherie was looking at, or more correctly, what Sherie had been waiting for.

A single shooting star struck through a dim constellation. Kate had never seen anything like it before in her whole life, and she was taken completely off guard by the unexpected blaze. "WOW! Did you just see that?"

Sherie ignored her. Within seconds, two more stars shot through the sky. Kate's mouth dropped, and stayed that way as another star followed. Then another, and another. Before long, the sky was full of shooting stars. They sat in silence watching the shower of raining stars that carved through the midnight sky. When it slowed down, Sherie wiped a tear from her eye. It did not go unnoticed by Kate, though she had the decency to pretend it did.

"That was incredible," Kate whispered.

"Tell me about it. And here I thought you weren't capable of shutting up for more than a few seconds."

Kate looked at Sherie, unswayed by her disposition. "What was that?"

"That was the Delta Pavonids. They're a meteor shower that rains through Pavo every year."

"Pavo?"

"A constellation," Sherie explained. "It means Peacock. See there, those stars? That's the head, and the breast." She motioned upward, outlining the constellation; or apparently outlining it. For all Kate could see, she might as well have been conducting an orchestra with the speed her hands were moving. Kate shook her head. She had no idea what she was looking at. Sherie moved closer to her, as if that would help her to identify the gas bodies in the distance. "Those in that arc there?"

Kate nodded. She could see the arc.

"Those make the tail."

Kate was suddenly unimpressed as she watched Sherie describe the peacock. "Hm. Nope."

"Nope what?" Sherie asked.

"It's not a peacock," Kate stated decidedly.

Sherie finally broke her gaze from the sky to look at Kate, blatantly offended. "I think you'll find it is. Pavo is Latin for peacock. It's a peacock."

"Well, then they should change the name. It looks more like a saucepan to me."

Sherie looked at Kate incredulously. "What? It's a peacock!"

"So you say," said Kate, enjoying being antagonistic. Sherie frowned, clearly frustrated.

"What are you doing here anyway?"

"Here on this hill? Or in a grander sense?" Kate asked.

Sherie rolled her eyes and stood up again. Kate stood too and held out her hand. "I'm Kate."

Kate watched as Sherie considered her introduction, looking at her outstretched hand. She didn't answer. Kate pushed forward her outstretched hand. "I'm Kate," she said again, more slowly this time.

Sherie gave in and took Kate's hand. "Sherie," she said.

"Nice to meet you, Sherie. And may I introduce you to my good friend the saucepan?" she asked, motioning to Pavo in the sky. This time, Kate saw a small smile cross Sherie's face as she turned to walk away, shaking her head as she went.

"Where are you going?" Kate asked her, unwilling to let her disappear so shortly after she had broken through her façade.

"Where in this town? Or in a grander sense?" Sherie shot back.

Kate laughed. "You're quick. I like it."

Sherie's response was deadpan. "Don't go spreading that around. It'll kill my business."

Kate had no response, and the silence was awkward.

"Sorry," Sherie added, "my sense of humor is sort of tainted."

"That's a bit sad," Kate said. Sherie shrugged.

"That's a bit life," she said. "Don't worry though; it's mine, not yours. I'll see you later, Kate." Sherie disappeared before Kate could say anything else.

Kate sat back down and looked up at Pavo in the sky. "It's a saucepan," she muttered to herself.

Kate descended the stairs late in the afternoon. She had stayed on top of the hill long after Sherie had returned to town, and she hadn't left until after the sun began peeking above the horizon. She wandered sleepily into the kitchen, where she bumped into Mrs. Flanagan, who was sprinkling flour lightly over the dough that she was kneading. Kate picked up a glass and walked over to the water jug, noticing the hawk-like observation from Mrs. Flanagan, who started to knead the dough a little more roughly than before.

"Where did you get to last night?" she asked tersely.

Kate poured the water into her glass. *Great.* She was in trouble. "Oh, I just went to explore the town a little." She sat down on a stool at the bench across from her aunt.

"Well, Sam was looking for you." Mrs. Flanagan selected a rolling pin from a pot of utensils and began rolling the dough out flat. Kate took a drink of water and used her index finger to make dots in the flour on the bench. After a few random dots, she realized that she had unwittingly dotted out the Pavo constellation.

"I'd be lying if I said I wasn't more than a little disappointed at your lack of enthusiasm towards making friends, Katie."

Kate blew on the excess flour, causing the smaller flecks of flour shoot through the Pavo she had dotted out. She knew it wouldn't be wise to correct her aunt and advise that she had in fact been very enthusiastic about making friends, and that it had taken a lot of effort on her part to crack the shell of the woman who hadn't escaped her thoughts since she found her on the hill the night before. No, that would definitely not be wise.

"Everything was just so loud, and when they brought out those torches…I needed to get away."

Mrs. Flanagan looked sympathetically at Kate as she pulled a biscuit mold out from a box. She started to cut shapes out of the dough and laid them on a separate baking tray. "It's okay. It will take a while to get settled, but it will happen eventually. This is your home now. I know you didn't choose for life to be this way, but it is and you need to start accepting that Katie."

Kate nodded. Her aunt was right—she did need to accept Richmond as her home and let herself settle in. A few days ago she probably wouldn't have been able to comprehend the idea, let alone consider it seriously, but for some reason the idea seemed now almost palpable. She had a feeling the reason was Sherie.

"What do you say we organize a nice lunch? Invite some people over after church so you can meet them in a less hectic atmosphere, hm? Not so much pressure that way."

Kate nodded again.

"And of course, there's always the masquerade ball. That's a fair while away yet, so you have plenty of time to get acquainted with everyone in town."

Mrs. Flanagan pushed the biscuit mold into Kate's hand before going to the sink to wash her hands. "I'll make a guest list. I'll be sure to call down to Sam's house personally to invite him."

Kate recalled her conversation with Sam about his horse, grabbing at the chance to use Mrs. Flanagan's determination for them to spend time together. She knew it couldn't hurt for her to indulge her aunt, even just a little. Encouraging her matchmaking would more than likely kick her in the rear later on, but if she could get a horse out of the deal, then it would be worth it. If she was expected to start putting down roots here, she was going to do it her way.

"I could invite him? I mean, I'm pretty sure I know which house is his...we went past it the other day, right? Weeping willow hanging over the pond near the front of the property?"

Mrs. Flanagan's face lit up as she nodded with an enthusiasm that could quite believably tear her head from her body. "Definitely, definitely! Wait until these have finished baking and you can bring him some!" she said with a bounce in her step as she slid the tray of biscuits and the remaining dough toward Kate.

Kate looked down at the biscuit mold in her hand and cringed when she saw the shape. She pushed the mold into the dough, picked the biscuit up, and laid it on the tray beside the ones already cut. The biscuits were love heart shaped. So much for less pressure.

It was late in the afternoon and the sun was high in the sky and at its hottest. Molly stuck her head outside to see her exhausted girls barely moving. "Maggie, can you give me a hand in here?"

Maggie lay on the couch in Claire's usual place holding a wet cloth over her forehead with one hand, her other hanging limply off the couch. Her skirt was hitched up high and her bare feet twitched every now and then as she kicked the flies off her toes whenever they got so bold as to land. She did not look well, on account of having enjoyed herself far too much the previous night. She grunted, and waved her hand in what Molly hoped was an affirmative.

Maggie wasn't the only one suffering the effects of the festivities. The front window of the Bucket sported a massive hole, smashed by multiple rocks of decent size that rested on the floor of the Suds Bucket inside.

Maggie shushed James constantly as the little taps from his tape measure proved to be too loud for her hammering head to handle. He did his best to avoid tapping the glass but it was unavoidable, since his attention continued to drift from his measuring tape to Claire, stealing glances at her as she sat curled in the swinging chair, her head buried in her book. Olivia looked almost as hung over as Maggie, her lump of wet clay spinning slowly resembling more of a molehill than a vase of any kind. She was making no attempt to craft it either, appearing to enjoy the feeling of the mud squishing between her fingers more than anything else. Georgina's forehead pressed against the copper bars of the birdcage, her arm completely inside the cage and covered in canaries buried up to her shoulders, which were only outside because they were too big to fit through the tiny sliding door.

The women outside ignored the presence of Constable Reid and Constable Smith, more commonly known to the girls as Smitty, who were inspecting the damage done to the main window of the Bucket and pretending to take notes. They all knew that it was a waste of everyone's time, but procedures had to be followed, even if it were just for show.

Within the Bucket, Sherie was behind the bar chopping up lemon slices in preparation for the evening. Molly came back in and launched herself up on top of the bar, hitting a rolled up dishtowel against her hand in frustration. Maggie still wasn't moving.

"Maggie, grab the broom and get in here! There's glass everywhere!" Molly's command was purposely tense, expecting the delivery of her order to bring about swift action as opposed to what she was met with, which was yet another unenthusiastic groan that drifted through the doors from outside and no further movement.

"I don't know why you're surprised. Something happens every year." Sherie said.

"I'm not surprised Sherie, I'm pissed off. We can't afford this."

Sherie put the lemon slices in a bowl and moved them to one side. Molly's eyes followed the bowl, and she picked it up the moment Sherie's fingers let it go. She inspected the slices, holding one up and motioning to the white pith outlining the flesh of the fruit.

"You have to cut these bits off. They look ugly otherwise," she said, shoving the bowl back into Sherie's hands. Without question, Sherie began to re-slice every portion of lemon, trimming away the ugliness that offended Molly so.

Molly knew she wouldn't take it to heart. Everyone should know by now that she got like this when she was angry. She didn't think it was a flaw to like to have control over things—it was just good business. When she couldn't control something she would go into overdrive, making sure that she had a firm grasp on everything else going on around her until the issue in question either fell under her control or disappeared completely.

James rolled his tape measure up. "Right, all measured. I'll be back soon." On his way out, he stopped on the veranda. "Officers, you might want to check out the rocks inside too. Evidence right there," he said.

The constables nodded and headed inside. James paused for a moment in front of the girls. His eyes lingered on Claire, but he addressed his goodbye to the group as a whole. The girls waved goodbye, but Claire, buried in her book, didn't look up. James looked at the utterly unanimated Maggie, who was no help at all. "Bye, Claire," he said, blushing.

Olivia gave Claire a swift punch in the arm and Claire looked up to smile at James. "See you later. Thank you for coming to fix the window."

James all but fell down the stairs in jubilation as he left the Bucket, all of this lost on Claire, who had already returned to her book.

The constables looked at the rocks on the floor. Smitty stood awkwardly, a clear attempt to pretend he had never set foot in the Bucket before. "It's obvious what has happened here," he said, "but without anything more solid we can't accuse anyone."

Molly hit the dishcloth against her hands. "We know EXACTLY who did it," she said.

"But you can't prove it," said Constable Reid.

Sherie put the bowl of lemons back down on the bench. "Can I offer you gentlemen a drink?" she asked.

Molly threw the dishcloth on the bench in fury. "I think if they have nothing useful to do here, they should be on their way."

Constable Reid nodded in agreement. "Can I use your outhouse?" he asked.
Molly shot daggers at him with her eyes. "Careful not to fall in."

"Watch it," Constable Reid warned her, walking in the direction of Molly's
outstretched arm that pointed the way to the toilet.

Smitty relaxed and wiped the sweat from his brow as Constable Reid left
the room. Molly, however, took the opportunity to get less than respectful with
the constable. "Are you fuckin' serious, Smitty? There's nothing you can do?!
You KNOW it was Josh's lot. Can't you even question them?"

Constable Smith threw his arms up in helplessness. "On what grounds,
Molly?"

"On the grounds that they're assholes in general," she suggested.

"You know I'd do anything to help if I could, but we really don't know if
it was Josh Flanagan," he said.

"That's bollocks! They're the only ones in this town who do things like this
to us. They act all respectable, but they have it out for us you know. It's because
we went to the festival, I'm telling you. They hate it when we come out of our
little cave here," Molly said, motioning to the room they were standing in.

"Why would they care if you went to the festival or not? You don't have
any proof other than a gut instinct, Mol."

"I don't need any God damn proof!" Molly shouted, slapping the towel
across the bar. "I just know, okay? I just know."

"Is there something you're not telling me? Because if you know something
that could help pinpoint them…"

Molly shook her head. "No. Forget it."

"Mol…" but Smitty cut himself off as Constable Reid came back from
the bathroom.

"If we get any further information, we'll let you know," Smitty assured her,
suddenly more rigid and stern sounding than before.

"Yeah, you do that," Molly spat sarcastically.

"Miss, I suggest you show a little more respect," Reid cautioned.

"You know if it weren't for us, this town wouldn't be what it is today," said
Molly.

Constable Reid turned and walked out of the Bucket. Smitty shot a final
look of apology before following him.

"We're the reason Richmond gets so many visitors, and you know it," Molly shouted at their backs.

"Molly." Sherie finally spoke up, and Molly knew it was time to calm down. The local authorities looked past their activities due to the fact that the Suds Bucket did indeed account for a lot of travelers who would otherwise not stay in town for the night, but a blatant admission of guilt would be something they would be unable to ignore.

Constable Reid stuck his head back through the broken glass window. "Tread carefully with your words Molly, because I know your grog isn't that good."

Molly kicked a rock on the floor in frustration. "MAGGIE! WHERE'S THAT BROOM?!"

It took a moment, but Maggie eventually appeared in the doorway of the Bucket, looking entirely disheveled, and her hair strewn about the place like medusa. She leaned on the broom as if it was holding her up. She swayed for a moment, and it was uncertain whether she would remain upright, but after a few seconds she was stable again, and she made her way toward the shards of glass.

Chapter 11

Surrounded by the original fence that had recently been painted white, the grand estate of Lawton Station and homestead stretched across one thousand acres, established by Sam Booth's grandfather over forty years before. Lawton Station's history was as rich as the estate was beautiful, and while Sam's family were proud to loudly discuss its foundation by Charles William Lawton, an American doctor who was granted the land as an incentive to settle in Australia around 1812, they were a little more tight-lipped on how their family came to be.

Charles and his wife Lydia had five daughters and no sons. Even more tragically, all of his daughters but one died in infancy after contracting scarlet fever. After his best efforts to keep his daughters separate failed, one by one they fell victim to the disease. When his eldest daughter Augusta fell ill, Lydia committed suicide in order to avoid further grief of losing their one remaining child. Augusta, however, survived the illness, and as soon as she was well enough to travel, they left their misery in New York and journeyed to Australia, for a new life. On the boat over, Charles met a Welshman who gave him 1800 sheep and 408 cows after he saved his son from choking. Charles tried to deny the extravagant repayment, but the Welshman insisted he take his due after already hearing of how he lost his family. Upon their arrival in Sydney, Charles was unable to find land to his satisfaction so he decided to travel further south, eventually ending up in Van Diemen's Land. When he reached Richmond (which was not yet named so) in 1812, he was granted one thousand acres of land and a number of convicts who worked to establish the station and homestead for him.

In 1817, when Augusta was 16 years old, she fell in love with one of the convicts who worked for her father, Henry Booth. Her feelings were immediately reciprocated, for Augusta was as beautiful as her mother and as clever as her father. Charles was not happy when he learned of their love affair, banishing Henry from the station, but since he had not yet carried out his sentence, he was re-assigned to build the Richmond gaol. It was here that he aided the police in capturing an escaped convict and was granted a pardon along with his freedom. Henry returned to Lawton Station in 1820 as a free man, and when Charles realized that the now nineteen-year-old Augusta's prospects were few and far between, he agreed to let them marry. As time passed, the convicts who were working at the station completed their sentences and were released, clashing terribly with the onset of Charles's severe arthritis, and he handed the running of the station over to Henry.

Few people living in Richmond today were around when Henry was serving his sentence, and the Booths tweaked their family history with ease. When anyone ever asked Henry where he was originally from, he had no moral misgivings in telling them "England" and leaving it at that.

Kate walked slowly down the red dirt driveway hedged by neatly trimmed grass that spread far across the front of the estate, a welcoming lush green. After walking down the path for five minutes she still could not see the house, though she was happy to admire the large weeping willow that blanketed a still pond with shade, providing the perfect playground for several ducklings that chased and prodded one another, and she stopped for a moment to laugh at their folly.

"Kate?"

She turned to see Sam approaching atop the most beautiful palomino horse she had ever seen. "You're riding my horse!"

Sam laughed.

"I'm serious."

"What are those?" Sam asked, pointing at the package Kate was holding.

"That depends," Kate said.

"On what?"

"On whether or not you are prepared to take payment in the form of oatmeal biscuits."

Sam laughed again and jumped down off the horse. "And if I'm not?"

"Well, then in that case they're just a gift from my aunt." She handed the package to Sam. "Do NOT take any notice of the shape."

They started walking toward the house, the horse trailing behind them obediently.

"Let me guess…love hearts?"

Kate blushed. "How did you know?"

"We're talking about Anne Flanagan here, the woman whose life mission is to pair up every living creature as if she were preparing to load them onto an ark."

"I'm starting to see that, yes," Kate said.

"She made the same little package for my older brother John, and sent Regina around to deliver them with an invitation to lunch after church a while ago."

Kate cringed.

"You've come to ask me to lunch too, haven't you?" he asked.

She nodded.

"I'd love to." Sam smiled at her, looking into Kate's eyes for a little longer than she was comfortable with, but she ignored the feelings for now. They approached the house, walking first through the most stunning rose garden, the beauty of which prepared Kate so that she was not as surprised when she finally set eyes on the magnificent homestead.

"They weren't wrong when they said your home was one of the loveliest in Richmond," she said.

"Would you like a quick tour?"

"Are you sure?"

"Of course. Come on. I'll just tie Bunny up around the back."

"Bunny? Are you kidding me? Bunny?" Kate looked at Sam, taken aback by the choice of name for such an impressive beast.

"My sister named her. It's short for Bunyip."

"You did not let your sister name this gorgeous…" Kate paused and looked under the horse "…girl, after a monster."

"Let her? I don't know how many nine-year-old girls you know Kate, but you don't really let them do anything…they just do."

Kate patted the horse. "Don't worry, girl. We'll get you a better name." She turned to Sam. "So let's get business over with before you give me the grand tour. I told you I'd give you double what you paid for her, remember?"

"I do, but I honestly didn't think you were being—"

Kate cut Sam off. "I was. I am. But if that's not enough, just name your price. Whatever you want."

"Do you know how to take care of a horse?"

"Sam, you're just getting to know me so I'll let that one slide. I grew up around horses. I probably know more about them than you do."

Sam grinned and Kate grinned back at him, knowing that she was pissing him off on purpose, despite his being too smart, or too polite to bite back.

"I'll have to take your word on that."

"You don't have to. I'll show you. How about a race?"

Sam didn't say anything, and Kate looked at him with silent hope. "How does racing horses prove you know more about them than I?"

"Do you have a faster horse than…" she forced herself to say the name "…Bunny, here?"

"Of course. She's just a filly. I've got a few stallions that would beat her hands down. Do you want to race one of those?"

"No. I want to race her."

"Against a stallion?"

"Against whatever you want to race me against." Kate wrapped her arm around the palomino's neck. "We'll beat you."

"Go on, Sam, race her!" A little voice from behind them piped up. A tiny girl stood barefoot on the railing of the verandah, holding on to the wooden post for balance.

"Harriet Booth, get down from there!"

Harriet hopped down and skipped over to them. She turned to look at Kate, her expression serious. "I hope you win," she said, reaching out and tugging on Kate's skirt.

"Thanks for the support, little sis!" Sam said, nudging her on the bum gently with his foot.

"Don't worry, Sam. She won't beat Derwent."

"Hey! I thought you just said you hope I win?"

"My mother taught me to be polite, even if you don't mean it."

Kate and Sam both exploded with laughter. Harriet frowned. "I'll go get Derwent," she said, heading in the direction of the stables.

"So, we're racing Derwent, my love," Kate said to the palomino.

"Honestly, Kate, I don't think we could even call it a race. Derwent's my best purebred Arabian. I'll race Chocolate."

"The stock horse? I don't think so. That'll even out the playing field."

'You don't want it to be a fair race?" Sam asked.

"I wanna kick your behind and shame you at the same time."

"To what end?"

"Yours, Sam Booth," Kate said with a wink, hoisting herself onto the palomino and distributing her blue and burgundy checkered day dress so that it draped evenly across the horse.

They walked toward the stables slowly, giving Harriet time to saddle Derwent.

"You're very different to the other Flanagan women," Sam said.

"I'm definitely more of a Walmsley."

"A what?"

"My mother's maiden name. We're farm folk," she said.

"So are we," Sam replied, pointing to the acres of land that surrounded them.

Kate chuckled and pointed to the Chinese men who were working in the distance. "We're that kind of farm folk. The ones doing the grunt work, in the dirt."

"Hey! I get dirty!" he said.

"And I bet you have a gorgeous tub to bathe in at the end of the day, don't you?"

"There's nothing wrong with that."

"Not saying there is. Just saying…I don't know. I'm just not from here."

Sam nodded. "I bet it's different living with the Flanagans then?"

"You have no idea." She grabbed at her skirt. "I don't think I've worn one of these since I was about six years old. Probably younger."

"Me too," Sam said.

Kate laughed, thankful that he was steering the conversation away from where it was headed.

"Nah, you'll get used to it soon. Once you learn the rules, you know, the codes and what not."

"Rules and codes…God, it makes me sick just thinking about it all. Wear this, don't talk to those people, don't buy from that blacksmith, never walk past the gaol alone…I mean, the last one I understand, but the rest are just…" Kate trailed off as Sherie's face appeared in her mind.

"People are different…not all of them should mix."

Kate shook her head. "Not true. You're right in that people are different, I'll give you that, but 'not all of them should mix'? That's nonsense. Not all of them get along, but that doesn't mean that we should make a point to treat someone differently to anyone else, just because they're not the same as us… does that even make sense?" She knew that it did, but she could see from the look on Sam's face that she was asking difficult questions.

"I think I know what you're saying."

"I just don't see how one person can say they're better than another, for the sake of social status."

"Isn't that what it is though?"

"I don't know…" Kate bit her lip. She decided not to say anything else on the subject.

Harriet appeared from within the stables, her arm held straight up above her as she led the stunning black Arabian horse almost three times her size.

"Whoa," was all Kate could manage to say.

"Impressive, isn't he?"

"He's got nothing on my love here," Kate said, patting the palomino as she bluffed. "Where are we racing to?"

Sam pointed to a large white gum tree a way back. "Out to that tree, then over to the water tower, through the quad past the second kitchen, through the rose gardens, and we'll end at the willow at the front of the property." He climbed onto Derwent.

"Sounds good to me," Kate said, mapping the race in her head and trying to take note of as many obstacles as she could.

"Harriet, go stand over near that post. You can send us off." Sam waited until Harriet was out of earshot before he continued. "So what are we racing for here?"

Kate leaned forward, wrapping both her arms around the palomino's neck and laying her head gently on top of his mane. "Do I really need to spell it out?"

"How about a date?" Sam asked.

"How about a horse?"

"A date, my final offer."

"A horse, my only offer," she said, digging her heels into the side of the horse and turning her to face the white gum tree.

"I'd say yes to both if you win."

"I'd only ask for the former if I win."

"I'd insist on the latter if I lose."

"When you lose, Sam Booth, when you lose." Kate untied her bonnet and pulled it from her head. She kicked her heels sharply into the horse, who bolted instantly on her command. "Yah!" Kate raced past Harriet and dropped her bonnet perfectly in place on top of her head.

Harriet threw her arms up in disappointment. "I didn't start it yet!"

"I'll get her, Harri!" Sam shouted from behind her as he kicked Derwent into gear, passing her the package of biscuits he was holding as he rode past.

"Giddyup! Hah! I'm gaining on you already, Flanagan!"

Kate and the palomino formerly known as Bunny galloped toward the white gum tree, a wild grin on her face as her hair flew behind her, getting more tangled by the second. Kate made it to the tree first, but Sam was right behind her, and she could hear Derwent's hoofs thundering behind her as they raced across the plain to the water tower. From the corner of her eye she could see Sam appearing, and she dug her heels in and pushed her pelvis forward, urging the horse to go faster. She knew his horse was faster, and her eyes scanned the area for anything that could give her an advantage. To her left, Sam was now riding directly beside her and she got the impression that he had slowed Derwent just a little so that he could match her pace.

"So what's first place?" Sam shouted, looking over to her quickly before returning his eyes to the front.

"That depends on who wins!" Kate said, her horse's nose edging slightly in front of Derwent's. "If I win, I get the horse. If you win—"

"I get to take you on a date," Sam said.

"God, you're persistent."

"No, I'm insistent," Sam corrected her.

Kate rolled her eyes. "Fine."

With that, Sam pushed Derwent harder and within a few seconds he was a few horse lengths ahead of Kate.

"Only if you win!" Kate shouted.

Sam looked back, his hand to his mouth in mock-fear. "Oh, gosh, how am I going to manage?" He laughed and kicked Derwent again, increasing the distance between them again.

Kate frowned and leaned forwards. "Come on, baby. Come on, my love." She looked up again to see that Sam was now a considerable distance ahead of her, and was already riding around the corner of the fencing toward the quad that separated the main residence to the outdoor kitchen and maids' quarters. *Who needs a second kitchen, seriously?*

Kate rode hard, but waited for Sam to pass the fence and cross onto the red ground of the quad, changing angles to where he couldn't see her. As soon as he did, Kate kicked the horse and leaned back in the saddle, leaping the fence and cutting across the entire corner of the field. She reached the quad a few moments later and snickered at Sam's surprised face when he turned around.

"Slowing down, Booth?" she called out to him.

"I must be!" he said, giving Derwent another kick and speeding up a little.

Kate looked for her next move, seeing it ahead as Sam rode around the kitchen and headed for the side of the house opposite the woolshed where he would follow the path through to the rose garden.

Technically, I passed the kitchen when I rode through the quad, Kate thought as she turned left instead of right, and shot straight toward the rose garden instead of circling the kitchen first as Sam had done. She looked up and saw that Sam was about to pass the woolshed. At this rate, he would definitely make it to the willow before she did. Ahead of her, the verandah of the homestead stretched out in front of her, blocking what would have been a direct line through to the rose garden. By the time she went around it, Sam would already be through the rose garden. Unless...

Kate took a deep breath and leaned as far forward as she could, and let out a loud yell of encouragement. "Yaaaaaaaaaaaah!"

She approached the house at full speed, and she closed her eyes tightly as she pulled back on the reins. She sailed through the air, time seeming to slow down and she forced herself to open her eyes. At the end of the rose garden stood Harriet, her mouth wide open as the parcel of biscuits she was holding dropped to the floor. Sam had passed the woolshed but had slowed almost to a complete stop to watch the jump. The jump was perfect, with the palomino clearing the railing completely and Kate crouched low enough that her head was nowhere near the wrought iron lacework that decorated the eaves of the verandah. Her landing was smoother than the jump, if that were even possible, and Kate found herself at the foot of the rose garden.

"Well done, love," she whispered to the horse. Her horse.

She looked back and saw Sam far behind her. She cackled and looked ahead again, easing into the final stretch of the race. She slowed as she made it to the weeping willow, taking care not to scare the ducklings that were still playing at the edge of the pond. She jumped down off the horse as they came to a stop, and stretched her legs. It had been ages since she had ridden like that.

Harriet came racing up and the ducklings scattered. "Wow! That was amazing! Kate, Wow! Where did you learn to ride like that? Can you teach me? Kate! Wow, Kate!"

Kate picked Harriet up and spun her around, bathing in the accolades. "Of course I can!"

"You cheated!" Sam rode toward them, a smile on his face.

"How did I cheat? I passed everything on the list."

"Technically, yes but—"

"But nothing. I hit the tree, the water tower, through the quad, past the kitchen, through the rose garden, all the way to here. I didn't even scare the ducks!"

Sam shook his head. "You bent the rules."

"Well, that just makes me smarter than you, doesn't it?"

Harriet chuckled.

"Oh, you think that's funny do you?" Sam climbed down off his horse and ran over to Harriet, tickling her. "Well, will you still be laughing when you find out that Miss Flanagan here just won your horse?"

Harriet shrugged. "I don't mind. She deserves her."

Kate smiled. "Does that mean it's okay for me to change her name?"

Harriet gave her a nod of approval, already more interested in the package that she had just discovered was full of biscuits as she skipped off back toward the house.

"Aren't you going to say goodbye, Harriet?"

"Bye!" Harriet's farewell was muffled as she shouted through a mouth full.

Kate turned back to Sam. "We should do this again sometime," she joked.

"I'd love to. And here I was thinking you weren't going to offer me a date if I lost."

"Oh…" Kate stopped herself. *Great. Put your mouth in it now. It was just start-ing to feel normal.*

"It's okay, if you'd rather not."

"It's not that, I just…"

Sam waited for an answer as Kate's mind rushed for the right words.

"It just feels like the only thing everyone around here cares about is getting married. Like it's the most important thing ever."

"Marrying someone you love isn't the most important thing ever?"

"Bingo! That's just it. Marrying someone you love. I kinda feel like my aunt doesn't really care if I love you or not."

"Well, you have to get to know someone first before you can love them don't you?"

Kate shook her head. "No, I don't think so."

"You're just supposed to know?" Sam took his hat off and wiped his brow.

"You're just supposed to feel."

Sam put his hat back on. "Ah."

"I'm sorry. I really like you. Just not…"

"It's alright," Sam said with a reassuring smile. "You know your aunt won't give up though, right?"

"That's okay. She's just looking out for me. As long as she understands that I refuse to settle for anything less than what my parents had…"

"True love?"

"The truest. Pure eternal love."

"Well, I wish you luck finding it, Kate."

"Friends?" Kate asked, holding out her hand.

Sam nodded and grabbed her hand firmly. He pulled her forward with a jolt, knocking her off balance and hoisted her over his shoulder. Kate screeched loudly but couldn't stop her laughter as he carried her toward the pond.

"No! Sam, no!" She hit his back playfully, but he was in no mood to give in and he launched her as far as he could into the air. Kate landed in the pond with a splash and a yell, before noticing that the cool water was actually refreshingly welcome to her hot and sweaty skin. She splashed up at Sam, who had already backed up in order to avoid getting wet.

"Friends," he confirmed with a laugh.

"You're a sly bastard!"

"Language!"

Kate climbed out of the pond. "You scared the ducks away."

"Correction, YOU scared the ducks away."

"Help me up?" Kate asked as her soggy clothing slipped against her horse.

Sam cupped his hand at the belly of the horse and helped her mount. "What's her name, then?"

Kate gave her a pat and kicked her into motion. "Aiko."

"What does that mean?" Sam asked, raising his voice as Kate rode further down the path, dripping into the dust as she left.

"Loosely translated? Child of Love."

If Sam replied, Kate didn't hear it. Without even needing to nudge her, Aiko had started to gallop down the end of the driveway, jumping the front fence as if it were only a foot tall.

"That's my girl."

Sherie walked beside Tom through a large meadow, wondering if they were ever going to decide on a place to stop and sit. He had invited her out on a picnic, not a walk, and she was not wearing the right boots. She was starting to get frustrated, the more he rambled.

"Everyone just seems to think they're better than me. I don't understand it. I'm polite, I dress well, hell my clothes are more expensive than all their wardrobes put together! They still don't invite me anywhere!"

"How long is it going to take you to realize that they're never going to accept you, Tom? You're not one of them. It's not about money, it's about breeding, and you're a convict."

Tom's face fell.

"I'm sorry. I didn't mean to be so blunt. I just meant…" Sherie took Tom's hand in hers, "They're all sods, okay? Why do you want to be like them anyway?"

"I don't want to be like them," said Tom. "They're all miserable."

"Well then, what do you want?"

"I want them to accept me," he said.

"Accept you for what? They're not exactly the most accepting bunch of people, in case you hadn't noticed."

"Accept me as part of Richmond. I like this town and I want to make it my home, but I can't even walk into church without being scoffed at!"

"At least they'll let you inside the church," said Sherie.

"I'm sorry. You probably think I'm an idiot for wishing I could be a part of it all,"

"Not at all. I wish I could be too. I used to be one of them, so it's hard, you know?"

Tom nodded. "I don't want to leave, that's all."

"So don't leave," said Sherie. "Simple as that."

"You're one tough woman, you know that?"

Sherie laughed. "I've been told once or twice, yes. Listen, they'll start to accept you when they realize that you're not about to run out of money any time soon. They're ridiculous like that. Until then, just keep being who you are, offer to help when you see they need it, and don't take no for an answer. I'm sure you'll work your way into their exclusive little social group eventually." They approached a boulder under a large tree and Sherie made the decision to stop and sit down. Tom sat beside her.

"Thanks," he said.

"Just don't treat us like dirt when they finally let you in," she said.

"I'd never do that."

"Yeah, well, we'll see."

Sherie inhaled and held her oxygen captive. It wasn't until she started to feel dizzy that she decided it was time to exhale.

"Are you hungry?" asked Tom.

Sherie nodded, and then, without so much as a blink, said, "Where's the picnic basket?"

Tom looked around him for a moment, before a look of disbelief passed across his face.

"Damn!" He leaped up and ran back in the direction they had just come from. Sherie chuckled as she watched him run. She had noticed he left it behind a while back and she was waiting to see how long it would take him to realize, but she was getting hungrier by the second and so she gave up the game. She looked down at the rock to the patches of moss she had been picking at. She had picked out a perfect formation of Pavo, but it was cast into darkness by the shadow of a head.

"What a nice saucepan you've made there." The sound of Kate's voice triggered a scowl on Sherie's face and she looked up to see her hanging above her in the tree.

"You again."

Kate grinned a wide toothy grin, scrunching up her entire face. "Me again," she said proudly. She jumped onto the boulder and dropped herself down beside Sherie. "So, what's with the peacock?"

Sherie laughed. "Oh, so now it's a peacock?"

"No, that's a saucepan," said Kate, pointing at the mossy Pavo. She jerked her head in the direction of Tom, who was still running toward the horse to collect their lunch from the saddlebag. "I mean him."

Sherie had no response. She wanted to laugh, but she didn't want to encourage this strange woman's company, so instead she shook her head and attempted to offer no facial expression whatsoever. "Who ARE you?"

Kate rolled her eyes, as she handed Sherie a single daffodil, seemingly producing it from nowhere. "Haven't we been through this? I'm Kate."

Sherie opened her mouth to say something, but Kate plowed on. "And you're not looking for fun. Or trouble. Lucky for you, I happen to be an expert in both, and present them to you willingly. No need to thank me." She bowed her head mockingly.

Sherie wasn't sure whether she should smile or scowl. She decided to continue with the lack of expression, though she suspected it was not going to plan as she felt the corners of her mouth curl into a smirk. "I'm not going to thank you."

Kate winked at her. "Not yet, anyway. First I have to rescue you from the peacock!" They looked over at Tom, who was carrying two rather large picnic baskets, hiding his face from view. He appeared to be walking a slightly zigzag path. Sherie chuckled fondly at the sight of him. Kate leaped to her feet and grabbed Sherie by the hand. "Come on! We can hide up the tree and watch him try to figure out where you went. It'll be fun!"

Sherie remained glued to the rock. She was smiling, but shaking her head. "I can't!"

Kate continued her attempts to pull Sherie up. "Of course you can! Quick!" Tom was getting closer. Sherie looked over to him and then back to Kate, but Kate had disappeared.

Sherie looked up into the tree. "Kate?"

She couldn't see her anywhere. A bunch of flowers appeared over her shoulder and made her jump. She grinned and turned around expecting to see Kate, but her grin disappeared when she saw Tom instead.

"Wildflowers?" he asked, offering them to her.

Sherie forced a smile and accepted the flowers. She laid them beside the solitary daffodil that Kate had given her. She picked it up and twirled it between her fingers, lost in thought as Tom continued to vent his frustrations about the faults of the Richmond townsfolk.

Sherie made sure Tom was out of sight before she threw the bunch of wildflowers into the bushes. When she got back to the Bucket, James was cleaning the new pane of glass proudly.

"Looks good," she said, nodding her approval. "How much?"

"Don't worry about it. Just give me a drink or two tonight."

"Apparently it's the only way we can get rid of the stuff," joked Olivia.

Claire looked up from her book and smiled at James. "It looks really good," she said.

James stumbled into one of the balcony poles as he turned around. Sherie chuckled softly to herself. "See you tonight."

James turned bright red and waved goodbye.

Sherie collapsed down onto the swinging chair and pulled Kate's daffodil out from her hair. She sniffed it, unable to stop the buzz that was generated by the sweet smell.

"You told me Tom only picked wildflowers."

"Hm?"

Claire pointed at the daffodil. "That's lovely. You said all he picked was weeds."

"Oh, yeah. Guess I was wrong," said Sherie.

"That's so thoughtful of him. He must really like you," Claire said.

Sherie nodded. She leaned back and kicked off the ground, launching the chair into motion, and closed her eyes.

Chapter 12

Night had long since fallen and the evening at the Suds Bucket was well underway, with a scattering of shady looking patrons throughout the bar who were laughing, joking, and most importantly, drinking. Tonight, Sherie was behind the bar, Olivia and Maggie were working the drinks, Claire and Georgina worked the men, and, as always, Molly floated around overseeing everything.

Claire was sitting on top of the piano, laughing loudly and flirting like she meant business (which, of course, she did) while Yin Yue belted out a lively song beneath her. Georgina was sitting on the knee of a man who was playing pool with a group of men in the corner, her arm draped around his shoulders, whispering god knows what into his ear—golden words to close the deal, as if there was any doubt left that he intended to take her upstairs at the end of the night. Every time he stood up to take his shot, she would feign disappointment for having to move off his knee, pattering him with kisses and running her hands over his arms. It didn't matter whether the man had muscles or not and there was usually a different man every night. The show worked, and even though deep down they all knew it was all an act, the men's behavior was enough to show that they allowed themselves to be convinced that Georgina really wanted them. Sherie chuckled while she watched Georgina using a strategy taught by Molly, whereby when their backs were turned, the girls would drink the patron's drinks to ensure they reached the bottom faster and, as a result, order more. It worked every time.

The girls had their work down to a fine art; Sherie would hear the orders being shouted from across the room and have the drinks poured and ready to go by the time the others came up to the bar to collect them, leaving empty glasses in their place. She usually had just enough time to wash the dirty glasses before they were needed again. It was an unrelenting cycle, but the money flowed just as fast as the drinks, so nobody complained.

Sherie was settling into her familiar work routine for an evening behind the bar, pouring drinks, washing glasses, and enduring the occasional squeeze on the bum from a patron. Some of the men were either very bold or far too drunk to care about the consequences of slipping behind the bar, though she did notice that Tom's presence had prevented that from happening as often as it used to. For that, she was grateful. Tom was sitting at the end of the bar chatting away with James, and Sherie wondered for a moment if marrying him wasn't such a bad idea. Pulled from her thoughts when she heard the front doors open, she looked up to greet her new customer, losing her breath as she found herself looking into Kate's eyes.

"What are you doing here?"

Kate slid onto an empty bar stool, a winning smile spread across her face. "Here as in your bar? Or here in the grander sense?"

Sherie shot her a look, making it clear that she was looking for a more specific answer.

"A girl's gotta drink."

Sherie raised an eyebrow as Kate flashed her the briefest of winks, and she felt something flutter inside as she pulled down a clean glass. "Mmmhmm. And where have you been drinking all this time before now?"

"Beats me."

Sherie didn't take her eyes off Kate. Why did this woman suddenly seem to have such a hold on her? "I'm sorry I was rude to you the other night."

"You were being rude?" Kate said, her smile not faltering. "I didn't notice. I guess I was too busy being cocky."

"Are you always cocky?" Sherie asked.

"Are you always rude?"

Sherie laughed, embarrassed.

"You'll just have to get to know me better and find out," Kate said.

"I guess so." Sherie felt a warmth start flowing from within. She could feel her heart was beating faster and she felt her face flush. She suddenly wanted to throw her towel down and follow Kate to wherever she was headed, but when the music died down, she fell from the tune that carried her excitement and she found herself back in the Bucket, full of smoke and liquor—the stench of reality.

Molly bustled past and knocked Sherie off balance as she dumped a tray of dirty glasses in front of her. "Present for you," she said.

"Ugh, thanks."

"Yin Yue, last song!" Molly called out as the pianist started up a new ditty. Billy danced toward Claire, who was still atop the piano, her leg swinging over the side in time with the song.

"Who are you?" Molly asked, looking at Kate.

"Molly!" Sherie was embarrassed by Molly's bluntness, which was usually easier to take when you knew her a little better.

"I'm new," Kate said.

"I can see that. You looking for a job?"

Kate chuckled. "Just a drink for now, thanks."

"Make sure you pay for it," Molly said.

Kate gestured to the shillings in front of her.

"Good-o." Molly nodded before disappearing again.

Sherie looked at Kate, unsure of what to say. She started to wash the dirty glasses left behind by Molly. She watched with interest as Kate played with the shillings, sliding them around the bar with a single index finger.

The last song finished and Claire climbed down from the piano. Billy draped an arm around her and whispered something into her ear. Claire laughed and shook her head, pushing his hand off her shoulder. Sherie wasn't the only one watching the interaction, as she noticed Maggie with her eye on the pair, moving closer to collect the empty glasses at a nearby table.

"Last call, people!" Molly yelled above the natter of unruly men making their way to the bar to collect their last drink for the evening.

"What? No! Come on the vase hasn't broken yet!" complained Billy.

From in front of the piano, Claire shrieked in pain and Sherie moved instantly to help her, stopping when she realized Molly and Maggie were already there.

Claire was pushing Billy's hands off her shoulders again. "No Billy. You don't have any money!" She shoved Billy hard and he fell back and hit the piano with a thud, causing Olivia's rectangular vase to topple and smash on the floor.

"There it goes! That's the night, people," Molly shouted, and opened the front doors.

"I'll pay for that," Billy slurred, pointing to the pieces of the vase on the floor that Olivia had already started to clean up.

Maggie grabbed Billy by the shoulders and attempted to steer him towards the exit. "You never pay for anything. Get home with you, Billy."

"Come on, Mags, give the guy a break." Warren shoved some money into Maggie's hands. "Here. Should cover the vase AND the girl for the night," he said, jerking his head toward Claire. Maggie looked to Claire, who only shrugged and rubbed her fingers together. It wasn't a secret that they needed the money, but even after all this time it still made Sherie's heart break to see the women she considered family putting themselves into uncomfortable situations for a coin or two. Business was business, though, and she appreciated the fact that they all understood this. Maggie shook her head and turned Billy around by the shoulders again, this time to face Claire. She put her mouth so close to his ear that he shuddered as she whispered something to him. Sherie knew Maggie well enough to assume that she had given Billy a very sincere warning.

Even with the male patrons who she knew were loyal enough to step in at the first hint of disorder, Sherie was surprised that there weren't more disturbances. It had to be in part due to the rumors that still floated around about their beginnings and the fate of the men who crossed them, which were mostly all falsehoods started by Molly. Occasionally a slither of the truth slipped in which could be verified by someone or another. Maggie's protective demeanor, combined with her size, also helped them early on before they made agreements with a hefty man or two to step in as security on nights when ships of officers were in town, or convicts up the trail were released on mass. Generally, most men were understanding of the rules and more than happy to abide by them if they didn't want to risk being 'strongly advised' never to come back.

Billy was too drunk to give a coherent response, but Claire grabbed him by his hand and marched him upstairs.

From the corner of the Bucket, James watched with obvious jealousy as they went upstairs, and turned to leave. Maggie dropped an arm over his shoulders and jerked her head in the direction of the stairs. With a nod, he dropped a coin into Molly's hand on their way up, Maggie's arm still around his shoulders. Georgina followed closely behind the pair with the man whose lap she had been sitting on all night.

The Bucket was close to empty by now. Olivia walked around the back of the bar and dropped the vase pieces into the bin. She waved goodnight to Molly, who flicked her tea towel out and hit her on the bum as she left the back of the bar.

Olivia squealed and she made her way upstairs with a weedy man who had been waiting for her to finish. Sherie dropped her head in shame for the first time in a long time, hoping that Kate didn't notice that most of the clientele of the Suds Bucket were hardly up market gentlemen.

Kate drained her glass and pushed it forwards as she stood up to leave. Before she knew what she was doing, Sherie grabbed Kate's hand. She gave her head the slightest of shakes and Kate sat back down. Tom stood up and put his empty glass on the bar.

"Do you still want to get a late dinner?" he asked her.

Sherie cringed and pointed to all the glasses. "I still have a few things to finish off. I'll come by when I'm done though?" she offered.

Tom leaned over the bar and gave her a quick kiss on the cheek, and Sherie felt herself blushing again. Kate looked away and Sherie felt the awkwardness intensify. She wanted to clarify very quickly with Kate that Tom kissing her was not a usual occurrence.

Tom turned to Molly with a wave. "See you, Mol."

Molly waved back at Tom as she wrote a few figures into the book, sighing when she started to count the last of the coins. Sherie took Kate's glass and filled it up again, and then looked at Molly. "Is it that bad?"

"Hand me those coins there," Molly instructed, pointing to Kate's shillings on the bar and ignoring the question. Sherie noticed that Kate had arranged them into a very familiar shape, and she admired the silver peacock from upside down. She glanced at Kate from the corner of her eye, but she was still looking somewhere else. Sherie wished she could speak to her alone and explain. She wasn't really sure what she needed to explain, but she knew she needed to be alone with her.

Molly slammed the book shut and threw it on top of the safe that sat below the bar. She bent down and picked up a crate full of empty beer bottles from the floor. She nodded to the glasses that Sherie was cleaning "You gonna finish those?" she asked.

Sherie shrugged. "May as well."

Molly kissed Sherie's cheek softly as she walked past her. "Have fun with Tom later," she said with a wink before she headed outside with the crate.

Sherie looked down at the glasses, this time too nervous to look up at Kate. "So, you and Tom, huh?" Kate asked.

Sherie took a deep breath as she picked up another glass. What did it matter? Why was it so important that Sherie made it clear to Kate that she was not in a relationship with Tom? *And why am I suddenly shaking?*

Sherie did her best to convey her lack of interest in Tom with an over the top eye roll. "Ugh, not really. He's a nice enough guy, but there's just no spark."

Kate nodded. "Molly seems pretty keen for you two to get together."

"She has her reasons," Sherie said, unable to remove the defensive tone from her voice. She could tell Kate noticed it, since she stiffened up very slightly.

"And you?"

"I have my reasons too."

Kate nodded again, an eyebrow raised, but she said nothing further. Sherie knew her defenses were high, her walls solid, and she had absolutely no reason to trust this woman, especially since learning she was a Flanagan, but for some reason all she wished for in this moment was that Kate was feeling the same way she was. What those feelings were exactly Sherie had no idea, but she knew she wanted Kate to pick up a hammer and smash her walls to the ground. Sherie knew Kate was going to have to work for it…she just hoped Kate was up for the challenge.

Sherie noticed Kate's glass was empty. "More?" she asked.

Kate shot her a cheeky grin and reached across the bar, picking up a clean glass. She put it beside her empty glass in front of Sherie and tapped it twice on the bar top.

"Is that an invitation?"

"It's a demand. Drink with me, woman."

Sherie felt the bubbles within her chest rise again and nerves reverberated through her body at the way Kate spoke to her. "Are you in the habit of walking into bars and making demands of the owners?"

"There's a first time for everything," said Kate, pushing forward one of the glasses. Before she could let go, Sherie reached out and grabbed it too, their fingers touching briefly. Sherie was certain the electricity she felt pass between them would shatter the glass, and she had to shake herself from the moment when it didn't.

"Well, Kate, I would be happy to be your first," she said boldly. Kate blushed, and Sherie celebrated silently. It appeared she felt the same way.

It took no time at all for Sherie to abandon her dirty glasses in exchange for multiple glasses of beer, and they were incredibly drunk soon after. They moved to a table in the bar where they spent the next hour laughing hysterically about any number of things, and the awkwardness that often comes with a new friendship evaporated almost immediately. Sherie felt more at home in the Bucket with Kate there than she had in a long time, and she was surprised that her walls had crumbled so easily. Certainly without the use of a hammer Sherie had willingly opened the gates.

"And they just crawled across it? Without even testing it first?" Kate had just heard Sherie tell the story of the day she and her sister convinced two brothers from town to crawl across a dangerous wooden plank that ran high between two grain silos on their farm.

"Yep. Molly put the plank down, we told 'em to crawl across it, and they did!" Sherie said proudly.

"And no doubt they fell?"

"Of course! About five meters! And their father never believed it was our fault. We were just two sweet, innocent little girls watching!"

Kate laughed and poured another two beers from a pitcher beside them—a sound time management decision made in order to consume more alcohol with fewer trips back to the bar. "After everything I've heard about you tonight, Sherie, innocent is the last thing I would ever consider calling you."

Sherie put her hands under her chin and fluttered her eyelids. "I have no idea what you mean," she cooed.

Kate pushed her hands away playfully. Sherie loved that Kate understood her without any hint of trying, and she especially loved that she could laugh without forcing it or faking it.

"And what about you? Naughtiest thing you ever did as a kid?" she asked, intrigued as she swallowed the last of the beer in her glass.

"I shot my father's dog," Kate answered, deadpan.

If Sherie hadn't just swallowed her mouthful of beer, it would have been spraying out of her mouth by now. "What?! Shot it with what?"

"With a feather," Kate said sarcastically. "With a gun, what do you think?"

Sherie went to pour more beer into her glass, but the pitcher was empty. "How old were you?" she stood up.

"Eight," Kate answered.

Sherie's eyes widened as she poured more beer into the pitcher. "EIGHT?!"

"No. Wait. That's a lie. I would have been six," Kate said.

"You shot your father's dog when you were six years old?" Sherie asked, making sure she had heard right.

Kate paused for a moment as she swallowed all of her beer. "I just had really bad aim. I still do, actually."

"You are so going to hell." Sherie chuckled.

"Says the prostitute!" Kate retorted. Suddenly the bar was silent, as Sherie took a moment to decide how she felt about that sentence. If anyone else were to have said it, she would probably kick them out, insulted and ashamed. She knew she was flirting with Kate, although she wasn't entirely sure why. Checking in with her heart, she noticed it was still smiling and she decided that was good enough for her. She was definitely very familiar with the feelings of shame by now, and since it didn't appear to be roaring across her face, she was satisfied that meant she was comfortable with Kate's gibe and suddenly burst out laughing.

Kate joined her laughter.

"Bad aim." Sherie laughed a lot longer than she would have done if she were sober.

"Well, what's your aim like, little miss perfect?" Kate asked.

Sherie shrugged. "I wouldn't know. I've never shot a gun."

This time Kate's eyes widened while Sherie continued. "Never done a lot of things. My life's been pretty stagnant." When Sherie finished her sentence, she noticed the mood in the room changed suddenly from light-hearted fun to a far more serious conversation. The full jug of beer sat forgotten for a moment.

"Interesting word to choose to describe your life," Kate said.

"I don't even think I'd use the word 'life.'"

"Why not?" asked Kate.

"Because I'm not really living. I'm existing."

Kate was silent for a moment or two before she spoke. "I feel that way too sometimes."

Sherie smiled at her sadly. "I know. You act like life's all fun and games, but there's something in your eyes that gives you away," she said.

"Aah. So you have been paying attention," Kate said with a slight smile.

Are we still flirting? Sherie paused as she thought about the type of response she was going to give. She didn't want to flirt flippantly if they were still speaking seriously, but she also didn't want to continue the sullen tone if Kate was trying to steer her away from the subject. Before she could decide, Kate spoke again.

"A darkness," Kate said.

Sherie leaned forward, paying no interest to whether whatever she was about to say were the right words or not. "What happened to you?"

"I was in the dark for a long time. One morning I woke up and decided it was time to find the light. Find my light."

Sherie sensed that Kate had decided that her explanation was good enough as she broke eye contact with her and looked down at the table. She of all people knew that the past could be difficult to talk about and she let it go without a fight. "That's what I need to do. I don't push myself enough. I guess I don't believe there's anywhere to go."

"There's always somewhere to go."

Kate smiled at Sherie, who wanted nothing more than to take her hand in hers. There was a certain fire in Kate's eyes, and she got the feeling that Kate's words, while seemingly inspirational, came more from a place of hurt than anything else. She knew what she was talking about. Qualified on the subject of suffering just as she was, Sherie took comfort in the knowledge that her newfound friend had enough of an understanding of a harried past to be the perfect person to talk to. *Doesn't everyone these days?*

Sherie found herself falling into the blue of Kate's eyes, and before she could stop herself she was reaching out for her hand.

"What do you mean you don't push yourself enough?" Kate asked. She pushed Sherie's glass across the table to her after having just filled it again. Sherie caught the glass instead of Kate's hand, feigning that was what she was reaching for in the first place. She hoped any blushing in her cheeks could be excused by the alcohol she had already consumed. If Kate noticed Sherie's awkward attempts to make contact, she did not let on, and to save herself a night of replaying the event in her mind to decide whether Kate's sudden movement was intentional or not, Sherie made up her mind then and there that it was nothing but bad timing. She took a big gulp of the beer and tucked her hand between her legs. Her moment of bravado was over for now.

"I'm just not good at stuff," she said.

"Stuff?" Kate questioned. "Like what?"

Sherie watched the amber bubbles rise to the surface of her beer. She wondered what happened to them once they reached the top. "Stuff. Like… shooting. Riding horses. You know, stuff," she said.

"You've never ridden a horse?" asked Kate, her mouth wide open in obvious shock. Sherie paused as she heard a noise out the front of the bar.

"It's Tom. Quick!" she whispered. She grabbed Kate by the shirt and sprang out of her chair, dragging Kate with her. In her haste, she bumped into the table, and the beer slopped over the edge of the jug and spilled onto the floor. She giggled, too drunk to stifle it, and pulled Kate down behind the bar. She stumbled, her grip tightening when she tried to keep herself upright. Kate fell on top of her as she toppled to the floor. They giggled again, and Sherie put her hand over Kate's mouth as they managed to regain their footing, crouched behind the bar.

Tom walked into the bar slowly, his footsteps slow. "Sherie?"

Sherie tried not to make a sound as she breathed; a hard task considering she had just leaped half way across the room to hide. She raised a finger slowly to her mouth, indicating that she expected Kate to remain silent and still. She peeked over the top of the bar. Tom was looking at the beer jug that was still sloshing about slightly, and Sherie cringed when she saw him notice the two glasses full of beer beside the jug. She ducked again as Tom turned toward her.

Sherie was centimeters away from Kate's face when she dropped back down. She let their eyes lock on to each other and she felt the ignition instantaneously.

The sound of Tom's footsteps came closer to them, and Sherie noticed that Kate's skirt was poking out slightly. Tom was moving dangerously close to the bar, and Sherie wondered what on earth she would say if she had to give an explanation about why she was hiding from him in the arms of a woman from the Flanagan family. If Tom saw the skirt, he would definitely look behind the bar. She leaned forward to pull it out of view and her body pressed against Kate's. Kate inhaled with a stab of breath and Sherie felt her freeze beneath her. She looked at Kate, her face so close that their noses were almost touching. She tugged on the skirt, pulling it back behind the bar. They stayed motionless while Tom's footsteps continued. Sherie looked at Kate, whose eyes were tightly closed. Tom paused for a moment, causing Sherie's heart to do the same.

Just leave.

As if on command, Tom's footsteps started up again, this time toward the front door. Sherie gave Kate's hand a squeeze, which was as much movement as she would allow herself to risk. After a moment, the footsteps disappeared completely. Kate opened her eyes slowly and Sherie felt her breath on her lips as she exhaled finally. Sherie swallowed.

Chapter 15

S herie was exhausted the following morning. Her best efforts to tell herself that Kate was interested in her were thwarted as she spent all night replaying the events over and over, analyzing beyond sanity what every movement, every flinch meant, and her reasons behind it. Kate had been flirting with her earlier in the night; of this she was certain. Whether or not she had come to regret it when Sherie returned her advances was what had her so conflicted. She could very well just be one of those over confident women who enjoyed the type of witty banter that came across as flirting, but Sherie refused to let herself be convinced that what Kate was like that. She was in the business and she knew when someone was flirting with her. So why couldn't she figure it out? In the end, she gave up on sleep and went downstairs to the swinging chair, where she sat alone and watched the sun rise over the gum trees, allowing herself the comforts that came with the early morning chorus of the bush birds. As the sunrise edged the moon out of view, Sherie was joined by the girls one by one. Olivia was the next one up, choosing clay over coffee. Georgina appeared quietly and padded over to her canary cage wearing her usual vague smile. Maggie carried out a plate of fruit, put it on the small table that sat in the middle of the group, and settled herself on Claire's couch.

Everyone appeared to be tired, and for that Sherie was grateful as she stared across the plains and out to the distant hills. She appreciated the silence.

Claire appeared later in the morning, her face buried in her book while she clumsily navigated her way toward her seat, accidentally sitting on Maggie. "Sorry!" she said, moving over.

"You know, Claire, it wouldn't kill you to look up from that damn book every once in a while," Olivia teased. "It can't be that interesting!"

When Claire didn't respond the way she usually would, Sherie knew something was up. She tried to catch Maggie's attention, but Maggie was already eying Claire up.

"Claire?" Maggie asked.

"Mmm?" said Claire.

"Put the book down."

Claire said nothing.

"Claire," Maggie said, this time more of a demand.

"I'm reading."

"No, you're not."

Claire did not respond.

"Claire."

"What?!" Claire snapped this time, but did not move her book.

"The book is upside down," Maggie said matter-of-factly.

Claire sighed and dropped the book. Her right eye was black and grossly swollen.

"Oh, what the hell!" Olivia dropped her handful of clay.

Maggie shook her head and reached out to move a strand of hair from Claire's face. "Oh, baby girl," she said.

"It's fine."

"That's it," Sherie said. "Billy isn't welcome here any longer."

"Oh, come on, Sherie, he's harmless."

Sherie scoffed, followed in unison by the others.

"Okay, fine, not...not entirely harmless, but he doesn't mean it. You know that. He's just...he's just Billy."

"He needs to toast his eyebrows and just die, if you ask me!" Olivia said.

"I'll toast them!" Georgina cackled.

"Settle down, girls," Maggie said.

"You're joking, aren't you? Come on, Maggie, this is going too far!"

"I'll be sending someone to have a word with him. Let's just worry about Claire."

"I told you, I'm fine," Claire said.

Sherie looked at Claire, who was definitely not fine. Her eye was weeping a brownish fluid, not thick enough to be blood but certainly not pretty, and she felt her eyes water as she stared at it. She stood up and went inside to find something to cover it.

She forced herself to contain her tears while she looked behind the bar for a clean rag that she could soak in some water. It wasn't the first time one of them had been hurt by a patron, but the guilt was rampant. She shook as she wrung out the wet rag, controlling her temper as best she could, lest she throw the bucket of water across the room or through the new window. Doing her best to ignore her fury for Claire's sake, Sherie took a deep breath and headed back outside.

Claire put the wet rag on her eye, wincing slightly as she did. "Can everyone stop looking at me now, please?" She picked up her book and turned it the right way up, but Maggie snatched it from her hands instantly.

"Oi!"

"Oi nothing, woman. You're not straining your eyes. Lie back and take care of yourself."

Claire frowned, but Sherie knew she was grateful. They'd all been there before, and despite all the insistence in the world that they were in charge of themselves, it was nice to know there was someone else out there looking out for them. Being strong wasn't part of their survival...it was pretending they were strong was what counted the most. Sherie knew that for sure, and so she was expecting Claire's answer before she even asked her question, but she asked it anyway. "Are you sure you're okay?"

"Splendid," Claire said, lying down on the couch, her head resting on Maggie's lap. "So are we going to talk about your little guest last night or what?" she asked.

"Huh?" Sherie had almost forgotten about Kate for a moment. Almost.

"Was that the woman from the other night? On the hill?"

"Oh. Kate? Yes." Sherie wasn't exactly thrilled to be talking about Kate, but she knew that Claire was just trying to change the subject, so she allowed her to keep going.

"What did she want?"

"Just to say hi, I guess," Sherie said.

Olivia's eyes narrowed and her clay wheel slowed down slightly. "Wait. You meet her, you ignore her, and then when you finally decide to speak to her you're rude, you tell her to leave you alone, and then you disappear...That about right?"

Sherie nodded. "That about sums it up, yes."

"So even after such a charming first meeting, she still felt the need to track you down and talk to you?" Claire asked.

"What can I say, I'm intriguing," Sherie said with a wink.

"An intriguing asshole!" Claire said.

"Hey! Unless you want your left eye to match your right, watch what you say, patch!"

"Olivia, throw some clay at Sherie, would ya?" Claire said with a chuckle.

"If you value your life you'll belay that order!"

Olivia shook her head. "We work so hard to have such winning personalities, and then here you come with your Sherie-scowl and your round little bottom that sways when you walk."

"What? I—" Sherie's protests were spoken over.

"That completely negates the fact that you practically tell the girl to jump off the hill you met her on…"

"And she makes a point to not only find out where you work, but to come and visit you, 'just to say hi'?"

Maggie chuckled at Claire and Olivia.

"It's just not right," said Claire.

"I do not have a little round bottom that sways when I walk!" Sherie said.

"Well, how would you know?" Olivia asked.

Claire took the ice away from her eye and looked at Sherie, staring her down.

"What?" Sherie asked.

"You were up all night," Claire said.

"Laughing!" Sherie protested.

"Exactly," Olivia said, as if Sherie had made her point for her.

Sherie looked at them, imploring them to go on. "Sherie, you don't laugh. Ever," said Claire.

Sherie gave up protesting verbally, and shook her head in defeat.

"What do you think, Georgina?" Olivia asked.

Georgina looked up from the canary that she was preening. "Foul play," she said.

Sherie scoffed and rolled her eyes. Olivia laughed as she bent over her clay and started to craft the mouth of her vase. Claire dropped the rag to the ground and winced slightly when she moved. The girls all winced along with her.

"I'll get you another one, love." Maggie picked up the rag from the ground and went inside.

"Morning, ladies!" Molly kissed Sherie's forehead from where she was standing. Sherie bent her head backwards to look at her.

"How did you go with Tom last night? Have fun?" Molly asked.

Sherie stretched out. "No, I was knackered after cleaning all those bloody glasses, so I just went straight to bed." She chose to ignore the glances exchanged by Claire and Olivia, and she hoped Molly missed them too.

"You work too hard, kiddo. Take tonight off."

Sherie's face lit up. "Are you sure?"

Molly smiled. "Of course. Just make sure we're right for stock and the night is all yours. I've got to head down and see Tom this morning so I'll let him know."

Sherie felt her face drop for a fraction of a second, but she hid it well. Molly plopped herself down beside her.

"You should wear your blue…" Molly stopped dead. She was looking at Claire. "What the…"

Olivia's demeanor returned to that of a livid dragon that had just realized her treasure had been stolen. "Billy," she spat, the B holding particular venom.

Molly's face was full of anger as she took in the bruise covering Claire's ordinarily beautiful face. "Well, I'll be having a little word with him tonight when he arrives. And by 'a little word' I mean I'm going to squeeze his damn balls so hard he'll wish he didn't have any," she said.

"Hopefully, when you're done with him he won't," Sherie said.

"It's my fault. I shouldn't have gone up with him when he was in one of his moods," Claire said. Sherie wished Claire wasn't so afraid of sticking up for herself sometimes.

Olivia's clay started to spin a little faster. "It is NOT your fault," she said.

The girls sat in silence while they watched Olivia, whose clay was spinning faster and faster. "Who is he to treat you like that? What does he think we are?" she continued.

"Whores," said Claire in a matter of fact tone.

Olivia snapped, and her hand turned white as it tightened into a fist around the clay that became mush in her hands. "Fuck!" she yelled.

Olivia

Four years earlier.

It seemed like it should be a match made in heaven: Olivia liked to have sex, a lot of sex, and so did Gil. The problem was that Gil wanted sex with more women than just Olivia. For all his life he had been successful in managing to convince even the most conservative and moral of women to lay beside him (as well as on top of him, underneath him, in front of him) and he wanted it to stay that way. Gil's life was one of leisure and he had no intention of giving it up. Traveling from town to town, enjoying his time by drinking, eating, and most importantly, flirting with girls, Gil was responsible for claiming the virginity of close to every woman from Hobart to Richmond (or so he liked to brag). He had an uncle in Launceston, his final destination, and his plan was to enjoy his journey north as much as possible before picking the right girl to settle down with. He could have walked away and left Olivia to deal with the situation, but deep down Gil wasn't heartless, and he argued with himself that his biggest flaw was that he loved women too much. Unfortunately for Olivia, his love was for the plural of the gender, and he was not at all happy with the end result of their relationship: marriage.

Olivia wasn't entirely sure why Gil had proposed to her. She certainly wasn't expecting it, and while she was delighted to accept, she couldn't help but wonder what on earth had compelled him to make an offer that seemed to contradict his candid intentions, or lack of intentions as the case may be. At sixteen years old, Olivia was proud of the fact that she was far more mature than the rest of the girls she had grown up with, and she was certain it was why Gil had picked her. She knew that every other woman in Richmond had been in love with Gilbert Sournois from the moment he arrived. No one knew whether he had been transported as a convict, and no one felt the need to ask. His hypnotic deep brown eyes were enough of an answer to any question they could think of. He was the epitome of a Frenchman. His voice was as smooth as the trickling river, and his words were charming. Olivia had gloated far more than she should have upon announcing her engagement, and it only took a few weeks for the unkind truth to reach her. She was expecting the rumor mill to start churning as it always did when the girls of Richmond were jealous of one another, and she had paid no attention to the gossip at first.

"This is just another reason why Gil chose me. I don't play silly schoolgirl games like *some* people."

Her best friend looked at her with a sympathetic head tilt, but Olivia stopped her before she could say anything. "Don't try telling me there's truth to any of what they're saying, okay? Yes, I know he's been with other women. We are open and honest with one another and I've accepted it. I'm not that naïve, please."

Olivia was steadfast in her conviction in the face of growing evidence that suggested she was not the only woman in Richmond Gil had put his hands on. It took her walking in on Gil and Regina having sex in the very same place she and Gil were caught by her father for her to wake up and acknowledge what she supposed deep down she had always known. She was not the only one in Richmond. She married him anyway.

Their wedding was a paradox for the little girl who wanted so badly to believe that her happily ever after was here. Adamance and pride overruled common sense and the truth that she refused to let slap her in the face for so long. They hadn't made love since her father caught them in the act, and Olivia told herself it was because Gil had promised her father that he wouldn't touch her again until they were married, despite discovering that he was fucking other women. He and her father had talked for a long time, but Gil refused to tell her what they had discussed. All she knew was that it resulted in him asking her to marry him, and that he hadn't touched her since. As they neared their new home, Olivia prepared herself for his touch again after what felt like an eternity of abstinence. Her smile held firm until she tried to kiss him when they crossed the threshold of the house. The door slammed behind them, and Gil dropped her from his arms.

"Don't touch me."

Olivia fell to the ground with a thud and the revelation hit her harder than the floor. It was all for show; the smiles, the cake, the music, the perfect dress…

her foolishness came crashing down on her in an agonizing shower of shame as she realized just how naïve she was.

Their first year of marriage, if you could call it that, was acrimonious at best, but their relationship tempered as time passed, and eventually they found themselves settling into roles that suited each of them for a peaceful lifestyle albeit lacking any happiness whatsoever. They opened a pottery shop on the side of the house where Olivia found her solace in throwing clay and Gil found his in making money from the sales.

By their third year of marriage, the absence of children was the favorite topic of discussion for most women in town, regardless of the occasion for gathering. Gil's resolve for withholding sex from Olivia seemed iron clad, strengthened by resentment of the entire situation, but the truth was that he was getting more than his fair share of sex from more than his fair share of women. Olivia on the other hand was lucky to be able to catch a glimpse of his naked body before he dressed in the mornings, and she had lost count of how many months it had been since she so much as attempted to get him to make love to her. It wasn't that he was not aware of her sexual frustrations, Lord knows she begged enough, but he simply did not hold an interest in her anymore, and hadn't since the day they got engaged. She didn't have to ask him if it was true to know that it was. Not even when she was doing her best to seduce him by lying on top of their bed sheets, naked and touching herself (the only touch she was familiar with these days) did he so much as cast a glance in her direction. Whether or not he was in full 'working order' was not the question, as he was most definitely functioning every single morning, but he refused to let her do anything about it. Olivia grew more frustrated while Gil grew more satisfied and the notches on his belt began to look like a small army that knew nothing but conquest.

Gil spent a lot of time away from the house working on a number of different projects. He had secured himself a position with the local school assisting the teacher with French lessons for the children. Despite the fact that he felt the young school teacher up on more than one occasion, the position was legitimate and it led him to concoct the most perfect excuse to be out late in the evenings giving 'French lessons.' Olivia had sworn to herself that she would never be as naïve as she had been at the beginning of their marriage, but she found that believing him took far less energy and hurt than waiting up all night for him to come home, only to leave a gap between them in the bed big enough to drive a plough through. Whether or not Gil was fucking other women, Olivia decided, was none of her business. As far as she was concerned, her business was pottery, and she had become very good at it.

Throwing pots was second nature to Olivia, and sales had been steady enough with her standard pots and vases for her to be able to try out a few unique styles that were a little more out of the ordinary. She wasn't used to people visiting her workshop, though it was open for business during the week, and she found she sold most of her inventory at the weekend markets in the heart of town, so she was surprised when she heard footsteps early one morning.

"Gil? Is that you?" Olivia squinted through the dark shop trying to make out the silhouette at the sunlit doorway. It certainly wasn't Gil's shape, and as they crossed through the light, Olivia noticed that there were three young men in uniform standing in front of her. She recognized their attire instantly, slightly excited that three soldiers from the Royal British Navy had found their way into her humble shop. All three appeared very tall, standing straight as if at attention, but certainly not rigid.

"Hello. Are you open?" A very British voice drifted over the sounds of Olivia's spinning wheel. She took her foot off the pedal and stood up, wiping her hands on her apron.

"We are. How can I help you?"

All three of the men were incredibly attractive, and whether or not it was just the uniform Olivia wasn't sure, but she felt a tightening between her legs as she held her hand out.

The man closest to her shook it first, placing his other hand on top to capture her tiny one completely. It was the first touch from a man Olivia had felt in almost four years, and it took all the effort she had to remain upright. He smiled at her; the twinkle from behind his blue eyes appeared to almost know what she was feeling within. Breaking from the moment, Olivia realized she had covered the man's hand with clay.

"My Gosh, I'm so sorry!" she said, reaching for a rag and handing it to the soldier.

"Please, don't apologize. I don't mind a bit of dirt on me." He smiled, wiping the clay from his hands before handing the rag back to her. Olivia wiped the excess clay from hers and reached out to shake the hands of the other two soldiers.

"Olivia," she introduced herself.

"My, what a beautiful name," her soldier said. "I'm not surprised, for someone who makes such beautiful vases."

Olivia blushed.

"I'm Marion Keegan. This is Thomas Mawson and Peter Macauley." Acknowledging the other two men with a nod, Olivia found it difficult to take her eyes off of Marion. He was the most beautiful creature, and while they had only touched for a moment, she still felt a tingling where he had held her hand. Reminding herself that she was a married woman, despite the lack of perks that came along with the title, she pulled herself together.

"Lovely to meet you. You're welcome to browse, and even more welcome to buy." She watched as they wandered down the room, perusing her prized work. "Are you in town for long?"

"Just passing through, I'm afraid. A few days at most. Lovely little town you have here," Marion said as he picked up a vase.

Olivia nodded. "Even our worst parts of town are better than most places." She deliberately held eye contact with Marion, and wondered if it was at all possible that he might be interested in more than just her pottery.

"We came in on St. Vincent a few days back, but only just arrived here today. We're camped just outside of town, but we've heard so much about Richmond we just had to take a look."

"Well, I'm glad you did," Olivia said, willing herself to come up with something a little wittier the next time she spoke.

Marion put down the vase he was looking at and walked closer toward her. "Me too."

Olivia took a deep breath as subtly as she could. "That's one of my favorites," she said, motioning to the vase Marion had just put down. "I'm sure your wife would love it as a gift on your return." She noticed Thomas give Peter a little shove, and she knew she had been less than obvious in her intentions, but she didn't really care.

"I don't have a wife," Marion told her, and Olivia could have sworn she saw him flash her the quickest of winks. "I have a niece who would love it though." He walked back over to the shelf and picked the vase up again. "How much is it?"

"Well, that depends. What have you got?" Olivia asked, forgetting her shyness as the businesswoman inside of her took over.

Marion laughed. His laugh was deep and Olivia felt it rumble through her body straight to her heart.

"Let's see, I've got shillings, a few sovereigns…if I need more than that, I'll have to return to camp."

"Two shillings is fine," Olivia said, dismissing the opportunity to make a little more money than she ordinarily might have. "Your niece will love it."

"I won't be able to give it to her for a while, I'm afraid. I'm stationed here in Van Diemen's Land for now, but I'm hoping to be back before she turns fifteen."

"How old is she now?"

"We set sail two days before her tenth birthday. She'll be half way to eleven by now." Olivia watched Marion's expression carefully as he recalled his niece. His face was kind and very soft for that of a sailor. Not that she had met a sailor before, but she expected most of them were rough and sea-weathered, but Marion looked practically angelic albeit rather sun tanned. She wished she could reach out and touch his cheek, for her heart was willing her to do so, but she had a little more sense than to listen to it. So far in life giving in to her heart's urges had landed her in nothing but trouble, though she argued with herself that it wasn't exactly her heart that had led her to marry Gil.

"Transporting convicts? Olivia asked him.

Marion nodded. "One hundred and twenty-eight days on a ship full of stinkin' angry men. It was a pleasure!"

Olivia chuckled and noticed Marion's smile widen.

"We're taking them through to the colony in Port Arthur, and I've got a posting there for a few years."

"That must be tough to be away from your family for so long," Olivia said.

"Aye. It's worth it for the coin though. More than a few bob for the work, so by the time I go home I'll be set up nicely."

"Unless you spend it all on rum and women!" a voice interjected. Olivia wasn't sure if it was Peter or Thomas—she hadn't been paying attention well enough when she was introduced, and to be honest Marion was the only one whose face and name she cared to remember.

Marion frowned, and he swatted the air in the direction of the soldier who had spoken. "Hush, Peter, you bastard!" He attempted to hide his blushed face by turning toward the other vases and surveying them for a moment, before looking back at Olivia.

"Please, forgive my language. I've been at sea for a long time, and I've almost forgotten what it's like to be in the presence of a lady."

"Perhaps we should get to know each other, Mr. Keegan. You'll soon discover I'm not so much of a lady as I appear to be." She allowed herself to grin ever so slightly, and her head buzzed as the rush of adrenaline that came along with her boldness washed over her.

Marion's blush returned and Olivia silently congratulated herself on her ability to turn his face the same color as his tunic.

"Perhaps we should, Miss Olivia."

"Keegan, it looks like she's Mrs. Olivia, just so you know," Peter said, pointing to her ring and elbowing Marion sharply in the ribs. Olivia scowled and twisted her ring back and forth, Gil entering her mind briefly enough for her to feel a pang of guilt but it was swatted away as instantly as it appeared when she looked directly into Marion's eyes. He held her gaze for a moment before he looked down at her wedding ring, and Olivia's guilt grew as she saw his disappointment.

What had he expected? He's leaving town in a few days anyway. Olivia felt slightly indignant as she considered where their little back-and-forth of dialogue would have led them were Peter not to have revealed her marital status. *Nowhere. It was just flirting.* But she knew it wasn't, and for that she felt very sad. "I'm sorry, I didn't mean to—"

Marion cut Olivia off with a short wave of his hand. "Your husband's a lucky man," he told her as he reached into his pocket and withdrew some coins.

"No, he's not. He's a bastard." The truth was liberating, and the unhappiness that was trying to claw its way to her soul was forced back down with resilience. Marion reached out and picked up Olivia's left hand, which was resting on the table. He held it in the palm of his own and Olivia felt the roughness that she had been unable to see. His rough hands weren't ungentle though, and Olivia felt more than the simple pleasure that came from the feeling of a man's touch. He uncurled her fingers and brushed his thumb over her wedding band a few times before opening her hand completely. He dropped the coins into Olivia's hand and curled it back up again, wrapping her fingers tightly around the metal that was still warm from his body heat. Squeezing her hand once more with the kind of gentle strength she knew Gil would never possess, Marion released his grasp.

"Thank you for the vase. Tilly will love it."

He smiled at her once more and then he was gone, disappearing into the sunlight. Olivia watched his silhouette walk away and fought the urge to race after him.

Peter put down the vase he was looking at, nodded politely at Olivia and followed Marion back out to the village.

Thomas lingered, and Olivia noticed that he was holding a small statue of a dog. "I love this," he said. "Reminds me of my sheep dog back in Yorkshire. She's got the same markings."

"What's her name?"

"Dawn. Perfectly behaved little thing. Shame she's bloody terrified of sheep." They both laughed.

Olivia remembered making the dog one particularly lonely Sunday morning. Gil had left for church early, but by the time it came for her to leave it was pouring down with rain, so she decided to stay home. Not in the mood to finish off the jug she had been working on, she started with a handful of clay that she was squeezing to calm her mood. She fashioned it into the body, and before long she had added little legs and a tail, topping it off with a cheeky head, the dog's mouth half open, and a tiny tongue hanging out which she eventually colored pink. It was hardly a work of art, and Gil had scoffed at it when he returned home later that day, but it had brought Olivia comfort for a moment, and she was proud of it.

"You can have it," Olivia offered.

"How much?"

"Nothing. Please, it's a gift. It can remind you of Dawn while you're here."

"Boy, thank you, Miss. Err, Ma'am…" Thomas trailed off awkwardly.
"You're welcome."

Thomas loitered for a moment longer and Olivia could tell he wanted to say something more but she let him speak in his own time.

"We were planning on going for a drink tonight at the establishment near where we are camped, in case you're interested in joining us?"

Olivia thought for a moment. She wasn't sure of any bars near where he was referring to, except for…she tried to recall the name. "The Bucket?"

"The Suds Bucket. Yes," Thomas confirmed for her.

Olivia was fairly certain that place was a little more than just a bar, and no one she knew had ever so much as placed a foot on the first step. It was not a place where her circle of friends would ever even consider going for a drink. "Thanks, but I'm not sure."

Thomas dipped his hat politely. "It would be lovely if you considered it. Marion will be there," he said with a wink, before dropping the small dog into his pocket and disappearing out of the shop.

"Maybe," Olivia called after him, hoping he heard her.

She crafted more vases that afternoon than she had the entire rest of the week. Her hands moved with an inspired buzz. Marion had evoked in her a kind of motivation she had never felt before. Unable to pinpoint exactly what it was about him that made her feel better about not only herself but her outlook on life in general, Olivia felt refreshed and excited. It was for that reason that she decided to visit the Suds Bucket that night, in the hopes of seeing him again.

Olivia watched from behind the pearly sheer curtains of her upstairs bedroom window as Gil slinked across the road. Moments before, she had said goodnight to him and asked if he would like to come to bed with her, but she knew his answer would be no before the words left his lips. He had told her that he had to tutor a new French student, and for the first time since they were married she allowed herself to recognize the fact that he was lying to her, so blatantly that he might have as well punched her in the face.

Well, if he doesn't care about fidelity, why should I?

Olivia watched Gil disappear into the shadows provided by the gum trees that lined their street, and then stepped back from the window and sat down on her bed. By this point, her greatest concern wasn't that she might get caught, or that she was about to commit adultery, but whether or not Marion would be at the bar.

The Suds Bucket had been operating for just over two years. She knew of its existence because a so-called "friend" had taken great pleasure in smugly advising her that Gil had visited the bar the night before their wedding. It was well known that the bar offered more than the services written on their menu, but for some reason the local authorities never seemed to prosecute any of the women that worked there. It probably wasn't a coincidence that they also happened to have a lot more money than their salary suggested they should. Olivia wondered for a moment whether she should tell someone where she was going, in case something happened, but who would she tell? She had no friends, and it was hardly the type of conversation she could see herself having with her parents. "I'm going to a brothel, to see and possibly seduce a British sailor I've just met. Where's Gil? Oh, I don't know, probably fucking the neighbor."

No, she would just have to take a chance, and as she considered what the risk entailed, she decided that it was worth it to see Marion again.

The smell of a burning wood fire filled her nostrils as she approached the Suds Bucket and provided her with an almost calming feeling when she tentatively placed a foot on the bottom step. She paused for a moment, inhaling the smoky aroma and giving herself one last chance to just turn around and go home—home to where no one was waiting for her, and more than likely never would be. She crept up the stairs and peered in through the window to the left of her. She was looking into a room that appeared to lead off from the front of the bar, and she couldn't see Marion anywhere. *Guess I'll have to go in and look for him.*

Olivia walked through the doors of the bar, and was surprised by what she saw. The place wasn't as dirty or as disgusting as the rumors made it out to be. There was a Chinese man playing the piano, groups of men drinking, and only a few women who just looked as if they were doing nothing more than serving drinks. Perhaps the rumors were just that...perhaps this was just a bar with a bad reputation.

"Can I help you, love?"

Olivia ceased her scanning of the patrons and turned her attention to the person who was speaking to her. A beautiful woman with a rounded face and contrasting sharp features, and hair that was pinned fashionably half up in a bun with the rest of her hair cascading down her shoulders.

"I was just wondering if there were any soldiers who had come in tonight?"

"There were, but you're a bit late. They're all upstairs with our girls." Molly elbowed her with a wink.

"Oh," Olivia said, dejected.

"Don't worry, love, they've been at sea for a long time. They'll probably be down again in ten minutes. Maybe even five, if you catch my drift. Why don't you have a seat and a drink while you wait?" She indicated the bottles of liquor lined up behind the bar.

Olivia managed a half smile. "No, thanks. I'll just go home, I think."

"Oh, no, look at that. One of them is still down here. Looks like he just went outside to use the dunny."

Olivia stopped where she was standing, too afraid to turn around in case it wasn't who she wanted it to be.

"Olivia."

Bubbles welled at the top of her throat in excitement as his voice caressed her ears. She spun around with a smile far too large to be misconstrued as anything but the most ardent happiness to see him.

"Marion! Thomas told me you would be here."

"I'm glad he did."

The pair stared at one another for a moment, before Molly broke the silence. "So what are we drinking?"

Tucked away in an intimate corner of the Bucket, Marion and Olivia drank a little, but not a lot, as they lost themselves in conversations that ranged from how Marion had found himself enlisted in the Royal Navy, to how Olivia had found herself in a miserable marriage to a man who refused to sleep with her.

"I just can't imagine being married to a woman as beautiful as you, and not wanting to make love to you every night."

Olivia noticed that at some point they had ended up holding hands as she felt him give her a squeeze along with the flattery. They were past the point of blushing when one gave the other a compliment, and short of declaring their love for one another, their respective souls had most certainly been bared. Olivia had known this man for less than half a day, but already she loved him more fervently than she had ever loved Gil. Marion stood up to get them another drink, and as she watched him walk, or rather, stride, over to the bar she was struck with the realization that she had never loved Gil. She had fucked him, not even more times than she could count on two hands, but she had not loved him, nor he her. At sixteen years old, a handsome man with an exotic French accent had appealed to her false sense of maturity and drenched her in forged sincerity in order to get between her legs. It worked, and she enjoyed it, but the moment that she noticed Marion look back at her from where he was standing at the bar, was the moment that she finally understood that there was a difference between making love and having sex, and in that moment, all she wanted to do was make love to Marion.

As if she were a mind reader, Molly appeared beside Olivia from nowhere.

"He's a good looking man," Molly said, stating the obvious.

Olivia agreed with a nod, as her head rolled backwards and rested on the back of the chair.

"By the looks of that ring on your finger I'm guessing you can't take him home?"

"No," Olivia said, not bothered to lie about why she was here. It was definitely not just a bar with a bad reputation. She knew she didn't need to maintain any form of moral integrity with this woman.

"Tell you what. I'll rent you a room upstairs for the night if you want. Two sovereigns to stay until the sun comes up," Molly offered as Marion returned with their drinks.

Suddenly, everything became very real and Olivia's reply came stuttered and unsure. "I'm, um, I don't have…"

Marion put a hand on her shoulder with silent reassurance. Reaching into his pocket, he pulled out two sovereigns and put them in Olivia's hand. "It's your decision," he told her.

Olivia's eyes made one last sweep of the room, in an effort to confirm that there was no one there that she knew, and as she looked, she saw a man coming down the stairs whose face seemed painfully familiar. It was Gil.

Gil trailed a very slender woman, his hands kneading her buttocks as if it were dough. He walked with a distinct lack of dexterity, and while it had been almost four years since she had seen it, she recognized his wobbly walk as an indication that he had had an orgasm very recently.

Gil didn't notice her as he left the building, and Olivia watched from the corner of her eye as he stumbled down the stairs toward their home.

Olivia looked back at Marion and then down to the coins in her hand. She held them out, offering them to Molly, who snapped them up instantly. Turning back to Marion, whose hands were already outstretched waiting for her, she placed her tiny hands into his and closed her eyes as she felt them wrap around hers. He pulled her in close, her head rested on his chest and she took a deep breath in time with him. This moment felt more like home to her than four years in the place Gil was headed.

Olivia looked up to find Marion's lips waiting for hers, and when they kissed she felt as if she could pass out at any moment. Marion swept her up into his arms without breaking the embrace and carried her up the stairs. That night, Olivia knew what it felt like to truly love and be loved.

Olivia and Marion spent the next day together, hidden on the banks below the edge of the Richmond Bridge. Not having slept much the night before, their conversations were interspersed with shared naps to the point where neither one of them could be certain when they were dreaming and when they were awake. Eventually though, the words Marion had been avoiding all day had to be spoken.

"I'm leaving first thing in the morning, you know."

Olivia said nothing, since there was nothing worth saying. She knew he couldn't stay with her and she knew she couldn't go with him.

"It wouldn't be safe, and I'm not meant to have—"

"I know." Olivia stopped him before they had the same conversation again. "Will you come back for me? On your way back to England?"

Marion held her so tightly that she felt like they were the same entity. "Yes, beautiful."

Olivia looked down to her wedding band. She pulled it off her finger and hurled it into the river before shutting her eyes tightly and burying herself into

Marion's chest. They slept a little longer before returning to the Suds Bucket for their final night in one another's arms.

Olivia stood stationary at the top of the stairs of the Suds Bucket in between the gap in the railing while she watched the hues of pink and gold turn slowly to blue as the sun rose.

She hadn't moved since she had kissed Marion goodbye. She watched him walk away, praying that he would come back for her one day.

She jumped when someone came outside from behind her.

"Sorry, I didn't mean to startle you," Sherie said, stopping beside her and resting her hand on her shoulder. "This is a beautiful place to say goodbye, you know?"

"What do you mean?"

"A stairway has no doors. Nothing to close it off. It will always be open and ready for the ones we love to return."

Olivia looked at Sherie, and her eyes brimmed with tears as she felt an overwhelming urge to hug her that she didn't fight. "Thank you," she whispered, speaking not only to Sherie, but to Marion too. "Thank you."

Olivia withdrew from the hug and took a moment to consider Sherie. She was quite pretty, and despite her line of work she seemed to carry an air of hopefulness that shone from within her like a light. Taking strength from Sherie's unspoken spirit, Olivia walked down the old stairs toward the place she had once called home.

She played the words she would say to Gil over and over in her head as she approached the house, but they disappeared from her mind almost as soon as she walked inside. She looked at the place on the floor where Gil had dropped her on their wedding night, those four years ago, and she knew that what she was about to do was the right decision for both of them. She wandered upstairs to their bedroom where she found Gil still asleep.

"Gil."

He didn't move.

"Gil."

Still no movement.

Maybe he's dead. That would make this a lot easier, she thought, but she could see his chest rising ever so slightly. She picked up a glass of water that was sitting on his bedside table and tipped it upside down, drenching him completely. Gil sat up with an alarmed yell, wiping the water from his face.

"Christ, Olivia! What the hell is wrong with you?!"

Olivia remained calm as she sat down on the edge of the bed. "Are you happy?"

"Are you crazy? Do you expect me to be after being woken up like that?"

"You know what I mean."

Gil looked at her, water dripping from his hair and onto his face. He wiped the droplets from his nose, but he said nothing.

"I'm sure you are very happy, what with all the women you've been sleeping with. Yes, I know about them. I know about them all, Gil, even the ones you pay for. See, the thing is, I'm not happy. Not in the slightest, but I'm going to change that. So I'm leaving you."

Gil blinked a few times as if he needed a moment for the words to sink in. "You're not leaving me. I won't allow it," he said.

Olivia laughed. "You won't give me sex, but you won't let me leave to find it elsewhere, but you can?! You make no sense at all!"

Gil lurched forward, grabbing Olivia's wrists and pushing her back onto the bed. "Is that what this is about? You want to have sex with me or you'll leave me?" He moved Olivia's hand down to between his legs. "Fine. Let's fuck, needy *putain*! But next time do not try to drown me."

Olivia tore her hand away from Gil and slapped him across the face. She pushed him away from her and got off the bed, taking a few steps away from him. "I don't want you anymore."

"Well, you have me. Tough luck, *c'est la vie*. We are married."

"I don't want to be married to someone who won't even touch me, Gil."

Gil moved toward her again. "So come here and I'll touch you as much as you want. You want it? I'll give it to you, Olivia. You must be dying for it. It's been a long time."

"Not for you." Olivia held her hand out to stop Gil from getting closer.

"Oh, so this is a jealousy thing? I'm sorry, princess, but your father pays me to put a roof over your head and keep up appearances, not to fuck you.

Monogamy was never part of the deal. You know, you should be grateful I even agreed to his terms or you would probably be dead by now."

Olivia was stunned. "What?"

"When your father caught us, he took me away and threatened me. He gave me a choice. I could walk away from you and never come back to this town, or I could stay and marry you. Of course, I told him I already had plans to leave, and he told me that he would kick you out of his house for acting like a whore and causing your family such embarrassment. He told me it was my choice to leave if I wished, but he was getting rid of you whether I helped you or not. He said if I reconsidered leaving, if I married you, he would give me money each month and find us a home to live. He said he would make sure we had what we needed, so long as we got married to save him from embarrassment."

"I can't believe it."

"What did you think? I would leave you to rot on the streets? I should have!"

"You pig!"

"I did you a favor, ungrateful shit. Do you think I wanted to marry a child? It wasn't just for the money, okay? I did it to keep you safe, but you cocked up my life!"

Olivia took a few steps backward to lean on the wall for support as she tried to process what Gil was saying. "That's why you never made love to me. You resented me."

"We need to stay married. My uncle in Launceston returned to France last year so I can't just say goodbye to you and resume my travels. I'm losing my charm, and no one wants a fat old French man."

"Is that why you have to pay whores to fuck you?" Olivia spat with absolutely zero sensitivity to his case.

"I'll have sex with you if that's what you want, but you need to stay. We need your father's money. You know those pots you sell won't make enough money to support you if you're alone," Gil said, his voice firm, indicating that the topic was not up for negotiation.

"Fuck appearances. Fuck my father's money, and fuck you, Gil."

"Don't be silly, Olivia. Calm down."

"*Nique ta mere!*" Olivia hurled the glass she was still holding at Gil, whose reaction to dodge it was swift despite his obvious surprise in Olivia's sudden proficiency in French vulgarisms. She thundered down the stairs and out the front door, not stopping to think where she would go but knowing she needed to get as far away from Gil and the house as possible.

"I'm not sixteen anymore, Gilbert!" she yelled up at him as he stuck his head out the bedroom window to call her back.

"I don't need any of you!" she screamed.

Olivia hid beneath the bridge on the bank of the river in the same spot she and Marion had lain together the previous day. Marion had told her enough about the convicts they were transporting to know she didn't want to be anywhere near them, and she knew that if his superiors knew of their relationship, he would be in serious trouble. Going after him was, unfortunately, out of the question, and she resigned herself to the fact that she would have to wait for his posting to end before they could be together.

Where can I go until then?

Based on what Gil had told her about her father, she knew she couldn't return home. She might not trust Gil's sincerity, but she knew her father well enough to believe what he said was true. Gil was right that business had slowed down so much recently that making a living on pottery sales alone would be close to impossible.

Olivia stayed beside the river until the sun started to disappear behind the bridge. She was still nowhere near closer to deciding where to go, and after her declaration of independence to Gil she was adamant that she would not return home with her tail between her legs. There was only one place left she could think of with a spare bed...Olivia reached into her pocket and pulled out the two shillings Marion had given her for the vase she sold him. She was close to one hundred and eighty shillings short from the two sovereigns she had paid for the room the night before, but with nothing left to lose Olivia decided it was worth at least seeing if Molly would let her stay.

Her walk through the town was lonely and she wondered whether she could do this for the next five years while she waited for Marion to come back for her. After not even a day of being apart from him, fear started to creep in, and she began to wonder whether she was certain his love for her was genuine. Overflowing with self-doubt, it was easy to second-guess their short-lived romance, and by the time she reached the steps of the Bucket, she wasn't sure she knew what she was doing at all.

She walked up to the bar and sat down in front of Sherie, who was pouring some drinks for a dark haired attractive young man. Olivia wondered whether he had a wife waiting for him to come home later that night.

"Well, hey, what are you doing back here?" Sherie asked her.

Olivia could tell she was asking in earnest, and she could see concern in her eyes. *Wow, I must look like shit,* she thought. "You know what, Sherie?"

Sherie looked at her, waiting for her to continue.

"My whole life, since I was a tiny little Olivia, I have done everything for everyone else." Olivia knew that she was about to launch herself into a rant and Sherie apparently preempted the same as she poured her a large cup of rum and put it down in front of her.

"Is this free? I have no money." Olivia picked up the glass and tipped it slightly toward Sherie, toasting to her kindness. Sherie chuckled, nodding, and Olivia threw her head back and drank half the glass in one gulp.

"I have. I've done everything for everyone else and nothing for me. I thought I was marrying Gil for me, but I was marrying him for everyone else. I wanted everyyyyone else to look at me and say 'Look at Olivia in that pretty white dress with that handsome French man. She's so lucky. I wish I could find someone who made me feel that way.' But guess what? It's all for show." She took another swig of the rum. Molly appeared from behind Olivia, draping an arm over her shoulders.

"Slow down there, kiddo!" Sherie warned her, but she topped up her drink all the same.

"It's all fake. All of it. This whole world, even. We want so badly to be happy that we snap up the first thing that looks like happiness and then before you know it you're God damn miserable, you're alone, and no one will fuck you."

The dark haired young man beside her moved a little closer, and in a slurred whisper admitted, "I'd fuck you."

His words set off the familiar burn of arousal within that she had only reacquainted herself with in the past day. She was surprised such a good-looking man showed interest in her, but her heart belonged to Marion. She looked at the coins that the man had pulled out of his pocket. Marion would be gone for a long time, and maybe if she were able to save up some money while she waited for him, it would set in stone their plans to escape this country.

"Oh, you would, would you?" Olivia asked.

Billy seemed surprised that his lame attempt of an advance was so well received. "How much, Molly?"

Molly's eyes scanned Olivia's body, her smile widening when her eyes passed Olivia's chest. "Six sovereigns," she said boldly.

Billy scoffed. "Are you crazy? That's triple what I pay for Georgina!"

"Well, Georgina's busy right now, and this one's brand new. Do you wanna be the first or not?"

Olivia wasn't sure if it was the rum or her current state of mind, but she felt as if she were floating above her body watching the situation unfold. Was this really happening? Did she even care? She needed a place to stay, and even more than that she needed to be touched again. She would have preferred it to be Marion, but that was impossible right now. She was happy just to go upstairs and let this man make her feel good, but as she caught up to the conversation that was taking place in front of her, she realized what was happening.

"Hang on, you're going to pay me?" she asked.

"He's going to pay me," Molly said. "I'll give you half."

Olivia split the figure in her head. It took her a while, as mathematics was something she hadn't paid too much attention to during her schooling. Three sovereigns was more than she would make in a week at the pottery shop. Her mind replayed the conversation she'd had with Gil earlier that morning, and how he was convinced she couldn't manage without him. She looked at Billy and took another step into him, hoping that her lavender scent would temp his senses.

"I'm worth it, Billy," she purred.

Molly slapped her fist down on the bar, her mouth wide open. "Damn Ma'am! I like you!" She laughed.

Olivia gave Molly a quick wink and looked back to Billy, who was already handing his money to Molly. "You wanna head upstairs now, Billy, or take her at the end of the night?"

"Let's have some laughs first, eh?" Billy said, pulling Olivia by the hips toward him. He gave her a squeeze, and while the whole scene appeared incredibly degrading, Olivia felt excited by the prospect of looking after herself.

"Give us a minute, Bill. Why don't you go sit over by the window there, and she'll be right over," Molly said. Billy collected his drink from the bar and waltzed over to the table, not needing to be told twice. Molly put five of the sovereigns in her pocket and gave one to Olivia.

"Just one?"

"I know a lost soul when I see one. You gonna be staying here after tonight?"

Olivia nodded tentatively. "Is that okay?"

"It's fine. Two sovereigns a week board. Everything else on top of that, you keep. Buy your own food or we can feed you for an extra sovereign a week, that's up to you."

Olivia gave the sovereign back to Molly. "Sounds good. I think I'm gonna need that drink after all. How much?" She pointed to the bottle of rum.

"Honey, you can drink as much as you want. As long as you're working, it's on the house." Molly picked up the bottle and filled her glass with the pungent brown liquor. Olivia threw the drink back in one gulp. What had begun as a disheartening evening was fast turning into an exciting one. All the liquor she could drink for free, an incredibly attractive man by her side who, granted, wasn't Marion, but was going to make her feel good all the same, great music… she was waiting for the catch!

"Olivia, isn't it?" Molly asked her. Olivia nodded, and Molly wrote her name down in a large book behind the bar, adding a small dash and a number six.

Olivia and Billy sat at the table by the window and drank while she shared her story. Billy found it hilarious that she was married to a man who didn't want to touch her. "Perhaps he prefers the company of other men," he suggested.

Olivia bellowed out with laughter. "Well, he is French!"

By the end of the night the whole room was captivated by her tale, and they almost drank the bar dry as they laughed and shared stories. Olivia found herself quite enjoying the evening, as she looked over to Billy, who, despite having drunk more than she probably weighed, still looked fairly bright eyed.

"So, are you going to take me upstairs or what?" she questioned him.

He put his hands on her knees and squeezed playfully, triggering her reflexes and making her squeal with laughter. When he trailed his hand a little further up her skirt, Olivia stopped his hand before it reached its intended destination, and pulled him up off the stool. "Come on, let's see what you're made of!"

The next morning, Billy and Olivia wandered downstairs bleary eyed. Sherie, Molly, Maggie, and Georgina were sitting out on the balcony. Olivia's arms were folded across her chest, and Molly motioned for her to come and sit down. She chose to sit on a long couch placed against the balcony railing and facing the right side.

"Rule number one: no overnight stays," Molly said, looking at Billy. "I only let you stay because you paid six sovereigns."

Maggie's eyes looked like they were going to pop out of her head. "You paid six sovereigns for her?"

Olivia looked at her, almost insulted by her surprise.

"She was worth it," Billy said with a grin, and shot a wink toward Olivia.

She shot one right back. "You're telling me. See you tonight?"

"I can't afford it tonight. Definitely next week though," he said with a smile and a wave, before heading down the stairs.

Olivia tipped her head back on the couch and giggled. "I can't believe I did that! I feel so…liberated!" She inhaled a deep breath of the fresh morning air. "What a beautiful day, isn't it?" she asked, smiling.

From the opposite side of the balcony, Georgina slowly opened the door to a small copper cage and gently deposited the two canaries she had been playing with. "Something's wrong with you," she said.

Her expression was vacant, and despite her words, Olivia got the feeling that she wasn't so much judging her as she was making a statement about her own situation.

"Don't mind Georgina. She's crazy." Molly waved a dismissive hand in Georgina's direction.

"It's okay," she said. "She's right."

Sherie smiled at Olivia, who returned the smile. It felt good to be around people who didn't judge her, though how much judgment could she realistically receive from a prostitute?

"Do you like strawberries?" Maggie motioned to the bowl of luscious strawberries that sat atop the balcony railing beside her.

Olivia nodded.

"Tuck in," Maggie offered.

Olivia took a strawberry and bit into it. The dew trickled down her chin and she wiped it up with her sleeve. She was surprised at how good it tasted, and found herself appreciating more than just the taste of the red berry. She took another deep breath of morning air and a calm settled within her. Georgina's canaries whistled a whimsical melody, and Olivia savored the moment for what it was. She didn't feel blissfully happy, but she wasn't utterly miserable either. She could wait for Marion here, saving as much as she could, and when he returned she would leave this country forever and go back to the majestic motherland everyone spoke so highly of. She would be the wife of a soldier, and have tea and strawberries with cream every morning if she so felt like it. Yes, she was willing to wait as long as it took for her dreams to become reality, and she knew it was only a matter of time before Marion came back for her. She let the sun drench her in rays. The only thing missing was a wheel spinning and her hands sunk deep into the brown clay she loved so much.

She sat for a while longer on the balcony, listening to the girls discuss the events of the previous night, and before she knew it, the evening was upon them.

Molly took her upstairs and gave her a room for her to prepare herself in. "The men will pay us no matter what we look like, but it's nice to pretty up just a little for yourself, if not for anyone else. I've found if you do your hair and put on a bit of rouge, you can get an extra few shillings. Don't expect sovereigns every night. Now and then yes, from folks who come from out of town. Standard payment is about three shillings; four or five if you can work yourself up a 'specialty.'"

Olivia looked around the room after Molly had left her. Suddenly, everything felt very real. She wondered what Gil was doing and how upset he was that she had left (or taken away his meal ticket!) but it was a mere few hours later that she found out.

Gil walked into the Suds Bucket that night and straight onto the scene of Olivia giving a particularly raunchy lap dance to an excitable and grabby patron.

"Olivia?!"

She was already very drunk and laughed at Gil's surprised expression, but she didn't stop dancing. "Hey everyone, this is my husband! Everyone, say *Bonjooour*, Gilbert!" She rolled the French greeting around her tongue with a distinct ridicule for his accent. A number of the patrons repeated her instructions, slurring the satirical greeting.

The music stopped suddenly as Gil's angry voice thundered throughout the bar. "You didn't come home all day! I've been worried!"

Olivia chortled. "How very perceptive of you, Gil! Although the whole point of me storming out and telling you that I was LEAVING YOU is generally a good indicator that I probably won't be back anytime soon, *Mon Cherie*." She stumbled as she finally climbed off the man and approached Gil. "As for being beside yourself..." She looked him up and down. "Clearly, so distraught that you had to come and visit Georgina here," she said.

"Georgina!" Gil watched as Olivia called over the woman who had slept with him the night before. "My husband here needs calming down...would you care to oblige? He's happy to pay you double what he paid last night."

Gil blushed. "Come on. We're going home."

"I am home. In case you hadn't figured that part out yet, Gil. You decided to fuck other people...I'm just doing the same."

Her retort was met by cheers from the onlooking patrons, all who by now had stopped whatever they were doing to watch the scene before them play out.

"Can I please take you home?" he asked, reaching out to caress her cheek.

Molly stepped in between them. "Touch her like that again and I'll have to start charging," she said. "You can take her upstairs if you want, but it will cost you."

"Excuse me, I'm talking to my wife here."

"No, you're talking to my girl. You gave her up the moment you stepped inside these walls, and how ironic, she did the same to you!" Molly laughed in his face.

Gil's narrowed eyes spat hatred at Molly.

"Last chance, Olivia," he told her.

"No, Gil, it was your last chance…and you blew it. Just like how I'm gonna blow this guy tonight," she stated with a distinct lack of sensitivity. "I'll be around tomorrow to collect my things. Make sure you're not." And with that, she climbed back onto the man she had been dancing for.

"YinYue! Music!"

The piano started up again with her command and the patrons crowded around Olivia, leaving Gil on the outside of their circle. He turned and slinked out of the Bucket, and was not at home the next day when Olivia went to collect her possessions.

Chapter 14

S herie counted the inventory slowly and methodically making sure she didn't miss anything. On the long list of 'stuff' that she was not good at, counting was close to the top. She scribbled down a number and moved on to the next row. She jumped when she heard the front door opening and looked up with a smile as Claire walked in. She gave her a quick nod of acknowledgment and went back to counting, restarting the row she was on. After a while of silence, Claire spoke. "You gonna be alright?"

Sherie looked up from her notepad. "Me?"

Claire smiled but said nothing more. Sherie looked at her for a moment before returning to her counting. She wrote down a few more numbers and looked up again, finding that Claire hadn't moved. "What?"

"Tom asked Maggie to help him look for a ring the other day," Claire informed her.

Sherie wasn't the least bit surprised or excited.

"I bet if I told Molly that, she'd be so happy she'd leap ten feet in the air," Claire added.

"Well, I just don't get excited about practical stuff like that," Sherie said.

"Lord, Sherie, getting married isn't supposed to be practical; it's supposed to be romantic!"

Sherie recounted a row of bottles before writing down a figure. She wished desperately that she could drown herself in the vat of whiskey beside her instead of having to endure this subject of discussion. "I don't believe in romance," she stated, attempting to be as nonchalant as possible.

Claire was silent, but Sherie knew her well enough to know she hadn't won the battle, much less the war. When Claire spoke again, her voice was soft and full of concern. "The Suds Bucket will be fine," she said.

Sherie slammed down her pencil. "No, Claire, the Suds Bucket will not be fine. Every week we're losing more and more money. Dad left us in charge of our home and we turned it into a bloody brothel! Yes, okay, I might not be in love with Tom, but he has a lot of gold, and he's a nice enough guy looking to move on from his shitten life and settle down. This way we all win. I don't let Molly down, the Bucket goes back to being our family home, and I don't let Dad down."

The swiftness of Claire's response indicated to Sherie that she had been expecting such an answer. "But it's clear he doesn't make you happy and that kills me to see. Aren't you worried about letting me down?"

Sherie looked at Claire's black eye. "I already have," she said sadly, caressing the bruise lightly and then closed the notepad and walked around the bar, disappearing upstairs.

Kate had spent the morning riding with Aiko as fast as she could along the bank of the Coal River, and didn't return home until it started to get dark. She knew her aunt would be worried, but a little quiet reflection on her part was far more important than keeping her aunt happy. She knew all she had to do was play the grief card and she'd be let off the hook yet again. It wasn't that she wasn't grieving, but that she had something to funnel her emotions into in the way of Sherie Kelly. The woman was beyond fascinating to her, and it had nothing to do with her chosen profession. She actually had thought it would have taken longer for her to convince Sherie to warm up to her—not that she was complaining.

She had fought the urge to go past the Suds Bucket all day, not just because she didn't want to come across as an obsessive stalker, but also because she really did need some time to herself to think about the evening before.

She always knew this day would come. The day where she admitted to herself, really truly admitted to the fact that…that she was different. Of course, this was a widely known fact, but the reasoning behind it was not what it seemed. It was not just a confidence that was respectful enough so as not to push the boundaries of arrogance. Kate's sureness in herself manifested in a playfulness that most other girls lose when they turn sixteen, or perhaps a year earlier. She truly was different, for reasons which, as she was realizing painfully enough now, were too difficult to explain to anyone, let alone herself. Even now, while she sat proudly on her horse in front of a trickling river set upon the most beautiful backdrop in the world, she could not even think it to herself.

Yet Sherie's actions the previous night betokened an understanding that needed no words at all. It was excruciating for Kate, who was a woman of words.

Her thoughts circled in similar patterns her entire ride home, but she had found no peace by the time she climbed down from Aiko at the front of the Flanagan estate.

She resigned herself to an unsuccessful afternoon of contemplation, and sent herself to bed.

"Kate?" Mrs. Flanagan called from the sitting room.

"It's me," Kate said, but she knew it was more of a summons than a confirmation of whether it was her who had just walked through the door.

Kate walked into the sitting room, where she was met with the unimpressed faces of her aunt and uncle. Mrs. Flanagan was cross-stitching with vigor, Mr. Flanagan was reading a newspaper, and her cousin Josh was standing at the fireplace, his back to the room.

"Something wrong?" Kate asked.

Mrs. Flanagan dropped her stitching. "You forgot."

Kate protested instantly. "I didn't forget!" she said, despite having no idea what her aunt was talking about. "Forget what?" she added timidly.

Mrs. Flanagan flapped as much as she could from the armchair in which she was sitting. "Lunch! That was arranged especially for you! The lunch that you never showed up to!"

Kate cringed. She had forgotten. "I'm sorry. I just really needed to be alone," she said.

Josh turned around and Kate could see that he was annoyed. "Come off it, Kate. John told me he saw you with one of the sisters in the valley the other day."

"Harriet?" she asked, knowing that was not the sister he was referring to.

"One of the Kelly whores," Josh spat.

"Katie?" Mrs. Flanagan asked, seeking an admission of guilt. Kate was lost for words, not wanting to lie to the people who had looked after her so generously when her whole world fell apart, but at the same time not wanting to disappoint them. She knew any answer could do both. Mrs. Flanagan put her head in her hands, full of shame, and Kate knew her silence was as good as confirmation.

"Katie, you stay away from that place. It's full of sin. It's dirty. Angus, tell her," Mrs. Flanagan said, flapping a limp wrist in her direction.

Kate remained silent, looking at the ground. Mr. Flanagan, who usually remained quiet during most family discussions, spoke now with unusual sternness. "Our people and her people don't mix. It's just not done."

Josh weighed in, his tone less suggestive and more commanding. "If you don't stay away from them, I'll make sure they stay away from you," he threatened.

Kate had had enough. "Okay, stop. You can't tell me who I can and can't be friends with."

Mr. Flanagan was clearly done with the pretense. "You will stay away from that girl," he said, pausing between every word. Kate understood that he was not asking.

"I'll do no such thing," she said, looking into his eyes and standing up.

"SIT DOWN, KATE," Mr. Flanagan yelled. Surprised at the outburst from her usually demure uncle, Kate complied instantly.

"Those girls in that bar, they're nothing but whores. And this ends. Now."

Kate looked out the window, still unable to meet her aunt's gaze. "Are we done?" she asked.

"For now," Mr. Flanagan said, as good as dismissing her. Kate turned on her heels and walked back out the front door, heading for the place she had just been banned from.

Sherie sat at the same dressing table that used to belong to her mother, and looked at herself in the clouded glass. Her blue dress was shabby and she knew it, but it was the best one she owned. In the top corner of the mirror, Pavo was dotted in lipstick. She pushed her hair behind her ears, paused, and then pulled it back over them again. She wasn't happy with how she looked either way, so she settled for hiding her ears just in case she hadn't managed to clean them properly, despite her scrubbing them until they were red raw. Her eye caught the lipstick constellation and she considered it for a moment.

"It's a peacock," she whispered to herself.

There was a knock at her door, and Sherie turned around to see it open a crack, her beloved Claire peeping her head in.

"You look beautiful," she said.

Sherie screwed up her face in an attempt to pull the world's ugliest face ever. Claire's laughter indicated that she was successful.

"You might want to fix that face up. You have a visitor downstairs."

Sherie felt her face sink and this time she made no attempt to hide it from Claire. Unimpressed, she sighed. "Tell him I'll be down in a minute."

Claire grinned. "It's not Tom," she said, flashing the bright whites of her eyes wide before closing the door and disappearing.

Sherie rushed outside and stopped dead in her tracks. Kate was at the bottom of the stairs, smiling and standing beside the most magnificent palomino horse. Kate tipped her hat toward Sherie, and Sherie blushed at the charming splendor of it all.

"What is that?!" Sherie asked with an air of shock and horror, staring at the horse.

"A horse. What our Latin friends referred to as 'equus,'" Kate replied.

"Why is it here?" Sherie asked suspiciously.

"Because someone has to eat all the hay," said Kate. Sherie's eyes narrowed in on Kate.

"I meant why it is here in front of my Bucket, not why is it here in the grander sense," she said.

"Are we going to stand here for the rest of the afternoon while you ask questions that force me to come up with witty yet irrelevant answers? Or are you going to get down here and come on an adventure with me?" Kate asked her.

Sherie needed no further convincing, and she skipped down the steps, taking them two at a time. She glanced back at Claire and Maggie, who were looking on, amused grins spread across their faces. Sherie knew this would give them enough conversation to last them at least a week.

Kate cupped her hand and put it beside the belly of the horse. Sherie had no idea what she was doing, and she just looked at Kate's hands.

"What's that?" she asked.

Without reply, Kate lifted Sherie with a display of strength that caused her to swoon a little inside. She heard Claire and Maggie's giggles, and shot them a smile as she struggled on top of the horse. Finally finding her balance, she shuffled uncomfortably in the saddle and held on for dear life. Kate mounted the horse with ease behind her and took the reins in her hands. Sherie looked back to the girls, who were still watching, disbelief and jealousy splashed across their faces.

"Will you tell Tom something came up?" she asked.

Kate kicked the horse gently, gave a few clicks of her tongue and they began to move, which provoked a yell of surprise from Sherie as her legs flew forward and she tipped backward. She felt Kate's solid body behind her and she relaxed a little…but only a little.

From the balcony, Maggie leaned against the railing, close to Claire. "I don't know about coming up, but something's sure about to go down," she mused. Claire agreed with a nod and a hum and watched the pair disappear.

When Kate began to slow the horse down, Sherie decided it was safe enough for her to open her eyes. They were in the middle of a paddock that was dimly lit by the moon.

"So, do you wanna have a go?" Kate asked.

"Honestly? I'm happy for you to be the driver," Sherie informed her.

"Hm. Well, Sherie, I'm very sorry to advise you that my question was more of a rhetorical one." Kate swung her leg over the horse and jumped down to the ground. She took the reins over the horse's head and began to lead it in a circle.

"What are you doing?" Sherie asked, terrified that she would fall off at any second.

"Seeing if you're good at stuff," Kate replied. "You seem to be. Wanna go a little faster?"

Sherie sat in the saddle with a rigid awkwardness. "This speed is fine."

Apparently, her answer was not good enough and Kate clicked her tongue again, setting the horse off into a trot. Kate ran to keep up with the horse while Sherie bounced wildly in the saddle, a train of girly noises coming from her mouth. Her legs were thrown backwards, her feet practically flying over her shoulders.

"I'm...not..." Sherie found it difficult to speak and stay upright at the same time. She slipped slightly and Kate grabbed her hand, helping to steady her. She tried again. "I'm...not sure...if this is working...for me," she said.

Kate smirked. Sherie was glad that at least someone was finding the whole ordeal incredibly amusing.

"Want to try something less bumpy?" she asked.

Sherie nodded, her arms flailing about frantically. Kate moved the reins back over the head of the horse and handed them to Sherie.

"Wait! What are you doing?"

Kate slapped the horse on the behind and yelled in a slow command. "Canter!"

The ride became instantly smoother and the speed increased too. Sherie was unprepared in the shift of momentum when the horse changed pace and rhythm, and her legs were thrown backwards yet again.

"What did you do?!" she squealed, and then decided that rather than receive an answer, she would like to add an instruction. "Undo it! Undo it!"

Kate laughed. When the horse became too fast for her, she came to a stop and was left behind as Sherie rode off. "Trust me, it's smoother! Just go with it!" she yelled.

Sherie vaguely heard Kate's instructions over her own squeals. She took a moment to sync into pace with the movements of the horse, and slipped into the rhythm fairly easily after that. Her yells transformed from fearful to excited as she embraced the sequence of movements she had figured out worked best with the flow of the canter. She leaned forward with her arms, her head lowered slightly, and when the horse shifted its weight to its hind legs, she was momentarily thrust into the air, defying gravity for a fraction of a second before she came back down into the saddle. It took just a few slams of her tailbone into the saddle to realize that the more of a curve she allowed herself to come down with, the smoother and more comfortable a ride it became. Kate got smaller as she rode further away, but her concerns dwindled when she discovered just how easily the horse would react to the slightest pull on the reins.

"Time for payback, Flanagan," Sherie said to herself, tugging the reins and turning the horse to face Kate. As she rode faster and faster toward Kate, she could see her face start to twist with fear when she realized they were heading straight for her. Sherie faked a scream that she changed to a yell at the last second, steering the horse around her and galloping away fast into the opposite corner of the paddock. She threw her head back with a cackle as she recalled Kate's face.

"Damn you!" Kate shouted, her fist in the air.

Sherie pulled the horse around again and rode past her in a blur, waving at Kate with one hand, the reins in the other, and a broad grin on her face. "Yieeeeeeew!" she yelled.

Kate laughed while Sherie kicked the horse to increase speed, disappearing again into the distant paddock.

Sherie realized quickly that riding hard was exhausting work, so she slowed the horse down and headed back toward Kate and pulled up beside her.

"Well, then, we can certainly tick that off the list."

Sherie beamed. "I'd say so."

Sherie was in control of the horse when they arrived back at the Bucket's front steps. She pulled up gently on the reins and they stopped. She let out a squeal and clapped her hands together.

"Nothin' to it!" she proclaimed. The novelty still hadn't worn off.

She climbed down from the horse and Kate moved up in the saddle.

Sherie gave the horse a pat on her soft nose.

"Aiko," said Kate.

"Bless you," said Sherie.

Kate laughed. "No, Aiko is the horse's name."

"Oh! Aiko. Beautiful name. Is that Japanese?"

Kate nodded. Sherie kissed Aiko on the top of her nose and rubbed her neck.

"I'll teach you something new tomorrow," Kate promised.

"Like what?" Sherie asked.

Kate winked before kicking Aiko into motion. "You'll see," she said. And then she was gone.

Sherie danced through the doors of the Bucket and kissed Maggie on the cheek with a giggle. Claire was sitting on the couch reading, and laughed at Sherie's enthusiasm.

"So you had fun then?" Molly asked.

Sherie walked around the bar and took down a glass and a bottle of liquor. She poured herself a drink and threw it back with vigor, letting out a happy sigh as she played back the evening's events. She didn't even care that she was supposed to be lying to Molly about where she had been. She wanted the whole world to know just how happy she was and every single detail surrounding the reason why. "Yes. Kate is the most fun ever. Oh, you have to meet her, Molly!"

Molly wrote a figure in the cashbook and looked up at Sherie, who recognized the false smile that had spread across her face. She was not happy. "Good. I told you all you needed was a break," she said.

Rather than force Molly to admit that she was angry, Sherie decided to take herself to bed. She danced over to the stairs, but paused as she reached the first step. "Quiet tonight? You didn't work?"

Maggie shook her head while she swept up the pieces of the broken vase. "Five minute Freddy," she explained.

Sherie nodded in understanding, and flashed a grin at the group. "I am off to dream sweet dreams. Goodnight, my beautiful girlies." She smiled and floated up the stairs.

Maggie threw the pot pieces into the bin and rested the broom against a wall before sitting down on a stool and closing her eyes. Claire walked over to the bar and spun the cashbook around to face her. After a few moments, she looked up from the book. "This isn't right," she said.

"What?" Molly looked up from under the bar, pulling her head out from the back of the hidden safe. Claire pointed to the place in the book where she had found the incorrect numbers. From her stool, Maggie opened one eye to watch.

"These numbers don't add up. Here." Claire tapped on a column in the book. "And here, it looks like there is money missing."

Molly was not looking at where Claire was pointing. She slammed the heavy book closed, narrowly missing Claire's fingers. "Who asked you?"

Claire was taken aback by Molly's sudden change. "I just thought I would practice my numbers," she said.

"How about you stick to being a whore and I'll stick to running the business?"

Claire stood still, looking at the ground, too embarrassed to know what to say.

"I'm going to bed. Claire?" Maggie asked. Claire was thankful for the opportunity to leave without looking like she had been shamed out of the room, even though that's how she felt. She followed Maggie up the stairs, not daring to look back at Molly.

"She's just stressed. You know how she gets. Especially when she's wrong," Maggie said.

Claire snorted. Molly was never wrong.

"She'll probably just recount it all again when we go to bed," Maggie finished.

Claire rolled her eyes. "Whatever." She walked into her bedroom, frustrated.

Chapter 15

The next morning, Kate arrived at the Bucket early and greeted the girls, who were sitting in their usual places on the balcony, the only difference being that Maggie sat where Sherie usually would on the swinging chair, beside Molly.

"Morning. Sherie around?" Kate asked politely.

Olivia threw back her head and yelled, "SHERIE!"

"What are you reading?" Kate asked Claire.

"Attempting to read, more like." Claire smiled. "I mean, look…" She handed the book to Kate and pointed to a word on the page. "What's a fugate?"

Kate was perplexed. "A what?"

Claire tapped the word on the page. "Here. This word here."

"Fugitive," Kate read.

"Ohh. Ugh, see what I mean? Attempting to read," Claire said.

Kate smiled at Claire and handed the book back to her. "Well, that was a hard word. You're doing great; keep at it."

Claire's face erupted with a beaming smile. "No wonder Sherie likes you so much," she said.

As if on command, Sherie appeared on the balcony, immediately shooting a stern look in Claire's direction. She was not moving with her usual sprightliness, and her sweet face cringed as she shuffled out the front door.

"Oh, she does, does she?" Kate looked at Sherie pointedly.

"I will kill you," Sherie told Claire.

"You'd have to move faster than the waddle you've currently got going, so I feel like I'm safe," Claire replied.

"Oh my, what on earth happened to you?" Kate asked, amused.

"Don't forget dinner tonight," Molly said, interrupting the playful atmosphere.

"My hips are killing me. They actually want me to die, I think." Sherie grimaced.

"Well, we think you look beautiful, don't we, Kate?" Olivia said with a wink.

Kate prayed her cheeks didn't betray her as she nodded in agreement.

Sherie twirled, or rather, attempted to twirl, letting her beige skirt flare out. She looked like an injured walrus, but a very cute one. It was hardly a pretty dress, Kate noted, but apparently Sherie could make anything look fabulous.

"Sherie. Dinner. Tonight." Molly was clearly unimpressed.

Sherie sighed. "Yes. I know. I'll be here." She turned to Kate. "Ready?"

Kate nodded, and they made it halfway down the stairs before Molly called Sherie back again. Sherie rolled her eyes and turned her body around as if it weighed a hundred kilos. "Yes?"

Molly tossed her an akubra from the hat stand beside the door. "Maybe Kate could come to dinner too," she said.

Sherie grinned at Molly and ambled clumsily back to give her a tight hug, grunting in pain with each step she took. "I love you, Mol," she said. Molly hugged her back tightly.

"Love you too, kiddo."

"So what are we doing today?" Sherie asked.

"You're gonna love it," Kate hinted, but that was all she said.

Sherie's legs screamed in pain when she climbed back up on Aiko, but she did her best to pretend they didn't. She was sure Kate had noticed though, because the journey to their destination was more of a stroll than anything else. Aiko didn't move faster than a brisk walk, and Kate made sure to slow her down whenever her movements started to jolt them.

Sherie's pelvis was tucked in a little closer to Kate than it had been the other day, and she enjoyed the warm pulses between her legs from the soft leather saddle as it moved forward, allowing her to press herself tightly against Kate's behind. She stopped when she realized that her thrusts were close to losing their subtlety, and she tried hard not to lean into Kate's body more than she needed to in order to maintain her balance on the horse.

"You can relax if you want; we still have a little while to go yet," Kate said.

Sherie wondered if she had noticed her pull back or if her words were just well timed. She leaned forward, rested her head on Kate's back, and closed her eyes. Kate reached behind and pulled Sherie's hands around her waist, bringing them together at the front. "You don't want to fall off."

Sherie squeezed her arms tightly around Kate. "Definitely not."

To say Sherie had no idea what she was doing would be a lie. She certainly understood exactly what she was doing. She recalled her feelings the other night, the electricity she felt when their hands touched. The same current flowed now, humming quietly as it shot back and forth between them. What she was curious about was where this was all leading to.

Do I need to know? How about enjoying the moment instead of figuring out what's going to happen next?

It was a habit that she found impossible to kick. Planning for the future and being concerned about the consequences of every action was a daily occurrence for Sherie, and as hard as she tried, she just couldn't allow herself to let go and enjoy her feelings without questioning them further. Her real concerns stemmed not from the tingling between her legs (as uncommon as that sensation was these days), but from the subject who induced it. *A woman.*

Generally, Sherie preferred the company of women to men, but it was never something she gave much thought to at all, because the attraction always derived from feelings of safety as opposed to sex. Unlike her horny clients, Sherie didn't look at either sex with an urge to whisk them away to a bedroom; she found her attraction lay predominantly in her ability to trust a person with her soul more than anything else. Having all but given up on love completely these days, Sherie had entrusted one person, and one person only, with the job of looking after her soul: herself.

What she wanted to know was why she felt like handing it over to this woman, and more importantly, why the notion didn't alarm her in the slightest.

"We're here."

Sherie opened her eyes. They were in a paddock that seemed to be on the far end of town by the looks of where they were standing in relation to the hills that surrounded them. Kate jumped down from Aiko and reached out to help Sherie down.

Sherie grunted as she climbed down and immediately bent over to stretch her legs out. Kate walked around to the other side of Aiko and pulled something out of the saddlebag. Sherie looked at her surroundings and took in a few more details. She could see the road that led back into town, and the trees that stretched toward the sky, housing the birds who sang down to them. There were bales of hay stationed in peculiar places, but what they were for she had no idea, since she couldn't see a single horse other than Aiko in the paddock. The hay had uneven wooden boards hanging from them and they appeared to be marked with something. She hobbled closer toward them. Above her, she heard the cackles of the Kookaburras, and she shot an annoyed glance at them. Apparently they found her movements amusing.

"You do look pretty funny," Kate said from behind her.

"Well, what's your excuse?" Sherie turned around to see Kate holding a shotgun.

"You wanna take that back?" Kate asked, cocking the shotgun with a grin.

Sherie looked at the bales of hay, realizing what they were. Targets.

Kate pointed out the different parts of the gun, and showed Sherie how to load it. She snapped the gun closed with an impressive one-handed movement that Sherie vowed to nail before the end of the day. She looked down the barrel of the gun as instructed by Kate, and did her best to point it at the red blotch marked out on the wooden board. She was terrible at holding the gun steady, completely unable to stop the barrel from moving in small circles. She was surprised at just how heavy it actually was.

Kate pulled one of the bales of hay over to where Sherie was standing. "Here, lean over that to steady yourself."

Sherie knelt down and propped her elbows on the bale. Kate stepped behind her and crouched over her. Sherie lost her breath briefly when she felt Kate's breast's brush over her back. Kate reached around and moved her hand slightly so that she was supporting the gun properly. "If you hold it there you'll melt your fingers the moment you fire it."

Sherie nodded. It took all of her strength not to tilt her head up to look at Kate, which would have put their lips just a whisper away from each other. In that moment, she realized…Sherie desperately wanted to kiss Kate.

"You ready?" Kate queried.

Excitement ripped through Sherie. "Oh, yes."

She pulled the trigger. The kickback surprised her, and the stock smashed into her shoulder. If Kate hadn't been directly behind her, she would have toppled over backwards for sure. She dropped the gun and let out a roar of pain as the initial impact was replaced by a burning throb. She knew she would have a bruise by the end of the day.

She punched Kate hard in the shoulder with her good arm. "You could have warned me!"

Kate burst out laughing, and Sherie punched her again.

"Look, though." Kate pointed at the bale Sherie had been aiming at.

She walked closer to it and squealed when she saw the tiny hole that poked almost dead center through the target mark. "I guess I have better aim than you!" she said proudly, puffing out her chest.

Kate prodded her sore shoulder, causing her to yell again and pull away.

"Now you just need the guts to go with it!" Kate taunted.

Sherie picked the gun up again. "Maybe it's time to try a moving target," she said, pointing the gun at Kate.

"Be my guest, but without any bullets, you're going to have a hard time shooting me no matter how good your aim is, little one."

Sherie laughed and held the gun out to Kate. "Load me up!"

Kate handed Sherie a bullet, but after a few seconds of trying, it became clear that she had no idea where the hinge was, let alone how to open it.

Kate took the gun back and broke it open as if it were nothing. She gave it back to Sherie, who dropped the bullet into the chamber and attempted to snap it shut with the same one-handed motion Kate had used earlier. Instead of snapping crisply into place, it swung back down and Sherie jumped backwards in order to avoid her leg being hit by the bottom of the barrel. Kate laughed and held her hand out, and Sherie gave the gun back to her again. She snapped it shut with ease and a wink. This time, Sherie was ready for the kickback when she fired, and though she did feel the same force as last time, it didn't throw her off at all. She stood up after the shot and walked over to the target. "Dead on!" she exclaimed.

Kate nodded her approval and re-loaded the gun.

'Your turn," Sherie said.

"Okay, but don't expect anything," Kate said.

"Please. You shot your father's dog. I'm hardly expectant."

Kate lined her shot up from where she was standing, and Sherie noticed she was able to hold the gun still without having to lean on the hay. She fired, and completely missed the target. When they looked at the hay bale, they couldn't even see a bullet hole. Sherie laughed and Kate pushed her playfully.

By the end of the afternoon, Sherie was loading the gun solo with ease. She snapped it shut as if she had been doing it all her life and took careful aim at a target that Kate had just moved further back.

"You don't want to move over a little more in case I miss?" Sherie shouted to Kate, who had only stepped a few feet to the left of the hay bale.

"Sherie, you haven't missed a single shot all day. I'm sure I'll be fine."

"I hope you don't regret saying that," Sherie joked.

Kate seemed to have complete trust in her, and despite the constant teasing, Sherie knew Kate was really proud of how quickly she had picked it up. She forgot about aiming for a second as she watched Kate standing there, waiting for her to take the shot. She was facing the sun, so her eyes were scrunched up in a squint, but her nose looked adorable when it was crinkled and it made Sherie smile. Strands of her hair caught the breeze and fluttered around her, dancing with a small butterfly that darted through the wisps, taking care not to get tangled up with her ponytail, which flapped far less delicately behind her.

Sherie's eyes scanned higher to Kate's hat, and as soon as the thought entered her mind, before she could stop herself from carrying out the idiotic idea, she pulled the trigger and shot the hat clean off Kate's head.

"FUCK ME SIDEWAYS IN THE BILLABONG, SHERIE, WHAT IN GOD'S NAME…" Clearly, Kate was less than impressed.

Sherie threw the shotgun to the ground and leaped in the air with a squeal. "Did you see that?!"

"See it?! I FELT it! My god, couldn't you have warned me first?!"

Sherie could see that Kate was shaking, and she reached out to steady her hands. "I didn't know I was going to do it until I pulled the trigger."

"Oh, well, that makes me feel better!"

"Besides, if I had told you, you might have flinched, and then what?" Sherie grinned and threw Kate's hands into the air with joy.

"Uh huh. Well, I tell you what, how about we just stick to the wooden targets for the rest of the day, huh?"

Sherie wasn't listening. She cracked the gun, dropped another bullet into the chamber, and snapped it closed one handed with a triumphant grin. "Admit it. I'm brilliant."

Kate chuckled. "Wow, so not only have I taught you how to ride a horse and shoot a gun, but I've taught you to be cocky now, too?"

"Watch it, woman, I've got a gun," Sherie said.

After another hour or so, Sherie had grown tired of shooting and her arm felt like it had been filled with lead and set on fire. She handed the gun to Kate, who took aim from where she was standing.

"No, no, no. I don't care how steady that barrel is. Your aim is horrible…" Sherie pointed to the bale of hay where she had fired her first shot. "On your knees, Flanagan," she ordered.

With a salute befitting a sailor of the Royal British Navy, Kate knelt down into position. Sherie came up behind her and adjusted her grip ever so slightly.

"This isn't how I showed you to hold it," Kate said.

"I know. I made some improvements."

"Mmhmm."

Sherie purposefully pressed her body against Kate, and her heart skipped a beat when she felt Kate press back. Kate tipped her head back slightly and Sherie dipped hers forward so that her nose nuzzled into Kate's neck. She inhaled deeply, drawing as much of Kate in as she could, and let her breath out in a slow and steady stream. She felt Kate's breath too, just as heavy, and suddenly caught herself.

"Sorry," she said, and pulled away. "I'm just tired."

"Maybe I should take you home," Kate said.

"Hah. You're not getting out of it that easily." Sherie jerked her head toward the target.

She wondered if Kate would be able to concentrate, because all she could think about was how it had felt to breathe Kate in and when she could do it again. She was jolted from her thoughts by the loud crack of the gun.

"Yes!" Kate's triumphant yell told Sherie that she had managed to hit the target before she could focus her eyes to see for herself.

Kate reloaded the gun and aimed a second time. Prepared for the shot this time, Sherie watched the target, which shifted abruptly when the bullet made impact. Splinters of wood flew out in every direction as Kate hit the board perfectly in the center. Sherie clapped loudly. "You did it!"

Kate turned around and took two big steps toward Sherie, picked her up, and twirled her around in the air. Sherie yelped when her muscles protested the sudden movement.

Kate dropped her gently on the ground and looked at her. Sherie found her eyes instantly and locked on to them.

"I brought you out here to teach you something, and look what happened."

Sherie smiled. "I think we might just be good for one another. Don't you?"

"I think you might just be right," Kate said with a tip of her hat and its newfound hole.

By the time Kate arrived at the Bucket for dinner everyone else was sitting at the table that had been set up in the main bar area, chatting amongst themselves. She gripped a bunch of daffodils tightly and leaned slightly to the left under the weight of the satchel that was slung over her shoulder as she walked quietly inside

Molly looked stressed as she put a bowl of bread on the table and she didn't seem to be a participant of the fun going on around her. Neither did Georgina, whose dark eyes appeared to look through everything around her. She was eternally lost in thought, or so it looked like it from the outside. Her hair fell around her face as if they were blinkers to the world around her but Kate got the impression that even if her hair was pulled back there would be an invisible curtain keeping her separate from the stains of her reality.

Kate looked at the other three girls—Maggie, Olivia and Claire. They were laughing and behaving so playfully that Kate wondered whether she had got it all wrong. Was their life really as unpleasant as she expected it should be, given their line of work? She felt like unpleasant was far too light a word to use to describe how they lived and what they were expected to do just to maintain a living. Repulsive, hideous, terrible, horrific. All seemed like much more acceptable words to use, but their faces really didn't indicate that she was right. Their laughter was genuine, extending to the eyes of all girls save Georgina and Molly, both of who were hardly active participant of the conversation at hand.

It was the first time she had seen Claire without a book in her hands and Olivia not in front of her pottery wheel. Without the loud music and the men they hung off of on an evening they just appeared to be a normal family sharing a meal together, sitting at a table opposite one another, joking.

"Knock, knock."

Everyone turned and looked at her, their faces welcoming.

"You don't have to knock at a brothel—we're always open!" joked Maggie.

Kate's eyes were drawn to Sherie when she heard her groan, presumably at Maggie's terrible joke.

It was as if Sherie was waiting for her to look at her, and Kate felt her body flood with heat when their eyes connected.

"Aaah, Kate!" Molly said, approaching her. Kate smiled and held out the bunch of daffodils she was holding.

"Thanks for having me," she said.

Molly looked at the flowers, back at Kate, and then over to Sherie, who was glowing brighter than the sun. Kate congratulated herself silently for her choice of flowers. Molly held her hand out for the flowers, and Kate got the distinct impression that she had not been successful in her attempts to 'win over' the big sister. Just out of reach, Kate had to step forward to give the flowers to Molly, who appeared to look down at Kate despite being a few inches shorter.

"Thanks for coming," she said with a smile that Kate noticed did not reach her eyes. She returned the smile however, and shook Molly's hand, but her smile disappeared when Molly's grip increased to the point where Kate had to bite her lip in order to avoid yelping in pain. She felt the knuckles in her hand crumple and just as she was about to pull her hand away, unable to take the pain, Molly let her go. This woman was not on her side at all, and her thanks were not in the least bit sincere.

"I don't think we have anywhere to put these," Molly said holding up the flowers.

Olivia shot out of her chair and swiped the flowers from Molly's hands. "Oh, yes, we do!" On the bookcase behind the table sat a newly crafted vase. She placed it in the middle of the table and dropped the daffodils in.

"They fit perfectly." She beamed.

Molly's eyes narrowed, and Kate matched them and shot her a smug half smile.

Georgina picked up a jug of water. "You must nourish that which is beautiful," she said seriously, pouring the water into the vase carefully.

"Oh, blast," Olivia said as she watched water spurt from the sides of the vase and leak all over the table.

Molly pushed swiftly past Kate and the others with a towel that hung from her apron and mopped up the water. "I've got it," she said.

Maggie snorted with amusement.

"Nice one, Da Vinci," Claire chimed in.

Olivia threw a disdainful look at Claire, her hands on her hips. "Da Vinci was a painter!"

"Bet he could throw a better pot than you can!" Maggie said.

Olivia reached across the table and punched Maggie in the chest. "You may call me Michelangelo," she said, each word accompanied with a punch.

Maggie continued her taunting. "Bet Michelangelo could throw a better punch too!"

Everybody laughed at this, much to the dismay of Olivia, who picked up a piece of bread and threw it at Maggie. It missed and hit Sherie by accident.

"And a better bread roll!" said Sherie. The group was in hysterics now, all but Olivia, of course, who appeared to be attempting to muffle the grin that was creeping up at the corners of her mouth.

Kate felt relaxed enough to slip into a seat at the table, between Claire and Sherie. She reached down under the table and gave Sherie's leg a squeeze just above the knee.

"And a better canary!" said Georgina.

There was a moment of silence before the group burst into further fits of laughter over Georgina's failed attempt to contribute to the joke.

As the laughter subsided a figure appeared at the door and Kate recognized him as the peacock formerly known as Tom.

"Knock, knock."

"You're too late! The joke's been made tonight!" Sherie yelled without even looking at who was at the door.

Georgina raised her fist in the air as she proclaimed, "ALWAYS OPEN!"

The girls whooped and cheered and clinked their glasses. Alarm washed over Sherie when she looked up and saw that it was Tom who had just arrived. She cast a quick glance at Kate, who was sitting on her hands, smiling politely. Tom gave Molly a kiss on the cheek as he walked through the room.

"Sorry, I'm late." He sat down beside Sherie and kissed the top of her head on the way down.

To her horror, he then picked up her hand and kissed it.

"Haven't seen much of you lately. I'd almost forgotten how beautiful you are," he said.

Sherie couldn't bring herself to look at Kate. Where this sudden display of affection came from she had no idea, and she wanted to wring Tom's neck for his impeccable timing. She was grateful for Olivia's proclamation of disgust by way of an embellished sound of vomiting as she jabbed her fingers into her mouth.

Maggie contributed to the mockery, batting her eyebrows at Tom. "Luckily, you've had me to remind you how beautiful I am," she said.

Olivia snorted. "Yeah, you're a real Mona Lisa. Much better to look at from a distance."

"Shut up, Michelangelo," said Maggie.

"Isn't Michelangelo a poet?" Tom asked.

Sherie stood up, her patience completely evaporated. "Molly! Need help?"

Sherie walked into the kitchen and was handed a bowl right away.

"Hold this," Molly said, motioning that she was going to ladle soup into it.

"You knew Kate was coming! Why would you invite Tom?" Sherie asked her in a low voice.

"I didn't think it would matter. I thought you would want to introduce your 'new best friend' to your fiancé," Molly said with an unsubtle air of sarcasm. Sherie set down the bowl she was holding.

"You're my best friend, Molly Kelly. You know exactly how I work better than anyone else in the whole world. You're always looking out for me. You look out for all of us. We all love you. No one is replacing you if that's what this is about."

Molly looked at the ground and nodded.

"Come here." Sherie took the ladle out of Molly's hands and hugged her. She came out of the hug and put her hands on Molly's shoulders, pulling back and making sure the look on her face was a stern one. "And he is NOT my fiancé!"

Molly picked up the ladle and pointed it at Sherie. "Yet!" she said, jabbing it at her.

They were interrupted by Maggie, whose head appeared through the doorway. "Plate another one up, ladies! James just arrived!"

Molly dropped the ladle into the pot, clearly unimpressed. "We're closed!" she said.

"We're always open," Maggie said with a stern look. "Besides, I invited him. He likes Claire."

Sherie picked another bowl up and held it out for Molly. "Maybe he could try talking to her then!" she said.

"He's just shy! I think he needs to get some confidence up around her."

Molly filled the bowl with soup. "Yeah, well, if he gets anything else up around her, he'll be payin' for it!"

Maggie rolled her eyes. "We're closed! If anything happens—" Molly cut her off.

"Whatever happened to 'We're always open!'?" Molly asked, but Maggie had no retort. She poured another ladle of soup into the last bowl, took it from Sherie, and handed it to Maggie. "If anything happens, he WILL be paying for it. Business is business. And we have mouths to feed. Extra mouths, apparently."

Maggie raised her eyebrows, but she said nothing as she took the bowl from Molly.

The evening progressed as awkwardly as Sherie expected it to, sitting between Kate and Tom. Tom flirted with her all night, and, not wanting to jeopardize their opportunity to secure the Bucket's future, or anger Molly any further, she forced herself to laugh at all his jokes, and behaved as coy as possible as per Molly's instructions that she come off as 'needy.' Personally, she thought it was a little stupid, but Molly's plans usually had a way of working out for the best, and she definitely knew better than to offer her opinion when Molly's mind was made up.

James sat on the piano stool, squeezed in between Maggie and Olivia. He was bright red and struggled to keep his soup on his spoon most of the time. Maggie and Olivia talked around him, and it looked almost as if he were trying to hide in between the walls of their conversation. Sherie knew Kate was ignoring her, but she didn't know how to stop what was going on. She had to keep Tom interested for Molly's plan to work. She hated that Kate's back was turned to her, but she was grateful at least that she could keep one ear to her conversation with Claire and make sure she was okay.

"So what made you want to learn to read?" Kate asked.

"We laugh," Claire said, pointing at Maggie and Olivia, who were smiling and joking about something. "But it's not because we're happy."

"I know what you mean," Kate said. She hoped her expression denoted her understanding as opposed to sounding like a condescending attempt to see it from her point of view. She hated it when her aunt told her that she 'knew how she felt.'

"We keep occupied. Distracted. Pretend that our lives are as carefree as people believe they are. Pretend we don't care what other people think. The morning after my first night at the Bucket, I woke up, washed myself, looked at myself in the mirror, and threw up. I don't think I've looked in a mirror since then. That was a long time ago. I remember when I was a little girl, and my sister would tell me stories. She would always get hung up on the tiny details… she made everything sound so real…but now there is no one to read me stories. So I read them myself."

"Wow," Kate whispered.

"We all need something to keep us going." Claire pointed at Olivia's vase in the middle of the table. "Do you really think Olivia doesn't care that her vases get smashed almost every night? Of course she does! But it also means she has an excuse to get up tomorrow. It gives her purpose."

Claire pointed at Georgina, who was eating her soup with one hand while her other hand was raised above her head holding a chunk of bread with a canary nibbling away at it. "And Georgina…you think she's insane, right? Barking mad. What's with the canaries? You're thinking it, right?"

Kate shrugged, not wanting to offend.

"Everyone does. But she's not insane. She has good reason to be, believe me. And with the amount of belladonna she drops into her eyes every night, you'd think that would make her insane…but she's not."

"And the canaries?" Kate asked.

"She gets a new one every year," Claire said.

"Like a birthday present?"

"Sort of. Have you counted how many canaries she has? There are four. One for each year that has passed since she lost her daughter."

The words came out of Kate's mouth before she could stop herself. "How did she die?"

"She didn't die. We all went to bed one night, and when we woke up the next day, the baby was gone. Disappeared just like that."

Kate felt as much shock as she did sadness and she could feel the hairs on her arms tingling. Claire looked up and saw Georgina looking at her. Georgina gave the slightest of a headshake.

"Anyway, it's an awful story, the details of which none of us are even sure of. My point, though, is that those canaries give Georgina a reason to get out of bed. That's what it's all about—having a reason."

Kate thought about what Claire had just said. She looked at Sherie, who was stroking Tom's arm gently. "Is he her reason?"

Claire shook her head. "That's the saddest part of all."

"What?" asked Kate.

"Sherie doesn't have a reason."

Kate glanced over at Sherie and Tom again and decided she couldn't look at them any longer. "I have to go."

She got up, and then realized she had forgotten something. "I brought this for you," she said, pulling out a leather bound journal from her satchel and handing it to Claire.

"Oh, wow," Claire said.

Maggie looked over at the journal. "Gosh, Kate, that's really sweet," she said.

Sherie looked down at Kate and smiled at her. Kate didn't meet her eyes, though she desperately wanted to.

"No use just learning how to read," Kate said. She suddenly remembered something else and started digging through her bag. She pulled out a pencil. "You'll need this as well," she said, handing the pencil to Claire. Claire took it, her face amazed.

"Thank you, Kate," she said.

"You're welcome." Kate stood, taking care not to look Sherie in the eye. "Thank you so much for dinner. And Molly, for the invitation. I appreciate it."

Molly winked at Kate. "Come back any time. And hey, if you're ever lookin' for a job…"

What Kate really wanted to do was dump her leftover soup on Tom's head and throw the bowl at Molly, but for the sake of diplomacy she simply nodded goodbye to the group and headed swiftly for the door.

Once outside, she paused at the edge of the top stair of the balcony between the break in the rail and rested her head on the pole. Sherie suddenly burst through the doors. She stopped fast when she saw Kate was still there.

"Are you okay?" Sherie asked.

Kate stiffened her lip refusing to let Sherie see she was hurt. "Fine. Just remembered I should probably get an early night. Big day tomorrow," she said.

Sherie took a step closer to her. "What are we doing?" she asked.

Kate continued to look away. "Nothing. I've got other stuff to do," she said.

"Oh."

"I'm sure you and Tom can find something to do," Kate said, her intent to hurt.

Sherie nodded. "I thought that might be what this was about. Look, I don't have time for games, so just be straight wi—"

Kate interrupted Sherie, stepping toward her and looking her directly in the eye. "No time for games, huh? That's funny, because it seems to me that's all you seem to be playing. We spend the day together, you invite me to dinner, and you spend the WHOLE night stroking his arm!"

Sherie stepped forward. "Kate, it's not like that," she pleaded with her.

"It's exactly like that! You can't have it both ways, Sherie. You can't act one way with me, and then another with him. Is it because the others were watching? Is it me?" Kate grabbed her skirt in her fists and held it up to Sherie. "This?!"

Sherie appeared close to tears when she answered. "No! It's business! I don't have a choice."

Kate rushed into Sherie with a mix of fury and passion. She took Sherie's head in her hands, roughly but not violently. For a moment, Kate thought she was going to kiss her, but at the last second, she didn't. Her nose was an inch from Sherie's. "Yes. Yes, you do," she whispered. "You do have a choice." She ran down the stairs, not looking back.

From the window inside, Molly watched Sherie cry while Kate stormed down the stairs, mounted her horse, and disappeared.

Chapter 16

S herie tossed in bed, unable to keep still. Why she was still trying to sleep was beyond her. Between the anvil of guilt that sat at the bottom of her stomach and the rain that hammered on the tin roof, she knew sleeping was not going to be an option tonight. She climbed out of bed and walked over to her dresser, kicking the chair out as she collapsed onto it and looked at herself in the mirror. She looked like hell.

Her eyes were swollen, a puffy pink mess that stung when she tried to wipe them dry. She shot herself a dirty look and dropped her head into her hands with a groan. She wished tonight had never happened. She wished she had explained sooner to Kate, if that would have even made a difference. Were her actions justified? Kate had laid no claim to her, nor could she ever. Her head pounded. That situation was an entirely different kettle of fish, and she wasn't even sure what 'that situation' was.

Outside the moon was high in the sky and there was still plenty of time to lie back in bed and attempt to sleep. Sherie was working the room the following night, and it usually took a lot more energy to keep her spirits high and pretend to flirt with men whom she would rather castrate than sleep with than it did to pour drinks, which was far more of a monotonous job, predictable, and much less grisly on the soul.

She thought about Kate and the look in her eyes when she had grabbed her face in her hands. If she was so furious then why did her touch not scare Sherie? Even in that moment, she was certain Kate's intentions were not to harm her. In fact, quite the opposite—she had almost leaned in to kiss Kate.

Unable to process the thoughts that were grating against her skull, Sherie stood up for half a second only to sit back down again. She threw her head on the table and it cracked loudly on impact. She knew her body felt the pain, but it didn't seem to register through the cloud of angst that overpowered everything else. She picked her head up and brought it back down again heavily with no concern for the marks or bumps it would leave, despite knowing that Molly would kill her for it the next morning. She didn't give a damn about Molly. If it weren't for Molly, this wouldn't be happening, and for the briefest of moments she wondered whether the entire circumstance had been arranged on purpose.

No, she wouldn't do that. She shook the thought from her mind. Molly loved her, first and foremost, and wanted her to be happy. Even though she liked to have control over situations, Sherie understood that it came from a place of concern, not malice.

Sherie looked at the daffodil Kate had given her earlier that week which had long since wilted. Even during its last few moments of existence, it was still beautiful.

The floor creaked from just outside her bedroom and a flickering light appeared under the crack of her door, casting an amber glow across the floor. She knew Maggie was asleep because she could hear the snores, and she hoped it wasn't Molly, since she was definitely not ready to deal with her when the events of the evening were still raw in her mind.

"Are you okay?" a voice whispered.

Georgina.

Not wanting to wake the whole house up, Sherie opened the door and let her in. "No," she told her honestly.

Georgina cradled a doll in her arms and she rocked it back and forth. She climbed onto Sherie's bed and tucked her feet beneath her. "Tonight didn't go well for anyone," she said.

"No. It didn't."

"It was a bad night." Georgina stroked the hair of her doll. Sherie twirled the daffodil between her fingers and nodded her agreement. Georgina's ability to read a situation with such clarity no longer astounded her the way it had when she first arrived at the Bucket. At first, she had thought that all the things she had seen, experienced, and endured had made Georgina wise beyond her years. After time, Sherie realized that Georgina's simplification of things hinged on the verge of insanity. She toed the line dangerously, but remained in-bounds of the realms of lucidity just enough for no one to be sure exactly whether she was actually mad, or just one of those queer individuals that you come across every now and then who aren't quite like the rest of us. Sherie had often wondered whether they were doing the right thing, allowing her to continue to work with them, but always came to the same conclusion. Georgina had just as much a right to be here as everyone else did, and the fact that she chose to vacate reality a little more often than the rest of them didn't mean she deserved to be locked away. Perhaps it made her smarter, even.

"That's pretty," Georgina said pointing at the daffodil that Sherie was still twirling. "Where did you get it?"

"Kate gave it to me."

"Don't be sad. It will survive."

Sherie smiled. "It's sweet of you to say, but I don't think even water could save it now."

"Not the flower, you fool," Georgina said.

Sherie was thrown. "Uh, Kate, I, uh…"

"Anything can be preserved if you try hard enough." Georgina kissed the baby doll on the forehead. "Shhhh," she whispered, calming the non-existent cries.

"Preserve? Or save?" Sherie asked.

"The difference depends on how you look at it," Georgina said. "Show me the rule book that says something is exactly so because of this or that and not because of what they say it is."

"What?" Georgina wasn't making sense to Sherie.

"Because who are 'they' and why do 'they' tell me if something is or isn't?"

"I don't know what you mean," Sherie confessed.

"But you know what you mean. And that is all that matters."

"I don't know what I mean," said Sherie.

"What you mean to her. What you mean to do."

"What? How do I know what I mean to her? That's just cra—" Sherie stopped herself. She tried not to use that word around Georgina.

"Everyone is crazy and no one believes it. If it's crazy, that just means it's real." Georgina laid the doll down gently, stood up, and left the room. Sherie had no idea what was happening and whether she should be following Georgina or staying to 'watch' the doll. Before she could decide, Georgina was back holding two books and a belt. She snatched the dying daffodil from Sherie's hand as she walked past her. She put one book on the dresser, placed the daffodil on it, and then slammed the other book down on top of it. She wrapped the belt tightly around the books, buckled it, and then threw it at Sherie.

"Some things you must force to exist," she said.

Sherie wasn't sure what to say. Were they still talking about her and Kate? The daffodil? Georgina? "Is this really existing, though? It will hardly be beautiful anymore, and it's already starting to stink," she said, holding the books up. "I mean, what's the point?"

"That depends on who you ask."

"I'm asking you," Sherie said.

"Georgina wants to know who gets to decide what is considered beautiful? The chicken shit we scatter on the vegetable seeds stinks, but it helps them to grow better than anything else. If you want good things to happen, sometimes you have to lie in the shit," Georgina said.

"Okay, you're starting to make sense."

"I always make sense. Who gets to decide who makes sense? This flower is a flower because someone told us that it is a flower."

"And the weeds are weeds because someone told us that they are weeds," Sherie said, understanding.

"We are the weeds, Sherie. Do you think Billy would have punched a flower?" Georgina took the books from Sherie again and put them on the dresser. "This dead flower might not be much now, but imagine what value it will hold in a hundred years. If you want something to last, you have to do something about it."

"We are not weeds," Sherie said.

"No. We're not." Georgina smiled at her.

"Georgina?"

"Mm?"

"Is this you?" Sherie asked, pointing at the books.

"Those are books."

Sherie looked at her, unimpressed. "Do you force yourself to exist?"

"I told you. Things are what they are because people say they are so. The rules don't have to be the same for every single thing. The weeds are weeds when we want them to be weeds, until we decide we don't want them to be weeds and then they are no longer weeds."

"Okay, you lost me again," Sherie said.

"I drink nettle tea and it's tea, but when it stings me, it's a weed."

"Okay…" Sherie said.

"I stand, I breathe, I talk, but I am not existing. I am living, but I am not existing."

Sherie processed her words, fascinated. "I had the same conversation with Kate, but I had it the other way around," she said. "I told her I wasn't living, but just existing."

"That is your truth. There's hope for you," Georgina said.

"But not for you?"

"Existing is innate. You are born, so you exist. Living is something you learn."

"But you said you don't exist?"

"I breathe in and out," Georgina said.

Sherie had no idea what to say. The conversation had become incredibly heavy all of a sudden, and she wasn't exactly sure what Georgina was talking about.

"All I am is a mother without a child. I live because she lives in me, but I can't exist without her. To disappear into oblivion would be to lose her, do you understand?"

Sherie wasn't sure she did. "It sounds like you're saying you don't have a soul," she said.

"You can't see that?" Georgina asked, picking up her doll.

"I think you do, honey. I think you still have a soul."

"You're wrong. Yours is missing too," Georgina said.

"My soul?"

"Yes."

Sherie felt a chill run through her. It wasn't that she believed what Georgina was saying, but being told her soul was not there caused a harrowing uneasiness. "What makes you say that?"

"Why do you think Kate is here?" Georgina asked.

Sherie was thrown by the sudden apparent subject change. "She won't talk about it. I don't know why she came to Richmond."

"She has it."

"Has what?"

"Your soul," said Georgina.

Sherie shuddered. This was one of those times where Georgina seemed as if she were discussing something completely rational, even though the topic was absurd.

"I thought you knew that?" said Georgina.

She did. Not a second before that instant, but as soon as Georgina said it, she knew that a part of her had known all along. "Okay, you're starting to get a little scary, Georgina."

"You wouldn't be scared if you didn't think I wasn't telling you the truth."

"So how do you know this?"

"That's the thing about living where I live. I just do." Georgina tapped her temple with her long index finger and then stood up and left the room. Sherie waited for a while, but as time passed, it was clear Georgina was not returning.

It was well past midnight and the rain had eased up. Sherie stood at the bottom of Kate's window with a handful of pebbles. She wasn't sure if this was a bad idea, but given that everything else up to now had felt like the right thing to do despite leading to disaster, she decided that perhaps the wrong thing would end up being the right thing to do this time. She threw the pebbles up at the window, her first few attempts failing miserably as they arced not more than a few feet above her head before gravity took control.

Come on, Sherie, you're going to have to try harder than that. She threw the next pebble a little harder, and a quiet tap affirmed her successful aim this time. She continued to throw the pebbles, one by one every few seconds until Kate's window opened and she appeared from behind the curtain, her face angry. Sherie offered a small smile with the hopes it would gain forgiveness, but she knew it wouldn't, and when Kate's expression didn't waver, it was confirmed.

"Can I show you something?"

Kate closed her window. Sherie turned around and started to walk away. Of course the answer would be no. She was an idiot for thinking otherwise after embarrassing her like that. From behind her, the front door opened and she turned around, hopeful.

Kate stood behind the screen door for a moment. "Okay."

They walked in silence, accompanied only by the chirps of the crickets along the roadside. Richmond Bridge stood magnificently under the moonlight, arching over Coal River, the silver moonbeams blanketing the water like a sheet of eternal velvet. Halfway across the bridge, Sherie stopped and sat on the side of the stone wall, her legs dangling over the edge. She looked at Kate, but she was not looking back at her.

"I don't know how to say I'm sorry," Sherie said.

"I wouldn't waste your breath on a lie," Kate replied, still not looking at her.

"It's not a lie. You have to know I'm sorry."

"The thing is, Sherie, I don't know anything about you. I thought maybe I did, but after your little show tonight, I really have no idea."

Sherie felt a pain in her chest. "Things are complicated…" She struggled to find the right words to explain the situation.

"Which is why I walked away. I don't want to be involved," Kate said.

Suddenly, Sherie was struck with realization. Kate did want to be involved. If she didn't, she wouldn't have agreed to join her. Sherie stood up on the ledge of the wall, liberated by the understanding that Georgina was right. As dramatic and ridiculous as it sounded, Kate was here for a reason, and whether it was to "give her soul back" or just to help her see that life wasn't as horrible as she had thought it was, Kate was here, and Kate was staying. She just needed to help Kate realize it.

"Stand up," said Sherie.

Kate did not look at her. "Oh, so now you've decided you're just going to order me about?"

"Kate." Sherie stared at her until she looked up. "Stand up," she said softly.

Kate stood up. She looked highly dubious, but she finally made eye contact with her for the first time since Sherie's face had been in her hands at the Suds Bucket.

"What?" Kate asked.

"Jump," said Sherie simply.

Kate looked down at the river below. "Sure," she said. She jumped back down off the ledge and onto the bridge. Sherie looked down at her and frowned.

"Ha. Ha." She held out her hand, inviting her back up onto the ledge. Kate stepped forward and looked down to the water below again.

"You've gotta be kidding me."

"Do you trust me? Enough to dive feet first?" Sherie asked.

"You mean head first," Kate corrected her.

"No. Feet first. Not even looking where you're going. Just take the plunge. Entirely on faith, knowing there's someone beside you looking out for you."

Kate was unswayed. "Are you beside me?"

Sherie looked at Kate, words failing her. Suddenly she felt very self-conscious. Her little plan hadn't gone the way she had wanted it to, and Kate was calling her out on her games.

Kate paused and sighed. "I don't know, Sherie." She stared up directly into Sherie's eyes. "I don't know if I trust you."

Sherie smiled sadly at Kate, who smiled back at her. "What do you say you take a chance?" She held her arm out. Kate looked at her hand and ran her index finger along the length of Sherie's thumb, moving across to brush over the creases in her palm. Sherie allowed her to contemplate her lifelines for a moment, before closing her hand, trapping Kate's hand in hers. "Jump. Fall with me."

Kate climbed back up onto the wall. "I have no idea why I'm doing this."

"I do," Sherie said.

The pair leaped from the bridge and plummeted into the river.

Sherie surfaced first. She looked around, but she couldn't see Kate anywhere. She took a breath and went back under, but the water was murky and she couldn't see very far at all. She resurfaced to find Kate's face right in front of her, and before she could say anything, Kate spat a jet of water into her face. Sherie yelled and splashed her. Kate grabbed her hands, causing a cease-fire. Sherie felt her smile disappear as Kate looked seriously into her eyes.

"I'm not as tough as I seem," she said.

"Neither am I," Sherie said, shaking.

The wind blew across the river and Kate moved closer to Sherie.

"Don't hurt me," said Kate.

Sherie let her hand move around to Kate's back and she pulled her closer in, feeling her skin when her shirt drifted up in the water. She curled her fingers gently, stroking her lower back. The current carried them down the river so slowly that they didn't realize they were even moving until they looked up and saw that they were under the bridge. Sherie moved her hands up around Kate's neck and she lifted her legs up and locked on to her waist.

She held her tightly, and pulled herself in further so that her body was pressed tightly against Kate's. She rested her head on Kate's shoulder, and as they bobbed in the water together, she could feel Kate's heart pounding through her chest.

"I won't hurt you," she whispered.

Molly snarled as she watched Sherie arrive home. She didn't know where she had been, but she didn't need to guess who she was with. She pulled a shawl on and left the Bucket quietly, the song of the larks in the sky above while the early morning colors started to stretch across the navy sky.

She arrived at her destination—a dirty shack of a house with no glass in the windows and a creaking front porch. She heard the cries of a baby from inside as she knocked on the front door, which was opened by Billy.

"What the hell do you think you're doing here?" he asked. He stepped outside and closed the door, hiding Molly from his wife inside. He looked past Molly to the street.

"No one's around. Trust me," she said.

"Who'd you bring with you to do your dirty work?" Billy asked, his face terrified while he continued to scan up and down the street.

"Shut up and listen, Billy. I'm not going to hurt you. I didn't bring anyone with me. A fair warning though, you lay a hand on Claire again and I won't just go to the police, you hear me? I'll tell your wife, I'll tell your boss, I'll tell everyone in town that will listen. Got it?"

Billy stepped closer to Molly and she could smell the alcohol on his breath. "You came all the way out here to threaten me?"

"No. That was a precursor, you asshole. I came out here because I have a job for you," she said.

"What's it pay?"

"The ability to come back to the Suds Bucket again without getting your ass kicked from here to Timbuktu."

Billy snorted and started to head back inside, obviously uninterested.

"Unless you'd like me to speak to your wife instead?" Molly added.

The sun peeked through the curtains, but Kate slept through, utterly exhausted. The only muscles willing to move were her eyelids, which fluttered open at one point in the early morning, but closed almost immediately after she decided that she would not be moving for quite some time. Her clothes sat in a soggy pile on the floor where she had stripped herself bare before collapsing into bed, not bothering to pull the covers over her.

She was afforded another few hours of sleep before Mrs. Flanagan burst through the door, her unapologetic air apparent from the second she barreled across the room and wrenched the curtains open.

"Goodness! Lord, girl, where are your clothes?! Where is your modesty?"

Kate gave a happy moan as she felt the warmth of the sun on her bare bottom. The heat felt good and she had no intention of moving. She felt a blanket drop on top of her.

"I didn't exactly expect anyone to be walking in so early in the morning."

"Early in the morning? Kate, it's past two o'clock," Mrs. Flanagan screeched. Kate grabbed a pillow and put it over her head, burying into the mattress.

Muffled reality sharpened as Mrs. Flanagan pulled the pillow away from her and threw it to the other side of the room. "Up!"

Kate groaned.

"We are due to arrive at the ball in four hours, and we've a lot to do in that short amount of time," Mrs. Flanagan said.

"Short amount of time? That's half a day!"

"Your friends have been here getting ready since eleven, and they're still rushing around like headless chooks. You'll be surprised how much there is to do."

"Oh, I'm sure I will be," Kate said, dreading what Mrs. Flanagan had in store for her. She wrapped her blanket around her body and tucked it under her armpits to hold it in place. "What friends?" she asked, uncertain who exactly Mrs. Flanagan could be referring to.

"Regina and your cousins," Mrs. Flanagan said.

"Oh." Kate had absolutely nothing in common with the other girls, and dreaded being in their company. When Regina wasn't scowling at her for getting along so well with Sam, she was twittering on about what shade of pale cream was her favorite against what pattern of lace.

She forced herself downstairs. Her legs weighed with reluctance as she appeared in the lounge room and realized that Mrs. Flanagan had neglected to inform her that nearly half the young women in the town were here. Apparently all these women, whose names she did not even know, were considered her 'friends'. She was surprised she hadn't woken earlier, with the amount of chatter that echoed across the room.

"I thought you said it was just my cousins?" Kate asked when Mrs. Flanagan bounded over to her, holding what Kate hoped was not meant for her.

"Put this on, dear."

Kate's stomach dropped. It was a dress. A very green, very lacy, very puffy, very fancy dress.

"Well, and your cousins' friends, and their sisters."

"And their sisters' friends?" Kate asked.

"Oh, hush, there aren't that many people here," Mrs. Flanagan said.

Kate struggled to find a familiar face in the room, uncomfortable with the idea that she was meant to undress in front of all of these women. Regina's voice squawked the loudest over the top of the other women, who all seemed to crowd around her, hanging off every word she said and admiring the two dresses that she was holding. "Now be honest, do you think I should wear this one?" Regina held up a cream dress covered in a flowing pearly chiffon, lined with brilliant red lace at the bottom.

"Or this one?" She held another dress, this one gray and a little less full of ridiculous ruffles. "I do just adore this one. Mummy made it for me herself, but it does look a little common, don't you think?" She paused long enough for the other girls to voice their firm agreement. "Broadcloth is just so common, and even this gorgeous lace doesn't make it stand out. It just looks like every single other dress out there. Perhaps if it were a nice pink, or even pale yellow, it would be so delightful and perfectly different, but…" She stopped to admire the dress for a second more, and then threw it down onto the couch beside her. "No, it's just not enough for tonight. I want all eyes on me." She held up the cream chiffon dress again. "This just screams 'Look at me, and make sure you take it all in because you'll be dreaming about me tonight.'" She pulled the dress to her chest and breathed in tightly as if it were the answer to all life's problems.

"I'm so excited!" she squealed and twirled and the other girls followed suit. Kate cringed, and decided that she would prefer to change up in her room. She turned toward the stairs.

"Kate?"

Kate turned when she heard the young voice of Harriet Booth.

"I'm glad you're here! I've been waiting for you to wake up." Harriet smiled.

"Hiya, Harriet. How are you?"

"Good. Jealous though. I want to go to the ball and I'm not allowed."

Kate leaned forward. "You can go in my place if you want," she whispered, "I'd much rather stay here."

Harriet grinned. "Maybe you can stay with me. We can talk about horses and you can tell me all about what you and Bunny have been up to."

"It's Aiko now," Kate corrected her. "And I wish, but my aunt will kill me if I skip this. She made me go to the dress shop about five hundred times to try this dress on." She held the dress up in her fist.

"Katherine! Hold that dress properly, would you!" Mrs. Flanagan screeched. Every head in the room turned in Kate's direction, and she suddenly wished that she could hide under the mountains of ruffles and lace.

"Oooh, isn't it beautiful?" One of the girls cooed, rushing over to touch the fabric.

"Look at that stitch. Mrs. Flanagan, that must have taken weeks to make!" said another.

Mrs. Flanagan's smiled, her round cheeks tinted a proud red. "It did. Judy spent a whole week on the edging alone!" she boasted.

Kate wanted to strangle herself with the edging. "I'm going to change," she said, turning once again toward the stairs.

"Can I come with you?" Harriet asked, her eyes pleading. There was no way Kate could say no.

"Sure." If there was one girl she didn't mind spending time with, it was one who knew how to ride a horse.

"So how come you're here, if you're not allowed to go tonight?" Kate asked.

"I came with Sam."

"Sam's here?"

"Aye. He's downstairs helping your uncle with something in the back yard. A broken crank or something I think."

Kate leaned out her window and tried to look around the side of the house to the back. She wondered if it would be possible to sneak downstairs and outside without any of the women seeing her and sucking her back into their excruciating little gathering.

Kate walked down the stairs as quietly as possible, Harriet following her on tiptoes, but her failure was instant, as Mrs. Flanagan was standing at the bottom of the stairs waiting for her.

"What's the matter? It doesn't fit?" Kate could hear the alarm in her voice.

"No, no it's not that. I just…" Kate tried to think quickly. "Need a glass of water."

"Harriet, dear, get Kate some water so she can change."

Harriet nodded and slipped down past Kate, giving her hand a quick apologetic squeeze as she walked past.

"Come on, Kate, we're all dying to see what you look like in something other than those plain brown pants of yours." Regina giggled with a snort.

Kate flashed her a dirty look, but she was quick to cover it up with a false smile, knowing that her aunt would chastise her for it later if she didn't 'do her best to make friends.' "Oh, Regina, I just don't even know why I should try, since everyone will be looking at you anyway."

Regina blushed at the false compliment, blissfully unaware that inside her mind, Kate was hurling mud at her perfect little face. The sarcasm did not go unnoticed by Mrs. Flanagan, Kate realized, when she felt one of her sharp fingers prodding her in the ribs.

"Hush with you. Get upstairs." She prodded her again. "Now."

Kate went upstairs, annoyed. She pulled the dress over her head and tugged it roughly down her body, squirming when the little bits of fabric twisted in the wrong places. She was getting frustrated, and the feeling intensified as the dress stuck below her shoulder, the boning poking into her ribs. She pulled it hard and let out a gruff shout, regretting her rash movements when the dress ripped down the side. "Damn!"

"Everything okay in there?" Mrs. Flanagan called from the outside.

Well, at least she's decided that walking in on me is a bad idea.

"Yeah, uh, I'm..." Kate had no idea how she was going to cover this one up. "I don't think it fits," she said. Thinking quickly, she pulled the dress back up over her shoulder and held the waistline in her hand so that she was hiding the rip. "Can you come in and help me, please?"

As if her hand was already on the door handle waiting for the request, Mrs. Flanagan was in the room. "What do you mean you don't think it fits? You had a fitting appointment less than a week ago and it was fine."

"I know. I must be doing it wrong..." Kate said, holding the rip firmly in her first. "Can you pull it down? I can't get it." She flailed her arms a little above her head for show.

"Stop moving, stop moving! Here we go..." Kate could feel her take hold of the fabric, and as she gave it a gentle tug down, Kate held on to the top of the ripped hole and let the other part drop down in sync with Mrs. Flanagan's short tug, causing it to rip even more.

"Oh, God, I've ripped it!" Mrs. Flanagan flapped her arms as she squeaked.

Kate wiggled the dress down over her ribs, pulling the chiffon away from her face. "Oh, no! You did? Where?" She hoped her face looked upset and she did her best to twist it up even more to convey her 'utter disappointment.'

Mrs. Flanagan pointed to the rip in the dress down her left-hand side. "Oh, dear Kate, I'm so sorry. I can't believe I did that!"

"It's okay." Kate started to feel bad. She knew her aunt would be upset, but she didn't realize it would be this bad. "Honestly. It's okay. I can just wear a coat all night."

"Don't be ridiculous. Take it off. I'll stitch it now."

Kate bent over and waited for Mrs. Flanagan to pull the dress carefully over her head. It took about five minutes to get the dress off, since Mrs. Flanagan refused to move it more than an inch at a time.

There was another knock at the door, and Harriet's voice floated through. "Miss Kate, would you like your water in there?"

"We'll be out in a moment, dear. Just leave it downstairs for her," Mrs. Flanagan called. Pulling the dress over Kate's head, she stepped back and draped it over her arm. "I can't believe I did that," she said, shaking her head. "I'll fix this. You go downstairs and calm yourself after all this. I'll let you know when it's ready." Mrs. Flanagan hurried downstairs again, cursing as she went.

"I'll just be up here, calming myself," Kate called to her with a chuckle. She pulled on a shirt and made sure to grab her brown pants just to spite Regina, and then headed downstairs. She whipped past the sitting room as quickly as she could, praying that she wouldn't be noticed by anyone.

Kate walked swiftly down the back garden path, along the rotting wooden fence until she reached the shed where she could hear men's voices. "Fixed it yet?"

"Kate!" Mr. Flanagan looked up from whatever it was that he was fixing, his face covered in grease. "You're awake! Missed some good pancakes this morning."

Kate laughed. "Damn! If I had known there were going to be pancakes I probably would have dragged myself out of bed!"

"The promise of a fancy ball gown wasn't enough for you?" Sam's gruff chuckle made Kate smile. She really did like the man. She drew a sharp breath in, pulling it through her teeth, letting it hiss. "You know, it really wasn't." She laughed.

"Give it another go now, Angus," said Sam.

Mr. Flanagan tugged on a wooden handle that stuck out from the barrel churn that they were standing over. It didn't move.

"Still nothing!" Mr. Flanagan said.

"I've got no idea then. We've cleaned the caps, replaced the bolts, I can't see any rust…"

"It must be one of the paddles inside," Mr. Flanagan said.

"Bugger, we'll have to take the hoops off then," said Sam.

"No time for that now?"

"It'll take some time. May as well call it a day for now. We can have a look again tomorrow."

"I'll tell you now my head won't be ready for it first thing. Henderson has been distilling whiskey for months and I plan on drinking as much as I can."

Sam laughed. "I'll come by in the afternoon. I plan on having my fair share of whisky tonight too," he said.

"Which is where I come in," Kate interrupted. "I came to ask if I could bring you anything, but perhaps some water is in order, to make sure you're hydrated enough for this evening's drinking?"

"You're a good girl, Katie. I'm coming in now anyway so no need to bring me anything."

Kate smiled at Mr. Flanagan as he walked past her on his way to the house. She walked beside Sam when he started to head toward the front of the property, down the side of the house.

"You might be able to fool your sweet uncle, but you can't fool me. What are you up to?" Sam asked.

"What are you talking about?" Kate did her best to feign innocence with a flutter of her eyelashes.

"You are hardly the picture perfect little woman," he said. Kate hit him. "Hey! I mean that in the best way possible. I highly doubt for one second that you came out here just to ask if we needed a drink. Tell me I'm wrong, and I'll…" Sam looked around. "I'll jump in this puddle right now." He pointed to a muddy hole in the ground that had filled with rain from the night before.

"You're not wrong," Kate smiled. "I came to talk to you."

"Ah ha! You've come to ask me on a date because you've realized that you are actually desperately in love with me and you can't imagine living a second longer without me?" He smiled.

Kate shoved him and he stumbled off the path slightly. He was a cocky git, but not in an arrogant way. She liked his playfulness, and there was something about him that Kate felt was trustworthy. "Actually, I think I went on a date last night…" she said.

"You did? With who?" She noticed that Sam was blushing slightly.

"Um, just uh, someone from around here. I mean, they don't spend much time with our family's circles. I don't think my aunt and uncle would approve," she said.

"Oh god, who on earth did you see? Not someone from the outskirts? Billy whatshisname?"

"God no! Not Billy."

"Well, who? Come on, how bad could it be? A soldier? A convict? I've got it! A Chinaman! One of the blokes who came down from Ballarat?" He chuckled, clearly not serious.

"No," Kate said. She was starting to wish she hadn't said anything.

"Well, come on then, who?"

She took a deep breath and mumbled Sherie's name quietly enough so that Sam could not hear it.

"Who?" Sam poked Kate in the ribs.

"Sherie Kelly." This time she said it much louder, the volume liberating as Sherie's name rang out across the garden.

Sam stopped dead in his tracks. "The…"

Kate nodded.

"Did you p…I mean, how much…"

Kate could see Sam didn't want to ask what he was trying to ask, so she saved him the pain. "It wasn't at the Bucket and I didn't pay for anything, if that's what you're wondering. We haven't even kissed. We've just…spent some time together…and it was amazing."

Sam started up walking again and Kate matched his strides. "So are you going to see her again?" he asked.

"I think so. I want to go tonight. I miss her already. Pretty sure I dreamed about her. Is that weird? It's weird, isn't it?"

"It's not so weird. If you like the girl then it makes sense that you'd dream about her," Sam said.

Kate was frustrated. Sam wasn't reacting how she thought he would. She wasn't sure why she expected outrage, perhaps even a little jealousy, but not this. "No, Sam, I mean…HER. She. Female. Is that weird?"

"Well, she's hardly the most wholesome girl in town that you could have picked, but then again it appears you aren't either, so perhaps it's a match?"

Kate couldn't believe his reaction. She was stunned to silence.

"I knew their father, Daniel. He was a good man. A very good man. You could do worse."

"She's a good woman," Kate said. She pictured Sherie, her golden eyes reflecting the soft river waves in the moonlight, surprisingly full of hope despite the way she spoke about life. She recalled what it was like to hold her close, to feel their hearts pounding together. She didn't want to go to this damn masquerade ball tonight. She wanted to see Sherie.

"Hello? Anyone home?" Sam was waving his hand in front of Kate's face.

"Sorry," Kate said.

"You're really done for, aren't you?"

"What do you mean?"

"You're in love with her."

Kate nodded. "I think I am." She paused for a second and decided to rephrase her statement. "I am."

"But you haven't kissed her yet?"

"No."

"How many times have you seen her?"

"Not enough. Nowhere near enough."

Sam cocked his head to the side and a strange look spread across his face.

"What?" Kate asked.

"She's beautiful. I mean, for a…" he trailed off. "I just can't believe you haven't kissed her yet. What do you do then?"

"Jesus, Sam, it's not all about that!"

"I know it's not! But I just assumed since she—"

"Don't be a twat. And don't mention that again," Kate said. It annoyed her that he was referring to Sherie's career. It was always going to be the first thing people thought of though, and she was going to have to work on accepting that.

"Mention what?"

"You know what," said Kate.

"You can't even say it," said Sam.

"Can you just stop talking and pretend I didn't say anything?"

"No. Can you stop talking for five seconds and listen to me, instead of jumping on the defense?"

"Unlikely, but I'll try," said Kate.

"I was going to say I assumed since she was so gorgeous that you wouldn't be able to keep your hands off her, knowing you like I do."

"Oh," said Kate. So perhaps Sherie's career bothered her a little more than she had originally thought it had.

"I'll take that apology any time, by the way," said Sam.

"Shut up," said Kate.

"So then, what do you do if you're not kissing her? Talk? Because to be honest, I can't think of anything else worth doing with a girl like that."

"What's that supposed to mean?" Kate asked reactively, spitting her words.

"Would you calm down? Can we just assume from now on that I am not referring to her line of work here? No judgment, okay?"

Kate nodded. "We talk."

This time Sam said nothing. Perhaps a little too scared his words would be taken the wrong way, Kate thought.

"We look at the stars, we ride horses…"

"Of course you do!" Sam laughed. "Riding horses…that's how you court everyone, isn't it?"

"Who is everyone? You?"

"Well, now I know that's definitely not what you were doing!" laughed Sam.

"No, I'm afraid it wasn't. I really was just after your horse."

"Taken for a ride, I was," said Sam.

"Hah. You think you're so funny, Sam Booth."

Sam stopped walking and grabbed her hands. "I wish you thought so," he said.

His actions didn't make Kate feel uncomfortable, but as she gave his hand a squeeze she did feel sorry that it appeared she had hurt him. "I do. Just…"

Sam dropped her hands. "Ahh, don't say it. It's fine. I'll just have to go out and find myself a girl."

"I hear Regina's looking?" Kate chortled.

"Now you're the comedian!"

They rounded the corner to the front of the house. Sam looked across the Flanagan's yard to the street out the front. "Maybe you can teach me how to find the right girl then. You've not even been here a month and you've managed to do it. What's this about looking at stars? Is that what women like to do these days?"

"Sherie isn't like most women," said Kate. "But the stars are amazing. Did you know there's a meteor shower every year that you can see here in Richmond? It cuts right through the Pavo constellation!"

"Pavo? What is that?"

"It means…" Kate stopped for a second. Saucepan? Or Peacock? She decided to let Sam form his own opinion. "It looks like this."

She picked up a nearby stick and drew the dots in the sand where the stars belonged in the constellation. "That is Pavo," she said.

"It kinda looks like a saucepan," said Sam.

"I knew I liked you, boy!" Kate laughed.

"Okay, so you're saying if I show a girl these stars she will fall in love with me?"

"I'm pretty sure you could show Regina a pile of rocks and she would fall in love with you."

"You don't think it would scare her, to see what was inside her head?" said Sam.

Kate punched Sam in the arm lightly. "Be nice."

They stood in silence a while longer. Kate looked down at the Pavo she had drawn in the dirt. "Do you think anyone would notice if I just didn't go to the ball tonight?"

Sam laughed and pointed to the window in front of them. Mrs. Flanagan was sitting with Kate's dress, feverishly pulling a needle through it.

"Yeah." Kate sighed. "Not a chance. I guess I'll just have to be patient."

"Come on, let's go in. I've got to collect Harriet and head home," Sam said.

"Sam." Kate stopped. "You won't tell anyone, will you?"

"Course not." Sam smiled. "I want to be sure I'm the only one with the dirt on you!"

Kate punched him in the arm again, harder this time, and he yelped in pain. "Kate!"

Kate spun around. Mrs. Flanagan was standing on the front porch.

"I asked for it, Mrs. Flanagan," Sam said.

"Mmhmm." She did not appear impressed at all. "Your dress is ready. Come on."

Kate gave Sam a smile and headed up the stairs.

"Harri!" Sam called.

Harriet's face appeared in the doorway. "Do I have to go, Sam? Regina's going to let me try her dress on."

"You're a good three feet shorter than her!"

Harriet threw her head back with a groan. "Yes, but it will fit me one day!"

"Not if you don't get your behind out of that house right now," Sam warned her playfully.

Kate smiled. She loved these two.

"Fiiiiine." Harriet disappeared into the house and came out a moment later with her bag. "Let's go."

Sherie was a disappointed that Kate hadn't visited her. Granted, she was still in bed at five in the evening, but she thought that if Kate had come by, one of the girls would have come to wake her. Unless it was Molly who had seen her. Sherie was sure that while Molly might not know exactly what was going on between her and Kate, the details of which Sherie herself was unsure of, she didn't like the fact that right now she preferred spending time with her as opposed to Tom. She didn't feel torn so much as frustrated, knowing that her responsibility to her family and her home was to make sure she lay a solid foundation with Tom. It was clear that Molly expected Tom to propose after a little bit of flirting and a promise to be the girl of his dreams, but after spending time with him, Sherie knew it would take a lot more than that. Tom might be looking for a girl, but after giving up Prue it would take a very special girl to convince him to propose. She had a feeling that deep down they both knew they weren't right for each other. She was playing along because Molly had asked her to. She had told her it was the best way to make sure the Suds Bucket not only stayed in the family, but had enough money to stay open, but then why was Tom playing along? Sherie sat up, her stomach muscles crunching as she reached up and flipped her pillow over, the cool side of it relaxing the side of her face when she flopped back down onto it. Maybe there was another way, so she didn't have to marry Tom, hurting Kate in the process, in order to keep the Suds Bucket open. She wondered if they could re-vamp the business somehow, bring in some more girls...no. That was not an option. Raise the prices? Run away with Kate for good and never look back? As much as she was tempted by the latter option, she knew she could never leave her family, the other girls, or the Suds Bucket. Besides, Richmond was her home and she always swore she would never leave it. She was stuck here and she had to make the most of it. So she didn't have an answer right away…treading water was what she had done best these past five years, so for now, it was going to have to do.

She begrudgingly pulled herself out of bed and dropped onto the chair in front of the mirror.

"Ugh." She hardly looked beautiful right now. She had twisted her wet hair into a bun on the top of her head before she went to bed, and it had dried that way. She decided she didn't care enough to do anything about it. She pulled a plain dress over her head, tugged it into place, and headed downstairs.

Molly was cutting lemons behind the bar and Maggie was wiping down tables. Claire sat on the piano stool, stretched out, her face hidden behind her book, and Georgina and Olivia were not around, presumably upstairs getting ready.

"Hey, kiddo. I was about to come and get you. It's going to be a slow one tonight apparently. There's some ball going on in town and everyone's going," said Molly.

"Oh, thank God. I need a quiet night," said Sherie.

"No, we need a busy night. I've sent Georgina and Olivia down to the soldier camp to see if we can encourage some new business."

"I wasn't sexy enough to go," said Claire.

"I didn't say that. I said I wanted you to go upstairs and make yourself look more appealing," said Molly.

"Same thing," said Claire.

"Well, same thing or not, you're still down here with your nose in that damn book. Are you going to make a move or what?" Molly asked, her voice losing patience.

Claire sighed and closed her book emphatically. She marched upstairs, pinching Maggie's bum on her way past. Maggie squealed and dropped the cloth she was holding.

"Both of you should rub a little rouge into your cheeks too," said Molly, looking at Maggie and Sherie. "We're going to have to work hard if we're going to fill the beds tonight."

"Aye aye, Ma'am!" Maggie said, stamping her foot on the ground and briskly saluting Molly. "We've got soldiers to fuck! Better have rosy cheeks!" She picked the cloth up and threw it in Molly's direction.

"I'm tired, Mol," said Sherie. She walked up to the bar and let the top half of her body collapse on it. "Do I have to work tonight?"

"We're not going to make anywhere near as much as we usually make on drinks tonight. We need to be pushing for all-nighters in order to make any kind of a profit at all."

Sherie sighed. "Do you know if Tom's coming tonight?"

"He came by earlier today and I told him you weren't feeling very well."

"Thank you," said Sherie.

"No worries. Listen, though, I think he's really keen to make a move. He's coming over a lot more, and he's even come up with some ideas for how he thinks he can improve the Bucket's structure."

"Wow, that's great." Sherie did her best to smile, but she knew it probably didn't look all that convincing.

"I know he's not your true love, but you've said yourself in the past you don't believe in love."

"Yeah…" Sherie wished she could tell Molly about Kate. Really truly tell her about Kate. She knew that was definitely not an option.

"Okay, so go upstairs and get yourself looking gorgeous," said Molly.

Hah. That was going to take a mammoth effort tonight. Sherie reached for one of the lemon slices Molly had cut. "I look like shit," she said, and tilted her head back to squeeze the lemon into her eye.

"I still don't understand how you can do that," Molly said.

"It whitens your eyes."

"Yeah, but doesn't it sting like a bitch?"

"Well, yes, but you did say you wanted me to get myself looking gorgeous, didn't you?" Sherie was squeezing the lemon juice everywhere but her eyes.

"Give it here," Molly said. She took the slice of lemon from Sherie and pushed her head back a little further. The juice stung her when it dropped into her eyes, but she knew she needed to do it if she was going to get rid of the red.

"Gah! Dammit, that hurts!"

"Wow. They're whiter already!" Molly said.

"Do I look better now?" Sherie asked.

"You definitely don't look as tired. As for looking better? You need to fix that bird's nest on the top of your head and blush your cheeks up a bit."

"Okay." Sherie headed upstairs.

"Go into my room and get some of that alkanet salve from that Greek fellow, George something," Maggie shouted up to her.

"Georgios," Sherie called back.

Sherie was surprised at how little effort it had taken to look as good as she did, and that was saying something for the oft-humble woman. Her hair cascaded down her shoulders, and large natural curls sat perfectly, the most convenient result of a lazy bun left to dry overnight. Her lips were enticing, stained a spicy sweet burgundy that would no doubt be irresistible to the clients.

Georgina and Olivia had done a good job at convincing soldiers to visit the Suds Bucket. It wasn't as busy as usual, but there was certainly a large crowd downstairs drinking happily and enjoying the company of the raunchy women who were flirting with such a resolve that would see most men unable to contain themselves, disappearing to the bathroom with a hurried embarrassment to clean themselves up, hoping another drink or two would sort them out and put them back in the running to spend the night with one of them. The girls took advantage of the men who rarely frequented the bar, encouraging them to place their deposit early in order to 'secure their spot' with their favorite girl, promising free alcohol for all deposits placed before midnight. Of course, as soon as the deposit was placed, the man was fed the strongest liquor in the bar, "saved especially for you, handsome," and passed out in the corner without fail, long before midnight. Molly kept his money and re-booked the girl. They would wake him a few hours before daylight, with just enough time for him to panic and race back to either his wife, the barracks or his boss. A quick kiss goodbye and a breathy whisper of "thanks for last night. You were the best I've ever had" to top it all off, and the scheme worked almost every time with a newcomer. It wasn't honest, but as Molly always said, "If you come to a brothel expecting to screw us, don't be surprised when we screw you."

It was still early in the evening when an incredibly handsome and well-dressed young man walked through the doors of the Bucket. He approached Molly and said something to her, but Sherie was too far away and the bar was too loud for her to overhear. He looked slightly familiar, but she couldn't recall his name. She poured a glass of beer and waived Georgina over. "This is for your man," she said, still looking at the handsome newcomer.

"He isn't who he says he is," said Georgina.

"Who? Him?" asked Sherie. Georgina took the beer and nodded. "Who is he?"

"Booth."

"Booth?" The name was definitely familiar.

"Booth. Booth. Not what he appears." Georgina's pupils were dilated, more than likely due to the belladonna she had dropped into them, but her eyes were wide too. "Booth," she said abruptly, and Sherie jumped.

"Sherie, this is Sam Booth. He's asked for you." Molly held up a hand full of coins. "He's paying a lot."

Sherie smiled at Sam. Now she remembered. Sam's father was friends with their father and they had played together as kids. He was one of the boys they used to play with when they were little. He was the one who had fallen off the plank of wood between the two silos. She held back a giggle and wondered if he or Molly remembered.

"Hello, Sam," was all Sherie said.

"I heard you were the best," Sam said.

What an asshole, she thought. "Well, that depends on what you're after, but I can certainly be whatever you want," she said with a wink.

"Give him the special draught, Sherie," Molly told her.

Sherie made sure to pour him a double of their special security deposit draught.

"Sounds good to me," he said.

Ugh. Pass out already, you creep.

Sam sipped the concoction and started to cough violently. Clearly, he didn't drink very often.

"Woah, don't die!" Molly slapped him hard on the back and Sam struggled to speak.

"I'm fine," he choked. "Maybe we can just go upstairs now?"

Sherie did her best not to roll her eyes. May as well get it over with, and she still might have time for another client later on.

Sherie led Sam into her room. She noticed that his eyes lingered on the Pavo pattern dotted out in the top corner of her mirror, and suddenly he appeared very nervous.

"You okay?"

He nodded precariously.

"Are you a virgin?" she asked him.

He wiped his hands on his pants and that was enough of an answer for Sherie. "It's okay, we can go slow." She smiled.

"No, it's not that, I just…I didn't expect to be able to get up here so easily. I mean, I had this whole plan worked out for how I would manage to get you alone, and…it was so easy," Sam said.

"We aim to please," Sherie said. "Literally." She stepped forward and reached for the button on his pants.

"Oh, gosh, no, stop, I need to explain." Sam stepped back, his hands held up in front of him. "I don't want to sleep with you."

"Ah. That's okay. That's fine," Sherie said. *Thank God.* "Did you want to play a game? Or…" She motioned to the bag he was holding. "Did you want me to wear something in particular?"

Sam took a deep breath and took another step back. "I'm here for Kate," he said.

"What?" Sherie was not expecting him to say that.

Sam pulled a beautiful, pale gray dress from his bag. Sherie wasn't usually one for admiring dresses, but she couldn't stop herself from staring at this one. A simple yet elegant black lace trim adorned the bottom of the dress, with black velvet that snaked down into spiral loops.

"Here." Sam handed Sherie the dress and pulled something else out from his bag. "I've been told this is called a crinoline," he said, pulling it apart with his hands in an attempt to reshape it. He looked rather hilarious, blushing furiously as he struggled with the wire contraption. Sherie held her hand out.

"I know what a crinoline is," she said.

"I have to get you out of here somehow. Is there a back way?" Sam asked.

"Why?" Sherie was suspicious. It was well known that the Booth family was very close to the Flanagan family, and she was concerned that if someone had found out about her and Kate spending time together, it wouldn't be well-received information.

"I told you. I'm here for Kate." Sam looked at the window. "You could probably climb out here, but I don't think you would fit through wearing the dress. You'll have to put the crinoline and the rest of it on once you get to the bottom." Sam tried to hustle Sherie over to the window. "Once you're dressed, you're going to meet Kate at the corner of Henry and Bathurst. It's a while away from the hall, but you'll be riding from there together."

"Wait. Who says I trust you? I don't trust any of you lot." Sherie folded her arms and dropped the crinoline onto her bed.

"Hang on." Sam reached into his bag again. He pulled out a handful of small candles and placed them one by one on the floor, lighting each one as he placed it down. It wasn't until he put the fourth candle in position and lit it that Sherie realized what he was doing. With the last candle in place, Sam stepped back to reveal the shining constellation of Pavo lighting her dim bedroom.

Sherie's face erupted into a smile and her mood transitioned from concern to delight. "Pavo!" she squealed.

"Right. Now we have that cleared up you need to hurry or you'll be late."

"Where am I going?" Sherie asked, curious and excited.

"A ball being hosted by one of the farmers," Sam told her.

Sherie's face fell. "I wouldn't be welcome. You know that."

"Ah, but wait!" Sam pulled a mask out from his bag. It was painted silver and lined with what Sherie assumed were fake pearls, cleverly dusted to look like the real thing, but as she looked a little closer, she realized that they were in fact, real. Feathers decorated the top of the mask, adding height and flair, and a piece of elastic ran from one side of the mask to the other. "It's a masquerade ball. No one will know it's you."

Sherie was entirely unconvinced. "You know if they found out who I was, they'd throw me into the pig slop."

"Well, let's hope it doesn't come to that. You need to decide now, though, if you're going or not, because Kate will be waiting for you."

"Wahhhhh, okay! I'll go!" Sherie grabbed the mask from Sam. "Thank you," she added. She dropped the mask on the bed and stripped off her dress unabashedly. Sam blushed a brighter red than earlier and spun around quickly to face the door.

"You're sweet," Sherie said to the back of his head. She gathered the gray dress in her arms and picked up the mask again. Halfway out the window, she realized that Sam had only paid Molly for a few hours. She pulled herself back inside, almost tripping over Sam, who was standing close behind her.

"Too high? Can't do it?" Sam asked. "That's okay. We can find another way down."

"Pfft. Please. I'll be fine. I just need to make sure Molly doesn't come up here. Do you have any more money?"

Sam reached into his pockets and pulled out about five sovereigns. "How many?"

Sherie resisted her urge to tell him all five. He was after all doing her a big favor here. "Just one will be plenty," she said.

Sherie raced down the stairs and hurtled around the bar, bumping into Molly. "Mol!"

Molly looked alarmed. "What's going on? Did he hurt you?!"

"No, no, I'm fine. He's actually really funny. He's paid for me all night," Sherie said, handing the sovereign to Molly.

"Jesus, he must be really keen!" Molly admired the coin and pocketed it quickly. "Are you sure you can handle him all night? He's okay?"

Sherie put her hands behind her back and locked her fingers tightly together. Molly always knew when she was lying because she would rub her ears. It was a reflex that she could barely control, and as she spoke her knuckles turned white behind her back. "I'll be fine. He has a very tiny willy. I can hardly feel him. Honestly, it's the closest to a night off I'll get. For a sovereign, trust me, it's worth it."

Molly cackled. "Poor guy. Well, you, uh, have fun then? I guess?"

Sherie kissed Molly on the cheek. "Night, sis."

She ran upstairs and waited until she got into her bedroom and closed her door to scratch her ear roughly.

"All good?" asked Sam.

"Let's go!" Sherie launched herself out of the window.

Sam had dropped Sherie at the corner under a lamp, and even though her face was obscured by the delicate mask, she felt terrified being alone in this part of town. The dress fit almost perfectly, with the sleeves just a little too long, but Sherie liked the way they extended past her hands. Almost every inch of her body was hidden, save her lips, which were still a rich burgundy, and her soft, flawless complexion, which required no powdering whatsoever. She had been blessed with her mother's skin. Sherie was starting to think Kate wasn't going to show up until she saw Aiko's silhouette approaching from the distance. Kate looked lovelier than ever, and Sherie felt her jaw drop open when she rode closer, the glow of the street lamp illuminating her beauty. Kate's dress was a striking emerald green satin and black floral brocade lined with a stiff black lace that enhanced her neck. She was wearing a bodice, and Sherie guessed from the way Kate was moving that it had been laced rather tightly. Her sleeves extended out into full bells from her elbow, and the bottom was lined with more of the stiff black lace, and beaded with green dyed glass to look like emeralds. She climbed down carefully from Aiko and Sherie noticed that she was also wearing a large crinoline, easily twice the size of the one she was wearing, and a long train trailed behind her. All Sherie could do was shake her head in awe.

"Sherie?"

Sherie nodded, still unable to find the words to convey her surprise at just how stunning Kate looked. The young woman who stood before her was still Kate, but a very different version.

"You look beautiful," Kate said. "I'm sorry I'm late. I had no idea Sam was going to do this."

"You didn't?"

Kate shook her head. "He told me last minute. I had to convince my aunt to let me go alone—she didn't think I would show up."

Sherie reached out and touched Kate's hair. It was pulled back into a stylish bun, with most of her bangs swept to one side, the other side with a lighter more gentle curl with sparkling earrings that peeked out from behind.

"I know. It's a bit much." Kate frowned.

"You are the most beautiful being I have ever seen," Sherie whispered.

"I feel like a fool," Kate whispered back.

"Well, you look like a princess."

Kate turned toward Sherie and kissed her cheek lightly. "So do you."

Sherie was terrified when she walked into the hall, which had been brightly decorated to look like the most sophisticated of ballrooms, but her apprehension eased as she realized that no one was anywhere close to making the connection to who she actually was. She received the kindest compliments throughout the evening, and for a second she almost forgot that she was not one of them.

She froze when she ran into Josh and John, but they simply smiled, bowed, and told her that she looked beautiful. The disguise had been working exceptionally well, and Sherie was having a wonderful time. She was actually enjoying the company of these people, in particular Mrs. Flanagan, who had had her laughing all evening. It turns out they actually had quite a lot in common, and Sherie found her to be most pleasant indeed. Guests were dancing with an air of lightness about them the atmosphere was very different to that of the Suds Bucket. Life was good in this room. Sherie fit in perfectly.

Kate and Sherie took turns dancing with Sam, as well as Josh and John, and Sherie sniggered silently as she made a point of stepping on their feet more than once while they danced.

"Your friend is beautiful, Kate, but I'm afraid she can't dance to save herself!" John taunted.

Sherie laughed. "I'm not used to dancing so elegantly!"

John sidled closer to her. "Oh, no? What kind of dancing are you used to?"

Kate swooped in immediately and stole her away. "I think we need a drink," she said.

Sherie threw John a little wave as she was escorted away by Kate.

"I know I told you to relax, but you need to watch what you say! You're going to get caught!"

"Katie, Katie, beautiful Katie, I'm not going to get caught. I'm wearing a mask!" Sherie chuckled as she pointed to it, lifting it off her face slightly and letting it go, allowing the elastic to snap the mask back down into place.

"Are you drunk?" Kate asked.

"Are you sober?" Sherie retorted.

"Oh boy, come on, let's get some air!"

They moved to the edge of the hall, close to an open window nearby Mrs. Flanagan and Regina. Across the room they could see Josh by the drinks table, surreptitiously pouring something into the punch.

Mrs. Flanagan leaned into Kate. "Katie, go set your cousin straight before he gets us all thrown out, would you?"

Kate made her way over to Josh, who had started to pour himself a large glass of whatever it was he had just used to spike the punch. Kate took the glass from him and tipped it back into the punch. He protested when she picked up the entire bowl of punch and tipped it out of the closest window. She put the empty bowl back down on the stand and grabbed Josh's hands, pulling him out onto the dance floor with her. Sam crept up from behind Kate and snatched the mask off her face. She spun around, struggling to get her mask back, but she was laughing too much to make any attempt that wasn't feeble. Sam played with her for a minute before handing it back. Kate snatched it from him and shoved it back over her face.

Regina leaned into Mrs. Flanagan and Sherie. "She seems to be settling in finally, considering..."

Considering what? Sherie realized suddenly that she knew absolutely nothing about why Kate had moved to Richmond in the first place.

"It's such a shame that she's so caught up with those whores over at..." Regina jerked her head toward the direction of the door, obviously indicating the Suds Bucket.

Sherie tensed instantly. She reached up and touched her mask to make sure it was still properly in place.

"I wasn't even sure she would come tonight. She's been awfully moody ever since we told her what those women were like. It's so nice to see her with different friends for a change," said Mrs. Flanagan, nudging Sherie. Sherie smiled with a cringe.

"I just hope she realizes before it's too late and people start talking," Regina said.

Mrs. Flanagan let out a sigh. "People are already talking," she said.

While Mrs. Flanagan and Regina were still looking at Kate, Sherie took the opportunity to slip away, out the nearest door.

Sherie stormed down the street, mask-less. Droplets of rain began to fall on her face, indistinguishable from the tears that were already streaming. She got perhaps a hundred meters before Kate appeared in the distance, running to catch up to her.

"Sherie! Stop. What happened?" Kate sounded out of breath, probably due to the corset she was wearing. Sherie didn't care.

"Why did you leave?" Kate asked.

Sherie didn't slow down. "I told you I didn't belong!"

Kate tripped as she tried to match Sherie's pace. "Can you slow down, please? Hey!" She tried to grab Sherie's shoulders. "STOP!" she shouted finally.

The rain started to fall a little heavier and thunder rumbled across the sky. Sherie pushed Kate's hand from her shoulders. "Get off me! Haven't you realized you're socializing with the scum of the town, Kate? I'm so fed up of being judged by you people!"

Kate stood there, looking stunned. "I thought you didn't care what people think about you?"

"You obviously don't know me at all," Sherie shouted, allowing the rain to fall down on her face and hide her tears.

She turned away from Kate and stalked off again, headed for home. She would have kept walking and not looked back if she hadn't heard Kate's yell behind her, not desperate for her to turn around but indicating that she was in pain. Sherie spun around to see Kate surrounded by Bucket regulars. Warren had her in a headlock and Billy punched her, first in the stomach and then in the face. Sherie screamed and ran back toward Kate without hesitation. She tried to pull Warren off Kate, but was about as helpless as a puppy trying to eat a great blue whale in less than twenty seconds. Warren swatted

Sherie off him like a fly and she flew into a bench outside a nearby shop. She looked helplessly at Kate, who looked back at her, suddenly furious. She threw Billy off her and into a pole holding up a veranda. The pole cracked and the roof of the veranda collapsed on Billy. Warren ran at Kate, but she was already on the offense. She blocked his attack and punched him in the gut. She grabbed the scruff of his neck and pulled down as she kneed him between the legs. Warren keeled over. Billy was back on his feet and made another move at Kate. Kate and Billy traded a few blows before she finally got the upper hand and finished him off, throwing him back into the rubble of the collapsed veranda roof.

Despite blood gushing out of her eyebrow and lip, Kate hurried over to Sherie. "Are you okay?" she asked.

Sherie nodded, but she was shaking inside and couldn't stop herself from sobbing. She folded her arms across her body, and tried to make herself as small as possible. Kate stumbled when she tried to put an arm around her. Sherie looked up and noticed how much blood was gushing out from her face. "I'm so sorry. This is all my fault," she said.

Kate coughed and spat some blood out of her mouth. "Not true."

"I'm damaged goods," Sherie told her.

The rain fell heavily on them now, and the thunder growled loudly. Kate took Sherie's head in her hands and stared into her eyes. "Sometimes a few scars make the soul more beautiful." She leaned in toward Sherie and kissed her on the forehead. "Come on."

They stumbled back up the road toward the hall.

Josh, Sam, and Mr. Flanagan were all outside the hall smoking cigarettes.

Perfect. Sherie looked for her mask, but she had lost it during the fight at some point. Mr. Flanagan noticed them instantly. "What the hell is going on?"

Kate wiped her face in an attempt to clean herself up, but she stumbled as she approached. Sherie held her up as best she could, and Josh rushed over to try and take her.

"I'm fine," Kate said, refusing to let go of Sherie. She held her tightly and pushed Josh away. "It's nothing," she said. Josh eyed Sherie furiously.

"Don't give me that, Katherine. You're a mess," Mr. Flanagan said sternly. He turned to look at Sherie, accusingly. "What happened?"

Sherie buckled slightly under Kate's weight but didn't let go of her. Sam ran to the other side of Kate to help hold her up. "It was Billy and Warren," Sherie said.

"No surprise it was your lot," spat Josh.

Sherie threw daggers from her eyes at him. "They are NOT my lot."

"I saw Billy talking to your bloody sister last night," he shot back.

"Molly?" she asked, confused. Sherie looked at Kate, but Kate was starting to fade quickly. Mr. Flanagan noticed this too and stepped in to take Kate from Sherie. "Come on, Kate, let's get you home."

"No! All of you, back off! I'm fine!" Kate pushed everyone away, including Sherie, and stood for herself. She shuffled over to Aiko, who was tied to a post a few meters away. Sherie remained in a standoff with Josh, who had moved to block her path, stopping her from following Kate.

Mr. Flanagan turned around and walked inside angrily muttering about stubborn kids who never learn. Kate pulled herself up onto the horse slowly and brought Aiko around in between Sherie and Josh. "Little one?" she asked, reaching down and offering her hand to Sherie.

Sherie turned and climbed onto the horse.

"Tell your sister to watch her back. This is your last warning," Josh said.

Sam stepped in, finally. "Josh, come on, mate, settle down," he said.

Sherie didn't respond. She took the reins from Kate's hands and kicked Aiko into motion. Kate rested her head on Sherie's shoulders and tugged the reins gently, steering Aiko in the right direction.

The ride back to Kate's house was a short one, but it was long enough for both of them to calm down. Sherie felt her heart slow, and once the adrenaline had left her body, she felt a splitting ache rip across her brow. She was very much sober now, and in a lot of pain. She felt Kate's legs gripping hers from behind her, and she reached around to rub her leg as they arrived.

"We're here."

Kate grunted and moved her body weight from Sherie. Sherie jumped down as smoothly as she could, and reached up to help Kate down. Taking her hand, Kate half slid, half jumped off Aiko, falling into Sherie's arms. It was dark, and Sherie wanted to get Kate inside in order to see how badly she was hurt. It was a difficult task, getting Kate up the stairs. She moved slowly, her breath heavy and uncomfortable. They paused in the middle of the stairs and Kate held on to the railing and took a break.

"Look at this ridiculous thing you're wearing—no wonder you can hardly breathe," said Sherie, playing with the green laces of Kate's corset. She untied the bows, which had been knotted tightly, and loosened the back of the dress. "Does that feel a bit better?"

Kate nodded. "Much."

Kate dropped onto her bed as soon as they got into her room. Sherie looked for a lamp that she could light, finding one on a nearby shelf. Checking quickly to make sure Kate was okay and not bleeding too badly, she rushed back downstairs, praying that the Flanagans had a water pump inside. She found the kitchen and looked around as fast as she could, sure that the rest of Kate's family would probably not spend too much more time at the ball after Mrs. Flanagan was told about what had happened. She felt curtains and pulled them open, hoping the moon would give her enough light to find what she needed. Luckily for Sherie, Mrs. Flanagan kept an impeccable kitchen, and though the light that shone through the window was dim, she was able to locate the items she needed quickly. Her evening gown didn't happen to boast any pockets, so Sherie shoved a few rags down the front of her dress, improvising. She found a bowl and dipped it into a bucket of water that sat on the kitchen counter, filling it to the top. She drew the curtains and rushed back upstairs.

When she returned, Kate wasn't on her bed, and Sherie lost her heart for a moment until she realized that she was sitting in front of a piano in the back corner of the room that managed to avoid the light cast by the lamp. Sherie picked up the lamp and carried it over to Kate, who winced at its brightness.

"I'm going to clean you up," Sherie whispered, hoping her gentle words would convince Kate that she wasn't going to hurt her. Not anymore.

Kate had pulled off the top layers of her dress, left wearing a loose fitting white camisole and matching drawers. Sherie could see discoloration had already started to form around her ribs, where Billy had punched her. She reached out and let her fingers skim across the top of Kate's bruised skin, barely touching her but feeling the energy leave her fingertips, willing it to scatter across her stomach and heal her. "I wish I—"

Kate put two fingers over Sherie's mouth, stopping her words and looking into her eyes. "Shh."

Kate's eyes were as fiery as ever, but Sherie noticed a small cut above her brow that was dripping blood onto her drawers, and a cut on her bottom lip too. She pulled the rag out of the bowl and squeezed it tightly to get rid of as much excess water as possible. She dabbed slowly at the cuts, taking such care that Kate didn't flinch even once. She dabbed carefully until the cuts were clean and the water in the bowl was stained a murky blood brown.

Sherie put the bowl and rags on the bedside table and sat down on the bed, facing Kate. She realized that the piano she was sitting at was covered. "Looks like you haven't played this for a while," she said.

Kate shook her head. "I haven't felt moved enough to play since..."

"Since what?" Sherie was reminded of the conversation she overheard at the ball, and remembered that she was desperate to know what exactly had happened for Kate to end up in Richmond.

"I just haven't felt a strong enough reason to play," was all she said. She walked over to her wardrobe and pulled the doors open. The top half of her body disappeared inside it for a moment while she searched for something, emerging with a charred wooden box. She gripped the box tightly with two hands as she walked back to Sherie and sat down beside her on the bed. She opened the box slowly, and pulled out a piece of paper that looked like it was sheet music. She passed it to Sherie, who admired it, despite not understanding a single note of it.

"You wrote this?" she asked.

Kate nodded. She looked at the music notes over Sherie's shoulders.

"Can I try?" Sherie asked, holding the sheet up in the direction of the piano. "I've never played a piano before."

Kate walked over to the piano and pulled its covers back. "Maybe it's something you're good at." She smiled.

Sherie grinned as Kate lifted up the heavy lid that covered the ivory keys, pulled out the chair and motioned for Sherie to sit down. Sherie put the sheets on the ledge and sat down. Kate sat down behind her and put her legs on either side of Sherie, forcing her to scoot forwards slightly to give Kate enough room to fit on the chair with her. She leaned back very gently and pressed her shoulder blades against Kate's chest. It was like the electricity had never left, but was just waiting to be ignited by the touch of their skin. Kate swallowed hard and pointed to the first note on the sheet music, and then to a key on the piano. Sherie pressed the key and the note reverberated across the room and lingered on the tension in the air. Kate pointed to the next note on the sheet music and then to the corresponding key. Sherie pressed it and held it for a moment before releasing it and let her hands drop to her lap.

She leaned back into Kate again and inhaled deeply, her breath shuddering as if even her lungs were terrified by the strength of her feelings. Kate placed her hands on the piano keys, and Sherie put her hands on top of Kate's. Kate started to play a few bars of a simple yet beautiful melody. Sherie tilted her head back into Kate's shoulders and she let the music drift through her as it gained in momentum. She felt her hand move up Kate's arm and then around to clasp the back of Kate's head while she continued to play. Sherie closed her eyes and let her hands act on their own accord, as if they were boldly doing the things they knew Sherie was too scared to follow through with. Her fears started to evaporate when she felt Kate dip her head into her neck, and she wondered for a second if she had felt a soft wet kiss on her collarbone, or if she was imagining things.

Their breathing deepened while the music began to growl with lower notes and a slower rhythm. Sherie lost her breath as Kate ran the tip of her nose up her neck, stopping when she reached her ear. She definitely felt a soft kiss dot the bone below her earlobe this time. She moved her other hand from Kate's, which was still playing music, and moved it down Kate's side, running across her rib cage and along her thigh, dragging her fingers softly over Kate's drawers, stepping them one by one past the ruffled seam to find her bare skin, rough with goose bumps and radiating warmth. Sherie turned her head in Kate's direction and Kate leaned forward too.

Sherie's heart rumbled and it felt like it had melted and started to rush throughout her entire body, causing her hair to stand up and her fingertips to pulsate. She leaned in to kiss her, but at the last moment, she rested her forehead against Kate's instead and moved both of her hands back to where they had started, on top of Kate's.

Kate continued to play for a few more beats, before she turned her hands up and grasped Sherie's tightly, their fingers interlocking when the music stopped instantly. In the sudden silence, their hands fell from the piano, down to their sides, remaining intertwined, and with all the courage she possessed, Sherie closed the remaining distance between them and kissed Kate passionately on her lips. She fell into the kiss, her soul melting into Kate's as her body collapsed and she felt Kate's arms wrap tightly around her. She had never felt so vulnerable and so safe at exactly the same moment. Breaking their kiss, they stood up slowly, neither one needing to communicate while they moved together. Sherie turned around fully to face Kate, their eyes locking instantly. Whatever was left of Sherie's heart stopped beating and froze when she found herself in Kate's eyes. Kate reached around and started to untie Sherie's dress, not breaking eye contact for a second. Sherie stared right back at her, holding her gaze as she stepped out of her dress toward Kate. She lifted Kate's camisole over her head, finding more goose bumps on her naked chest that rose up and down in the moonlight with her heavy breathing. She touched her stomach against Kate's and she rolled her body upwards, slowly closing the gap until there was nothing between them and she could feel their hearts pounding together, completely out of sync but creating a perfect rhythm between them as they beat. She placed a light kiss on Kate's collarbone and pulled back to trace her fingers along Kate's chest. She dotted Pavo out on Kate's breast with her finger and then followed the same pattern with her lips, giving gentle kisses.

Kate pulled her closer and Sherie knew that even if the entire surface of her body were touching Kate, it would never be enough. She let a short hum escape, happiness encapsulated as she allowed Kate to pull her down onto the bed.

The rain pelted hard down on the window, and through it, Pavo shone brightly above them in the night sky.

Chapter 17

Molly cleaned the last table and wiped her brow with a cloth before putting it in her apron pocket. It had been a very long, very slow evening, and even though all the girls had managed to secure a client who wished to spend the whole night with them, they hadn't sold anywhere near as much alcohol as they usually did, which was a big problem for her, considering that was where the bulk of the profit came from. On top of the piano, Olivia's latest vase stood triumphantly, still in one piece.

She sighed and turned off the gas lamp on the wall by the front entrance. She was about to turn off the lamp on the opposite side of the door when it suddenly opened, and Tom appeared.

"Evenin' darling." Tom's grin faded fast as he looked around at the empty, silent bar.

Molly shrugged. Great—this was just what she needed, for Tom to see the Suds Bucket on a quiet night. Hardly the most brilliant investment. This was why she needed Sherie to convince him to invest in *her*, not just the Bucket. "Sherie's with a client all night. Sorry, Tom," she said.

"Well, maybe I didn't come to see Sherie."

Molly sighed. This was perfect. He really didn't appear all that interested in Sherie, and her damned sister didn't seem to care. Her plan was not working and she really didn't have enough time left to let the pieces fall into place gradually. She was going to have to do something about it herself if she wanted things to move faster than they were doing.

"Drink?" Molly asked.

Tom nodded and took his hat off, setting it at the end of the bar. Molly poured him a double of whiskey, his liquor of choice.

"Cheers." He gave her a wink and tipped the glass to the ceiling.

"Thirsty?" Molly laughed.

Tom swirled the liquid around in his glass. "You gonna have one?"

"Me? No." Molly took the rag from her pocket and threw it into the pile of dirty washing behind the bar.

"Come on, Mol, have a drink with me. If we're going to be family, then I'd like to get to know you," said Tom.

He had a somewhat childish grin, and Molly liked that about him. *If we're going to be family.* So he did still plan on moving things forward with Sherie, despite what appeared to be every effort on her part to ignore him. Tom walked behind the bar and pulled a bottle of whiskey from the shelf behind him. He poured a long, golden stream into a glass and put the glass up to Molly's lips. Molly found herself laughing with Tom as she pursed her lips and refused to drink, shaking her head with a giggle.

"What's wrong? This delicious drink isn't good enough for you?" Tom put the glass to his own lips and downed it in one. "How about something sweeter, just like yourself?"

"Okay, now I know you're full of shit," said Molly, lamely pushing his arms away as he tried to capture her, wrapping his arms around her waist. He picked her up and pointed her in the direction of the alcohol.

"Pick your poison," he ordered her.

Molly looked over their selection of liquor on offer. They distilled a lot of different alcohol to kill time, but they rarely sold anything other than whiskey, rum, and beer. She plucked a bottle of port from the shelf and waved it down at Tom. He dropped her quickly and without warning and she squealed, but he caught her before she could hit the ground. He held her tightly for a moment and Molly could have sworn she felt something throb as he slid her slowly down until her feet touched the sticky wooden floorboards. Tom eyed the bottle she held.

"I knew you liked it sweet," he said.

Molly poured herself a glass of port and topped Tom's glass up with whiskey. She placed a palm on the bar and jumped up on top of it, swinging her legs around so that they dangled down the front and she faced Tom.

"Aren't you quite the little acrobat?" he taunted.

Molly raised a single eyebrow at Tom and took another swig of port. "So when are you going to propose to my sister?"

"There it is! I wondered how long you'd last before bringing it up!"

Molly blushed. "You know me. I'm a business woman."

"Seriously, Molly? You're putting love in the same category as business?"

Molly leaned forward. She could smell the port on her own breath. "Come on, Tom, you and I both know that it's not about love."

Tom reached out and tugged Molly's hair mischievously. "So what's it about then?"

"I've told you. This is a great opportunity for you to invest your money into a growing business," she said.

"So why all the talk of going broke, and needing my money to keep it open then? Hm? And the repairs to the structure? Is that an investment opportunity too?"

"Who have you been talking to? Claire?" asked Molly.

"It's the talk of the town. The wealthy are hoping you'll go broke and the others are drinking as much as they can afford to in order to keep you open," Tom said.

Molly smiled. She liked the sound of that, and made a mental note to talk about the possibility that they might close in front of a few more people. Boosting sales was always a good thing.

"Besides, what if I don't want to invest in a brothel? I'm having a hard enough time as it is trying to get the people of Richmond to accept me into their circles, and I've got more money than most of them combined! Do you really think they'll let me in to their exclusive little parties if I'm the part owner of the Suds Bucket?" Tom was no longer joking around.

"So, what if we don't keep it open as a brothel? What if we turn it back into a home?" Molly took another drink of port and held it in her mouth, the liquor burning her gums.

"What would happen to the other girls?"

"They can be relocated," said Molly.

"Relocated?" Tom's head reeled backwards slightly, but he stepped in closer toward Molly. "As in, what? Kill them?" he whispered.

Molly threw her head back with a roar of laughter. "Of course not! Come on!" She ruffled his hair and jumped down off the bar. She stumbled when she landed and Tom caught her. "All these girls came here a long time ago, broken and messy because they had nowhere else to go. I gave them an opportunity to muster up a little self-confidence and get their lives in order. If we told them we were closing, I'm sure they would all go find jobs somewhere else. They like what they do. I don't think they'd stop doing it just because we closed our doors."

"Are you sure? I'm not so convinced they wouldn't take the opportunity to better themselves," said Tom.

"Better themselves? Why, does sleeping with men for money mean they're automatically assigned a lower station in life?"

Tom looked at her quizzically. She realized it sounded like a trick question.

"People assume that just because a woman uses her body to earn a living it's something temporary, and that she's looking for an out. Have you spent five minutes talking to Olivia? She loves what she does!"

"I have. She told me her story, how she's waiting for Marion. She said she used to love it, but that something changed," Tom said.

"When did she say that?"

"The other night at dinner. We actually had a long talk. When was the last time you spoke to the girls? I think you'll find none of them are particularly happy."

"What the hell is 'particularly happy'? Who the hell is 'particularly happy'? No one in this God-forsaken country is 'particularly happy,' Tom. Why don't you bugger off back to England then?" Molly spat.

"Calm down, Mol."

Tom tipped more port in Molly's glass and she picked it up and took a swig before he had finished pouring. It sloshed out of the bottle and spilled all over the floor.

"Damn it, Tom!" Molly shouted.

Tom grabbed Molly's hand as she slammed her fist onto the bar. "Molly!" She looked up into his eyes. They were bloodshot and frustrated, and suddenly she noticed that she was very drunk.

"I need to go to bed," she said.

"D'you want me to help you up the stairs?" Tom asked.

Molly shot him a blank stare and she struggled to release her wrists from his grip. "I can manage by myself."

Tom let go of her. "I don't doubt you can, but would you humor me?"

Molly pushed him back forcefully with both hands. "Fine."

She stumbled up the stairs, wondering how she had become so drunk so quickly, until she remembered that she had barely eaten anything at all today. That and the fact that she had been feeling worse and worse lately about everything in general. Being concerned with her own health was hardly the most important thing on her long list of things to worry about.

Tom was the perfect gentleman, holding her up without trying to grab her anywhere inappropriately. She gave him a pat on the back as he led her over to her bed.

"Come by in the morning if you want to see Sherie," Molly told him.

"I will," Tom said. He squeezed her elbow affectionately and turned to leave.

"Tom," Molly said. Tom paused in the doorway. "Come here."

She watched him hesitate, probably unsure as to whether she was going to make a move on him or not. She appreciated that he seemed reluctant to take advantage of her. This was why she wanted him to marry Sherie. She knew she could trust him.

She stood up, somewhat unbalanced, and shuffled over to the jewelry box that had once belonged to her mother. She opened it and pulled out her mother's wedding ring. It wasn't extravagant—a delicately beautiful silver band with a small pearl in between two diamonds. Whether or not they were actually diamonds, Molly wasn't sure of, but the fact that the ring had belonged to her mother added enough value to it, so the makeup of the actual stones was irrelevant.

"Here. This was my mother's." She handed the ring to Tom.

"It's beautiful," he said. "Keep it for now. I'll think about it a little more."

Molly refused to take it back from him. "No, take it," she said.

"What if I want to give it back to you?" asked Tom.

"What, and buy Sherie a ring of your choosing?" She supposed that would make sense, though she didn't understand why he didn't think this ring was perfect for Sherie.

"No, I mean what if I want to propose to the other Kelly sister?"

Molly froze as she processed what he said. "What?"

"I could marry you instead," he said.

Molly laughed. "Believe me when I say you would get far more than you bargained for."

"Well, what would be wrong with that?"

"Trust me, you don't want to know," said Molly.

"You're not telling me something."

Molly pushed him out the door. She didn't like that he could see past her jokes. "Tell me it wouldn't work exactly the same way if I married you instead of Sherie. At the end of the day it's the same result, isn't it?"

"You made a promise and I expect you to keep it," said Molly.

"Wait!" Tom struggled as Molly tried to close the door. "Hang on now, why won't you—"

Molly slammed the door shut, locked it, and ran over to her bed, collapsing on it and pulling a pillow tightly over her head. She screamed and sobbed into the pillow, wishing things could be different, until she passed out.

Molly stood at the window with her arms folded, waiting. Her dark disposition complimented the somber mood at the Suds Bucket that morning. She knew Sherie wasn't in her bedroom because she hadn't raced downstairs with the rest of them earlier when they heard Georgina scream. The scream was rich with horror and Molly felt the uneasiness soak through her body as the decibels stabbed at her ears, cutting across what had been up until that moment a peaceful dawn. They had only heard this particular scream one time before—when they woke to find Georgina's baby missing from her cradle, so when the same pitches woke Molly this morning she flew downstairs with alarm, Claire and Olivia in front and Maggie just a heartbeat behind. They had found Georgina on the front porch, her legs wobbling as she faced the dead bodies of her four canaries. They littered the balcony amongst an array of headless crows, a sea of motionless black and yellow save their feathers, which were fluttering in the breeze. The entire front wall of the Bucket, including the window, had been slapped crudely with red paint that read 'WHORE HOUSE.' Blood marks made spattered circles across the words and oozed down to the chair where Molly and Sherie usually sat, currently hosting the decapitated crows' heads, the source of the bloody blotches on the wall above.

The stench was powerful. It smelled almost like hay, but instead of the pleasant wooden taste, it was an overpowering dirty iron, mashed with slowly rotting guts and flesh, and marinated by the tiny feet of a thousand flies. Georgina dropped to her knees and wailed. Her mouth fell open and saliva spilled out from both sides. It was as if her muscles had stopped working, and she collapsed sideways. Olivia caught her before she hit her head on the bench next to her, and with some help from Maggie, they scooped her up and carried her inside.

A few hours bad passed and Georgina was still a complete mess. She sat on the floor, slumped forward, propped up by Olivia and Claire. She was shaking, and only lifted her head very slightly to take sips of water that were being offered to her by Maggie every few minutes.

From the window, Molly saw a cloud of dust in the distance. *There she is.*

She wasn't disappointed by the horrified looks on their faces as Kate and Sherie walked up the steps. Sherie buried her face into Kate's chest, and Kate folded her arms over Sherie's head, taking the lead and directing her into the bar. Molly's eyes narrowed. She had no idea that this little relationship was… she couldn't even describe it to herself. Whatever it was, it was time to put a stop to it.

Sherie looked at Georgina. "What happened?" Her voice broke and trailed away before she could manage to utter both words properly.

Georgina looked up. She stood up and walked towards them, stopping within inches of Kate's face. She reached up and touched the cut above Kate's eyebrow softly and then glanced down at their hands. Molly looked too. Kate's and Sherie's little fingers were hooked around each other, and Kate was rubbing the top of Sherie's hand with her thumb. Georgina looked up again into Kate's eyes before giving a sharp nod. She turned away and walked up the stairs.

"Let's sort the birds out," Olivia said. Maggie followed her outside, while Claire motioned that she was going after Georgina and disappeared upstairs. Sherie grabbed a slop bucket from the bar and took it outside. Kate moved to follow, but Molly stopped her.

"You're ruining her life, you know. You're running it into the ground. If you cared about her, you'd leave today and never come back," Molly said.

"Excuse me?" asked Kate.

"Don't play dumb with me. We both know who did this." Molly jerked her head over to where the red paint had marred the window, drenching the sunlight that poured through the glass with a blood red stain.

Kate looked almost amused, and this infuriated Molly even more. "Please. I'm not so quick to believe this pathetic 'best friend' act you've got going on Molly. You know, if you hadn't arranged that little beating last night, this probably wouldn't have happened, and the Bucket would have been fine." Molly opened her mouth to reply, but Kate wasn't finished. "But then again…we all know you don't give a damn about the Bucket, don't we?"

"Do you really think you can come between my sister and me?" Molly's voice was dangerous. She stepped in closer to Kate, but stopped when Sherie re-entered the room holding a bucket full of dead crows.

Kate retreated toward the front door. "I've gotta go." She squeezed Sherie's hand as she passed her.

Sherie held on to her hand and pulled Kate back in towards her. "Come by after?" she asked.

Kate leaned in and planted a kiss on Sherie's head. "Of course," she said, shooting a defiant look at Molly before she turned around and walked out the door. Sherie walked through the Bucket and out the back door with the bucket of crows.

Molly debated on chasing after Kate and warning her not to come back, but after considering her options for a moment, she changed her mind. She walked behind the bar, opened the safe, and pulled out a bag of money. She put the bag at the bottom of an empty crate and then tipped a pile of empty beer bottles on top of it. She hoisted the crate onto her hip and followed Sherie outside.

Sherie sat on the ground, poking holes into the dirt, to form the shape of the Pavo constellation. Molly needed to remind Sherie what was important. She disappeared under the Bucket and put the crate down as far back as she could, deep in the shadows where she was certain it would not be seen, and then hurried over toward Sherie. "You okay?"

Sherie looked up. Her face was red, and there were still tears in her eyes. She shook her head. "Not really. When did everything start to get so hard?"

Molly wished she could answer her truthfully. "It's all going to be alright," she said.

Sherie prodded the ground with her stick.

"Tom's coming over later to help clean up the window," Molly said. Sherie rolled her eyes, annoying Molly. "Sherie, you know how much money we're losing every day, don't you?"

Sherie nodded.

"And you know how much Tom loves you?"

"I'm not so sure about that," Sherie said.

"Well, get sure. Marrying him is the only way you're going to survive this."

"I think we've done pretty well so far," said Sherie.

"Gee, Sherie, you're right! You've been fucking men for money since you were sweet sixteen, Claire thinks she's fine when she's used as a punching bag, she's more colorful than a bloody rainbow, Georgina's bloody nuts and she thinks that doll of hers is a real baby, and I…" she trailed off, stopping herself from getting carried away. She took a calming breath and continued when she was certain she had regained composure. "Imagine how disappointed Dad is going to be when he comes back and sees what our lives have become."

Sherie sighed and looked at Molly sideways through her hair. "Can I tell you something?"

Molly put her arm around her. "Of course you can."

"Part of me hopes Dad never comes back. You're right, you know." Sherie started to cry again. "We have screwed everything up. We were meant to look after this place, and look what we've done…we've turned it into a…into a…" Her sobs became audible and her body started to shake as she cried. "Whore house!" She collapsed into Molly's arms, wailing.

Molly held her tight. "It's okay, it's okay."

"We're working so hard all the time and it's for nothing." Sherie's words melted together as she wept.

Molly kissed the top of Sherie's head, tears forming in her own eyes. "I know, kiddo. But sometimes working hard isn't good enough. We have to do whatever it takes to be happy, right? Whatever it takes."

Sherie's cries died down slowly and the two sat in silence for a while.

"Whether Dad comes home or not," Sherie took a few deep breaths, "I don't think I can keep this up much longer. I don't think any of us can. You too, Mol. I know you try to be strong, but I hear you crying still sometimes. You used to let me in and tell me everything, and I wish you still would. You look terrible, you know. Oh, Mol, I don't mean it in a mean way, but you've lost a lot of weight and it's like you're always sick. You're not healthy like you used to be. I know you know what I'm talking about." She looked up at Molly, who avoided her eyes for as long as she could before she gave up and looked at her.

"You're right," Molly said. Sherie pulled her in for a tight hug. "I'll try to open up to you a little more, okay?

Sherie nodded.

"You know how we can get out of this mess, don't you?"

Sherie didn't say anything. Molly gave her shoulders a shake for an answer.

"I guess," said Sherie.

Molly smiled. "I talked to Tom about you last night."

"You did?"

Molly nodded. "He said he didn't want the Bucket to be a brothel anymore either."

"Oh."

"Oh? That's what you just told me you wanted, didn't you?"

"Yes, but isn't he looking for an investment?"

"I think more than that he's looking for someone to love," said Molly.

Sherie chuckled. "Isn't everybody?"

Molly laughed with her and gave her shoulders another squeeze. "Maybe, if we closed down the Bucket and turned it back into a quiet little home, then Richmond would start talking to us again."

"THAT will not happen," said Sherie. "We're scum."

"Nonsense. Don't you ever believe that for a second!" Molly snapped.

"I don't," said Sherie.

"Good. You'd be surprised, Sherie. If the right people spoke up for us, everyone else would follow suit soon enough. Maybe then you could spend time with your friend in public instead of, oh, I don't know, sneaking around and lying to your family about where you're going," Molly said.

Sherie blushed. "I'm sorry, I—"

"It's okay," Molly cut her off. "Just don't disappear without telling me again, okay? Look what happened to the Bucket last night. What if those people had found you?"

Sherie scoffed. "Yet you still think they'd forget how much they hate us if we just decided to close down?"

Molly shrugged. "Maybe,"

"Well, that's a nice dream to have."

"It starts with you and Tom, you know?"

Sherie nodded.

"Good girl. Now, get yourself upstairs and clean your face up. He'll probably be around soon."

Sherie wiped her eyes and went back inside the Bucket. Molly stood up and kicked dirt over the constellation. She waited to make sure no one was going to come outside, and then disappeared back under the Bucket to retrieve the crate. She carried it around to the front of the building and walked nonchalantly up the steps. The balcony was clean of dead birds now, despite the bloody words that appeared to have stained the wood. She reminded herself to talk to Tom or James about replacing those panels. She peered through the window but didn't see anyone inside. She walked back down the stairs, stopping in the middle and crouching over the third step. She pulled out a loose nail and peeled the wood back, revealing her hidden stash of money. She reached into the crate trying not to jostle the glass bottles, and pulled out the bag of money. She dropped it gently into the hole and it thudded against the other bags already in there. She did a quick calculation of roughly how much she had by now. It was definitely enough. She dropped the step back into place and replaced the nail. Now all she needed was for Tom to propose to Sherie, and everything would be as she had planned.

Back inside, she returned the crate to its place behind the bar and headed upstairs.

The day passed quietly. No one went out onto the balcony at all, the girls instead spending most of their time in Georgina's bedroom comforting her, except for Molly, who chose to spend the day alone in her own room. From Georgina's room, Sherie could see the road below and she couldn't stop herself from glancing at it every few minutes to see if Kate had come back yet. Disappointingly, she didn't show up, but neither did Tom, which made Sherie feel somewhat better. Whether or not Tom actually loved her (and she didn't believe that he did) was not the point. She needed Kate the way she needed to breathe, and even though she wasn't naïve enough to believe Molly when she said that things could go back to the way they used to be, part of her wished it could be true. She could freely be with Kate, and laugh with Mrs. Flanagan without hiding behind a mask…but Mrs. Flanagan's voice sounded in her head: *Those women.* Suds Bucket or not, Sherie knew Mrs. Flanagan couldn't be convinced to accept them, not even with some of Molly's usual blackmail. She wondered exactly what Molly had done to earn them such a disgusting attack. It was surprising, because as much as she understood the townsfolk dislike for their establishment, they usually didn't go out of their way to express it in such a manner, opting instead to ignore them, or spit at them if they happened to cross paths. She knew it was something Molly had done. It had to be. She recalled what Josh said about having seen Molly speaking to Billy the night before. There was no way Molly would have arranged for Billy and Warren to attack them. Molly would never do that to her, and for all their faults and horrible tempers, Sherie also knew there was no way Billy and Warren would attack her for no reason. Unless Molly had some sort of blackmail on them too, but she couldn't think what that would be. No, she wouldn't believe it. Molly was probably chastising Billy for laying a hand on Claire. Of course! That's what it was. So then why would Billy and Warren have attacked them, and why the hell would someone do what they did to the Bucket? Sherie had no idea what was happening, let alone any idea of what she was going to do about Molly's insistence that she marry Tom. The ambivalence sat like a churning weight at the bottom of her stomach, curdling the contents. She could no longer take it.

"I need to get out of here," she said.

"Good idea," said Claire.

"Up for a walk?" asked Olivia.

Maggie sat up from where she was lying on the bed next to Georgina. "That sounds good to me. What do you say, George?"

Georgina didn't move or say anything.

"Actually, I think I need some alone time," said Sherie.

Olivia nudged her. "That means she's going to visit Kate, I bet."

"Exactly what is going on there?" asked Claire. "You two seemed very close this morning."

Sherie blushed and rubbed her face in an attempt to hide it.

"When did you even leave last night?" asked Olivia.

Sherie stood up. "I'm going."

"Stop, stop, you have to tell us! I'm dying here," said Claire.

"I'm dying here," whispered Georgina sadly.

The women looked at Georgina, who had sat up. Her hair was wild and stood out at all angles, uncaring as much as the rest of her. Her nightgown drooped down at the front, her breast slightly exposed, and Maggie pulled the material across to cover her up.

"Sorry, George. We shouldn't be joking," said Olivia. She reached out and tucked a strand of hair behind Georgina's ear. Georgina reached up and pulled the hair back over her face again.

"Come on, let's all get out of here," said Claire.

Sherie didn't wait, and she disappeared out of the house before any of them could ask her any more questions.

The songs of the birds outside started to change, and Molly knew that it would be getting dark soon. She put the lid on the ointment she had been using and wiped her hands on her skirt. On her way downstairs, she knocked on Georgina's door. The girls had been quiet for a while and she thought it would be a good idea to wake them now, to make sure they had enough time to prepare for the evening ahead.

"Hello?" The door opened a crack when Molly knocked on it, and she peered in to see that there was no one there. She walked downstairs to look for them.

"Anyone here?" Downstairs was deserted too, and after Molly looked all over the Bucket, back upstairs and downstairs again, she realized she was alone.

"I'll just do everything myself then," she grumbled as she emptied a box of lemons out onto the bar. Chopping them roughly without any care at all, Molly almost cut her finger off when a noise from the front balcony made her jump.

"Girls? Are you back?"

The door opened slowly and a silhouette entered. She couldn't see who it was, the sunlight streaming into the dark room behind them as they entered, but she knew it definitely wasn't one of her girls.

"Well, well, Molly bloody Kelly."

Molly gripped the knife she was holding tightly when she heard the voice she would never in all her life forget. She felt her blood turn cold when realized who had just walked through the doors. It was Edward Smith.

"I wonder how long it's going to take those coppers to see the writing out the front there," he said, phlegm mixing with the words as they came out of his mouth. "Some good advertising for you, isn't it?" he gurgled.

"Get out," she said.

"I don't think so dear. You see this?" Ed reached into his pocket and pulled out a piece of paper. He unfolded it slowly and held it up to Molly, shaking it in front of her face. "Your father gave me this before he left Richmond."

Molly snatched it off him and read it. She saw her father's scribble below a wordy agreement.

"It says when Daddy's dead, this place belongs to me. First and only cousin. Perks of the job," he said.

Molly spat on the agreement. "You can't prove he's dead."

"I don't have to. He's been gone for over five years, and that's good enough as dead according to the law. All I have to do is show up and tell the ol' Constables that he hasn't been seen or heard from, and this old piece of shit," he kicked the bar, "will all belong to me."

"You're the damned devil."

Ed smiled and Molly noticed he had fewer teeth than the last time she had seen him.

"How's about you come here and bend over my bar for me? Lift up that pretty little skirt of yours while you're at it," he growled.

Molly lunged forward at Ed and drove the knife she was holding deep into his neck. She screamed in unison with him as she twisted the knife, digging it in as hard as she could. She stabbed him again, this time into his chest, pulling it out swiftly and thrusting it back in again, over and over again. Ed stumbled forwards, blood spurting out from his wounds, and Molly raised the knife over her head and brought it down between his shoulder blades, feeling his spine crunch against the blade when she shunted it in. She dragged the knife down his back, slicing his flesh open and letting the blood gush freely.

"Go to hell, you bastard!" she roared. Ed fell to the floor, landing on his back. His agonizing screams only fueled Molly's rage as she stabbed him again and again until his entire body was peppered with weeping gashes. She kicked his bloody legs apart and knelt over him, straddling his thigh. "You want me to ride you? Like this? Tell me, Ed, how does it feel?" She plunged the knife between his legs. "How does it feel to be fucked?!"

Ed was silent and no longer moving, but Molly continued to stab at his crotch, enraged. "This is how it feels, you bastard." Stab.

Stab,

Stab,

STAB.

"This is how it feels."

She stopped when the muscles in her arm stiffened and she could no longer move. Ed's crotch was shredded, the blood just trickling out slowly now. Exhausted, she dropped the knife and walked back over to the bar. She wiped her hands on her skirt, dipping them into a bucket of water to get rid of the blood. She filled a glass with clean water and took a long drink.

What just happened?

She looked at the lifeless body in the middle of the room, and the knife that lay beside it. She finished her glass of water and calmly put it down on the bar, her blood covered fingers leaving marks on the glass. She could hear the cicada's chirping outside, fighting for volume against the crickets. The noises grew louder, and suddenly she felt like the sounds were carving at her eardrums, the ringing ricocheting throughout the room, bouncing off Ed's dead body and slapping her across the face. She covered her ears with her hands and shouted. Curse words, prayers, more curse words, pleading and begging it would all stop. Stop. STOP JUST STOP!

Silence. Suddenly nothing but silence. Molly knew there wouldn't be much time until sound returned to haunt her. She picked up Ed's ankles and started to drag him out through the back door. He was very easy to move. Did blood weigh that much? Or had she slashed some pieces off without realizing? She looked back, but there was no flesh left behind, and all his appendages seemed to be in place. At least, the ones she hadn't minced. Perhaps it was her own strength she did not realize. She was strong; she had to be, for her family. This was all for her family. The whole plan, everything. The puzzle. She needed to focus on the puzzle. The pieces were in place, almost. She would be gone soon, and she needed everything perfectly in place. Ed's appearance had almost threatened that, but once again she had done what needed to be done for the sake of her family. She had taken care of it all. She dropped Ed under the Bucket and moved a table in front of him. That would do for now. She could deal with him later.

Inside, she scrubbed and scrubbed the blood soaked floor. As she scrubbed, she rationalized, and the sounds slowly returned, normal this time.

When Tom opened his front door, Molly walked straight in, not waiting for an invitation.

"Tom. Listen, no more games. You need to propose to Sherie. Tonight." She paced back and forth while she waited for him to say something, but all he did was look at her with a ridiculously gormless expression.

"You have the ring still, don't you?" Still he said nothing. She launched herself at him, grabbing his shoulders and shaking him. "TELL ME YOU HAVE MY MOTHER'S RING!"

"I have it! I have it!" Finally, he started to speak.

"Good." Molly licked her lips, but her mouth remained dry. "You can do it then, tonight?"

He looked uncertain.

"I'm begging you, Tom, please, I'm begging you. Look after my sister," she said.

"Let's just talk about this a little more, see if we can explore options," he said.

"There are no other options and you agreed to this!"

"I said I would help in any way I could, but I never agreed to—"

Molly threw herself at Tom. "Why are you doing this to me? What more do you want?" She pounded on his chest. "Please, Tom."

He held her tightly and she cried with her eyes open, too afraid to close them for what might appear in the darkness. "You know what I want," Tom said.

"More money? The Bucket makes plenty of money; you saw the books. We're making more money than ever now people thing we're going broke. Even the girls are working for less because they're afraid we'll close," she said.

"That's not what I want."

She pulled back to look at Tom, and he slid his hand up the back of her neck, tangling his fingers in her hair. He pulled her into him, pressing his lips on hers and kissed her. She was surprised at the softness of his kiss, despite his apparent passion. "I want *you*, Molly. Why can't I marry *you*?"

She let her legs give way, but Tom held her up. He lowered her gently to the floor and knelt beside her as she cried. "Tell me why I can't have you? Tell me what's gone so horribly wrong. I can help you," he said.

"I'm poison," she said.

"I don't believe that," he said.

Molly laughed. *If only you knew.* "The things I've done, the lies I've told... the blackmail."

"We've all done things we wish we didn't have to, for the sake of our families," said Tom. "I don't believe you're a bad person. Beneath that hard exterior, you're just scared. You don't think I can see that?" He kissed her again, but this time she pushed him away.

"You're a damn idiot," she said. "You can't see anything. I told you, I'm poison. Literally. POISON, Tom. I have syphilis."

Tom didn't seem at all phased. "When? It's treatable, you know? There are—"

Molly cut him off before he could get his hopes up. "A long time ago," she said, more calmly now. "Very early on. A one-time customer, and the bastard shortchanged me too. I've been treating it, but it's starting to get worse."

Tom looked at the ground. Finally, she was getting through to him.

"You didn't wonder why I didn't work with the rest of the girls?" she asked.

"I just assumed you didn't want to, or were too busy running the place," he said.

"I'm a good liar."

"Who knows?" he asked.

"No one. It's going to stay that way too. I need to leave, Tom, before it gets any worse. I don't want Sherie to see me this way. I've got enough money to last me for the rest of my life…" She paused for a moment and closed her eyes. "Or whatever's left of it."

"What are the girls going to do without you?"

"Oh, believe me; they'll be able to do a hell of a lot better with me gone. They're in this whole mess because of me," she said.

"What about me? What will I do without you?"

"I'll tell you what you need to know in order to get into the right circles," she said. She handed him a wad of papers. "This gives you as much information as I could remember about almost everyone in town. All the dirt. You hint to anyone that you know something about them, they'll want to keep you close."

Tom took the papers from her and flipped through them quickly. "What kind of details?"

"You'll see," she said.

Tom reached out and grabbed her arms, pulling her across the floor until she was in his lap. "What if I take you to see the doctor, see if there's anything else he can do?"

"There's nothing he can do. It's all been done. It's over, Tom. This is the ending I deserve, trust me," she said.

"But I love you," he said, holding her. She could feel him shaking. She pulled his arms off her and stood up, noticing her mother's ring on the kitchen table.

"You don't know me. You know the person I've let you get to know, and she's not me. Besides, there's no such thing as love." She picked up the ring, walked back over to Tom, and dropped it on the ground in front of him. "Propose to my sister, or never go back to the Suds Bucket again. I'm leaving either way, so if you really do love me, you'll look after Sherie." Molly turned and walked towards the front door.

"For someone who doesn't believe in love, you seem to care an awful lot about your sister," he called to her.

She didn't turn around.

"Molly!" Molly refused to let herself look back.

"I'll do it," Tom shouted. "I'll ask Sherie to marry me. I promise I will look after her."

"Goodbye, Tom." She walked out the door and closed it behind her.

Tom didn't move from his spot on the floor as he opened the pieces of paper that Molly had left him.

Molly

"I can't stand that baby crying." A frustrated patron put his head down on the bar and covered the back of his head with his hands.

The evening had slowed down since Sherie and Maggie had both taken men upstairs. The newest edition to their clan, Georgina, was not doing anything at all to earn her keep. Instead, she was having the opposite effect—her crying baby was driving clients home before they had even finished their drinks.

"*You* can't stand the crying? Try being me. I haven't had a single night's sleep since the damn kid was born. Not even a week old and louder than half our clients!" Molly threw a soaking wet towel on the bar and picked up a fresh one.

"You don't understand," he said. "My wife's at home, in a coma."

Molly's brow creased and she felt genuinely sorry for the man. No wonder he hadn't been interested in Maggie when she danced alongside him earlier in the evening. Some men came here legitimately to do nothing but drink. Granted, it didn't happen very often, but when it did, Molly liked to look after them.

"I'm sorry," she said, filling his glass up again. "On the house," she told him with a smile.

"She went into labor last week, but she lost a lot of blood during the whole thing. She passed out before the baby was born. It came out dead."

"Jesus." Molly didn't know what to say. "Is your wife going to be okay?"

"She's starting to wake up, slowly," he said. "That's the worst part."

She looked at him, confused.

"She's going to wake up and ask me whether we have a baby boy or a baby girl, and I'm going to have to tell her it's neither." Molly turned around to let the man wipe the tears from his eyes in private.

"The doctor didn't even bother to stay. Blamed man just told me the baby would likely not make it, but my wife would be fine after a few days, and he'd come by in another week to check on her."

"Doctors," Molly spat. "Let me guess, Patterson?" The man nodded.

"Useless excuse for a human being," she said. "I'd rather rub mud on myself and hope for the best than trust a treatment from him."

The man chuckled at her through a sniff.

"I'm just about finished here. Would you like some company on your walk home?"

"Oh, no, I'll be fine. I haven't had that much to drink," he said with a grateful smile.

"You'd be doing me a favor, getting me away from the wretched baby screams," she said.

"Don't be talking about one of God's children like that," the man said sternly, but then added more gently, "Your company would be lovely, thank you."

They walked for a while in silence. Molly played with words in her head, trying to decide the best way to phrase what was going through her mind. Eventually, unable to think of any way that would make what she was about to suggest sound anything but insane, she chose just to go ahead and say it the best way she knew how—bluntly. "Do you want the baby?"

The man looked at her, eyes narrowed. "What do you mean?"

"You saw how empty my bar was. It hasn't been that empty since the day we opened, just over a year ago. The kid's bad for business, and honestly a brothel is no place for a baby. Do you agree?"

"I suppose, yes, if you put it that way."

"The mother of the child is only a child herself, did you know that?"

"How old?"

"Not yet even fifteen!" she said.

"You're serious?"

"I am if you are. I have some conditions."

He looked at Molly with great interest, and she felt a buzz of success within her. The suggestion had been a risky one, but it looked like it was about to pay off.

"Number one: You never come into the Suds Bucket again. You don't know me and we never spoke. Number two: This isn't a gift. I want money."

"How much? We don't have much; the doctor cost us a lot."

"Ongoing payments. Once a month."

"How much? For how long?"

"However much you feel warrants the gift of a child. If it's not enough, I'll let you know."

The man sighed. As long as he kept agreeing, Molly would keep pushing the boundaries. "As for how long, well, let's just say that as long as the money's coming in I'll have a reason to keep my mouth shut."

They reached a handsome fence, and Molly guessed they had arrived at the edge of his land. She could see the house a little further up the pathway. It looked like he would definitely be able to afford it.

"I'm not sure about this. My wife...what if she—"

"Look, mate, that's up to you. Let her wake up and find out her baby's dead, or hand her a newborn baby girl. She is beautiful, by the way, when she's not crying. Lots of energy."

The man kicked the fence post. "Can I let you know?"

"It won't work if your wife wakes up and there's no baby in the house, so don't take your time. I'll check for the money tomorrow night. If you agree, make sure it's there before then."

"Wait. Where?"

"Front stairs of the Bucket, third step. It comes up. Drop it there, and make sure no one sees you," she said.

He nodded.

"When's the doctor coming again?"

"I'm not sure," he said.

"Well, make sure it's not before you get your daughter, okay? And make sure you start practicing how you're going to tell him. You're going to need to make it sound like a miracle."

"Okay. I'll drop the money tomorrow," he said.

"Not during the day. If anyone sees you, the deal is off. And remember what I told you—never speak to me again."

The man exhaled loudly. "You'll want nothing to do with the baby after this?"

"I already want nothing to do with that baby. She's yours."

"What's her name?"

Molly laughed. "Are you really that stupid? Listen, the police won't be looking for the baby, but my girls will be. She's going to be YOUR baby. You name her!"

He looked around nervously as Molly's voice got louder. "Wait, the mother won't be told about this? You're just going to take her?" He dropped his voice to a whisper.

"Listen. You don't need to know the details on my end, okay? All you need to know is that your wife is going to wake up, and you are going to hand her a beautiful baby girl and tell her congratulations. Anything you may or may not hear about a missing child somewhere else in town is just a sad story about a woman who obviously couldn't keep her legs closed, okay?" Molly made sure to lower her voice.

"Right. Yes. Of course," he said. "But—"

"But nothing. I'll take care of my side of things, and you take care of yours. Understand? Now, I'll see you tomorrow night, if the money's right." Molly started to walk away. "Oh, hang on." She turned back around. "I suppose you'd better tell me your name." Her hushed voice cut across the quiet evening.

"Angus," he whispered back to her. "Angus Flanagan."

From the moment Molly woke up, she was fired by raw adrenaline. She hurried into town as early as she could.

"Good morning, Miss Molly. You're up early, aren't you?" The apothecary's son was handsome and charming, and he gave Molly a quick wink as he greeted her. If he wasn't so young Molly might have flirted back and encouraged him to visit the Bucket, but at sixteen years old and not yet having sprouted much more than a bit of fluff on the sides of his face, Molly decided to let him keep his innocence a little while longer.

"Morning, James. Your father about?" She didn't have time for pleasantries this morning, and as excited as she was, she knew that what she was about to ask for could bring about suspicion if she didn't do it properly.

"Pa!" James called loudly up the stairs. "Molly Kelly's 'ere!" "How's your new friend?" he asked.

"Settling in," said Molly.

"I hope she's feeling better soon."

Molly gave him a half smile. He was a sweet young man. "I'm sure she will, with your expert care," she said.

James blushed.

"Back again so soon?" The apothecary appeared from upstairs.

"Afraid so," said Molly. She waited for him to shoo his son away, as he always did when she came in.

"James, would you go around the back and mix up another willow bark salve for Molly? We'll try one more dose, and if you're still not getting any relief, then it might be time to look at something a little stronger," he said. James disappeared around the back. Molly was about to tell him that she didn't need more medicine for herself yet, but his suggestion had left her curious.

"Stronger?"

"I was thinking it might be time to try mercury," he said. "But it comes with a price tag, so I thought I'd give you some notice, so you can start to save."

"Don't worry about money," Molly said. "If it's going to work then I'll take it."

"I can't say it will work for sure, but I definitely think it's worth a try. You still taking a break?" Molly nodded.

"Good. Best you're not social while you're still..." He looked her up and down. "...unwell."

"Agreed. Actually, Clancy, I was wondering if you could help me with something else."

"Something else?"

"I can't seem to sleep. At all."

"Itching?" He pointed between her legs. "Or are you starting to see lights when you close your eyes?"

"No, it's not me. It's Georgina's baby. It cries and cries and no matter how hard I bury my head into my pillow, the noise gets through."

Clancy chuckled. "In that case, I don't think I need to help you. Georgina was in here yesterday and I gave her a mixture that should help all of you get some sleep, baby Adelaide included."

That was not what she expected him to say. "Would you mind just giving something to me anyway? Just in case? I can't go another night without sleep, I'm telling you."

Clancy walked into the folds of the shelves beside the front counter and reappeared with a small bottle. "You won't need much," he said, putting it down in front of her. "Dab the smallest amount on a cloth and hold it up to your mouth after you get into bed. Breathe deeply, and you should sleep the whole night through without a peep."

This was perfect. "Thank you."

"Ten pence," he said. Molly pulled the coins out of her purse and handed them to him.

"The smallest amount," he repeated.

"Okay. I'll probably be back next week for the salve too."

"Shall I order the mercury? It'll take a few months to come in from the mainland, so if you're interested I'll send for it now," he said.

Molly flashed him a grin. "Sounds great, please."

"One last thing," he said. Molly paused in the doorway. "My James is a good boy, but if he ever shows up at the Suds Bucket…"

"I'll beat his behind and send him home faster than he can realize what has happened," she assured him.

Molly waited until all the clients went home and the girls had gone to bed before she checked the step. Georgina's baby was still crying loudly, so she didn't bother to be quiet when she pulled back the plank of wood on the stairs, and found a bag waiting for her. It was very heavy as she pulled it out, and she had to stop herself from giggling when she opened it to see all the silver coins looking back at her. She had not expected anywhere near as much money. She noticed a note, which she opened. Scrawled with ink, in impeccable handwriting were instructions from Mr. Flanagan.

Two a.m. Do not ever speak to a member of my family after this day.

She screwed his note up and threw it back down into the hollow step. She dropped the money back down into the step, and pushed it to the side so that it wasn't visible at first glance if someone were to pull the step up, or god forbid, fall into it. She walked up the stairs and knocked on Georgina's door, opening it without waiting for an answer.

"You alright?" Molly asked kindly.

Georgina looked absolutely exhausted. Her hair was stuck to her face and her eyes had black rings around them. "I've tried a few drops of this like the apothecary said, but it's not working," she said hopelessly.

"Try a little more," Molly suggested.

"He told me not to. He said only a few drops every night,"

"He's too cautious for an apothecary," said Molly. She walked over and picked up the glass bottle on the bedside. "Bring her here."

Georgina moved closer to Molly, cradling her daughter in her arms. "Don't worry, little darling," she whispered, rocking the baby gently as she moved. "It's all okay. It's all going to be okay."

Molly poured as much of the reddish-brown liquid as she could fit onto the spoon. It wobbled when she moved it toward the infant's mouth, but it didn't spill over, almost as if it was surrounded by an invisible bubble that let it extend just slightly past the edges of the spoon. She delivered the mixture to the child, who coughed and was silent for a hopeful second, before bursting back into tears.

Georgina pulled her into her chest and started swaying back and forth. "Thank you for trying," she said.

"Give it a little while to work," said Molly. "Here, why don't you put her down into her cot and let the medicine settle her?"

Georgina kissed her daughter on the top of her head. "I can't let her cry alone. She needs to know I'm here."

"She'll need to learn to cry alone," Molly said, her tone harshening. She realized she wasn't getting anywhere with kindness. "You're going to need to start working again if you want to stay and earn your keep, so she needs to learn how to settle down by herself. You hear?"

Georgina nodded. Her lips trembled and she pursed them together. She kissed her daughter again and walked over to the cot.

Molly held her arms out. "Give her here," she said.

"I can do it," said Georgina, as she lay the baby gently down into the cot and pulled a white shawl over her. The baby screamed when she let her go, and Georgina started to cry too. She picked the baby back up. "I can't. I can't leave her to cry, Molly. It's not right."

"Sooner or later you're going to need to sleep, aren't you? For heaven's sake, Georgina, she's not going to remember that you let her cry when she was a few weeks old. You need to sleep, and so do we!"

"No, Molly!" Georgina wouldn't let down. "She's my daughter, and I'll calm her how I want to." She pulled the cot beside her own bed. She climbed into bed and reached her arm through the bars of the cot so that she could stroke the baby's head while she rested.

Molly folded her arms and shifted her weight onto one leg as she watched. After a few minutes, the screaming started to die down and was replaced by the occasional sob.

"You see?" Georgina whispered.

"Good job," Molly said with a half-smile.

"You can go to sleep now," Georgina told her.

Any other person would have copped an ear full for telling Molly to do anything, but given that the child was starting to calm down finally, not to mention Georgina, Molly decided to let it slide.

"Sweet dreams to the both of you," Molly said. She left the room, but waited outside, listening to Georgina's soothing hushes every time the baby whimpered. Eventually, when the hushes stopped but the whimpers continued, Molly pushed the door open to find Georgina asleep, her hand still in the cot, the baby cuddled around it. Out of her pocket she pulled a cloth that she had dipped into the sleeping medicine given to her that morning. She pressed it on Georgina's face, covering her nose and mouth, and held it there for a few seconds. When she pulled it away, she poked Georgina in the cheek hard, but she did not move. She looked at the baby, who wasn't quite sleeping, but who was sucking on Georgina's index finger. Her little hand gripped it tightly, not even wrapping all the way around. She appeared dozy enough for Molly to risk moving.

She reached into the cot and pried her from Georgina's hand. The baby didn't cry while Molly wrapped her in the blankets and carried her downstairs, out of the Bucket and into the night.

Sherie floated between sleep and wakefulness as the first light started to sidle through her curtains. She used her big toes to pull her socks off and she reveled in the freshness of the morning while she let her feet breathe, rubbing them against the soft bed sheets. She inhaled the early air and stretched her body, letting it shudder as she extended her arms and legs, and arched her back. She nuzzled her pillow and sank deeper into her mattress as she relaxed her body again and fell back into a happy dream.

She was jolted from her snoozing by a blood-curdling scream that stiffened the hairs on her arms and scraped the back of her neck.

Chapter 18

Anne Flanagan raced across the landing, shaking the entire upstairs level. "TALLY HO!" She launched a ball through the air at Josh, who had just leaped out into the landing. He ducked the ball and retreated back into his bedroom, closing his door just in time to deflect a second ball that bounced off and flew back towards Anne. She caught it with expert reflexes and scurried over to the wall beside his door. She waited silently, breathing heavily, for him to open the door.

Click.

The doorknob turned, but Anne stayed perfectly still. The hinges creaked when Josh pulled the door slowly open, and he let one eye peer out to the supposedly vacant landing. Swinging it open quickly, he slinked across the open area to the stairs and started to descend down them quietly, not noticing Anne until she had ambushed him from above, throwing the ball over the railing, and bopping him square on the head.

"Got you! I win again!" She laughed with an air of evil genius as she danced overhead. Josh reached through the rails and grabbed her ankle tightly, halting her celebrations and causing her to squeal.

"Anne! Josh! Stop your bosh and behave yourselves! Your father's sleeping!" Mrs. Flanagan squeezed herself past Josh on the stairs, a basket of washing in her arms.

"I'm *trying* to sleep!" Mr. Flanagan's muffled voice came from behind a nearby door.

"Sorry, Papa," called Anne. She rushed into the room and placed a kiss on his forehead. "Want me to get you some water?"

"No, Annie." He patted her head fondly. "Just go outside and play." She raced out the door. "Quietly!" He added.

Mrs. Flanagan shook her head while Anne and Josh raced down the stairs. "Josh Flanagan, you are eighteen years old! Start acting like it!" she called to him as he disappeared around the corner with a loud roar. "Or perhaps not," she said to herself.

Kate sat at her piano playing a sweet tune. She tried not to think about the events of that morning, afraid that what had happened to Georgina's birds was because of her. The notes plinked out, the tune sounding pretty but not as smooth as she would have liked it to be.

The melody was interrupted by a knock at her door, and Mrs. Flanagan walked into the room and dropped a pile of folded washing at the foot of her bed. Kate smiled in thanks, which Mrs. Flanagan apparently interpreted as an invitation to sit down.

"It's nice to hear you playing finally," Mrs. Flanagan said. Kate nodded. "It's nice to see you with new friends, too. That girl at the party last night? She was lovely."

Kate suppressed a grin. "She was, wasn't she?"

"Not like that harlot we all know you've been spending all your time with recently," Mrs. Flanagan said.

Kate couldn't stop herself this time, and she let out a laugh.

"What's so funny?" Mrs. Flanagan asked.

"That was Sherie," Kate said, taking care not to so much as blink, for fear she might miss the reaction.

Mrs. Flanagan's mouth dropped open, but before she could speak again, Kate stood up, deciding she didn't want to hear more of the same words. "Can't you see how happy she makes me?"

Mrs. Flanagan shook her head. "But, Katie, she's—"

"She's what? Huh? What? She's kindhearted? She's brave? She's in a tough situation, doing what she needs to in order to protect her family?"

Mrs. Flanagan said nothing.

"When are you going to realize that I love this girl, and I'm not going to judge her for who her family is?" Kate started to storm out of her bedroom, but paused to add another thought, "I'm just lucky she doesn't judge me for MY god damned family."

Kate stormed down the stairs into the lounge room where she found Josh doing a puzzle with Anne.

"Anne, will you go pick me some flowers?" Kate asked. Anne leaped up and dashed outside. Kate loved how eager she was to please others. As soon as Anne was out of earshot, Kate turned to Josh. "Did you really have to kill all of the birds?" she accused him.

"Angus!" Mrs. Flanagan had followed Kate downstairs and started to pace behind her, ringing her hands in her skirt. "Angus, get down here, please!" she called.

Mr. Flanagan ambled down the stairs slowly, dressed in bedclothes, a newspaper in his hand. "What's going on?" He walked into the room, not happy to be interrupted from his hangover.

"Your son completely trashed the Bucket last night!" Kate said.

"The Suds Bucket?" Mr. Flanagan sat down in his chair. "Katie, aside from you, no one in this family wants or has anything to do with that place. I hardly think Josh would—" but his sentence was cut short.

"Yes, we did," Josh interrupted him. "They clearly haven't been getting the more subtle messages we have been sending them about how disgusting their lifestyle is."

Kate was surprised to see that Mr. Flanagan appeared livid by this news. His jaw clenched, and his head started to shake as he processed the words.

"Josh, we don't involve ourselves with them." He spat his words. "We don't concern ourselves with their business." His anger grew as he spoke. "We have nothing to do with them, and in return they have nothing to do with us!" He was yelling now, and he stood up and faced Josh, who looked regretful. "Haven't I always told you this?!"

Josh nodded, but he didn't appear apologetic. "But they're disgusting. It's about time someone did something about it. They'll ruin the town!"

Kate paced back and forth, looking from Mr. Flanagan to Josh as they spoke, the beautiful sunset outside completely marred by the disdain from her ignorant family. She couldn't stay silent any longer, but her next words were not angry ones, as she pleaded with her family.

"You know nothing of them. Of their lifestyle. They are human beings. Beautiful women. Who are you to judge a person when you so evidently know nothing about them? They laugh, they dream, they FEEL, Josh. They love. Just because they do it a little differently to you doesn't mean you have any right to tell them that they are doing it wrong. They're like family to me."

"Yeah, and when two of their scum customers beat the shit out of you, did it feel like they were family then?" asked Josh.

"You're missing the point. If we keep going with this eye for an eye drama, we're all going to end up blind," said Kate.

Josh shook his head. "Look, you just can't come from nowhere and demand we change our opinion overnight."

Kate turned toward her family, disgusted. She wanted to say something, but there were no words remotely useful for what she was feeling.

Mr. Flanagan spoke next. "If you think they're good people, Kate, then I can't argue that you're wrong. You're a good judge of character, just like your mother was. You're strong willed like your father was too, and it's an endearing trait, my dear, but you need to trust me now, and obey to me when I ask you not to associate with these people. I've worked hard for this family, and I can't allow you to ruin that."

"What if I was more careful? Made sure no one sees me with her?" Kate asked, feeling tears in her eyes. It appeared there would be no reasoning with her family. She was disappointed and heartbroken.

"I don't expect you to understand, but I do expect you to listen to me. Discontinue these friendships. If they are good people as you say, then they will understand," said Mr. Flanagan.

A tear fell onto Kate's cheek. "I've already lost one family. I can't believe I'm about to lose another one."

Josh scoffed. "Please. You can't tell me you think they're family?"

Mr. Flanagan moved toward her and put his hands on her shoulders. "It will become easier with time, and you have your aunt and me, who will support you. You can work in the stables to get your mi—"

"No." Kate cut him off and pushed his hands off her. "I mean this one." She walked out the front door before anyone else could say another word.

Chapter 19

On the balcony of the Suds Bucket, Maggie sat on the swinging chair, stroking a sleeping Georgina's head in her lap. Olivia sat in front of her wheel, her eyes closed as she leaned back in her chair, her vase for the evening already completed and sitting on the balcony railing to dry. Claire sat in her usual spot too, sitting up and leaning on the arm of the chair while she wrote slowly in the journal Kate had given to her. The walls were still stained red, though it was difficult to work out what the words said anymore. Kate arrived quietly and the girls jumped when she spoke.

"Hi." Kate felt embarrassed when she saw them all recognize the redness around her eyes, giving away the tears she had managed to stop just before she had arrived.

"Sherie's not here, sweetie." Maggie's voice was soft as she spoke over Georgina's head.

"Oh," said Kate. "Would you mind if I sat with you, girls?"

Olivia opened one eye. "As long as you're quiet," she said.

Kate nodded and sat next to Claire. She folded her hands in her lap and looked at Georgina. She looked so peaceful, so angelic.

Claire finished writing something in her journal and looked up. "I need to talk to you," she said.

"Claire," said Olivia. The word sounded like a warning.

"Inside," said Claire. She looked very serious and suddenly Kate felt there was something more going on than just Georgina's grieving. Maggie smiled sympathetically at Kate when they walked past her and into the Bucket.

"I am so sorry for everything," Kate said as soon as they were inside, pointing to the blood smudged window.

Claire held up a hand to stop her. "It's been coming for a long time. I'll admit I wasn't quite expecting what happened to the birds, but the rest…"

An unpleasant smell reached Kate's nose, and her nostrils flared as she got her first whiff of the stench. "God, where did you put the birds?"

Claire crinkled her nose. "Stinks pretty bad, huh? They're out the back for now. We want to bury them properly when Georgina's ready," she said.

"Ah," was all Kate could think to say. They stood, a little awkwardly for a while before Kate realized that Claire had asked to speak with her. She looked at Claire, who looked almost sick to her stomach all of a sudden and was picking at the palm of her hand, wincing. "Are you okay?" Kate asked.

Claire nodded. "I need to tell you something," she said.

"What's wrong with your hand?"

"Oh, it's nothing. I just got a splinter, that's all."

"Looks like a pretty bad splinter," said Kate, reaching out to pick her hand up and inspect it. The piece of wood floated under the surface of Claire's skin, completely visible. It was large, and the area around it was very red and inflamed.

"Jesus, it looks like you've got half a tree under there!" Kate said with a smile. She rubbed her thumb over it. "What did you want to tell me?" she asked as she applied pressure to Claire's wound, gently trying to coax the wood back out of the slit of skin it had entered through.

Claire took a deep breath and pulled her journal up to her chest with her free hand. "It's Molly."

As if summoned, Molly walked in from downstairs, stopping short when she noticed Claire and Kate. "Didn't think I'd be seeing you around here anymore." Molly's eyes flicked down to Kate's hand that was still holding Claire's. "I guess you've heard the news. Moving on already, are you? Bit close to home, isn't it? You know, Kate, we're going to have to start charging you soon."

Kate dropped Claire's hand and took a step towards Molly. Her demeanor didn't scare her in the slightest, and she wasn't afraid to make that known. "Am I supposed to know what you are talking about?" she asked.

Molly's smile was a mile wide, and smug as hell. "Tom's proposing to Sherie tonight."

Kate felt like the words slapped her across the face. She looked at Claire, who appeared to be just as surprised by the news.

"She's saying yes, by the way…but you got that part, right?" Molly crowed. "Celebratory bubbles, Kate?" She walked behind the bar and held up a bottle of champagne. She laughed while Kate processed the information. "Come on, Kate. You can't honestly believe Sherie was ever going to pick you. You don't belong here."

Kate didn't believe her. She was lying. Molly didn't know what she and Sherie shared, and there was no way Sherie would ever say yes to Tom…would she?

Claire's brow creased and Kate knew she was thinking the same thing.

"She's right," Claire said quietly.

"What?" Kate looked at Claire, hurt.

Molly popped the cork off the champagne. "Woo!"

"All you bring is trouble. You think it's a coincidence that you show up and all of a sudden we're being attacked? Georgina's canaries were murdered today. Because of you."

"That was my family, not me…Claire…you know I didn't…" Kate's words trailed off as she tried to deal with what was unraveling before her. This wasn't happening. What did Molly have over them?

"You just said it yourself. That's your family. Well, this is my family, and you don't belong." Claire threw her journal at Kate, who caught it before it hit her. "You should leave."

Kate studied Claire's eyes, searching for reason. She saw nothing but anger. She tried to hand the journal back to Claire. It had been a gift, and she wanted her to keep it.

Claire shook her head. "No. Take it with you."

Nodding, Kate looked at Molly, who was smiling now more than ever. "You win," Kate said.

"I always win," Molly spat at her.

Kate walked out of the Bucket, without looking back.

The evening at the Bucket carried on as if nothing had ever happened. Drinks flowed, girls danced, and cheeky boys copped cheap feels. It was business as usual, except for the stench that permeated through the floorboards of the Bucket. Lucky for Molly, she was able to pass it off as the smell from the bird's carcasses without anyone being suspicious, but she knew she was going to have to do something with Ed's body sooner or later, because it was turning the customers off.

Most of their clients went home early, unable to deal with the smell. Those who were desperate for a shag either held their breath or drank double shots of whiskey until they had burned enough of their nose hairs off that they couldn't smell anything any longer. Unfortunately for the girls, that meant the men were falling down drunk early on in the night, stopping most of them from being able to go upstairs and take care of business. Of the men who remained, Billy had been told he would be paying triple from now on if he wanted to go upstairs, much to his chagrin, and he left a very unsatisfied customer.

"You coming up tonight or what?" Maggie asked James, who had been drinking the same beer for the last few hours.

"What? Oh, sure," he said, dejected.

"Well, don't look so excited about it," said Maggie, and she pushed him playfully.

James pointed at Claire, who was wiping down tables.

"I've told you, James. As long as you love her I won't let you pay for her," Maggie said.

"Oh, but you'll let me waste my money with you?" he asked with a grin.

"Get upstairs, you rat bastard." She pinched his bum as she chased him up the stairs.

"Hey, hey, hey!" Molly held up her hand to James and rubbed her fingers together expectantly. James handed her two shillings and leaned into her. "Got more mercury arriving tomorrow," he said.

"Good. I'll be round first thing," said Molly.

"You sure you need so much? You're not going to take it all at once, are you?"

"Of course not," Molly snapped. "Get upstairs, you rascal, before I send someone to tell your father where you are."

"He gave up caring where I was a long time ago," said James as he followed Maggie up the stairs.

"He never stopped caring, James. He stopped remembering," Molly called to him. James waved his hand at her.

"Night," he said.

Molly took the money James had given her and put it into a bag behind the bar with the rest of the evening's takings. Claire and Olivia had come up empty with no one to take upstairs, so the cleaning was finished much faster than usual.

"Georgina upstairs?" Molly asked as she started to tally the books.

Olivia nodded. "Figured you wouldn't mind if she took the night off." She collapsed into a chair in the front bar area next to Claire. Molly enjoyed the silence while she pretended to count the books. As soon as Olivia and Claire went upstairs, she was going to collect the money from the front step and load it up into the horses that she had arranged to be waiting behind the Bucket. She would drop by the apothecary in the morning on the way out of Richmond to pick up the mercury. She knew it wasn't curing her, but at the very least it was stopping the pain. The pustules continued to blanket her body, and she knew it wouldn't be much longer until they started forming on her face and hands. No more hiding. Knowing Tom would take care of Sherie meant that the final piece of the puzzle was in place, and she could leave without regrets. Or so she would keep telling herself.

The silence only lasted a few moments longer, before the front door crashed open and Billy stumbled back into the Bucket. "I found six shillings on the street!" He held up the coins up in his fist triumphantly.

Olivia stood up unenthusiastically. "Wonderful," she said flatly. Billy slammed the coins down onto the bar and followed Olivia upstairs.

Claire leaned back on her chair legs and reached behind her head for a book on the nearby bookcase. She put her feet up on another chair and opened the book. The silence returned unbothered for a few more minutes, until once again the Bucket doors opened and Sherie walked in.

Molly was surprised to see her back. "You're back early. I would have thought you would be celebrating with Tom all night."

Sherie looked at Molly for a moment, eyes cold, and took a deep breath in. "I told him no," she said abruptly.

Molly stared at Sherie in horror. Claire's face lit up with a smile and Molly wanted to punch them both. "What the hell is wrong with you, Sherie? I had to work so hard to get Tom to even CONSIDER dating you, let alone proposing. What are you going to say to Dad, when he comes back and—"

"DAD IS DEAD!" Sherie shouted with a ferocity that Molly had never heard before. Molly threw one of the bags of money into the safe and slammed the door shut.

"Yeah. And a good thing too. He'd be disappointed as hell with you."

Sherie shook her head slowly. She didn't appear to care. "Where's all the money, Molly?"

Claire's head snapped toward Molly.

"What are you talking about?" Molly asked, feigning complete ignorance.

"Tom says you told him that if he married me, he would be investing into the Bucket, and all the money we had. Which is funny, since you keep telling us how broke we are."

"You've seen what's in the safe, Sherie...you know exactly how much money is in there." Molly bent down and pulled the money bag back out from the safe, and tipped it upside down, letting coins spill out all over the top of the bar. "Come here and count it for yourself. This is all we have."

"Well, Tom said you told him differently, so you're either lying to him or you're lying to us," said Sherie.

"Who are you going to believe? Him or your own sister?" asked Molly.

Sherie narrowed her eyes. "Well, then I'd sure love to know how you managed to convince Tom that we were doing so well..." She maintained eye contact with Molly a little too long for Molly's liking. "So which is it, Molly? Are we broke, or are we stinkin' rich?"

Molly broke the eye contact and slammed the book closed. "You really said no?" she asked, hoping that Sherie was just telling her that to piss her off.

"Yeah, I did," she said.

Claire lowered her book and looked across at Sherie. "Kate thinks you said yes," she said quietly.

Sherie looked up at Claire. "What?"

"To Tom. She thinks you're gonna marry him."

Sherie ran out the door. Molly marched upstairs furiously. She had done everything in her power to make sure her sister would be looked after, but if she was going to throw it all away to become a spinster, then there was nothing more she could do. She threw her mother's jewelry box across the room in a rage. That ungrateful tramp could tip the velvet for the rest of her life for all she cared. She was finished with the lot of them.

Kate's house grew bigger as Sherie ran towards it. When she got to the front door, she didn't hesitate to bang her fist as hard as she could against the solid wood. After a moment the door opened, and Sherie found herself facing Josh. He took one look at her and slammed the door shut.

Sherie ran a few steps back to where she could see light coming from Kate's window.

"Kate!"

Sherie grabbed a handful of stones and began to pelt them upwards at Kate's window. The front door re-opened and Sherie ran toward it, hopeful that it might be Kate, but it was Mrs. Flanagan. Holding a shotgun. Fear drenched Sherie's body and she turned around and started to run away from the Flanagan's house.

"She's not here!" Mrs. Flanagan yelled in fury.

She cocked the gun and fired it in Sherie's general direction. It missed by so much that for a fraction of a second Sherie almost felt comforted that she could have been trying to miss her on purpose, and only trying to scare her. The second shot was slightly closer than the first, and Sherie decided that either way she didn't want to stick around and figure out whether her theory was true or if Mrs. Flanagan was just as bad a shot as her niece was. Sherie ran as fast as she could until she could no longer see the Flanagan's house. Out of breath, she stopped when she reached the middle of town, and collapsed onto a bench out the front of an upscale teahouse that she would usually cross the street and double her pace in order to avoid. Right now, whether or not she was seen near places she had been explicitly told to stay away from, she did not care. She tried to calm herself down while she compiled a list of locations where Kate might be if she really wasn't at home.

Upstairs at the Bucket, the girls were none the wiser about anything that was going on. Maggie was lying on her bed, arms behind her and legs slightly apart.

"Come on, James, give it to me."

James sat in the corner of the room at an easel, in front of charcoal portrait of Claire. The lines were detailed and delicate. He shot a look of annoyance at Maggie over his shoulder. "I can't," he said.

"Come on, pretend I'm Claire and just say how you feel!" Maggie looked at James through her legs. James shook his head. "If you can't give me a good enough reason as to why you won't tell her that you're desperately in love with her, then I'll have to do it myself," she said teasingly.

James put his piece of charcoal down and turned around completely to face Maggie. "You wouldn't."

"You don't think so?" She made a move to stand up and go downstairs.

"Stop! Don't!" protested James.

"You're telling me you can't just go up to her and say, 'excuse me, Claire, I think you're just absolutely beautiful and amazing'?"

"I've tried. But she's always taken for the night by the time I get the guts to—"

"No, James, you can't PAY for her. You have to tell her how you feel if you want to make love to her. Otherwise, you're just a fuck. Claire deserves better than that, and you know it," Maggie said.

James nodded and looked down at the ground.

"What baffles me is that you are brave enough to challenge Billy to a fight for laying a hand on her, but you can't tell the girl that you love her. Come on, which one honestly sounds scarier?"

"Telling Claire. Definitely," James said.

"I'm not satisfied," Maggie replied.

"That's not something a man likes to hear, Mags." James grinned.

"Good job I don't see a man anywhere then, ain't it?" she said with a wink. James threw a piece of charcoal at her. "Honestly, you'd think with an apothecary for a father that he would have come up with some kind of cure for you when he realized you had no balls!"

"What did you just say?" James stood up and held his black charcoal covered hands out to Maggie threateningly.

"Oooh, what are you going to do, little lobcock?"

"That's it!"

Chapter 20

Downstairs, Claire was still reading her book when Molly stormed downstairs with a bag over her shoulder. "Good to see you're earning your keep," Molly said with a sneer in her voice.

Claire looked up at Molly, annoyed. Clearly she had already forgotten the loyalty Claire had showed earlier with Kate, but she had known Molly for long enough to know that she was picking a fight on purpose to fuel her bad mood, and Claire simply refused to play. Instead, she looked back down to her book and continued to read, knowing that Molly was still looking at her. She could feel her gaze drilling into the back of her head.

"We should probably cut your rates to half price. Then again that probably wouldn't do any good either."

Claire snapped her book shut, unable to hold her tongue any longer. "What did Sherie mean when she asked you where all the money was?"

Claire looked up and found Molly's eyes, locking onto them. She saw the anger within, but she refused to break eye contact.

"Sherie will believe anything anyone tells her. Tom has no idea what he is talking about," said Molly.

Claire maintained eye contact. "You better than anyone know that Sherie will believe anything she's told. She refuses to see the bad in people, even when it's punching her in the face."

Molly walked slowly towards Claire, the floorboards creaking with each step that she took, her voice poisonous. "Ooh, well, aren't you confident this evening? A far stretch from the scared little girl who stood at my front doorstep all those years ago, begging for us to take you in. My, how you've changed."

Claire

Claire listened to the paper scrape against the blanket over her head as her twin sister Mae turned another page. Their mother was still working, and they weren't allowed out of their room until she was finished, and her client had gone home.

"Are you listening?" When Mae stopped reading, they could hear their mother's shouts, often overpowered by the men she slept with, who groaned and heaved in rhythmic grunts.

"Yes, I'm listening!" The noises made Claire want to rip her ears off. "Keep reading, please!" She focused her attention on Mae's voice.

"She held her in the palm of her hand and she cried as she looked at the beauty before her. *'You promise me that you'll look after me still?'* Her mother sat down on the spongy pad of soft skin just below her thumb, and put her hand on her knuckle. *'I promise you, my dearest child, that I will look after you always. Nothing shall ever halt my love for you, and that love will be the strongest it can be, whatever form I take.'* She cried and cried, her teardrops alternating between happy ones and sad ones, for she knew that her mother's greatest dreams had come true, and that she could now be free forever. *'I love you,'* she whispered, and her mother whispered it back. *'I loved you then, I love you now, no matter when, no matter how. I'll love you here, I'll love you there, I'm with you, I am everywhere.'*"

From the pocket under the blanket they heard nothing when Mae stopped reading. Their mother was finished working.

"I love the ending," Claire said, and hugged her sister tight as they heard the front door close. They knew well enough to stay where they were until their mother joined them in bed.

"Me too," whispered Mae. The comforting sound of trickling water meant that she wasn't far away. The noise of the sponge scrubbing across her skin stopped, and then they heard the water splash. Claire threw the blanket back and stared at the door in anticipation. First her hand appeared, wrapped around the door, and pushed it open slowly, always very quietly, in case they were sleeping, but they never were.

"Hello, my little princesses," her mother whispered.

Claire and Mae sighed in unison, happy that she was finished for the night. They hated her job as much as they expected she hated it. At sixteen years old, Claire knew that she should be emotionally stronger, but her mother never forced her to be. Claire felt safe in an environment that she knew very well was not at all safe, and she felt that was a testament to her mother's care. She knew her friends laughed at her and Mae, but it didn't bother her and it never would, because they didn't understand.

Claire watched her mother dry herself with the only towel they owned, and pull on a shift. She scooted over to let her climb into bed beside her.

"What did you read tonight, my girls?" her mother asked. "Do I need to ask?" Claire could hear her smile, even though it was too dark to see anything.

"Guess," said Mae.

Their mother felt around the bed until her hands passed over the book that Mae had been reading from. "Ah hah! *The Littlest Mother* again?"

Claire giggled. "Yep!"

"Mum, you cheated!"

"Ohh, Mae-mae!" their mother reached across Claire and poked Mae gently in the ribs. "How are your words?"

"They're perfect, Mum. She's an expert!" Claire boasted for Mae.

"I still need some work, but I'm getting there," Mae answered, Claire agreeing that she was probably being a little more truthful.

"I'm so proud of you, my girls," their mother said. She curled an arm around both of them and they snuggled into to her.

"Goodnight, Mum," Claire whispered, but her mother was already asleep.

The next evening, Mae and Claire hid under the blankets again, waiting for their mother to finish work, but that night was not the same as usual. Their mother's voice was different, and everything lasted a lot longer than it usually would. Claire and Mae jumped in time with the noises they could hear, as something in the next room whipped through the air, hitting what they could only assume was their mother as she uttered cries in time with the violent cracking sounds.

Claire shook while she cried, afraid for her mother's life.

"Should I read the book?" Mae asked, crying too.

"No. Shh, let's be quiet," whispered Claire.

Their mother's shouts became louder, injected with pain, and so excruciating that by the time they reached Claire's ears she was hurting too. Claire and Mae heard it all, and while the man outside raped and beat their mother, they clung to one another under the false safety of their blanket, terrified that he would find them.

Claire didn't even realize it had stopped and everything was silent until their bedroom door creaked slowly open. She froze, terrified at who was coming through the door. Mae pulled the blanket down and they peered out, but they couldn't see anything. Something moved on the floor and the sound of raspy breathing edged closer toward them. Claire looked over the edge of the bed, her fingers interlocked tightly with Mae's. Crawling along the wooden floor, leaving a trail of blood behind her, was their mother, her face smashed and swollen, her neck bruised and no clothes on her bloody, bottom half.

"Mum!" Both girls leaped to their mother's aid.

"Get her on the bed," instructed Mae.

Claire picked her up from the shoulders and Mae took her legs. They put her gently on the bed.

"Fetch a doctor. I'm going to get something to try and stop the bleeding," said Mae.

"Girls." Their mother's dry whisper was almost unheard.

"Mum?" Claire moved closer to her mother.

"Girls, come here." She patted the sides of the bed beside her. "Come lie next to Mama."

Claire and Mae climbed onto the bed on either side of their mother, who was as white as the sheet she was lying on. She stroked their hair and kissed them both on the temples as she always did before they fell asleep together. Claire and Mae started to cry.

"Shh, shh, my princesses, it's all going to be okay," she said. Claire draped an arm over her mother's stomach, taking care not to bump her wounds.

"I love you," said Claire.

"I love you too. I love you both. How does that story go, Mae? Read it to me, please." She was speaking so quietly, so faintly.

Mae reached under the pillow and picked up the book. She started to read through her tears.

"*'I promise you, my dearest child, that I will look after you always. Nothing shall ever halt my love for you, and that love will be the strongest it can be, whatever form I take.'* She cried and cried, her teardrops alternating between happy ones and sad ones, for she knew that her mother's greatest dreams had come true, and that she could now be free forever. *'I love you,'* she whispered, and her mother whispered it back. *'I loved you then, I love you now, no matter when, no matter how. I'll love you here, I'll love you there, I'm with you, I am everywhere.'*"

Their mother's chest stopped moving.

"Mama?" Claire whispered.

She wrapped herself around her mother, holding Mae's hand where they met on her chest, and there they stayed until the warm, softness of their mother turned cold and rigid.

It had taken them all day to bury their mother, and by the time the sky was dark, Claire and Mae were exhausted. They walked back to the house in silence and covered in dirt. Claire noticed him first when they walked through the door. A regular client of their mother's was waiting for her. Their mother had always referred to him as Furzman, and they didn't know his surname.

"Hi, girls," said Furzman.

The girls nodded their welcomes. They were never permitted to speak to any of their mother's clients, and they were usually sent to their room long before any man was due to arrive.

"Your mother here?" he asked. His voice was gruff, and he had a strange accent.

Claire shook her head.

"She's not?"

"No," said Mae, stepping forward.

"When she coming? She owes me money. Lot of money," he said.

Mae turned to face Claire. "Go upstairs."

"What? No!" Claire knew her sister well enough to understand what she was trying to do.

"Claire. Go upstairs and read our book, and I'll come up soon," said Mae.

"No, Mae, I'm not letting you do this."

"I am going to the police," Furzman said. "Your mother owes me."

"Claire, please." Mae's eyes were desperate. Claire knew she was terrified, but she didn't know what else she could do. She was too scared to even look at Furzman's face.

"I can't read," said Claire.

"I'll start teaching you tonight, okay? Go look at the pictures. Go on, go." Mae pushed Claire toward the hallway. She didn't want to leave Mae alone with Furzman, but she knew their options were limited. Their mother told them not to trust the police, and she was starting to realize that there weren't many people in this world that she could trust. She ran into her bedroom and threw herself onto the bed that was still stained with her mother's blood. She peeled the sheets off and threw them into the corner, and pulled a new sheet out of the cupboard. She put it on the bed and smoothed the creases out, over and over until Mae appeared a long time later. She had washed herself down and her wet hair dripped onto her nightshirt.

"Do you want to read?" Claire asked.

"Not tonight," said Mae, her face sullen. She dropped onto the bed and pulled her knees tightly to her chest, hooking her arms under them. Claire turned the lamp down and clambered in behind her, pulling her in and holding her tightly.

It was around about a year after their mother died that Mae started to get sick. She had been teaching Claire to read every night after she finished with whatever man was visiting, but eventually she lost more and more energy and it had reached the point to where she could hardly eat or drink any more.

"When I die, you need to leave here. Don't bury me, and don't stay here any longer than you need to. You get away and you never come back," said Mae.

"Don't say that. You're not going to die." Claire climbed into bed beside Mae.

"I can feel it," said Mae.

They had this conversation almost every night, but tonight Claire felt that something was different. Mae's face was pale and her eyes were bloodshot and cloudy. Her breathing was different too, and she wheezed in and out as if it took as much effort as it did for her to stand up, which was a lot for Mae lately.

Claire decided enough was enough. She climbed out of bed and stormed about the tiny house, locking the windows and doors. "No one's touching you," she said when she walked back into their bedroom.

"No one's touching you either, you hear me?" said Mae.

Claire nodded.

Mae coughed, and coughed, and after about a minute she gripped her sides and screamed in pain. "It hurts! Claire, help!"

Claire ripped the covers off and started to rub Mae where her stiff fingers were digging into her ribs. "Okay, it's okay." She uttered the same reassurances every night, a bold-faced lie that she tried to tell herself as much as she told Mae.

There was nothing she could do to help, and it broke her heart. She wiped the bloody saliva from the corners of Mae's mouth, and kissed her sweaty forehead.

"Will you read to me, Claire?"

Claire picked up *The Littlest Mother*. "Already got it ready to go," she said with a gentle smile. She wished she could read as well as Mae could. She still stumbled over some words, and she had no rhythm at all, but she kept reading because she knew it wasn't about that. Mae breathed deeply and Claire could almost hear the liquid inside her, bubbling as she inhaled.

"It's happening. I can feel it," Mae murmured, interrupting the story.

"What does it feel like?" Claire asked.

"I've been so afraid…" Mae spoke slowly. "But I know there's nothing to be afraid of. It's gentle, it's rolling. It's very dark, but it's not scary."

Claire closed her eyes and tried to imagine what Mae was describing.

"No one's here yet, but they will be," said Mae.

"What do you mean?"

"Mama. Mama's coming."

Claire opened her eyes and looked at Mae. A delicate trail of blood trickled down her chin, and she dabbed it away tenderly.

"I'm so proud of you for learning how to read. You are going to be a great woman," said Mae.

"I learned from the best," Claire whispered.

"Loved…then…love you now…when, how," Mae tried to recite the last line of the book as she drifted in and out of consciousness.

"I'll love you here, I'll love you there," Claire said the words with her, trying to hold back her tears. "I'm with you," she sniffed, "I am everywhere."

"I've been so lucky," Mae's voice hissed and Claire knew she was taking some of her last breaths. "We lived with love."

"I love you, Mae-mae. Tell Mama, too," said Claire.

Mae held both of Claire's hands clasped to her chest, and she pulled them up to her lips and placed a soft kiss down gently onto her thumb, and then Claire was alone for the first time in her life.

"So where is the money, Molly?" Claire asked pointedly and full of confidence this time. She waited to see the change in Molly's eyes as she understood that this was a lot more than just an innocent question. Claire smiled, pinpointing the exact moment that Molly realized she had figured it all out, when the horror registered across her face.

"Something wrong?" Claire asked, the innocence returned to her voice. She intentionally broke eye contact with Molly at just the right moment, allowing her eyes to drift over to the front door and the steps outside.

"Where's the money, Claire?" Molly whispered with a frightening air of uncharacteristic calmness.

"Gone," Claire whispered with a hiss, letting the word be carried out the front door with the wind. Her exterior was unflinching, but she was shaking inside. Molly turned and stalked out suddenly to the third step of the Bucket. Claire swallowed and sat very still while she listened to Molly's movements. She heard her pull the third step back, and counted the seconds it would take her to feel around frantically inside for the hidden money. No matter how far she reached in, she wouldn't find anything. The money was gone.

Molly was livid when she returned, her hair streaming behind her as she lunged toward Claire and ripped the book out of her hands. "Don't you dare lie to me for a second longer. Where is it?!"

Claire lost her confidence as Molly towered over her, her face a brilliant shade of purple. She stood up and stepped backwards, tripping over her own feet as she did. She grabbed the chair and held on tightly to avoid stumbling. "I don't know."

Molly threw the book at Claire. The spine hit her hard in the face, and she shrieked as blood began to gush out of both her nose and the corner of her eye that had split open from the impact. Molly launched herself toward Claire, wrapping her hands around her neck, and pushed her against a wall. Claire's arms flailed outwards, and as she tried to pull Molly's hands away from her neck, she knocked one of the gas lamps on the wall off into the curtains. The alcohol-soaked curtains ignited instantly as a mane of fire roared to life and crawled upwards with intense speed and heat. Claire continued to lose strength, while Molly's grip tightened. She tried to form a few words, but nothing escaped her mouth other than gurgles.

"Speak up, Claire, I can't hear you." Molly jeered, her knuckles white.

Claire gasped when Molly released her grip slightly. Claire forced the words to form. "You. Lose."

Molly pulled Claire back from the wall. She held her tightly, and as much as she struggled, Claire was unable to break away from her. Molly shoved her back against the wall even harder. Claire was weak, and her neck snapped backwards and rolled sideways. As Molly slammed her back again, her head hit hard against the sharp corner of the bookcase and split open.

Claire fell into an unconscious oblivion, her life ending in a fiery heartbeat.

The contents of the bookshelf fell to the ground and into the pool of flames that had started to lick the floor. Molly stepped back from Claire's crumpled body. She watched as the flames started to devour the books. The fire had built a lot of momentum and was past being put out by a few buckets of water.

Molly heard someone coming, and she stepped back from Claire. James appeared through the smoke half way down the stairs.

"Maggie!"

Maggie's voice drifted down the stairs. "Come on, James! Be a man! Just tell her you love her!"

James raced down the stairs and threw himself over Claire's body, grabbing her face with both hands, not yet noticing all the blood on the floor underneath her.

"Claire's hurt!" he bellowed to Maggie through the smoke, and she appeared almost instantly at the top of the stairs. Olivia and Billy had also come out of Olivia's room, and they raced downstairs directly behind Maggie.

"Georgina!" Maggie turned on her heels and rushed straight back upstairs the second she saw the smoke and flames.

"Oh, my," Olivia screamed, and raced over to Claire, pushing James off her and shaking her shoulders in a violent attempt to wake her. Molly stepped backwards quietly into the kitchen, hoping the smoke would allow her to slip away, but Olivia saw her before she could disappear. "What happened?"

"It was Josh Flanagan."

James stood up with anger. "That—"

Billy slapped James in the face before he could get carried away. "Focus, both of you! We need to move Claire!"

Olivia stepped back, unable to move Claire after two attempts. None of them had noticed the blood yet, and as James and Billy lifted Claire up to carry her outside, James slipped in the blood and fell to the ground.

"Oh, God!" Olivia screamed, horrified.

James clambered back up, his feet slipping in the blood that still dripped from Claire's head and pooled at their feet.

"Maggie! Georgina!" James threw his head back to yell for them while he staggered clumsily out the front door, his steps short as he struggled with Claire's body. Maggie and Georgina ran down the stairs, the room now dangerously thick with smoke, and followed the others out of the burning Bucket. Still in the kitchen doorway, Molly rushed behind the bar to grab as many coins as she could, stuffing them into the bag that she had tipped them out of earlier that night. She coughed as she inhaled the toxic air, and staggered outside, grasping the bag of money.

James and Billy had laid Claire in Maggie's lap, all of their clothes completely soaked with blood. Georgina pulled her skirt off and wrapped Claire's head up with it, either unaware or refusing to realize that she was already dead. Olivia threw up in the grass further back, and Molly stood behind them all as the flames climbed higher inside the Bucket.

Billy raced off down the street, and whether he was a coward or he was going for help, Molly was unsure, but she knew she needed to disappear before the ashes settled and they discovered that Josh Flanagan was nowhere near the Bucket.

No one noticed when Kate dismounted before Aiko had come to a complete stop. She took in the scene before her and the whole world stopped as she looked at the Bucket.

The smoke.

The flames.

The burning wood.

The heat punched her when she moved closer. The scene reflected off her face just as the horrid memories did.

Kate

Kate was woken violently by her father. Smoke was seeping into the room that she shared with her younger brother, Rory. An orange glow flickered off the bedroom door.

"Kate! Kate!" Her father's call was frantic. He shook her quickly and then moved over to Rory's bed and scooped him up. "Rory, wake up!" She heard her brother moan softly, and then shout when he woke up fully. "Come on! Quickly!" her father said, putting Rory down and leading the way out of their bedroom.

Kate and Rory followed their father to find their mother waiting for them. The family moved toward the stairs in a hurry, the fire loud. Kate blinked, unable to see much of what was in front of her. The smoke stung her eyes and she halted for a moment on the stairs to rub them.

"Keep moving, Katie," her father commanded. She took another step, but she misjudged the distance and tripped. She fell down the stairs and landed at the bottom with a thud. Rory raced to help her, and she took his hand for support, but when she tried to stand, pain shot through her ankle and she screamed. Above her, a beam groaned dangerously.

"Come on!" her father shouted, taking her mother's hand. They only managed to take a few steps before the beam fell. Kate and Rory screamed and she felt like she was being stabbed by a thousand burning needles, pelted with blistering embers that burst from the beam as it crashed down. Only after the noise and the dust from the crash settled could Kate hear her mother's screams. She looked up and saw her, trapped under the beam, her face contorted in agony. Her father and Rory turned back to help her mother, and Kate pulled herself up using the banister and started climbing the stairs despite the pain in her ankle. Her father picked up the smoldering beam with his bare hands, shouting in pain when it hissed at contact with his skin, but he didn't let go. He tried to move it, but it was too heavy. Rory, all but helpless at nine years old, held his mother's hand from under the beam. Kate finally made it to where her family was stuck. She took the beam in her hands and tried to help her father, but her skin felt like it was melting the instant she touched the wood. Her mother's eyes were closed tightly to avoid the smoke, but Kate reached out and took her other hand and kissed it. She tasted like ash and burning. Another beam crashed from the roof and more embers exploded around them. It would have been pretty if the roaring fire and burning embers weren't so terrifying.

Her mother opened her eyes, black and radiating pain. "Get the children to safety, Paul!" Her words were dry. She grunted loudly after she spoke, and closed her eyes again. Paul grabbed Kate from behind and pulled her away from her mother. She screamed and reached out for her, but he hauled her and Rory outside and put them down under a tree, a few meters away from the house.

"Stay here!" Paul commanded before running back into the burning house. The air was as hot as an oven, and even Kate's tears burned her cheeks as they streamed from her eyes. She could taste the cinders in her mouth, gritty and sharp.

Rory tried to get up and follow his father back in, but Kate grabbed him and pulled him back down. "Dad said to stay here!" she shouted. She had never been so afraid in her life. Rory pulled his hand out of Kate's grip.

"Mum's still in there!" he said, and stepped out of her reach before she could seize him again. Kate couldn't move. She wanted to chase Rory and bring him back into her lap, but her body wasn't listening to her brain as it fired a million commands of action to move. She was stuck, watching in fear as he disappeared into the house. There was a burst of flames and Kate could hear more beams collapse inside the house. The roof would barely be supported by now. She watched the door and she willed for her family to come racing out. Each second that passed was another second of anguish as nothing but smoke bellowed through the front door. Kate heard a scream inside the house. Her mother.

The house groaned and there was another loud bang. High-pitched screams joined those of her mother's, and she knew Rory was trapped. Finally her body started to move and she forced herself to stand, the searing pain in her ankle not enough to stop her from limping toward what was left of her home. She could hear her father's screams now, and she wailed as the sounds and smells of her burning family tortured her senses. The heat formed a barrier that stopped her from entering the house. She tried and tried, but she just didn't have the power to overcome the heat that blasted her whenever she got close. Her eyelashes melted together, her hair singed, and she was forced back by the intensity of the flames.

The house groaned again, and then collapsed, fire exploding around her. She tripped over tree roots when she ran backwards, and fell into the nook at the base of the tree. She screamed with her family as they burned to death.

Kate stared at the burning Bucket, the sounds of her family haunting her as if it had happened just yesterday.

Chapter 21

Olivia wiped her mouth and climbed to her feet. She wobbled a little, but she managed to make it back to the group. She stood beside Molly, who appeared to be lost in thought, her eyes glazed over, and Olivia put her arm around her. She couldn't imagine how it would feel to watch her childhood home burn to the ground.

"What happened?" Kate shouted from behind, causing them to jump.

Molly pointed to the burning Bucket. "Sherie's inside!"

Kate ran into the Bucket, no further questions asked.

Olivia dropped her arm from Molly's waist and stepped back in shock. Maggie looked at Molly in horror.

A hand tapped Molly on the shoulder, and she turned around to see Sherie's furious face in hers. Before Molly had a chance to step back, Sherie had punched her hard in the face, and she dropped to the ground instantly.

"Where did you come from?" Olivia asked.

"I was on the hill, and I saw the smoke," said Sherie as she stepped over Molly's body and ran into the Bucket after Kate.

"Sherie, stop!" Maggie called out to her. Olivia tried to grab Sherie when she ran past, but she missed. She ran after Sherie, feeling the temperature rise as she ascended the stairs that wobbled beneath her feet.

"Why do people keep running INTO the building that is on FIRE?!" shouted Maggie. Sherie accelerated and managed to duck under the top of the doorway above her as it fell, narrowly missing her. Olivia shrieked and retreated when a spray of the embers spat in her direction, and Sherie disappeared into the smoke filled bar.

A crowd had started to form at the steps of the Bucket, and in the distance, Billy led a large group of townsfolk, carrying pails full of water.

Sherie ran into the burning Bucket, her eyes frantically darting left and right while she searched for Kate.

"Kate!" Sherie screamed her name. She knocked over bottles as she used the top of the bar as a guide to help her run through the thick smoke.

"Kate!" Sherie ran across the room, her arm accidentally hitting the most recent vase off the piano. It smashed to the ground.

Sherie coughed a little, and paused to look around the bar. There was no sign of Kate. She heard a loud crash upstairs, and without hesitating, she dashed in the direction of the noise. When she reached the bottom of the stairs, she saw Kate stumbling down them, her skirt lifted up and held over her mouth.

Kate saw Sherie, and her eyes lit up. "What are you doing here?" she asked.

Sherie flinched as more noises came from upstairs, and dust fell onto her from above. "Here in this burning Bucket? Or in a grander sense?"

Kate shook her head. "Are we really going to play this game right now, in the middle of all of this?" She smiled.

Sherie took a few more steps toward Kate and took her hands. "I'm saving you."

Kate grabbed Sherie and forcefully pulled her out of the way of a falling beam that crashed in the place she had been standing seconds before. "I'm saving you!" she said.

The flames crackled and the debris thundered loudly as it fell around them, but to Sherie, the world had gone completely quiet. She stepped into Kate, placed an arm around her neck and the other hand on the back of her head. "I think we're here to save each other," she said.

Kate looked into Sherie's eyes for what seemed like a lifetime. Sherie moved in slowly, and kissed her with a passion more intense than the fire that surrounded them.

The Bucket groaned loudly and Kate interrupted the kiss.

"I know that sound," warned Kate. "It's about to give way." She took the lead, pulling Sherie by the hand. The front door was blocked by the collapsed frame, and Sherie was about to turn around and look for another way out when she saw Billy's face appear as he pulled the frame aside. They ran until they were a safe distance away from the Bucket, further back than they had been before. Sherie wondered how Maggie had carried Claire's body so far back by herself, until she realized that it was actually Olivia who had collapsed in her arms, sobbing while Maggie stroked her hair. Georgina was standing alone, entranced by the flames. Molly was further away from them, on the other side of the road speaking with two police officers, one of whom was holding what looked like Claire's journal.

Sherie looked to see if the doctors had arrived. She saw something on the ground that was covered in a cloth. It was the shape of a body.

"Claire. Claire, who has Claire?!" she cried and her heart raced when she saw that Kate was looking at the body-shaped cloth too. She wanted to run over to the body and rip the sheet back. She wanted to confirm what she was sick to the stomach for even assuming, but Kate held her in a tight embrace, and Sherie couldn't move. "Where's Claire?!" She screamed at Maggie and Olivia, and Maggie dropped her head. Sherie knew. She knew it was Claire under there, and that she was gone. She buried her head into Kate's chest and cried.

The group watched in silence while the Bucket burned to the ground.

As the flames subsided, so did the drama. Eventually, when they had all calmed down, they walked over to where Claire lay. Sherie held her breath as she felt her heart galloping beneath her chest, and she felt Kate grab her when she swayed, the world dimming into blackness for a second. "I'm okay," she reassured her.

Sherie uncovered Claire's body and they stood around her, staring at her porcelain face. Olivia, Maggie, Georgina, Kate, and Sherie cried silently and whispered their goodbyes to their sister. Sherie reached inside Claire's pocket for the piece of paper that she knew was tucked inside. She unfolded the page, and through the tears that flowed down her face, she read the words out loud to Claire. She read to her as Claire had read to her sister and as her sister had read to her mother.

"She held her in the palm of her hand and she cried as she looked at the beauty before her. *'You promise me that you'll look after me still?'* Her mother sat down on the spongy pad of soft skin just below her thumb, and put her hand on her knuckle. *'I promise you, my dearest child, that I will look after you always. Nothing shall ever halt my love for you, and that love will be the strongest it can be, whatever form I take.'* She cried and cried, her teardrops alternating between happy ones and sad ones, for she knew that her mother's greatest dreams had come true, and that she could now be free forever. *'I love you,'* she whispered, and her mother whispered it back. *'I loved you then, I love you now, no matter when, no matter how. I'll love you here, I'll love you there, I'm with you, I am everywhere.'* Sherie folded the page again and popped it back into Claire's pocket, and Kate caught her as she collapsed with grief.

Tom walked into Molly's prison cell. It was dark and damp, and she deserved every last second of it. "Get up," he said.

Molly was curled up in the corner, and she shivered when she pulled herself off the ground, her wet clothes sticking to her body. Tom felt sick as he looked at her, a pathetic shadow of the figure she used to be.

"You're due to face the judge tomorrow morning, and he will probably send you to the firing squad," he said. He expected her to cry, or beg, but she didn't. She nodded. "You were going to run away, weren't you?"

"Yes," she said.

"Tonight, at some point, Smitty will let you out."

Molly looked at him, a dash of hope crossing her face.

"Don't get excited. There are conditions."

"Okay." She stood up and looked at him. Her eyes were empty, her soul missing.

"You're going to marry me," he said.

"What?"

"The land that the Suds Bucket was built on will transfer into my name. You're going to take this money, and you're going to leave and never come back." He dropped a small bag of coins into her lap.

"I need my mercury," said Molly.

Tom shook his head. "The mercury never arrived."

"But it's been a week! James said it would be here by now," she begged.

"Perhaps it went missing," Tom said, his eyes burning into hers until she hung her head.

"I see," she said.

Tom reached into his pocket and pulled out the marriage papers. "Sign here." He pointed to a line on the page.

"What, no vows?"

"I vow to kill you myself if I ever see you near Sherie again," he snarled.

"Finally caught on that I'm no good, have you?"

"Save me the pity talk. You're getting what you always wanted. I'm looking after Sherie, you've got a bag of money, and you're leaving Richmond."

Molly signed the piece of paper and looked into the bag on her lap.

"What's the matter? The money not filling you with happiness like it used to?"

Molly started to cry finally. "Do you think I'll ever be able to find peace, after this?"

Tom stared at Molly for a moment, resisting the urge to spit on her. He turned around and walked toward the cell doors, and a prison guard arrived to open the door for him. The door clanked and echoed down the long hall as it was locked again, and Tom looked at Molly through the iron bars.

"I hope you don't," he told her, and walked away.

Tom walked up the path to the Flanagans' house and rapped the brass door-knocker loudly. Almost instantly, a sprightly young girl answered the door with a toothy grin. "Who are you?" she asked.

"My name's Tom. Are you Anne?"

"Yep!"

Anne smiled at him and picked at the peeling paint on the front door.

"Is your dad about?" he asked.

"He's in the back shed. I'll take you, come on!"

Anne led him around the house, skipping as she went. Tom watched her, blown away. She was the image of Georgina, now that he knew what he did. He wished he could go back and tell Georgina that she was happy...perfect even, but he knew that while his intentions would be to bring her peace of mind, it probably wouldn't. Nor would it be the best thing for little Anne.

"Hello."

Tom looked up to see that they had arrived at the back shed. Mr. Flanagan was holding a wrench, and he put it on the side as he stood up from his work.

"Can I help you?" he asked.

"I'm Tom. Tom Burnes." Tom held out his hand.

Mr. Flanagan looked at his hand for a moment. "I know who you are," he said. Tom was ready to withdraw his hand and save himself further embarrassment, but Mr. Flanagan shook it at the last moment.

"I was wondering if I could have a word with you." Tom looked at Anne. "Privately."

"Annie, go and get Mr. Burnes here a drink please," said Mr. Flanagan.

"What d'you want to drink, Mr. Burnes?"

"Water would be lovely, please, Annie." Tom smiled.

Anne skipped off, and Tom decided to get to the point before she returned. He handed Mr. Flanagan a piece of paper.

"What's this?" Mr. Flanagan asked.

"Something that I don't think belongs in the hands of anyone else," said Tom.

Mr. Flanagan opened it and started to read, his eyes getting wider with every word he took in. "Molly gave this to you?" He looked furious.

"She did. She told me I could use it as blackmail material. Mr. Flanagan, I'm here to tell you that I won't be doing that. I'm sure you heard about what happened to the Suds Bucket? To the third step?"

Mr. Flanagan nodded, but said nothing.

"I came to tell you that you don't need to be putting any more money in that step. Molly's leaving town and she won't ever be back. She hasn't told anyone about Anne, and neither have I. I don't plan on it either. As far as I'm concerned, little Annie is your daughter. She belongs with you."

Whether Tom saw a tear in Mr. Flanagan's eye or not was something he would never know, as Mr. Flanagan turned around for a moment, took his hat off, and leaned against a rusty plough that looked like it had been out of commission for a long time. He wiped his brow and looked at Tom again, a grateful smile across his face. "Thank you," he said.

Tom nodded.

Anne arrived with Tom's glass of water, her hand wet. "Sorry, I spilled a bit," she admitted. Tom chuckled as he took the water off her.

"Thank you, Miss Annie," he said.

"Mum told me to tell you that dinner is almost ready, so you have to come in and wash up," Anne told Mr. Flanagan. "Are you staying for dinner, Mr. Burnes?"

"Oh, no—" Tom started, but Mr. Flanagan interrupted him.

"Yes, he is. Run and tell your mother to set another place for him, please." He turned back to Tom. "If you're willing?"

Tom smiled. "I'd be honored, thank you."

Chapter 22

Claire's funeral was small, but just perfect for what it was, and Sherie knew Claire would have loved it. After the last shovel of dirt was dropped on to her grave, James knelt down and placed a few daffodil bulbs just below the surface of the soil. They would grow during the upcoming winter and start to blossom in the early spring along with the rest of the new life.

"They're going to be like Claire." He smiled. "Growing under difficult conditions, and coming out the other side, strong and beautiful."

He stood back up and Maggie gave him a nudge. He leaned in and whispered quietly to the stone that bore her name. "I love you, Claire."

Sherie gave him a hug and a kiss on the cheek. "She loved you too, James." He shook his head and she took hold of his shoulders and gave him a shake to insist. "She did."

After the funeral was over, Tom invited everyone in attendance back to his house for a meal, but Sherie chose to be by herself. She wandered to the place where she used to sit with her father, the place where she met Kate, and sat alone at the top of the hill.

She didn't move, not when the sun started to sink, not through the beautiful sunset that emblazoned the sky while she cried for Claire's soul, and not when the view below her sank into darkness as night fell. She sat still, staring at Pavo above her.

In her hands she was holding Claire's journal, which she had been given by the police after Molly had been convicted. She shuddered. She still couldn't believe it had all happened, and that Molly had done such a thing. So many horrible things. They had found the mutilated body of Ed Smith under the Bucket too, and she wondered how long he had been there for, and whether there were any other bodies that they hadn't found. She would never know. She flipped through the journal for the ten thousandth time, the pages depicting in full detail what Claire had figured out, and what Molly had been up to. She looked at the drawing of the third step, and the money hidden beneath it. She had walked over that step almost every day. How could she not have known? She had even caught Molly hovering above it, with a nail in her hand, and yet she had believed her when she told her that it was just broken. She wondered if Claire would still be alive if Sherie had opened her eyes and not looked past Molly's strange behavior. She flipped the page. Words scrawled in childish handwriting, with figures and sums that added up to the actual profits the Suds Bucket had made—thousands and thousands of pounds more than what Molly had led them all to believe.

Kate appeared quietly, and said nothing as she sat down beside Sherie.

"So we weren't going broke after all," Sherie said.

Kate gave her a kiss on the cheek and smiled. She looked up at Pavo.

"Not that it matters anymore," Sherie continued.

"We can rebuild," Kate said, finally speaking.

Sherie sighed. "We can't rebuild the Suds Bucket. It wouldn't be right."

Kate pulled a piece of paper out of her pocket, unfolded it, and handed it to Sherie. "What about '*The Peacock*?" she asked.

"Did you draw this?" Sherie was amazed. Kate nodded. On the page was an intricate drawing of a peacock. "It's breathtaking," Sherie said. She looked up at Pavo again and then back to Kate. "Not 'The Saucepan'?" She grinned.

"We could make it a music bar," Kate said. "I'll play piano and Maggie can be head of security." She giggled. "You can sing."

Sherie frowned.

"Can you sing?" Kate asked.

"I don't know. I guess we'll find out." Sherie laughed.

"Olivia can sell her pottery too," Kate said.

Sherie nodded as she pictured what Kate was describing. "And a garden out the front for Claire," she said.

"Absolutely. Where anyone is welcome to read," Kate agreed.

Sherie smiled at the idea, but she felt her smile fade as the dream inside her head was spoiled by reality. "But we don't have any money, and don't tell me to ask Tom, because he's already done enough for us," she said, expecting Kate to suggest that first.

"We don't?" Kate's response surprised Sherie.

"The money under the stairs wasn't found," she said.

Kate smiled. "Wasn't it?"

Sherie's eyes were drawn to a small brass key that Kate pulled from her pocket. "What's that?" she asked.

"It's a key." Kate winked. "Are you ready for another Latin lesson?"

"Clavis!" Sherie shouted.

"I'm impressed!"

"I know some words in Latin," Sherie said, pinching Kate's arm. "Hello? Pavo!" She chuckled and kissed Kate on the cheek, but Kate turned her head to catch Sherie's open mouth with hers. As they kissed, Kate pressed the small key into Sherie's hand.

When they pulled apart, Sherie looked back up at Pavo. "What made you come up here? The night of the festival?" she asked. She noticed that Kate's eyes sparkled so much more than they had the night she had looked into them for the first time.

"I was looking for a reason," Kate said. "I was looking for my reason."

"You found me."

Kate nodded. "I've been looking for you for a long time, Sherie."

"You weren't happy with your family before they…?" Sherie trailed off.

"I was. I was very happy. I miss them every day and I always will, but I think I've been looking for you for longer than that."

"What do you mean?"

"I think in every life I've ever lived, I wander about aimlessly, until I find you. Something brings me to you."

"All of this wasn't for nothing," Sherie said.

"It's true," said Kate.

"I miss my family too. My mum, my dad, Claire…" Sherie paused in thought. "Molly."

"But we have each other now."

Sherie rested her head against Kate's and followed her gaze into the sky. "We do."

"From now on, we tackle life together."

Sherie smiled at her, warmed by the hope that she could now feel in her heart. "Feet first," she said.

Pavo twinkled in the night sky above with a promise to watch over them forever.

About the Author

An English born Australian writer, Penny now lives in Illinois, USA, with her wife Kat. She has written two films: Lightswitch and Star Cross'd Jammers. When not writing, she is coming up with new stories, spending time with her family, or running around a Xena: Warrior Princess convention with friends. Her mission is to tell stories and inspire people, igniting within them a passion that might not otherwise exist. For more information, visit www. glasswellcavanaugh.com

www.ingramcontent.com/pod-product-compliance
Lightning Source LLC
Chambersburg PA
CBHW051246260626
47162CB00002B/638